MW00795464

The
Maid's
Secret

BOOKS BY SHARI J. RYAN

The Bookseller of Dachau
The Doctor's Daughter
The Lieutenant's Girl

LAST WORDS
The Girl with the Diary
The Prison Child
The Soldier's Letters

SHARI J. RYAN

The
Maid's
Secret

bookouture

Published by Bookouture in 2022

An imprint of Storyfire Ltd.
Carmelite House
50 Victoria Embankment
London EC4Y 0DZ

www.bookouture.com

Copyright © Shari J. Ryan, 2022

Shari J. Ryan has asserted her right to be identified as the author of this work.

All rights reserved. No part of this publication may be reproduced, stored in any retrieval system, or transmitted, in any form or by any means, electronic, mechanical, photocopying, recording or otherwise, without the prior written permission of the publishers.

ISBN: 978-1-80314-752-9
eBook ISBN: 978-1-80314-751-2

This book is a work of fiction. Whilst some characters and circumstances portrayed by the author are based on real people and historical fact, references to real people, events, establishments, organizations or locales are intended only to provide a sense of authenticity and are used fictitiously. All other characters and all incidents and dialogue are drawn from the author's imagination and are not to be construed as real.

To all those who wander, may you always find your way to the place you want to be

PROLOGUE

MILA

A woman can be strong but lack the willpower to carry her to greater heights. She can also be weak, but with iron fists held out in front of her.

"Say something, please—we're running out of time," Ben pleas. My heart is pounding against my chest and sweat is beading across the back of my neck beneath my loose braid.

"It would be a mistake," I warn Ben. "You don't understand what you are asking me to do—what you will inevitably cause your family. I will destroy your lineage."

Ben runs his hands up the sides of his flushed cheeks. "Is this about religion? My mother? What—what is it? I must know." The desperation in his amber eyes causes my chin to twitch, threatening to unmask what I keep hidden.

I swallow against the sensation of grief and stare over his shoulder, toward the courtyard lined with red roses. "I am not like you," I say, glancing down at my borrowed black dress, trimmed with white ruffled hems.

He reaches out, grazes his fingertips against my shoulder, but I pull away as if I'm a fire that will burn him. "Mila, I don't want you to be like me. Can you not see this for yourself? I want the freedom to explore the world, sleep beneath the stars, feast off the land, and take pride in every feat I endure." He's speaking nonsense, and his portrayal of my life—my past—is something he has conjured up like a fairy tale. The life he dreams of is one I've run away from. Only a stupid man would run toward the shadows of my past, and he's anything but senseless. We're living within a fog—one that will lift and expose the truth. We all face the threat of losing how much or how little we have, and I can't help wondering what the point would be in destroying something that has survived much longer than either of us.

"I need my job. The rest will have to wait," I reply hastily, because each word is a lie I must believe.

"The rest can't wait. We're on borrowed time and I'd be a foolish man to give up on what I desire the most."

"You want to keep your life. That's all you should want right now."

My stomach is in knots, and I can hardly stand up straight as I clutch my hands over my chest. I've been taught so much over the course of my lifetime, and I've seen every example of what I shouldn't want to become. Ben is everything that is wrong with my world, and I know well enough to walk away from temptation.

ONE
RUNNING FROM OUR SHADOWS
MILA, SEPTEMBER 1938

The sputtering of stone and gravel catch beneath the wooden wheels of our horse-drawn vardo wagon, and the dirt road ahead stretches out so far into the distance, it may lead us to the end of the world—a ledge from where we will plummet into oblivion. The sun will prove my theory wrong once again though as I watch it descend into a place of nothingness only to rise again some hours later. The sky is a mix of citrus shades and I wonder if the air is in fact sweeter ahead. Regardless of whether the next stop is worse or not as bad as the previous one, I can rest knowing we won't be there—wherever there is—for long.

"I'm going to need you to help your mama in the morning," Papa says.

I glance over at Papa, unable to steady my focus on the long hairs of his gray beard as I bounce upon the wooden bench. "How long will you be away for this time?" The question is not one he can answer, and I know this all too well, but sometimes he establishes connections prior to setting off in search of unwanted horses.

"Not too long. I have a meeting set up with a man at the

base of Tiske Steny. If all goes well, I should be back within a few days."

I refocus my attention to the last few rays of sunlight kissing the white peaks of the mountain tops. "What is it that's bothering you, Mila?"

"Why would you think something isn't right?"

Papa's hand settles on the back of my neck. "I know you better than anyone else in this entire world."

"Even Mama?"

"Even your mama. You are my firstborn, the one I have spent the most time with, the one who used to tell me her every imagined story before bedtime... The road in front of us—it isn't a road at all, is it?"

"I don't understand." But I do.

"It's a far away land up ahead, one full of possibilities, where music drowns the silences and spring blossoms permeate the cool mist—a place where the sun never sleeps. Those who are like us cannot be taken as we have nothing to give—it's the answer to having everything." Papa speaks in riddles and often the words slip in through my ears and stir within my mind for hours before I make sense of it all. I want to disagree with his thoughts, but who am I to argue another person's right to see through their unique eyes, even if he is my papa?

"I believe that's called a dream," I reply. "No such place exists. We of all people should know this by now." To have nothing feels as empty as it sounds. My dreams aren't what they used to be. They go beyond what he has described as his version of perfection and the misconception draws a line between him, Mama, and me, but it's not something I can control.

Lela's head slips off my shoulder and falls against my chest as her inky black hair sweeps across her face. "I see you've won this bet. It's hardly past dusk," Papa says, leaning forward to get a better look at my sister. I'm surprised she was able to stay awake for as long as she did. We take turns up at the front of the vardo, but whoever is up here needs to stay alert to keep Papa awake. Lela is only ten; she doesn't understand how tiring the road becomes after hours of moving along a straight path. She promised she would keep her eyes open so she could stay up front with me, but the swaying motion never fails to put her to sleep. The only ones who can stay awake aside from Papa, Mama, and me are Broni and Morti, my two younger brothers. The other two, Lela and Bula, aren't old enough to sit up front alone yet. Of the five of us, I'm the oldest at seventeen, and feel it's my responsibility to help Papa whenever possible—even if that means forcing my eyes to stay open while we travel along an endless road in the dark.

"Do you know what separates us from the rest, my little dordi—what makes us special?" Papa asks, his eyes softening. He only calls me dordi, his dear, when he's trying to teach me a life lesson.

"Are you trying to tell me a joke?" As if I don't know what separates us from the others—the rest of the world. There's a long list of what makes us different. Most distinctly, people know who we are with one passing glance because of our deep olive skin tone, lack of modern amenities, raggedy clothing, and unique use of the Romani language. It wasn't long ago that our kind were nothing more than slaves to the wealthy. Many still view us in that light. According to society, we don't belong here. We don't belong anywhere.

Papa twists the frayed rope around his hands a little tighter, reining in Bell, our older vanna horse of the two shires we own. She likes to be one step ahead of Basil and causes the vardo to wobble more than it should. "I'm entirely serious," he says.

For the life of me, I can't imagine what he can say that would make me or our family feel distinct for any noble reason. "I'm not sure."

"We could run away and become ghosts of mankind. While everyone is living in fear of what laws will impact their lives next, we can move on to our next destination and leave the grim reality behind us."

"Because we're used to living this way," I suggest. "I'm not sure that makes us special."

"Well, of course it does. Nothing has changed for us, not like it's changing for every Jewish man, woman, and child in Germany. The incoming laws are a shock to their race and culture, but this is the way we've been living for centuries."

"It makes me feel sorry for each of them, knowing what it feels like," I reply. "No one should be treated differently because of their race or religion. If anything, people should be learning from their past mistakes, but instead, they are made again and again. It's disappointing—that's what it is."

Papa looks over at me as I run my fingers through Lela's dark ringlets. "You never cease to impress me with your ability to see life from other perspectives. But as your father, I want you to find peace for yourself, in whatever form that may be."

"I don't want to live my life on the run as a traveler—a 'Gypsy,' as we're called. I want to plant my roots in the ground and build steel walls around me, ones that not even the greatest powers can break through."

I can't look Papa in the eyes when I make statements like these because I know it goes against our way of living and I don't want him to think I'm ungrateful. He has always worked harder than most to provide for each of us, and my dreams may be impossible to achieve, but I pray for change so that our culture and race will someday be accepted by others. Perhaps, it is possible for all of mankind to see eye-to-eye without the prejudice that is currently eating humanity alive.

TWO
TEATIME ISN'T FOR THE FAINT OF HEART

BENEDIKT, SEPTEMBER 1938

The pings and pangs of our teacups rattling against each saucer is the only other sound to be heard in the round room decorated with shelves of books lining the walls. The drapes are bulbous and block out the sun, making the room feel darker than normal. The scratchy orchestral music hums from the radio's speakers and we all stare mindlessly around the room with glossy eyes. Our family has never been known for being quiet, but recently, as the conflict with Germany continues to grow, a silent fear has taken over, leaving us all with less and less to say.

To counter the silence, the radio adds a layer of noise but not one I enjoy much anymore. I never thought I would miss the days before we had a source of modern entertainment in our home, but over the last year, it's become the centerpiece of the tea table in our library as we listen to Germany's daily updates. It's become difficult to acquire bulletins from the country our village borders. It's as if Czechoslovakia has become detached from Germany. Yet, we're less than a hundred kilometers from the German border. The news is grimmer each day, and it sounds as if today will be no different given the despondent tone of the broadcaster's voice:

"At this late hour of the afternoon, I'm here to report that Germany has invaded Austria with the motivation to incorporate non-Jewish Austrians into the Third Reich. Reports of violence in the streets against the Jewish people and their business doesn't come as a surprise, but—"

Mother leans forward in her seat and cranks the radio knob, leaving the six of us in silence as we stare at the walnut-wood tube like it will answer all our lingering questions.

"Why did you turn it off, Mother?" Pavel asks, his voice high-pitched and innocent. By the time he understands the meaning of what we hear on the radio, I'm sure he won't be asking questions like this. He's the youngest of us at ten, and I would do anything for a piece of his innocence at eighteen.

Mother gently sweeps her hand over the tight roll of her auburn hair. Father stands up, places his teacup down and trades it for the burning cigar resting on the saucer. He pinches the tightly wrapped brown paper-like leaf between his fingers so hard I expect the seam to burst. I'm not sure how any of us could explain to Pavel how different life is in our neighboring countries. All he's ever known is the luxury of living in an estate with staff who tend to our every need. He believes all people look up to us and admire who we are, but it's far from the truth. It only appears as if we have everything.

"Boys, I'd like to speak to your father privately," Mother says.

"What is it that we aren't old enough to hear?" Filip asks. He's three years younger than I am, but more acquainted than necessary with the truth outside of the land we own, but Mother still thinks she can protect us from the destruction of the world around us.

"I'd prefer to stay," Tobias says, taking a pull of his cigar, which is identical to Father's. My older brother by just over a year thinks he has already become the reigning heir to our estate even though Mother and Father are still quite young. Tobias's dream of running this former aristocratic family-owned structure is the bane of our existence most days. The idea of power goes to his head in a way it never should. He thinks his ability to verbalize his thoughts is all that's required of him to maintain this lifestyle. I believe people like Tobias are the reason aristocrat titles no longer exist. Now, we only carry the blood of those who were known for being born into high class.

"Tobias, no, please go with your brothers," Mother says.

"Mother, please don't treat me like a child when I am a man of this house just as much as Father is. It's important that I am a part of any discussion regarding our well-being or the estate. Am I wrong?"

Mother stares directly into Tobias's eyes and I can't decipher whether she is ready to concede or argue, but I know she has grown tired of the disagreements he causes between us all. Rather than stir up more tension, I place my teacup down on the saucer and rest it on the table in front of the radio. Filip and Pavel follow my lead as they often do. I stand up from the sofa and straighten my coat and the three of us leave the room without further question. We wait in the foyer for a moment to see if Tobias will join us. Instead, he appears in the doorway with a smug grin and closes the heavy door in our faces. The echoing thud sends a chill down my spine. It's hard to ignore Tobias's behavior, but it's our only option if we want to live in peace within these walls.

"What do you think they're talking about?" Filip asks. My brother looks as nervous as I feel—both of us know right well what's happening.

"I don't see what else there is to discuss aside from what we just heard over the radio," I reply.

"How does that affect us, though?" Filip continues.

"It doesn't. Not yet anyway. Though, I might suggest we all say a prayer for Austria tonight. The fight has only begun for them."

Filip agrees with a subtle nod and Pavel leans the side of his face up against the door to the library. I'm not sure he can hear through the thick wooden slab, but his ears likely work better than anyone else's here. "Father is proposing to purchase more horses," he says, posing his statement as more of a question.

"We sold the last two. Why would we need any more?" Filip questions.

Father doesn't suggest anything without having thought through every detail of a potential outcome. He must have a good reason for suggesting such an unusual idea at a time like this.

"Why are the Jewish people in trouble?" Pavel asks after listening to more of what's taking place in the library. "We're Jewish. Are we in trouble?"

Filip and I share a look above Pavel's head. "No, you don't have anything to fret over. Go outside and play in the gardens for a bit."

"I'm too old to play outside," he says, snapping at my suggestion. "I'm nearly a man like you both. I want to do whatever you're doing."

"I have to tend to some work for my economics class," I say.

Pavel's shoulders drop and he lowers his head, leaving us to feel guilty. "I'll go prepare the stable for the horses," he says before turning the corner.

We used to have someone who tended to the horses, but we've been forced to cut back on staff over the last couple of years due to the recession, so the horses had to go too. Mama and Tobias think the one staff member we have can handle everything, but all we've done is ask for more hours and assign more responsibilities to them without offering additional compensation. It's not right, and I've said so, but Mama and Tobias act as if we've been left with no other options. Filip, Pavel, and I try to help lessen the burden, but it still doesn't seem like enough. I sometimes wonder if we will ever be able to truly repay her...

THREE
A NEW PATCH OF GRASS TO CALL HOME

MILA, SEPTEMBER 1938

The stars are fading in the azure dawn sky, and I wonder where my mind has been for the last couple of hours. I haven't fallen asleep as promised, but I've been less talkative. "Are you okay, Papa?"

"Who, me?" he questions. "I'm not the one who fell asleep with my eyes wide open." A laugh rumbles deep in his throat before a yawn steals his breath. "Don't worry, my dordi, we're just about there."

Our definition of the word "there" is the place we call home. It's always our "here" as Mama says. I can't say I'll be sorry to have left Besednice or the southern region of Czecho-slovakia behind. We were only there for three months, and I'm not sure one night went by when all of us were comfortable sleeping at the same time. There was always commotion of some sort, whether by other travelers or locals who didn't want us crowding their village. We keep to ourselves and don't cause anyone trouble, but our kind are often treated as if we're a rare contagious disease. There's hope that we'll find a place where people don't see us in that light, but I keep my expectations at bay.

We've turned off onto an uneven dirt road with the vague outline of a village in the distance. "Is there no other way around the village? Why make a show of ourselves if it isn't necessary?" I ask Papa.

He twists his head, giving me a brief look of puzzlement before dropping his gaze to the worn and crinkled map he has drawn across many times. He presses his finger down on a circled spot. "Not unless we'd like to travel another dozen miles for no good reason. We're cutting through the village. It won't take long." These are the only times I wish I was inside the wagon covering with the others. I could climb over the bench and go in through the small entrance of the covered shelter, but I would be leaving Papa on his own, especially since I helped Lela inside a few hours ago so she could sleep more comfortably.

It's not that I can't handle what's to come. I would rather be blissfully ignorant to the truth of the new location we're going to be residing in for however long we can last here. "You've never cared much before. Why now, my dear Mila?"

I force a small smile across my dry lips, feeling my parched skin pull. I haven't had anything to drink in hours. "I don't care. It was only a question."

Papa presses the pad of his thumb against my bottom lip. "You're thirsty." He pulls his hand away, showing me a spot of blood on his thumb from my dry, cracked lips. It isn't a surprise to see. The air is so dry, and we've been traveling and inhaling nothing but dust and dirt for almost a day.

"I can wait," I say.

"Rebecca," Papa says, knocking on the flimsy door behind our bench. "Mila needs water."

It doesn't take long for Mama to open the door enough to poke her head out. She seems surprised to see the sun as she winces and squints before lifting her arm above her face to shield from the glow. "We're out of water. Bula had the last of what we had just a few minutes ago. How much farther is the new settlement?" Mama runs her hand across the top of my head while waiting for Papa to respond.

"Just a little further. We must cross through the village up ahead and it's just down another two roads from there."

"Sorry, my sweet," Mama says, grabbing my chin and kissing my forehead. "Thank you for sitting with your papa all night. I don't know how you two manage to keep your eyes open for so long."

"You don't have to thank me, Mama. I don't mind." Though we try to take turns up front, I'm the only one who offers. As the eldest daughter, I try to set a good example for the other four. With a prideful smile, Mama backs away from the vardo door and secures the slab shut.

She disappears just in time to avoid our entrance into the village. The vardo leans heavily to the left then the right as the dirt road bleeds into wobbly ragged cobblestones. It sounds as if we're riding over a pile of wooden blocks. If anyone in the back was still asleep, they aren't now.

Most of the locals are on foot, along the curbs outside various shops. We might not have stood out as much as we do if it weren't for our old vardo, the tomato-red wood-paneling, the sea-green tapestry draped over the roof, and the excessive, extravagant flourishes embossed in a honey-yellow hue that once looked like gold. The first crowd we pass yell a string of profanities at us, questioning whether we are part of a traveling circus. *We are not.*

The next several locals we clomp by stop short in their steps to watch us meander through the center of their village. Some appear to be whispering to each other—those are the quiet types. The children never seem to know much better, so as usual they tag each other and make a show of us moving through the street by pointing and giggling. I'm not sure what they always find so funny. I like to think it's the vardo's contrasting colors, but it might very well be us.

A shop owner must have heard the racket from inside as he steps onto the curb, arms folded over his chest, wrinkling the white apron looped around his neck. "We don't need any more of you here. Už dost! Enough! No more Cikáni!" He spits in our direction as we pass by. "Damn Gypsies. They just keep coming to steal more." I'm not sure who he is talking to as no one appears to be listening, except for me, but I know he isn't alone with his thoughts. He's just the loudest who has noticed us so far.

I'm grateful when Papa turns down a narrow road, one that appears empty except for a couple of mice scampering about between the closely settled buildings. Papa doesn't say a word about the village. His expression doesn't falter, and I don't think he allowed any of those words to ruminate. I wonder if we all feel the same inside but grow better at deflecting the pain and hate we endure. Maybe one day I'll be able to block out the awful things they say and act as though the sound is nothing more than a howl of wind.

My revolving thoughts continue to ravage my mind, distracting me from noticing that we've turned onto another dirt road that leads to an open field with overgrown grass, one with several stationary vardos and caravans in the distance.

"Louisa is already here," Mama says, her voice taking me by surprise since I didn't hear the door reopen behind me. I recognize my aunt's vardo. They planned to arrive yesterday, and we see now that they did. We always travel together, but Papa had to finish some business yesterday before we left, which was the reason we had to travel through the night.

Aunt Louisa is standing in front of her vardo, one that looks like ours, but the colors are slightly more faded and the embellishments blend into the overall red paint. She's waving her arms in the air as if we might miss her. She's the only one standing in the immediate vicinity, and it would be quite hard to avoid seeing her.

It takes less than a few minutes for Papa to settle the vardo next to Aunt Louisa's, and it takes even less time for each of my siblings to fling themselves out of the enclosed wagon walls as if someone had shot them out the door with a slingshot.

I step down from the platform and stretch each of my limbs to help my blood move through my body, but I'm sore from sitting in the same position for so long. Papa is too. I can tell by the way he's bent over, holding the angry spot on his lower back that always bothers him.

Aunt Louisa strangles me with a quick hug and a wet kiss on the cheek before moving on to one of the others. She and Uncle Bosco have two daughters, Eldra and Gille. They are younger, around Bula's age—seven and eight.

"Mila," Papa calls after me while checking the horses' hooves for damage.

"Papa, look what I made," Lela interrupts, holding up a small woven hand towel. "It's just like the one Mila made last week."

"Very beautiful, dear," he says, smiling to give her the reaction she was looking for before refocusing on the horseshoes he's inspecting.

"I already know," I say. "I'll make sure to help Mama while you're gone."

He shakes his head. "I know you will. I'm sure Lela will help too since she seems to be living in your shadow lately. She truly looks up to you. It's so wonderful to see."

Lela is very much like me, even down to our appearances, but she's much younger, and I'm sure once she finds more confidence in herself, she'll become as unique as each of us are.

Papa gently places Basil's back left leg down. "Once I collect the two new horses from the breeder, I'm meeting with the buyer. I've been told he's easy to please and it won't be a difficult sale. I shouldn't be gone for more than a day." Papa reaches into his back pocket and pulls out a folded paper. "I've got a map and have traced the route I plan to take. It should be a simple trip."

I agree with a nod as he places the paper back into his pocket. "Yes, well, you should eat something before you go, and you need water as well," I remind him.

He also needs sleep, just some rest. I worry he is going to keel over and never stand back up again with the way he continues to march forward as if he's not human like the rest of us.

"Of course, dear," he says.

Mama already has a bowl of rice with vegetables and a mug of water prepared for Papa. I watched Aunt Louisa retrieve the food and water from her vardo. She must have had it waiting for Papa, knowing he would be leaving shortly after we arrived today. Papa's income from trading horses is usually our only source of money, and we do what we can not to take that for granted.

As Papa typically does, he clears his bowl within a few short moments and gulps the water as if he's racing against a clock. "Wonderful. Thank you," he says, handing the empty dishes back to Mama.

"Be safe, Doran, please," says our mother.

"I always am," he says, cupping his hands around her face and leaving her with an endearing goodbye kiss.

"Children, come say goodbye to your papa."

While he hugs each of my siblings and leaves them with a kiss on their head, his gaze holds steadily on me. I don't know why he seems worried about me, but it's clear he is. "Will you be okay?" he asks.

"Papa, you don't need to fuss over me. Worry about the horses and the buyer. Everything will be fine here." I kiss him on the cheek and give him a hug. He reaches into his pockets then pats his hands down and across his body, checking to make sure he has everything he needs—the money for the horses, his lucky handkerchief, and pocketknife.

Everyone is so used to Papa leaving that it sounds more like a celebration than a solemn event. It seems that no one thinks twice about the dangers he faces when conducting business outside of the Romani community. It would only take one bad trade to cause unthinkable damage to our family.

FOUR
A WILD MANE
BENEDIKT, SEPTEMBER 1938

I toss an old, ragged sheet across the wooden garden table, which does nothing more than collect dust most days. The outside furniture beneath the covered porch hasn't been used for years so I tend to make myself comfortable out here when working on a project I've taken on. It's hard to find a quiet space despite the large plot of land we own. There is always activity, whether it be a luncheon, afternoon tea, a business meeting, tutoring or private lessons, structural repairs, landscape maintenance—the business lifestyle here never ceases.

I lift the greasy engine block from the mess of newspaper I had it wrapped in and place it on the table. There's something very satisfying about taking a rusty broken part and making it look and work like new again. Of course, I'm the only one in the family who enjoys such a grubby hobby, but to each their own.

When I turn to the outdoor storage closet to collect my toolbox, I hear the doors to the back terrace open and close. Heavy heels clomp against the stone patio, warning me Tobias is likely on the prowl. Father doesn't feel the need to make his presence known as much as my older brother, and Filip and Pavel are typically heard running around the estate rather than walking with intention.

"Even on a lovely autumn day, I can smell the fragrance of motor grease wafting through the air," he announces before appearing around the hedge of bushes at the corner.

I release the handlebar of my toolbox and reach in to search for the proper wrench I need to loosen the bearings so I can work on removing some of the rust from the crankshaft. The last guy didn't take care of this thing, which isn't a surprise since I found it in pieces at the dump.

"You smell like Castrol oil, not grease," I correct.

Tobias stands on the other side of the table, his hands resting in the pockets of his freshly pressed pants. "You know, Ben, people are going to start thinking you work for us, rather than being a son and brother of this family."

I straighten up from my hunched position and stretch my shoulders. "Who—what people? I'm in the back courtyard and no one aside from our family is here. However, if someone was here, I don't think they would be as ignorant as you, so there isn't anything to brood over, brother."

The smirk on his face is different from anyone else's snide expression in our family. He's the only one with the look of something devious brewing in his mind. We're the same height, same build, and have similar facial features except for the scar running diagonally from my left eyebrow to my right cheek. Thankfully, and yet, not so thankfully, for that one mark, no one ever confuses the two of us. The irony of Tobias being the cause of the scar is something I've forced myself to forget about over the years.

"Well, Father should be home shortly with the new horses."

"And the horses have strong opinions on what I'm doing here?" I question him.

"I meant the horse trader will likely be with him," Tobias corrects his statement.

The only reason he's mentioning any of this to me is because the stables are across the courtyard from where I've set up the table to work.

"I'm sure you can distract them while they make their way over to the stables." I reach back into the toolbox for a second wrench, trying my best to ignore him.

Tobias spins around, his chin up, as if taking in the fresh air while admiring the landscape. I can only estimate how long he plans to stand here until the next idiotic statement spills out of his mouth.

"I think Father's plan is brilliant. Wouldn't you agree?" he says, exhaling.

"I know nothing of Father's plan, nor is it any of my business." It shouldn't be Tobias's business either, but he seems to think every decision made around here should include him since he will become the heir to this estate when Mother and Father pass away. We can only hope this not to be sooner than forty to fifty years from now, but Tobias seems to think otherwise. Unless he is expected to know imperative information pertaining to our livelihood, he avoids bulletins, worldwide news, and updates about the German conflict inflicting Europe. He believes that wealth can protect anyone from the harsh realities of the world.

"They're here now. Clean up the mess or put the sheet over the grimy metal box you're working on. What an embarrassment," he says, eyeing the tabling.

I lift my gaze to search the distance for a hint of Father approaching, but I don't see anything. "You should go greet him. I'm sure the horse dealer will be eager to meet the future heir to an estate we likely won't be able to afford in the coming yea—I apologize, brother. I forgot you don't follow any updates on the economic crisis we're going through. Forget I said anything. You should really go greet them though. It's the proper thing to do."

"You fool. We aren't losing the estate. We own it. It's been in our family for more than four hundred years. Perhaps you should study a little harder and pay less attention to the mess of grease you're toying with."

I learned long ago there's no sense in arguing with Tobias. Even if he doesn't win, he will convince himself he has.

Father, another gentleman, and two horses appear in view as they walk toward the stables. They must have been at the bottom of the hill when I looked moments ago.

Tobias straightens his tie and scurries toward Father, looking as if the excitement is too much for the seam of his pants. He can talk the talk, but like a monkey in a suit, most people aren't blind to the truth of what they're dealing with.

Pavel and Filip make their presence known as the back door swings open, followed by the slapping sound of the leather soccer ball puttering against the patio. "Play catch with me," Pavel demands. "Go far this time."

"Not now," Filip says.

"You won't ever play ball anymore. Why is everything else so much more important to everyone all of a sudden?"

They both round the corner, Pavel flapping his lips, begging Filip to play with him. "What are you working on?" Filip asks.

"The motorbike I found."

"I thought you said the engine was broken?"

"I found the parts I needed for the engine, but I need to clean it up first."

"Oh," Filip says, turning toward the stables. "Father's back?"

"The new horses are here?" Pavel asks.

"I would wait here until the dealer leaves. Then you can meet the horses," I say to Pavel.

"That man doesn't look like a horse dealer to me," Pavel says as Father and the other gentleman step out of the stables with Tobias on their heels.

"That's rude," Filip says. "Keep your voice down."

"Well, he doesn't," Pavel argues.

"What does it matter what a man looks like?" I ask. Pavel is picking up some poor traits from Tobias and I try my best to be a better influence over him, but at his age, it's easy to assume that Tobias is above others due to the way he acts.

"He isn't completely wrong," Filip says. "The man looks more like a beggar than a horse dealer."

"I honestly don't understand what difference it makes. Father has his reason for wanting two more horses, and it shouldn't matter who he acquires them from."

Pavel tosses his ball into Filip's stomach, igniting a chase and ensuing brawl.

While carefully loosening the bearings, I spot an awkward exchange between Father and Tobias. I can't hear what they're saying from here, but Father is pointing toward the estate, then Tobias walks away from the discussion between the dealer and Father. The closer he gets, the more fury I notice along Tobias's face. I could poke the lion, but I'd much prefer to work on the engine instead.

Tobias narrows his eyes at me as he walks by and the repeating sound of clapping heels against the stone patio tells me a door is likely to slam. I'm not sure I understand the point of acting rich and powerful if he's going to storm off like a spoiled child minutes later.

The sound of laughter floats through the air from Father and the horse dealer and I spot their exchange ending with a handshake. Father pats the man on the back and opens his arm to the side to guide him off the property.

I have a few minutes as Father disappears over the hill toward the front lawn, and Filip and Pavel sneak over to the stables for a peek at the new horses, to gain access to the crankshaft and start brushing some of the rust off before Father returns.

"Do you want to meet the new horses?" Father calls out to me. "I see your brothers are already becoming acquainted."

I pull a rag out of my toolbox and clean the black oil off my hands before walking toward the stables.

When I reach the stables, I hear one of the horses before I see them. It's an alarming sound of panic, which can happen from time to time when a horse is relocated, but this one seems very upset.

"Two young thoroughbreds for a great deal," Father says. "Nova and Twister."

"Should I take a guess which one is named Twister?" I ask with a quick laugh.

"She's just a bit nervous, but she'll settle down."

Nova seems to be the complete opposite of Twister as she stares at the other side of the stable as if there's something more to look at than a solid wall.

"Will we all be taking turns training the new horses?" I ask. We had to let our horse caretaker go about a year ago. Father said their salary was impeding the wages of the staff in the house. Just before we sold our last horses, we were down to minimal help and had a caretaker come once a week to clean and check them over, but between those times, Filip, Pavel, and I checked on them and brushed them, and sometimes cleaned out the stables if necessary. The burden was one of the reasons Father made the decision to give them up. No one asked us if we wanted two new horses on our hands now though, so hopefully there's a plan to go along with them.

"No, in fact, I've just made a wonderful bargain with the horse dealer. He has a daughter who has been looking for work and she knows everything about horses. She will also take the place of a new maid to replace Karolina. The rate was quite reasonable, which will be an enormous help." The family thinks we have been suffering without Karolina. She was wonderful to have around to handle all the housework, but I believe we are capable of picking up the extra slack, too.

"Father, the man looked like a beggar. Are you sure this is a good idea? Perhaps the rate was so reasonable because there are ulterior intentions?" Filip questions.

"I've heard there are a lot of beggars trying to trick the wealthy right now," Pavel adds. I'm not sure where he would have heard such a thing since we don't talk that way, but I assume Tobias said something suggestive.

"This man is not a beggar, son. He's a horse dealer. I assure you there's nothing to worry about."

"When does the girl start?" Filip asks.

Father loosens his tie and unbuttons the cuffs of his shirt to roll the sleeves up to his elbows. I'm certain he wants to calm the frantic horse—Twister—somehow. Though, I'm not sure he knows how to do that. "While I wish it were right this very moment, she will be here first thing tomorrow morning."

"I'll work on calming the horse, Father," I offer.

"Yes, well I suppose you're already dressed for the occasion," he says with a wink. Father doesn't mind my hobbies. In fact, I often wonder if he's jealous that he doesn't have the time to get his hands dirty sometimes.

"I'll take that as a compliment," I say, wiping the excess oil still left on my hands down the front of my white tee shirt.

Father pats me on the shoulder and heads out of the stables. "I'll let the others know about the new maid so we can prepare for her arrival."

"Something is wrong with this horse," Pavel says, watching Twister whip her neck from side to side.

"This one too," Filip says, running his hand down Nova's mane. She still doesn't move a muscle and continues to stare ahead.

"I'm sure they just need to adjust. I wouldn't worry just yet."

I'm not sure I can convince myself, but hopefully Father knows well enough not to take on horses that we can't care for or can't race like I'm sure he intends for them to do. There's an obvious disconnect in Father's recent decisions. Between the staff we've had to release and taking on an additional financial burden now, I'm not sure I understand the need for such a gamble.

FIVE
A DISCREET WORK FOR HIRE
MILA, SEPTEMBER 1938

We've been at the new settlement for just over a day. I walked a fair distance around the perimeter today, checking out how far into the woods I could go before spotting the village, which spans around half of this land. The other half is bordered by factory buildings, but the surrounding trees make us feel like we are in the center of the universe, alone. So long as there is a water pump and land without laws, our family is content.

As per my typical nightly chores, I wash the dishes after supper. Lela dries and then stacks them up neatly for the next day. We have two wooden buckets, one with soap and water, and the other just water for rinsing.

Morti and Broni are keeping a fire going and Mama and Aunt Louisa are telling the littlest of children bedtime stories. Uncle Bosco appears to be asleep already, his hands folded beneath his head, legs stretched out and crossed, facing the fire, with a tall grass straw dangling from his bottom lip. It's not fair that he's allowed time to rest while Papa is still on the move trying to secure our next load of income.

"Do you think Papa is okay?" Lela asks, staring out toward the darkening forest of trees.

"Of course, he is. We've been through this so many times. Why worry now?"

Lela sighs and drops her gaze to the rag in her hand as she rubs at the same clean spot on the bowl she's been drying for several minutes. "We're moving more frequently now. It seems like we can't stay in one place for very long, and we're going through money quicker than before too. Something must have changed."

Our only need for money is to buy certain foods we can't forage, but no matter where we go, the cost of every grain has increased, and continues to do so with each passing month. The pressure from the world's conflicts is taking a toll on Europe. "There will always be horses to buy and sell," I remind her. "Papa knows what he's doing."

Truth be told, I've offered to help Papa many times, but he insists on going about his business alone, claiming there are dangers and risks involved when trading animals. I've considered this statement many times, but still don't understand what problems could arise. Trades aren't new and they keep the world revolving. I often feel like Papa leaves out part of the truth behind the business he conducts. If so, I'm not sure I want to know any differently.

"Ah, everyone is still awake. Is there any food left for this old man?" Papa's voice carries through the wind between the trees like in an enclosed corridor. He's back.

"Papa!" Lela shouts, dropping the clean bowl to the ground beside the bucket.

I drop the dish I was cleaning back into the soapy water and pat my hands off on my white apron. Papa is like royalty to our family, always greeted as such with warmth, love, and excitement. While everyone is taking their turn welcoming him back, I'm busy studying the look on his face, the weariness within the swollen pockets beneath his eyes. I enjoy waiting to be the last to greet him when he returns because I will have the chance to hear stories about his travels and experiences.

Papa makes his way over to me with his arms stretched out to the sides, ready for the tight embrace I always promise to give. "My darling. Was everything all right while I was gone?"

"Of course, Papa. What about you? Did everything work out okay?"

Papa places his dry, calloused hand on my cheek. "Yes, yes. I need to talk to your mother for a moment before I tell you anything more."

"Is everything okay?" I take his hand off my cheek and hold it between mine. "Did you sleep somewhere last night? Please say you did."

"Yes, I came across another settlement of travelers, and I had a place to rest. No need to worry, my dear."

I release Papa's hand as he searches around our enclosed circle for Mama. "She's telling Bula a bedtime story inside the wagon," I say, pointing him in her direction.

Papa disappears around the corner of the vardo, and I watch the structure sway from side to side as he moves around inside the tight space.

"What's wrong?" Lela asks, returning to where we were washing the dishes. "You look like you've gotten bad news."

"No, everything is fine," I lie while wondering what Papa could need to speak with Mama about, something more important than telling me about his travels as he always does.

"You have that worry line on your forehead, the one you always try to hide with your hair," Broni says while dropping another pile of dry sticks into the fire. I sweep my hair behind my ear, loosely so the top of the strands falls diagonally across my forehead, covering the worry line Broni speaks of. "Mila, we still know it's there. What's the use in hiding it?" Broni likes to tease me about the amount of concern I take on just because I'm the eldest child of the family. I'm sure if he was the oldest, he might feel differently, but I also pay attention to more than he does. He'd rather pretend we were only surrounded by the grass and sky, and there's nothing more to life than the food he's handed each day. It isn't his fault that he thinks the way he does —Mama has always had a way of making us believe our lives are nothing less than perfect, but the older I become, and the more I see and witness, the less I'm able to believe her smiles.

The door to the vardo slams shut, followed by the crunch of grass beneath footsteps. "Mila, come on over here and talk with me for a moment," Papa says.

Lela glances over at me, her hands still moving as she dries another bowl. Her curiosity must be like mine based on the wide-eyed look she's giving me.

She takes the clean dish from my hand and places it on the tree stump she was sitting on earlier.

I drop my hands into the pockets of my apron and follow Papa toward the center of the settlement where the horses congregate. "What is it?" I ask, trying to hide the worry threatening to stifle my voice.

"An odd turn of events took me by surprise today," he begins.

I press my lips together firmly, feeling the dry cracks stinging in the wind. "What do you mean?"

Papa runs his hands down the sides of his face—a sign of unease, one he doesn't often show. "The horses I acquired last night were said to be healthy thoroughbreds. The man assured me with paperwork. His knowledge was unquestionable. However, it was dark when the transaction took place, so I carefully checked both horses over several times. They seemed to be as described—healthy, young, purebred."

"Are they sick?" I question, wondering what else could be wrong.

"I believe one of them was medicated during the purchase because this morning, she was spooked—or acting as though she was spooked. I couldn't calm her down. She was nothing like how she was last night. The other horse, she was almost exactly opposite—quiet, hard to get her attention. I'm no horse doctor, but something was quite wrong with both. The dealer was long gone in the morning, and I had no choice but to continue the transaction as planned. The family I had arrangements to sell the horses to had quite a few questions. The gentleman was about to walk away from the sale and—"

"Papa, how did you sell the horses?"

"The man told me he couldn't afford a full-time horse trainer and they were already in need of a housemaid. Even the wealthy are struggling these days."

I have a suspicion of where this conversation is heading. "You offered me up to help the man?"

"They have offered to pay," Papa says, his gaze dropping to the grass between us. "It isn't much, but it's income rather than a loss I could have faced."

"You would like me to act as a slave for this man?" It's all I can take from this conversation—a way of life our family has been running away from for centuries.

"You would be hired to help, Mila. You've offered to find work many times so you could contribute to the family. What better opportunity than to work with horses. For you and your adoration of horses, it sounds like a dream come true, doesn't it?"

"And clean up after wealthy people," I add.

"A job of any sort is a blessing to all people today, not just us."

"The man doesn't know who you are, does he?" I question him.

Papa stands a little taller, lifts his chin, and returns his stare to my face. "I am a man—a father to five children—and a husband to my wife. What more should I have told him about myself?"

"We are Romani—the most disliked race in this country."
Papa's skin isn't as olive-toned as mine and Mama's, but I
inherited his light blue eyes. My appearance is made up of a
combination of several races, but I fear it won't be hard to
figure out I'm a person the wealthy would never want in their
home.

"They have a uniform for you. You will fit right in, and no
one will question who you are. If you don't tell them, they won't
know."

"You want me to lie?"

"Call it what you want. You are protecting yourself and
helping our family like I do."

"I should have had a choice," I argue.

"Yes, darling, you should have, but if given the choice of us
all starving until I earn enough money to buy new horses rather
than you taking on some work, as you've requested to do, I
didn't expect you to think about the answer."

He's correct in what he's saying. I would never let anything
bad happen to my family, and I will protect them at all costs just
as Papa does. "I understand, and I want to help."

Papa places his hands on my shoulders and kisses my forehead. "I believe you will find a way to help the horses too. We've
always said you have a magic touch with them, right, my
darling?"

"I will try my best."

"Good girl. They will be expecting you in the morning. I
will take you there."

I tried to sleep, but Lela was tossing and turning most of the
night and kicked me several times. Bula had to go to the bath-
room twice, and Morti had a coughing fit that wouldn't cease.
The top platform bed we all share above Mama and Papa's bed
was rattling from the moment we tried to fall asleep until just a

few moments ago when I snuck out of the bed to brush my hair and change my clothes.

When I step out of the vardo, I find Papa washing his face with the bucket of clean water. "I'll be ready just as soon as I wash up too," I say.

"Did you take some padda from the cupboard?" Papa asks. "Your identification papers too. You must keep those on you at all times."

"Yes, I have the papers in my pocket as well as a bit of bread."

The water isn't as cool as I'd like, wishing a refreshing splash would offer me a bit more energy to push away my exhaustion.

"Everything is going to be fine," Papa says as we start down the dirt path that leads to the main road.

"I'm sure."

"The family seems fairly common, from those I met."

"A family?" I ask.

Our feet scuffle against the dirt-covered pebbles as Papa takes a moment to respond. "I believe Mister Bohdan said he and his wife have four sons. I met the eldest. While he seemed a bit aloof, Mister Bohdan was as pleasant as they come. I imagine the rest of them to be alike."

"Are there other maids or staff?"

"I would imagine there must be by the size of the estate."

The walk takes us about twenty minutes when an over-whelmingly large estate seemingly rolls over the hill we are climbing. The Baroque façade envelopes the curved frame, indented by dozens of arched windows, and embellished with twists that spill into columns around the front entrance. As if the estate is a centerpiece in an exquisite painting, with its lush gardens, and a diverse plethora of trees blurred around the edges like a warm encompassing vignette. "It's magnificent."

"It is very grand and lovely," Papa agrees. "It might be a

wonderful opportunity." We both know the likelihood is slim, but I'm doing this for our family, and that's that.

"I'm going to let you go the rest of the way through the arched gate. Knock on the door and ask for Mister or Madam Bohdan and let them know you are the new horse-keeper and maid."

"I'll find my way back to the settlement after I finish working," I say.

Papa places a kiss on my forehead. "Thank you, Mila. I don't know what we'd do without you."

Papa's words replay over and over as I make my way down the pristine, white-washed stone driveway, lined with gardens on each side. Before I make my way to the front entrance, I hear a wailing moan from what sounds like a horse. I circle around in search of the stables, but with the estate settled on a hill, I can't see much beyond the front edifice.

The front door opens before I reach the long, wide steps leading up to the marble lion statues that embrace the entrance on each side.

"You must be Mila," a middle-aged gentleman says, jutting his hand out with fervor. The man's cheerful greeting along with a mustache-lined jovial smile and bright-eyed gaze contrasts with his austere appearance—pleated slacks, stiff white button-down shirt, and a maroon tie that hangs straighter than an arrow along his tall and slender form. His elation doesn't quite match what I'm feeling.

"Yes, sir."

"Good, good. We've been eagerly awaiting your arrival. I'm hoping you are as gifted with horses as your papa mentioned."

"He does speak highly of me, but I know a fair amount about caring for horses. I hope I can help."

"Thank goodness. I'm Josef Bohdan. It's a pleasure to meet you," he says, stepping outside rather than inviting me in. "Please follow me to the stables. Madam Bohdan will be ready shortly and can introduce you to our other staff member here as well as give you a tour of our home and cover all the details."

I follow Mister Bohdan across the lawn and around the estate to where I see the stables settled in the back corner of their land. "Sometimes horses have trouble adjusting to new locations," I say, recalling Papa's difficulty with selling these two to this family.

"Yes, your papa mentioned the same."

When we arrive at the stables, I find two young men around Lela's age trying to pet the horse that seems to be in some type of pain. They both turn toward me, a look of surprise on their faces that doesn't come as a shock to me. As I feared, they will all likely assume what I am, or what it is that they wouldn't want around their high-end belongings.

Mister Bohdan takes a quick glance at my attire, as if he doesn't notice the rags draped over my body—the ones I refer to as clothes. "My wife will supply you with a uniform when she comes out to greet you."

"Perfect. Thank you."

"Boys, introduce yourself to the young lady."

"I'm Filip and this is Pavel," the older of the two says. "A pleasure to meet you."

"Good. Go on now and let Miss—" Mister Bohdan must not know my last name it seems by his questioning.

"Leon. Mila Leon."

"Miss Leon, yes. Well, I'll let you get to it. My other two sons, Tobias and Benedikt, will come around to meet you at some point this morning, as well."

"No need for later introductions, Father. I'm already here," a man says from behind us.

"Ah, Tobias. This is my eldest son," Mister Bohdan says.

"The heir to this estate," Tobias continues. Unlike the others, Tobias wears a smug grin like it's a badge of merit. His personality seems to match his pristine wardrobe, specifically the way his tight shirt collar hugs his neck. He's tall with broad shoulders, and he's handsome, but there's something very off-putting about him. It's hard to keep the word, *congratulations*, to myself. With a deep inhale, I lift my hand to shake his but, as expected, he looks at my hand and declines the greeting. "Well, Mother should be out soon to get you settled and to bring you a uniform," he says, his eyes tracing a line from my head down to my toes. He's not nearly as subtle as Mister Bohdan.

I wonder if they all dress so nicely every day. It seems so early in the day to have buttons clasped so tightly around their neck and wrists. Perhaps he does business with his father.

"Let's let her try and help Twister here," Mister Bohdan says. "Nova is much calmer but also seems unwell."

"I'll check them both out," I say.

"Wonderful." Mister Bohdan and Tobias both turn on their heels almost at the very same moment and clasp their hands behind their backs as they walk out of the stables.

"Father, did you hire a damn Gypsy to work in our house?" I hear the eldest son say.

While I can't say I appreciate his candor, I do know it takes a much bigger man to ask such a question while facing someone rather than doing so while walking away.

SIX
A VERY TELLING SIGN
BENEDIKT, SEPTEMBER 1938

The moment I hear Tobias shouting accusations from the foyer, I realize I have spent one minute too long savoring the warm sweet cake that Marena prepared for us this morning. She's been cooking for our family since I was about three years old, and she's the last of our staff we would dare let go. She's like family to us. In fact, I might starve if it wasn't for her.

Tobias and Father make their way into the breakfast room, my brother still shouting nonsense. None of which I can decipher as spit flies out of his mouth.

"Son, will you do us all a favor and take a breath. Your questions and assumptions aren't relevant or necessary."

There was a point in time when I wanted to know everything everyone was talking about. Tobias would love for me to question the meaning of the argument just so he can tell me it's none of my business, so instead, I prefer to stay silent and continue reading this morning's newspaper.

"Anything interesting this morning? I haven't had a moment to flip through the pages," Father asks me.

I refold the paper. I don't usually take it until he's had a chance to read through it. "My apologies, I didn't know you hadn't—"

"Ben, you don't need to apologize for reading the newspaper before me but thank you for being considerate." Father raises an eyebrow, silently questioning my abundance of politeness. It's my way of rattling the lion cage without having to get too close. Tobias likes to cause a ruckus and I try to be respectful —it's just a fun little game I sometimes play.

"What could be so important in the newspaper anyway?" Tobias asks, taking the sterling silver pot of tea from the center of the table just as Father was reaching for it.

"Aside from talk of Hitler threatening war if our country doesn't surrender its land to the Germans, absolutely nothing." I take the last nibble of sweet cake with hopes of making a quick escape from this room before more tension rises.

"Has the threat evolved at all or is everything hearsay?" Father asks.

"Britain and France are planning to discuss the situation, but there isn't much of a hint to which direction this will go."

Father exhales a sigh of frustration and retrieves the teapot Tobias placed back down on the table, filling his cup. "That man isn't going to stop until he has what he wants. I fear for what's coming."

"As do I," I reply.

"You fear for what's coming?" Tobias scolds Father. "Yet, you hire a Gypsy to work in our house?"

Father's aggravation presents itself with a loud clank of china when he drops his full teacup onto the saucer, causing the liquid to spill over the sides. I'm surprised it didn't crack. "You have no right to talk about people the way you do. I did not tell you she was a Gy—Romani. You are making allegations which make you sound like an imbecile. You embarrassed this family in front of her without a care in the world for how you make others feel. If I were you, son, I would take a long, hard look at the man you think you want to be, rather than the one you may end up as. I don't want to hear another slur about that young lady."

Tobias grits his teeth, his jaw muscles flexing as he inhales sharply through his nose.

"On that note, I have matters to tend to this morning before I take my economics exam this afternoon," I say.

"Ah yes, I'm sure you'll do fine as always," Father says.

"Of course, he will, Father. Ben is perfect in every way. He doesn't even need to study for an exam because he's far more intelligent than the rest of us, but only by God's given right, of course."

"Perhaps you should enroll at the university as well, and you won't feel it necessary to berate someone for seeking an education," I add in defense.

"What's the purpose? My future is already planned out."

I clear my throat and push my teacup and saucer toward the center of the table. The moment I stand from my seat, Mother arrives with Filip and Pavel following in her footsteps. "What's all the commotion?"

"There's nothing to fret over, dear," Father assures her.

"Except for the Gy—"

Father clears his throat, interrupting Tobias.

"The *traveler* he hired to be our new maid," Tobias grunts, along with a forced cough.

"Don't mind what he says. Tobias is having a bad day for whatever reason, and feels the need to let the world know," Father says.

"Is it true?" Mother asks.

"Is what true? That the young lady is a—? Of course not."

"Did you see the way she looks or how she's dressed?" Tobias continues.

"You are aware of how Germans are treating Jewish people right now, yes?" Father replies, a snap to each of his words. "You are Jewish. Someone wouldn't need to come in here with a ruler to decipher that your nose is not one that belongs to someone of Aryan descent, yet no one says a word to you because we have not lost the battle to Hitler. But, son, you don't know what the future will bring, and you might find yourself to be very sorry for the things you have said. I suggest you take a look at the world around you before you discriminate against an innocent person."

Rather than retaliate, Tobias runs his finger down the bridge of his nose. "There's nothing wrong with my nose."

After attempting to leave the room for the last several minutes, I finally excuse myself from the fiery words blazing across the table. I didn't have the chance to accomplish much with the motorbike's engine yesterday, and since everyone seems to be tongue-tied right now, it might be my only opportunity.

As I unwrap all the pieces on top of the sheet-covered table, I come to realize the horse, Twister, isn't making the awful noises we heard all night. The silence is refreshing, but I wonder what trick got her to calm down.

I've managed to remove most of the rust from the crankshaft and have tightened the bearings back to where they were as I notice Mother making her way through the back gardens, heading toward the stables. It looks as if she has a dress of some sort draped over her arm. I gather she's preparing to meet the young woman Father hired.

With curiosity nagging at me, I wipe my hands on a rag and follow Mother's trail to the stables. I know she can be easily persuaded by Tobias's opinions.

I stand off to the side of the stables, out of sight but within hearing range.

"Hello, dear," Mother says. "Mister Bohdan told me I would find you out here. I'm Hana Bohdan, and you are Mila Leon, correct?"

"It's nice to meet you, madam. Yes, I'm Mila," she says. A sense of confidence laces her words, but the honeyed sound of her voice is alluring.

"Well then."

The pause makes me wonder what look Mother might be giving the poor girl.

"I—I've brought you a uniform and a pair of proper shoes, but of course you can change inside the estate rather than out here."

"Thank you, madam."

The girl speaks with a sense of confidence, certainly not shy but not over assertive either.

"I see you've managed to calm down the poor horse too. How impressive," Mother says in a questioning manner.

"She seems very timid and scared, but I'm not sure why," Mila says.

"Maybe just a new location," Mother responds.

"Oh, no, it's not that. I think she may just need some extra care and love."

Mila's answer isn't typical for someone who is well versed in handling horses. At least, not from what I've heard from the specialists we've had here.

"I see. Well, I'm sure we can give her that," Mother says.

I don't have to see Mother's face to picture the stare she's giving Mila. I know that she's making direct eye contact and yet somehow still scrutinizing every part of the girl. "Thank you for this opportunity," Mila says. "Mister Bohdan mentioned you would be showing me around the estate this morning?"

"Ah, yes, yes, let's—uh, let's go on inside and I'll show you around and introduce you to the other staff member, Marena. Follow me."

I take a few steps back to make sure I'm out of sight when they exit the stables. The girl is nothing like what I was expecting according to Tobias's ranting. She may not be dressed like royalty but everything about her is neat and tidy, including her long honey-brown hair. She isn't quite as tall as Mother, which is unusual since she's much shorter than most women. Mila looks very young from behind. Perhaps that's why she looks smaller.

A stick snaps beneath my foot, one I didn't realize I was standing on. Luckily, Mother seems unaffected and continues walking.

Mila peers over her shoulder in search of the sound, finding me leaning against the stables. I instantly see why Tobias has labeled her, but I'm not sure why he would say a word when the girl is so startlingly beautiful with the light-coloring of her eyes in contrast with an olive skin complexion. Her features are rare to find here, but when we do, it's typical to assume they aren't born locals of the area.

She turns back toward the estate, following Mother inside. She must already think I'm as rude as Tobias. I wouldn't blame her for coming to such a conclusion.

Once they're inside, I step into the stables to check on the horses. The moment Twister acknowledges my presence, she begins to buck and make the same awful noises we heard last night. "It's okay, shh," I say, trying to calm her down. With each step closer I take, the more frantic she seems. I wish I knew how Mila got her to relax when all I seem to be doing is infuriating her.

Before I turn to leave, feeling unwelcome in the stables, I notice Nova's tired stare. I reach into the pen to touch her muzzle, but the moment my fingers stroke her hair, she jumps backward as if she didn't see me coming. Both horses buck, and groan. I leave the stables as quickly as I can, hoping they calm down, but they only become louder and more agitated. Mother and Mila return after likely hearing the noises. Mila runs past me as if she knows exactly what to do, but Mother stops beside me, holding her hands against her chest.

"What in the world did you do to them?" she asks.

"Why would you ask me something like that? I came in to visit them," I reply, watching as Mila effortlessly helps them both calm down within a short minute.

"Looks like a little bit of witchcraft to me," Mother mutters near my ear.

SEVEN
TO TURN A BLIND EYE...
MILA, SEPTEMBER 1938

This poor thing has had a rough start in life. Before reaching out to touch Twister's muzzle, I hush her, giving her a moment to sense my calmness. Many people don't understand that animals mirror our internal feelings and sometimes our outward behaviors. They are a better judge of character than we are, but in Twister's case, it seems she finds everyone to be a threat unless proven otherwise.

I almost forgot Madam Bohdan and... I can't recall what this son's name is, but they're still standing outside the stables watching me try and calm the horses down.

With a momentary glance toward their direction, I notice Madam Bohdan has her arms folded over her chest and her gaze is pinned to the face of her golden watch. "Mila, why don't you finish up out here and come inside when you're through? I'll be waiting for you in the library, which is the first room on the right once you enter the front foyer."

"Yes, madam," I reply, keeping my gaze on Twister's eyes, which seem to be focused on mine.

"Come along, Benedikt," Madam Bohdan commands. I try not to alter my expression despite what I'm thinking. Her son is clearly old enough to make decisions for himself, and I believe there's another son somewhere inside who desperately needs a good scolding—though they strike me as one and the same.

"Mother, you go on," Benedikt says.

From the corner of my eye, I watch her give him a questioning look. Benedikt defies her glare by stepping back into the stables.

Madam Bohdan huffs before walking back toward the estate.

"I'm sorry about my mother," Benedikt says.

It would be easy to forgive everyone for the way they speak to me, in front of me, or even behind my back, but I've come to learn that forgiveness won't mend much. Rather than the apology on behalf of someone who isn't ashamed, I'm more curious to learn the reason why Benedikt was standing outside the stables listening in on our conversation.

Twister is breathing heavier again as Benedikt steps closer. "It's all right, hush," I whisper.

"She mustn't like me," Benedikt says, speaking in a gentler tone than he was a minute ago.

I can imagine why. This entire family seems very tense.

Twister allows my hand to move in closer to her muzzle and I lightly sweep the back of my knuckles against her silky hair.

Benedikt takes another couple of steps toward Twister and me, but it's immediately obvious that he's too close to her when she whips her head back and forth, letting out a loud groan. "I don't understand why she seems afraid of me," Benedikt continues.

I glance over at him, finding a look of defeat in his brooding amber eyes. His full lips part as if he's about to speak again, but it seems the air has been stolen from his lungs because not a word comes out. I notice he isn't dressed like his brothers or parents. He's wearing a simple pair of gray slacks, though pressed perfectly, paired with suspenders and a white cotton shirt. If I didn't know better, I would think he might be another worker at the estate.

"By the volume of your silence, I should assume you must feel the same way about me as Twister does," he says. He isn't entirely incorrect. Twister doesn't trust him because she doesn't know him, and I feel the same. "I heard you speaking to my mother, so I am taking the lack of response personally," he says, when I still don't reply.

Benedikt clearly doesn't have an issue speaking about the way he feels, and I'm not surprised after the other introductions I've experienced with his family.

"I've been told by many people that I can carry on a conversation all on my own without the need of anyone ever responding. In fact, I find it to be a positive attribute, especially in situations when one person doesn't want to speak. However, it has gotten me in trouble too, I suppose. A person who likes to talk often doesn't pick up on the cues of another pleading for silence, which can cause a great deal of irritation. Oddly enough, the irritation will often provoke the quiet person to speak up. That way, there's no longer an uncomfortable one-sided conversation."

I'm trying my best not to laugh at the ridiculous chatter coming out of Benedikt's mouth, or the attempt he's making at trying to get me to talk. I wasn't purposely being silent as he has accused me of. I was looking for the proper words.

I've noticed him taking small steps, inching forward in my direction. It's not for my sake, but for Twister's. She is watching him like a hungry lion, ready to pounce. "You know, I'm willing to bet I get Twister to talk to me before I get a word out of you," he carries on. "But I'm okay with that, just so you know." This son is clearly the relentless type, but it's better than being arrogant. On the contrary, I find his motivation intriguing, making me want to play along with him.

Once again, Twister allows me to sweep the back of my

hand against her muzzle, even as Benedikt gets closer. It's good progress, and more of a confirmation of what I fear she has been through. Due to Papa's experience with the gentleman he bought the two horses from, it doesn't come as a surprise that the man might have been rough with her and Nova too, for that matter.

"Just in case you decide to speak to me, you can call me Ben rather than Benedikt. My mother is the only one who feels the need to be so formal, and without reason I should add. I'm not sure who she's trying to impress these days, but I assume it can only be her reflection in the mirror. I can only imagine what you might be thinking of us so far, but on the off chance that you aren't aware, we're just a Jewish family living in fear of our present and future. It may look as if we have a lot, but in my opinion, tangible items don't make a person rich. Many of the people we are friendly with—were friendly with—in the area, have distanced themselves. Aside from the business meetings Father conducts and attending the university, we don't converse with others. Not like we used to, anyway." I didn't think I would learn so much of Ben's life story so quickly, but it's obvious he has a lot to say.

I also wouldn't have assumed they were a Jewish family, which makes me as guilty as his family is for making assumptions about my background. It doesn't matter one way or another to me. That's the difference. Race and religion are our histories—what we're made of—and to be held accountable for whatever it is we are demonized for is nothing more than belligerent stupidity being passed down from one generation to the next.

Benedikt—Ben—has made his way up to the stall's gate, directly beside me. He gently reaches over to Twister's head, hoping she will allow him to touch her. Her ears fold back, showcasing her fear, but the moment his fingers graze her muzzle, her ears relax and she dips her head over the fence, resting it on my shoulder. *Poor girl.*

By the small smile forming along Ben's lips, it's easy to see he's pleased that Twister doesn't seem to hate him as much as she did a few minutes ago. "I thought you had a magic touch, but now I'm not sure anymore," he says in a whisper.

I feel the need to roll my eyes or give him a look like one his mother must have trained him to read, but as I turn to look at him, our hands brush against one another while we caress Twister's muzzle. The unexpected sensation of his rough skin and the warmth emanating from his touch startles me, and I flinch. Twister whips her head, knocking me backward while letting out another loud groan. It all happens in the blink of an eye, and I didn't realize Ben had caught me by the arm before I'd lost my balance and fallen onto the cement ground.

Once he's helped me regain my balance, I try to brush off the embarrassment, which leads to me breaking my silence. "I think she was hurt by the man who sold her to my father. She's young and it may be all she knows. She feels our emotions," I finally say.

"That was a lot of effort to get you to speak," he replies with a warm laugh. His cheeks brighten into a rosy shade as he clasps his fingers around the back of his neck. "Thank you for explaining what might be wrong with Twister. Now that you mention the thought of her past, it explains a lot."

"Whatever the case may be, it seems you might be better with horses than you are with people, so I'm glad she's here now."

It takes Ben a few seconds to extract the insult from my statement and once he does, his brows knit together, and his bottom lip drops. "I don't think I'm going to take that as a compliment—at least, half of what you said."

"Horses are nicer than people, so at least you have that in your favor," I say with a hint of a smirk.

He can't argue with that statement. Twister is calm again, hopefully realizing neither of us are going to hurt her in any way. I'm sure it will take some time to earn her trust, but it's a start.

While Ben is giving Twister his attention, I move over to the next stable to check on Nova. She's quite the opposite as she doesn't budge when I move to her right side. I wave my hand around in front of her muzzle, keeping the motions slow so they don't startle either of them. She still doesn't move. "I'm just going to rub your head," I mutter while reaching up to run my fingers through her dark mane. She reacts to my touch, drawing back at first before turning her head toward me. I hold my arm out to the other side of her muzzle and she presses her head into my hand. "Nova is blind in one eye," I say to Ben. "But she'll be just fine."

"She's blind," he states, as if needing to repeat the words to hear it again. "That means she won't be able to race."

"That's not true," I reply, running my hand through her thick mane. I keep my gaze on her, wondering what emotions she can pick up from us.

"I don't enjoy watching horses race like my father and brothers do, but I know that's why my father bought these two. It's more of an investment for him than anything else."

From the corner of my eye, I notice Ben's discomfort as he presses his hands against his hips and shifts his weight from one foot to the other.

"I see. I'll do what I can to help her so she can race as intended." The moment I turn to face Ben, he drops his hands and folds them behind his back as if he didn't want me to witness his concern.

"I'm sure my father will appreciate it." With what seems like hesitation, he steps in closer to Nova and me, but with an investigative look in his eye. Maybe he's hoping I'm wrong. I wish I was.

After a moment of acquainting himself better with Nova, he shifts his attention to me, fixating his stare to the side of my face as if there's something he wants to say. My heart thumps, wondering what might be going through his mind. With a warmth spreading across my cheeks, I turn and interrupt the mystery of silence, knowing I should tend to Madam Bohdan to start the real work she has waiting for me. "I should find your mother. I don't want to keep her waiting."

Ben clears his throat and moves to rest his arms on Nova's gate. "Yes, of course. Also—uh, if you want to take any advice from me—I wouldn't pay attention to anything negative you might hear. My older brother doesn't know what he's talking about most of the time, and my mother sees every person outside of our family as a threat to our livelihood."

"I'll keep that in mind. My best attribute is having the ability to be silent when necessary, so you don't have much to worry about."

"It seems you have that ability when it isn't necessary too," he says, a smile unfurling into his dimples.

An unfamiliar flutter surges through my stomach, forcing me to press my lips together and look away.

EIGHT

THIN WALLS

I haven't been to one area of this house where there isn't chatter brewing about Mila. It seems as though we haven't seen a new human in years, but no one is saying anything pleasant and I'm nearly positive no one knows a thing about the girl aside from the lack of upscale attire one should evidently be expected to arrive in when starting their new position as a maid. This is the exact reason why I refuse to "dress to impress," as Mother calls it, every single day. If I'm not attending classes, I don't see a reason to put so much effort into how I look.

Upon walking past the library and finding it empty, I take the opportunity to push through one last round of studying before my exam. One of the two tall leather wingback chairs faces the wall of windows, making it my favorite place to sit in this room. I ease down onto the forgiving cushion and rest my head against the chair, trying to convince myself I'm not too tired to run through the material once more.

Voices suddenly disturb me. "You failed to mention you were purchasing horses to further your habitual need to gamble this family's money away." I should have figured the silence wouldn't last long. Mother and Father must not realize how loudly they're speaking.

"This isn't about gambling, Hana."

"Then what is it about?" I don't know when she became so shrewd, but I often wonder if it's a complex she has from being a wife and the mother of four sons, without any other female influence.

"Has it occurred to you that we might come to a point when our only source of income might be from luck? Every day, we are another step closer to becoming another playing piece under Hitler's thumb."

"Stop talking like that. Why must I ask this of you so often? I don't see the point in fearing the worst-case scenarios while we are living contentedly for the moment," Mother says, irritation lacing her voice.

No one can ignore what's happening in Europe. We can't turn our heads away from the headlines.

I stare down at my thick economics book, spiteful for having to choose this subject for any hope of a promising career in the future. With Father questioning the risk of every one of our financial assets, I can't assume there will be a job waiting for me in his investments.

"Fine, Hana, I will keep the concerns to myself while you mosey about living your life like it's still 1925 when everything was luxurious, flashy, and overflowing with booze. We're coming out of an economic crisis, and for us, I don't believe it is the end. But this will be the last I mention any of this to you because you'd rather ignore our reality than stand beside me and handle our future together."

There's a long thread of quiet between Mother and Father and I'm assuming one of them is regretting what they have just said.

"I'm terrified, Josef. There's the truth you want to hear. I am beside myself with worry, and sitting in this house morning, noon, and night, with nothing to do but think, is making it much worse."

"You live in a chateau in the highest form of class next to royalty and I'm supposed to feel bad that you have to sit in this 'house' every day? No one asked you to lock yourself inside. You are still free to go about your life, which I would suggest you do before we no longer have that freedom."

It's clear there is no regret from Father's side.

"Wonderful. Thank you for the lecture. By the way, I believe both of those new horses you purchased with our family's money are broken."

I close my eyes and drop my head toward my lap. *The horses aren't broken.*

"What in the world are you talking about?" Father asks.

"One of them is very aggressive, and the other seems plain dumb."

I can't stop myself from interrupting this ridiculous conversation. I slap the cover of my book closed and drop it onto the chair before making my way out into the foyer. "The horses are not broken, Mother. One of them seems to have been abused, and the other has a bad eye. Both are still capable of racing, but you wouldn't know that because you were too busy scrutinizing the new maid's attire and contemplating whether she is some sort of a witch."

"A witch?" Father responds.

"Never mind any of this. The girl is in the next room, dusting. We should discuss this later, not while she can hear us," Mother says.

"She could hear you this morning," I argue.

"Enough, enough. Benedikt, just go back to your studies," Father says.

I should have kept my thoughts to myself. Mother and Father don't feel the need to move their conversation anywhere else. I'm just not allowed to take part in it.

"Why are you being rude to the young lady?" Father lowers his voice, trying to be quieter at least.

"Rude? I would hardly consider anything I've done today to be rude. I've given her clean clothes, showed her around the estate, introduced her to Marena, and—"

"And?" Father presses.

"That's all."

"If you want any help around here, treat the girl with some respect. There's no way I'm going to find anyone else to work at the same rate her father and I bartered for. We will be on our own if she leaves, and for good."

They're still so loud that I can't block them out. They're also loud enough for Mila to hear what they're saying. I hope she doesn't.

The conversation between them seems to end abruptly and Mother's heels click and clack toward the back of the house.

At least there's quiet again. I open my book back to the page I had marked for review and make it through the first line when a stack of books crashes to the ground. My heart pounds inside my chest as I whip my head around, finding Mila collecting the books into a pile. "I'm so sorry," she says. "I didn't see the stack resting there and backed into it."

The wall of books is on the right when walking into the room, so I'm unsure how she could have backed into the shelf. Perhaps she saw me when she stepped in and turned to leave. "Are you all right?"

"Yes, of course. I'll leave you to your reading. I didn't mean to interrupt." She seems far more tense than she did out in the stables. I wonder if she's ever worked in a large home before. I doubt she's as proficient a caretaker for horses as well as a former maid.

The black linen uniform Mother gave her is far too big and the hem of the dress falls between her knees and ankles. The shoulders are slipping all around and I assume the neckline is pestering her by the way she's clenching the fabric in her hand. "Don't worry about interrupting. Trust me, an interruption here is as common as breathing." I'd much prefer a distraction from her than anyone else.

"It certainly sounds like there are more than six members of your family living inside." Mila sweeps her loose strands of hair behind her ears, adding to her look of discomfort. Maybe I should be the one to leave so she can work without feeling like I'm watching her.

"How about I go and find somewhere else to study so I'm not in your way," I offer.

"No, no, you shouldn't have to leave. This is your home. Please, just go on and act as if I'm not here."

"But, you are here," I reply. I didn't mean to sound so serious, and I think she took my statement differently to how I intended. "I'm kidding. I'll continue reading and you do whatever it is you're doing."

"Okay," she says with an uneasy smile.

I try to refocus my attention, but the movement I detect in the corner of my eye is leading my mind astray. She's polishing the wooden shelves, removing small stacks of books, one at a time, and wiping down every nook and cranny, all while adjusting her uniform every few seconds.

"Pardon me for noticing, but you look quite uncomfortable in that uniform," I say, unable to help myself. "I'll have my mother find one that fits you better. Is that all right with you?"

"I don't want to bother your mother for anything. It's okay. I can hem it, so it fits better. I'll do so tonight before bed."

"You can sew too?"

"Of course. Most women sew, don't they?"

I chuckle, knowing Mama wouldn't know how to thread a needle if it meant saving her life. "I'm sure many do."

"I didn't mean to be offensive," she says.

"Please, stop worrying so much." I wish I could make her

more comfortable. I get the feeling it doesn't matter whether I stay or go, she's going to think it's her fault. My only guess is that she overheard Mother and Father's conversation.

I manage to hold my attention on my book for the length of time it takes Mila to clean her way over the wall of windows, but the longer I sit here, the more questions I want to ask her.

"Where do you live?" The question shoots out like a firecracker I didn't intend to light. I shouldn't be asking her, or anyone who works for the estate, a question like that. I never step out of line, but there's something about her causing me to break the rules I set for myself. "You know what—I don't know why I just asked. It's clearly none of my business. Don't mind me."

She's up on her toes, reaching up to the top of the window with a rag, but twists her head to look over her shoulder at me. "Just down the road a bit. Not too far. My family and I are new to the area."

This area doesn't see many new people moving in, not lately with this territory falling under Hitler's scrutiny. If anything, we've had a lot of people leave. "I see. Welcome to Bohemia. Are you finding the area pleasant so far?"

She doesn't turn to answer my question this time. Instead, she agrees with a curt nod, keeping her focus on the window she's cleaning. The people here are fickle, stick to what they know, stay close to the ones they've been around. We're all silently afraid of what's to come, but it's not an excuse to treat an outsider as if they don't belong. I've tried explaining this to my family but it seems as if I'm speaking a different language, aside from with Father.

"I'm a bit embarrassed that I was a bartered deal for your father," she says, refraining from looking at me still.

What can I say in response? I wasn't aware of the deal made and I feel awful that she knows this truth. "You overheard my parents talking in the foyer, I assume?"

"It was hard to miss," she says. "However, my papa had given me a warning of sorts."

"I wish I could make an excuse for every person in this house, but they would be just that—a made-up story."

"What makes you different?" she asks.

"I don't want this life you see here."

She hums as if lost in thought. "Well then, what type of life do you want?"

I close my book, knowing I'm done preparing for the exam. There's no possible way I can focus now. "That's an easy answer. One without expectations, schedules, uncomfortable clothing, or hierarchies of people."

Mila laughs as if my answer was something of a joke but stops herself. "I'm not sure such a place exists."

I'm aware my hope for such a life is unlikely, but to dream of that type of freedom is all I have some days. "I'm sure you're right." I stand from my chair and fold my book under my arm. With a quick check of my watch, I confirm it's time to leave for the university. Yet, I'm not sure I want to leave now. I'd much rather find a way to console Mila and take away the pain she is trying so desperately to hide behind her tell-all eyes. I find myself staring at her for a second too long while noticing her long, dark lashes—they conceal a mystery I want to solve. With an attempt to recenter my thoughts, I clear my throat and drop my gaze. "Yes, well—ah, I must be going. My exam is in an hour, and I need to make my way. Good luck with the rest of your day here. Hopefully, I'll see you again tomorrow." I dip my head to be courteous, realizing if my brothers, Mother or Father caught me showing this form of respect to a maid, they would criticize me for being an embarrassment to the family. "Good day, Miss Leon," I say before walking out of the library.

"Good luck with your exam," she responds in a hushed voice.

NINE

PROMISE ME YOU WON'T FOLLOW

MILA, SEPTEMBER 1938

Madam Bohdan asked me to see myself out through the laundry room in the back of the estate. She said it's the entrance and exit the house staff use. Of course, that door is the furthest location from the stables, but I won't complain about the fresh air after being cooped up and inhaling dust for the last several hours. My legs are tired, and my arms are sore from so much physical work, but I keep telling myself it's good to be active and I'm earning some pay too.

The reminder of money makes my blood boil, though. I can't understand how Papa would trade me as a bargain.

In my attempt to unwind from the long day, I focus on the blinding sun, flush with the horizon. The warm glow distracts me from all that I witnessed, heard, and I try to forget today. The family doesn't seem very united on any one topic, and most of them fit the description of an aristocrat—it must be in their blood.

I do wonder why Ben is so different from the rest of them. Even his younger brothers seemed to have a bit of an edge or a hint of Tobias. He was by far the rudest of them all with Madam Bohdan trailing right behind.

At the bottom of the Bohdan's estate driveway, I take the turn I recall from this morning, finding the opposite direction to be brooding with darkness as I face away from the sun.

The rumble of a car engine growls from somewhere behind me, and when I turn to see how far away it is, I can't see anything because of the angle of the sloped hill. The sound fades for a moment before it returns.

I move a bit faster, a wave of discomfort sending chills down my arms. I feel as if I'm being watched by the surrounding trees. I'm not used to being alone. There are so many of us always traveling together that the opportunity for quiet is rare. At least there are birds chirping, and frogs croaking. Also, the rubber crackling against rubble…

I turn around again, checking behind me. This time, I spot a car crawling at a snail's pace not too far down the road. With hopes that whoever it is will drive past me, I step off the road and onto a patch of grass hiding beneath the shadows of the thickly covered branches.

The pops and snaps between the tires and road grow deeper, hollower, warning me that the driver is coming to a stop. The inside of my chest feels like paper beneath the hammering of a swift typist on a typewriter. A Romani walking alone on darkening streets would be easy to remove from this village.

"No one offered to give you a ride home?" a voice calls out from inside the vehicle, but the tree branches are obstructing my view. I swallow hard, forcing a lump down my throat as I peek around the dangling leaves.

A long moment passes while I search for a familiar face, but the rim of a dark newsboy cap is casting a shadow over his face. He lifts the brim up a bit, revealing his luminous eyes and brilliant smile. My pulse shifts into a different rhythm. *Ben*. I wait for my heart to settle, and I try to take a deep breath, hoping to calm my fraying nerves. "I don't need a ride," I say, trying not to sound as petrified as I am.

"You don't need to be walking around alone when it's nearly dark out," he counters.

"I live just a few minutes down the road. I'm fine, I assure you."

"You're cold too," he points out.

I'm not, but I am holding on to the clothes I wore to the estate this morning, clutching them firmly against my chest. "No, I'm not."

"Mila, let me give you a ride. Please. I can't just leave you to walk home when I have another seat beside me." The thought of sitting in the seat of a beautiful car is nothing but a dream to me. I've never been in any type of automobile. *We have our vardo and don't need anything else,* Mama and Papa remind me.

Even out here on an empty road with nothing around us but trees, the distinct difference between our lives is like night and day, embarrassingly so. Even though I'm proud of who I am, I wouldn't dare show him where I live. We are from two different worlds, ones that don't see eye to eye.

"With all due respect, Ben, I don't want you to know where I live. I hardly know you." I hope my reason is suitable enough to close the discussion.

He lifts his hands off the shiny black steering wheel and holds them up in the air, as if he feels the need to defend himself. "I respect that. How about a compromise? What if I drive you close to where you live and agree to let you walk from there on your own? I'll sleep better knowing I didn't leave you on this road with nothing other than darkness ahead."

My turn is no more than another ten-minute walk, which would only take a couple minutes in the car. "If I agree, do you promise not to follow me home after?"

He nods his head. "I'm not someone you need to fear. I can promise you that."

I hug my clothes a little tighter. "Ben, I need you to promise me you won't follow me home."

He places his hand on his chest. "I promise."

I step out from under the tree and walk toward Ben's door. In a frantic motion, he swings the door open and hops out to allow me in.

He's wearing a rust-colored herringbone tweed coat and trousers like the other men in his family were dressed in today. There isn't a single crease in his matching vest, and the navy-blue tie is neatly knotted and perfectly straight down his center, clipped to his shirt with a silver bar clasp. I can't decide if he looks better while in casual clothes or in the sharp style he's sporting so well now. I try to avoid the thought and focus on slipping into the car.

The seats are leather, cool against the backs of my bare legs. I've ridden along the outside of the vardo behind the horses more times than I can remember but that doesn't compare to the speed we're moving, with nothing over our heads to block out the wind. I must be leaving marks on my legs from my finger-nails as my stomach lurches around, sensitive to every bump and sway. "How far up should I drive?"

I point up ahead. "Just another minute or two up the road."

"Did the rest of your day go smoothly?" he asks. It's hard to understand how he could be so calm and composed while driving at this speed—it's like he's been doing so his entire life, which is impossible.

"Yes, everything was fine," I say, failing to release the breaths I'm holding in.

"How—um, how was your—" Another bump causes me to slide along the seat right up to Ben. "I'm so sorry." I try to pull myself back but the curve we're traveling around won't allow me to move much.

He glances over to me for a quick second with a wry smile tugging at his mouth. "I'm not going very fast."

I beg to differ. Although, I've never been in a car so I can't say for sure what might be fast or not. Once the road straightens out, I'm able to put a bit of space between us, though I realize I'm also leaving the comfort of his warmth behind.

"I was trying to ask about your exam. How—" Again, another curve. Again, my shoulder is pinned to his arm. I close my eyes and inhale the scent of soap swirling through the piney air. My heart is racing again but not from fear. It's something else, and I'm not sure what it is.

"I think I did well," he says.

I should be trying to pull myself along the seat to give him space to move his arms, but I fail to do so. I also forget to tell him to stop when we pass the dirt road I was supposed to turn onto.

"You should drop me off here," I say, holding my breath again until the car comes to a stop.

"Here? We're still in the middle of nowhere."

"There's a shortcut I can take. It will bring me home within a minute of walking," I lie.

"Through the trees?"

"You promised you wouldn't follow me home. That includes asking questions or waiting on the side of the road until I begin walking again."

"I am a man of my word," he says, opening his door to step out. "If I don't see you in the morning, I will have to assume you've gotten lost in the woods, and I'll have to come looking for you." He isn't smiling or laughing through the words he's speaking.

"I appreciate the concern, but I will—"

"You'll be fine. I know."

"Thank you for the ride," I say, sliding out while trying to keep a grip on my crumpled clothes. "I will see you in the morning."

He bows his head at me, something unfamiliar I've seen for the second time today. No one has ever greeted me with any form of high-class respect. I can't help but snicker, wondering why he would be so polite to me of all people. "I'm just the maid. You don't need to try so hard to be nice."

He tips his head to the side just a smidgen. "You're not just a maid."

"A caretaker for your horses too," I add. "Pardon my mistake."

"That wasn't what I was going to say."

His pause leads me to believe I may never know what he was going to say, but it serves me right for responding so quickly. "Well, good night, Ben."

"Yes, it is a good night," he says, his eyes squinting with a measure of question and wonder. "Take care of yourself."

I wait until he settles back into his car and makes a turn to head back to the estate. Once he's out of sight, I make my way back to the dirt track we passed and check once more to make sure no one can see the path I'm taking toward the settlement.

The fire is blazing in front of our vardo, and Mama and Aunt Louisa are both cooking with metal pans perched on top of a stack of bricks. Bula is the first to spot me, making sure everyone else is aware that I've arrived home too.

Papa steps out from behind the vardo, making a point to greet me before I'm enveloped by the family. "How was your first day?" he asks. His face is pale, but his cheeks are burning with a red hue. He looks both hot and cold at the same time.

"Fine," I reply.

"Good, good. And the horses? Were you able to help them at all?"

"Nova is blind in one eye and the other, Twister, I believe, was mistreated before you purchased her."

Papa runs his hands through his hair. "I didn't know."

"They'll be okay," I tell him.

I take a step to the side, planning to make my way into the

wagon to disrobe from this awful uniform that hangs from me like a bulky curtain.

Papa catches me by the arm before I get too far. "Mila, what is wrong?"

"Should something be wrong?" I question him.

A look of empathy swims through his eyes and it ignites a wave of guilt that rushes through me. I know Papa would never maliciously do something to hurt me. We live on prayers some days, and each source of income we receive is a blessing. I should assume if there was a way to bring in more money, he would have made sure to create that opportunity instead of the one I'm in. My anger was tainting my common sense today.

"I would hope not. Did the family treat you well?"

I place a hand on his shoulder. "Everything is fine. It was work and that's all there is to it."

"I wish you would say something other than the word 'fine,' Mila."

He and everyone else, but it's hard to tell a lie. "I'd like to change out of these clothes."

"I understand. Go on," he says, patting me on the back as I leave.

When I step into the dark vardo, facing the narrow space my family and I are accustomed to, it makes me understand how accepting I am of the difference between our life and the Bohdans' life.

At least the change of scenery will give me something new to dream about, even if I can only witness it all from the outside looking in.

TEN

IT ONLY TAKES A CRYSTAL BALL TO SEE

BENEDIKT, OCTOBER 1938

The last few weeks have been steadily unraveling into a sense of normalcy around the estate. To have help around the chateau again seems to have offered a bit of relief to everyone, which has put a stop to the unnecessary comments about Mila. At least they haven't been as vocal about their feelings toward her.

She arrives earlier than necessary each day but takes the extra time to be with Nova and Twister. I offered to pick her up in the mornings, knowing she doesn't have any mode of transportation to get here, but as soon as I offered and she declined, she began showing up much earlier than necessary. I can't help but wonder if she's avoiding my help. It even seems as if she sneaks out at the end of the day to make sure no one notices her leaving. The obscurity of her life outside of this house has me constantly wondering. It's clear she's hiding something, but I haven't a clue as to what it could be. I shouldn't care as much as I do, but I'm drawn to a good mystery.

I pull a sweater over my head and make my way to the bedroom window, which overlooks the back courtyard and gardens. Filip and Pavel are off to the right, standing near the stables, watching something as if it's an entertaining production.

I assume Mila must be feeding the horses or brushing their manes. I'm not sure what's so fascinating about it all but my younger brothers clearly enjoy watching.

Pavel cups his hand around his mouth and takes a few steps back, but Filip stands in place, staring straight ahead. A minute doesn't pass before Pavel is off and running, screaming as if he's in danger. His voice echoes in the main foyer. He tends to be more dramatic than the rest of us, but I better check on him.

I comb my fingers through my hair, pushing it off to the side and step out into the hallway. He's still yelping and I'm contemplating whether he's hurt so I move a bit faster to make my way downstairs. "What's the matter?" I call out to him. I'm not sure why no one else is questioning the screams, but maybe everyone else is tied up.

His eyes are bulging as he stares at me from across the foyer. "Something is wrong with Twister," he says.

"That's why you're making all this commotion down here? It's early in the morning. You know that, right?" I'm not trying to be insensitive, but we've had a rough start with Twister and despite the hurdles, Mila has helped her overcome a lot of the early aggression she was showing.

"No, it's more," Pavel says. "It's Mila."

"Is she hurt?" My pounding heart plummets to the bottom of my stomach.

"No, she's not—she's—" I head for the door, assuming the worst.

I turn around, continuing to walk backward as he stutters through his words. "I think she's a real Gypsy," he says. "She has powers. Ones that aren't normal."

I drop my head to the side, realizing I'm talking to a ten-year-old and hearing the imagination of a young child come to life. He doesn't realize how terrible his words are.

Now knowing Mila isn't hurt, I take a minute to catch the panic-stricken breaths that have escaped me over the last few seconds, then try and clarify the situation with Pavel. "Listen, I'm not sure you understand what the word 'Gypsy' means. It's an offensive name for someone of the Romani culture. We should be more careful with how we speak about others, especially when we know how it feels to be called certain names."

"You don't understand," Pavel argues. "She said she can see the future."

I place my hands on my hips. "Mila told you she could predict what is going to happen?" I ask.

"She said she has a crystal ball too," he continues.

I purse my lips, wondering if any of this conversation is true. "Did she tell you what might happen next?"

"Yes."

"Well then, continue. What does she see in our future?" Despite myself, I can't help but wonder if any of her visions include me. I'd be lying if I acted as though there isn't an unspoken connection between us.

Pavel swallows what sounds like a rock in his throat and his eyes widen again. "She said Twister is going to have a baby fawn, but not for another few months."

The tension in my shoulders eases as I come to understand Pavel's confusion. "And she saw this happening when looking into her crystal ball? Do you by chance mean a foal?"

"Yes," he whines. "And how else would she know?"

"Why don't you go get ready for breakfast and I'll have a word with Mila? I'm sure we can sort all the confusion out." Although, I might tell him the same story rather than explain how pregnancy comes about.

Pavel runs up the stairs, clomping his feet so loudly, I doubt anyone is still asleep, even if they managed to block out his screams.

During the minutes it takes me to make my way to the stables, I ponder why everyone in the family is so hung up on Mila being Romani. The people in our village don't speak highly of those who pass through, only stay for a short while, and then leave us behind after completing their so-called devious acts. But Mila's eyes are telling, and I believe she's a good person, though I can't explain my reasoning to everyone else without proof either way.

"That doesn't make any sense at all. You do realize that?" Filip seems to be interrogating Mila as I approach the stables.

"Go inside," I tell him. "Leave Mila to her work."

"But she—"

"Go. Now," I repeat.

"Why are you treating me like a child all of a sudden? I'm only three years younger than you."

I stare at him for a long minute, waiting for him to take in my glare and understand its meaning. It doesn't take him long to roll his eyes and turn to leave.

I don't see Mila when I step into the stables. "Everything all right?" I ask, wondering where she is.

"Not exactly." I follow the sound of her voice, finding her sitting on a pile of hay next to Twister.

"Well, I've heard one version of the story already, but I'd rather know the truth."

"Do I need to explain to you how a horse becomes pregnant too?" she snaps, obviously frustrated by the situation. "Horses are pregnant for almost a full year. We wouldn't have known any sooner, but it likely happened just before my father sold your father the horses."

"I'm sure it will all be okay. There will just be another horse to care for and—"

"It's not that simple. Twister won't be able to race after the foal is born, and we don't know if the foal is a thoroughbred, or even if it will be capable of racing. Caring for a pregnant horse can be costly as well. I'm worried your father might not take kindly to this news."

I open the gate, letting myself into Twister's stall, where she greets me by nuzzling her head into my neck—something I patiently waited for her to do over the first couple of weeks she was here. I may be the only one in the family she likes aside from Mila.

"This isn't your fault," I explain, taking a seat on a pile of hay next to Mila.

"Filip seemed to understand the complexity of this situation before I could wrap my head around it. Your father purchased Twister for a purpose she can't fill. I wouldn't blame your father for being cross with mine, but I'm the one who is here in his place, facing the consequences."

"How long have you known she's pregnant?"

"I had a suspicion a few days ago and after talking with my father last night and checking Twister over this morning, I'm very confident she's about three months pregnant."

"Your father is worried, I assume?"

"Terrified," she replies.

"My father is a reasonable man," I try to explain. Though, I'm not sure how to reason with a man who is desperate to keep his family financially safe in these trying times.

"Can anyone truly be reasonable these days? Your family will claim to have been right about me from the start. It was all a trick to sell a horse. That's what they'll assume."

I want to tell her she's wrong. I wish I could offer her comfort like that, but she's right. The days of forgiveness and understanding are something of the past. Every person living in this village is worried about what the future holds and not one of us has a say in the matter. "Give me some time to sort things through with my parents."

"They won't believe you. They've made it clear that they know a Romani when they see one, and I'm quite sure I know what they call me behind my back."

ELEVEN
OPAQUE SHADOWS OF THE SKY
MILA, OCTOBER 1938

The truth sometimes hurts more than a lie, but deceit causes a different level of pain, especially when it's by family. Maybe I shouldn't make assumptions but it's hard to avoid when I'm staring at the vast space of greenery in the settlement where I left my family in this morning. There isn't a vardo or caravan in sight. Not one. Even the other travelers we didn't know have left too.

The night sky has almost fully taken over any hint of daylight and I'm standing in a field alone, wondering how they could leave me here without a trace of where I can find them.

I circle around the area where the ashes from last night's fire burned, searching for a clue as to what may have happened.

The closer I walk to the tree line, the darker the sky becomes. Even if I wanted to walk into the woods some ways, I'm afraid I won't see much. There's no sign of life, not even the chirp of a lonely cricket.

We've had to leave a settlement without notice before, but that was when the village rebelled against us living in their territory. They came with torches at night, shouting at us to leave or they would burn our vardos and caravans. We've never had intent to bother anyone around us, but it comes with the territory of who I was born to be.

I'm shaking through every muscle in my body, terrified of what's happening, or what may have already occurred. Papa was concerned about Twister being pregnant, but I don't think he would desert me here amid his worry that Mister Bohdan might come looking for him or that I might be left to deal with the consequences.

My footsteps feel heavy as the overgrown grass sweeps against my stocking-covered ankles, but I make my way back to the main road before the dirt path is swallowed by the shadows of the sky. Before stepping foot onto the road, I think about what others will see if they spot me walking the streets at night alone.

I pull my scarf off my head and shove it into the pocket of my uniform. My hair is a mess, some strands are matted and sticking to my sweaty forehead, and the rest are likely sticking out in every direction. No one would look at me and consider the possibility that I may not be a beggar or a thief. The hairpins holding my hair up against the base of my neck slip out easily, releasing long tangled waves that cascade down the center of my back. I add the pins to my pocket along with the scarf before combing my fingers through my hair to smooth out the mess left behind from a day of hard work.

My uniform speaks for itself, and I suppose it's better that I'm seen as a maid than anything else at the moment.

When I arrive at the fork in the road where I can head toward the village or go back up to the Bohdan estate, I make the quick decision to return to the stables. The family won't know I'm in there tonight. It may be the only place Papa would come looking for me too.

The hike up the hill at this hour and after being on my feet all day is strenuous, but at least I know for sure Twister and Nova will be there to greet me.

I watch each step I take, avoiding any loose sticks or rocks, my nerves getting the best of me. Both Twister and Nova snort, one after the other, likely happy to see me, but also concerned about my presence in the dark of night. Their muzzles stretch over their stall gates as if they're reaching for me. "It's okay. Shh," I whisper. "I hope you don't mind me staying with you tonight." I hope my calm demeanor eliminates their possible worry.

Before long, they appear to relax.

Once I'm settled in the stables, my mind begins to race with question after question, wondering how my family could leave me behind. There must be an explanation, but without one, I have two choices—be angry or be terrified.

The straw hay bales are more comfortable than sharing a bed with my siblings. I can hardly remember what it feels like to stretch my legs while trying to fall asleep.

As exhausted as I was, I thought I might fall asleep rather quickly, but Twister seems concerned with me being in here and has been prodding me with her nuzzle once every few minutes. I know she isn't used to sharing her pen with anyone else. But right now, we only have each other.

"Good morning, pretty girl. I didn't expect to see you here without your favorite person this morning." My eyes flash open, wondering why anyone would be talking to me in a high-pitched voice as if I was a baby. And why would someone be referring to me as a *pretty girl*. I push myself up to my elbow, waiting for my eyes to focus. It doesn't take me long to remember where I am and why I'm here, especially when I see Ben staring at me with a hint of shock and a lot of perplexity. "I —I didn't realize you were—"

I stand up quicker than my body wants to, finding the need to grab onto the short wall for support. "I wasn't."

"I didn't realize you were in here when I came in to see how Twister was doing."

I'm not sure what to say... whether I should admit to sleeping here last night. Although there's no other good reason why I would be asleep on a pile of straw and hay. "I must have—"

"Have you been here since last night?"

I wish that wasn't the first question he asked. While many will assume Romani can tell a lie without much trouble, I'm not capable of hiding the truth. I'm only able to keep quiet.

Silence will almost always answer every question.

Ben leans over the gate, pressing his elbows against the top. "You can be honest with me. I've been trying to prove to you that I'm not like my brothers and mother. Yet, you treat me like I am."

I don't treat him in any way other than a person I essentially work for. I understand he'd rather not think of me as a maid, but it's a reality he must come to terms with. "This isn't about you," I say.

"Did something happen between you and your family last night? Is that why you slept here?"

If there's one thing I've learned about Ben, it's that he's relentless when trying to find answers to his questions.

I hate that he knows which precise question to ask, knowing the truth must be written in the sadness in my eyes.

"Was there an argument?" he continues.

"No." It's the only honest answer I don't mind offering.

"Did something happen to your home?"

I don't have a home. I consider answering with another question, but the response should be a simple yes or no.

"Was there a fire?" This won't end until he finds the answer he's desperate to hear.

"No, Ben. There wasn't a fire."

"Then what is it?"

I cross my arms around my torso, wishing the squeeze would alleviate the ache in my body. All I can do is stare into Ben's eyes, finding more than just wonder; there's worry as well. The lines on his forehead deepen and his brows knit closer together. "Tell me, Mila."

"Why do you care so much?"

His gaze floats to the dirt-covered ground between us, seeming ashamed, as if I'm accusing him of doing something wrong. Maybe I am.

"I don't know how to answer your question," he says.

"And I don't know how to answer yours."

He huffs, sighing with frustration. "I care about you, okay? What other reason would I have to ask these questions?"

It's not that I didn't suspect that he felt something more than the others do for me, especially since I feel quite different about him compared to the rest of the family, but saying so out loud is inappropriate when I'm a worker in their home.

"Do you care about all of the people who work for your family?" It's an insulting question. He's been nothing but polite to anyone who crosses his path. Of course, he cares about others.

Ben tips his head to the side and his gaze intensifies. "Yes, but not in the same way I do about you."

"Your parents would be cross if they heard you say such a thing."

Ben opens the gate and steps inside the pen, removing the only barrier between us. "I don't care what my parents or brothers think. You intrigue me. I find myself yearning to learn something new about you every day, but at the same time it irks me that you can't find a way to trust me... even a little."

I trust him more than my own family at the moment. That might mean something to him, but not if he finds out what they did.

"Trust is something we earn, not an object that is taken away when it's too late."

"I'm not sure how to prove you can trust me," he says.

I press my lips together and close my eyes, dreading what I'm about to say. "My family is gone and I don't know where they went."

The frustration drawn along his face melts into an empathetic grimace. "How—they left the home you just moved into?"

My heart pounds like a church bell—slow and guttural. "We live in a vardo—a caravan. My parents, and my four siblings. The settlement we were occupying was empty last night. They left, and for what reason I don't know."

The short answer he desired will fill in the blank spaces of every query he's asked of me. I'm Romani, just as the family assumed. "You're a traveler?"

I appreciate his attempt to be polite. "A Romani. Yes. I don't like to brag about being on the run more often than not, since it isn't by choice."

"I'm Czechoslovakian. Does it matter?"

Of course it does. He knows very well how Romani people are viewed. No one wants us around. We make a village look poor and bring trouble wherever we go. Or so these assumptions continue as they have for centuries.

"Your parents would not want me here if they knew. That is, if they even still want me here after finding out about Twister."

"My father isn't upset about Twister. He was welcoming to the idea of raising a foal. Mother didn't have much to say, but likely because she knows she won't be asked to lift a finger to help with it."

Relief washes over me regarding Twister, but the feeling is short-lived as I follow up on my other concern. "They still don't know I'm Romani. I fear they will care much more about that than a pregnant horse."

Ben's eyes open wider, as if the realization has just struck him. He holds his finger up as he jogs through his thoughts. "I saw a bulletin yesterday about the Munich Agreement. Hitler is annexing the German-speaking regions of Moravia and Bohemia to form a new German province, Sudetenland. It means the borders of Czechoslovakia will be weak with defense. Basically, it's another step closer to occupation. Your family may have been warned to leave."

My chest tightens and I press my fist against my sternum, wishing to alleviate the ache. "I can't imagine they would leave me behind the way they have."

"You're safe here. Maybe that's why."

"Am I? Correct me if I'm wrong, but Jewish people are in no better position than the Romani."

"I assume your family must know my family and I are Jewish?" Ben asks.

It didn't cross my mind to bring up the religious beliefs of the people who employ me. "I'm not sure."

"If it wasn't brought up, they must think you're safe, and for now, you are."

For now. His statement doesn't comfort me. When the safety of my family is ever in question, we run. That's what we do. They chose to do so without me this time.

TWELVE
THE NERVE BEHIND PAIN
BENEDIKT, OCTOBER 1938

I have two options: I keep Mila's identity a secret or tell my family the truth and force them to accept her for who she is. We have plenty of space here and I can't let her sleep in a horse stable if she doesn't have anywhere else to go. Her placid reaction makes me wonder if she's used to this type of neglect. "You're going to need somewhere to stay, and I'm going to inform my parents that it's going to be here with us. Is that okay with you?"

The blood seems to drain from Mila's cheeks. "They'll want me to leave, never mind take up space inside," she says. It's embarrassing to know how true her statement is, but I won't allow them to make that decision. "I need the day to figure out where to go or what to do. Please, before you tell anyone, allow me a moment to pick up my pieces."

She doesn't believe I'm capable of convincing my parents into allowing her to stay. Perhaps I shouldn't be so confident that I can. "Of course. In the meantime, is there anything I can do to help you find your family? Do you know what direction they might have gone?"

She shakes her head and shrugs her shoulders. "Away from danger."

I'm not sure how much she may know of recent headlines and bulletins, but she seems wise enough to keep up with the daily changes occurring in all the surrounding countries. She knows we're boxed in and it's not a matter of *if*, but *when*.

"Would they travel deeper into the woods with hope of finding a safe area that way?"

Mila sweeps her hand across Twister's back, focusing on her coat rather than my question. "We've never had to hide per se, but it seems we've come to a brick wall and there aren't many options left, not without the means to flee Europe."

My family has discussed the possibility of leaving Europe, but Mother and Father fear it would lead to the ultimate surrender of our family's estate, along with the aristocracy of our family roots. It would force us to start from scratch and neither of them are prepared to make such a drastic change, not with the hope that this will all be over soon. I don't feel the same as they do. I'm not sure there will be an end to Hitler's plans any time soon.

"Come with me. You look quite uncomfortable. I'll find you a place to clean up." I reach toward her, taking caution not to make her more uncomfortable. She has straw poking out of her uniform in several places. Gently, I pull the first piece out from behind her elbow.

Mila's eyes widen and she glances down to inspect herself for more straw, finding the others. She moves quickly, trying to pull each single piece off her dress. "I can't imagine what I must look like," she says.

I can't help but chuckle as I reach for a wavy strand of hair dangling over her ear with straw woven through it. "I may go out on a limb and say you might feel far more uncomfortable than you look."

"That doesn't imply much to make me feel better at the moment," she replies.

"Come, follow me. It's safe. I promise."

She hesitates as I figured she might and smooths her hand across Twister's back once more before peering up through her lashes at me. "If you're sure?"

I don't have a choice but to be sure now. I open the gate to Twister's pen and hold my arm up so she can step out first. The back of her uniform is covered in twice as much straw as the front. I can't imagine how she managed to sleep at all last night.

I lead her around the back of the estate, to stone steps that descend to the bottom level that we hardly use for much more than storage these days. Before my time, an entire crew of staff members lived down here, but it feels rather abandoned now.

The corridor is dark and dusty. The scent of mildew fills the damp air, and I'm worried it's been so long since anyone has been down here that the piping might not work in the wash closet or toilet room.

Mila is trying to take in every detail of the grimy walls, the cobwebs that look more like thin curtains, and the many doors we're passing. "This might be a good place to go on a warm day," she says. It's always very cool down here, but it's uncomfortably cold come wintertime. There's no purpose in releasing heat down here when we hardly use the space.

The washroom is on the left and I turn the doorknob, hoping the slab of wood won't be stuck from the continuous temperature changes. Thankfully the door gives without much of a struggle but complains much louder than I anticipated. Hopefully Mother and Father are still on the second floor in their bedroom, far enough away from this hall.

I twist the faucet, hearing the water spit through the pipes before shooting out like an automatic weapon.

"Good. The pipes are still in working condition. Here, allow me to show you the toilet room as well." I take her across the hall and go through the same steps of pushing my way through the sticky door.

"You don't have to worry so much. I appreciate you offering me a place to clean up. I'll just be a moment," she says, walking into the wash closet.

"I'll wait out here. Take your time."

As I stand in the dark hallway that hasn't been maintained in years, I cycle through the ways I can convince Mother and Father to allow Mila to stay in a bedroom upstairs. It shouldn't be a question, especially with how little they must be paying her. In addition, the number of unoccupied rooms we have should be reason alone to offer the space to someone less fortunate than ourselves.

I don't think I will have much trouble convincing Father. Mother is the one who is stuck in her ways and afraid of any human being threatening the little amount of security we have left.

Tobias certainly won't be of any assistance. Keeping him out of the conversation will be imperative.

I lean back against the abrasive wall and fold one foot over the other, feeling the stretch in the backs of my legs and neck.

"Is someone down here?" The shout bounces like a ball from one wall to another. *Tobias.* I consider slipping into the toilet room, but I worry he will begin checking each room down here if he hears my clatter from upstairs. "A man must protect his property," he says more often than I'm able to block out. *This isn't his property and I'd be amiss to call him a man.* With concern that he might find Mila, I lunge toward the wash-closet's knob, thankfully finding it unlocked. The door doesn't complain like it did the first time and I slip inside, keeping my back to Mila in case she isn't decent.

"What are you—"

I turn my head to the side, holding my finger against my lips, warning her to keep quiet. I slip the lock bar through the metal hinge, careful not to twist the bar to where it will create a scraping sound.

"I heard someone down here!" Tobias continues searching for whatever he thinks he heard.

"I'm dressed," Mila whispers, likely wondering why my nose is practically touching the back of the door.

I turn to face her, stepping in closer to reply in her ear. "My brother must have heard us. We don't need to deal with him at this time."

Mila swallows what must feel like a lump in her throat. Through every attempt to calm her nerves about Mother and Father, I managed to glaze over the thought of Tobias.

"He hates me," she utters.

"He dislikes everyone," I reply.

The doors are opening and closing, one by one, each with a forceful slam.

I hate seeing a hint of dread swimming through her ice-blue eyes. She's been through enough since last night and I promised everything would be okay. Her gaze is pinned to the doorknob, watching for it to move.

Without thinking beyond the moment, I place my hand on her cheek, urging her to look up at me rather than the door. It takes her a couple of quick breaths before she complies and gazes up at me. "I'll keep you safe," I say.

Her cheek is burning against the palm of my hand, but her eyes are reeling me in. She doesn't bat an eyelash while studying me. Although I'm apprehensive about how far Tobias will take his search, my heart pounds for a much different reason. It's as if the walls around me don't exist. I hardly contemplate the consequences when my nose draws down toward hers. I gently trace the fingertips of my free hand across her other cheek.

The fading freckles on her nose hint at a childhood spent beneath the summer sun for hours on end. I spot some tiny markings on her top lip too. There is something so unique and mesmerizing about her that I'm distracted from the terse knocks hammering against the wash-closet door. Mila clutches her fists against my chest, fearing the likelihood of Tobias charging through the door and the only way I can steal that terror is by touching my lips to hers, selfishly losing myself among the warm silky sensation I have shamefully imagined too many times. Her hands grasp at the fabric of my shirt, holding on to me for safety, or maybe strength. Her grip encourages me to clasp her tighter, kiss her harder, inhale more of her. The noise disappears, the worry, the world—nothing matters around us. A long thread of silence urges me to take a breath, but I don't want to break the moment—a moment she may regret or one that might never happen again. Everything feels so wrong but so incredibly right that nothing makes a sliver of sense to me. "I think he may have left," I say, feverishly. "I don't hear him anymore."

Mila's breath shudders as I catch mine and she places her hands on her chest, staring with wonder... "Do you think he'll return?" she asks, her words escaping through gasps for air.

"He might be looking for something to pry open the door. We need to leave."

I slide the lock bar to the side and pray the door is as quiet as it was the last time it opened. Following the hush of air, I poke my head out into the corridor, checking both directions as quickly as possible, finding the space clear. I turn back for Mila and grab her hand, holding it tightly as I guide us back to the door we entered through.

Just as we're two doors away from the exit, the clack of dress shoes scrapes against the stone steps descending to this floor. He's already returned. I open the door to the right of us and pull Mila in behind me, hiding us in the corner where the door would conceal and trap us if opened. I wrap my arm around her shoulders, pulling her in closer. There's a shiver running through her body, and I want to make it stop. "I'm sorry," I whisper.

Her body seems to relax as she rests her head against my chest. "Don't be," she replies.

Tobias's footsteps clobber by the door and down the hall. I wait for the hint of him fighting with the wash-closet door. He must have been leaning on it while trying to pry it open, because the door screams against the rusty hinges and slaps against the wall.

I take the opportunity to open the door of the room we're in, just enough for us to squeeze through and make it to the exit, hopefully before he steps out of the wash closet.

I keep my eye on the corridor, while blocking the view of Mila making her way up to the outside door. Tobias must be doing a full investigation of the wash closet because I also manage to make my way out before he steps back out into the corridor. We both run toward the stables, coming to a sharp stop once inside where we hunch forward to catch our breath. Nova and Twister stir at the abrupt interruption but calm quickly upon recognition of us.

"I bet we just made him a bit crazy," Mila says, covering her hand over her mouth.

"I can only hope."

"He will be the one who makes it impossible to help me. You know this, right?"

I take another deep breath, hoping my heart will stop racing. "I know what you see when you look at Tobias."

"An uptight, egotistical aristocrat?" she follows.

"I can't argue with that description, but what you see is a façade, one he will never admit to."

"I don't understand. What could he possibly need to hide?"

My memory jogs back in time, recognizing the handful of moments I recall feeling sorry for my older brother. "He's a tortured soul, but it isn't because he was raised to be."

Mila is listening intently as she threads her hair into a long braid. "What happened?"

"It was about three years ago when he was traveling with my father to Nigeria. Father was in search of his next investment project and wanted Tobias to shadow him with hope that he would someday be able to conduct business in the same way.

"The country was in desperate need of funds to help their economy and it was a golden opportunity for someone like my father to plant his roots in territories outside of Europe. The area they visited was very undeveloped, and while the visit ended with success for the locals and my father, Tobias contracted a mild to moderate case of leprosy. The doctors couldn't do much aside from treat him with an oil, which didn't work. Therefore, there were some long-term side effects he was left with once the bacterial infection cleared up. The doctors think it might be something he has to live with indefinitely."

Mila releases her grip on the braid and folds her arms over her chest. "That's terrible. I'm so sorry that happened to him."

I appreciate the meaning behind her words, but I'd be remiss to think she truly feels that way about a man who has been utterly disrespectful to her since the day she arrived.

"In any case, he has on and off nerve pain, which we often use as an excuse for his aggressive and agitated behavior. While I'm fortunate enough not to deal with something so detrimental, I'm not sure I understand how it's an excuse to treat others poorly. In truth, I think his confidence was damaged more than his nerves and that's the part that has changed who he once was. Though, even before he got sick, he wasn't the most pleasant brother a child could ask for."

"I see. Well, maybe I understand why he might view others who are of a lower class to be a danger to him. We're all affected by different degrees of trauma throughout our life, aren't we?"

"It isn't hard for you to find the good in everyone, is it, Mila?

Does it come naturally? It appears you can't find fault in anyone no matter how they treat you."

A small smile forms on her lips. "It's much easier to forgive than to hold on to unnecessary feelings."

I dip my hands into my pockets, finding myself more intrigued by her with every word she says. "Well then, I hope you forgive me for my behavior in the wash closet."

She bites down on her bottom lip and her nose scrunches as her cheeks flush. "I can't forgive you for something I'd rather hold on to."

THIRTEEN

IT ISN'T THE SHOES THAT HURT
MILA, OCTOBER 1938

My head is floating between contrasting clouds. On one side, I can only see a dark and stormy horizon, with foreboding patches of fog. On the other, the sky is cornflower blue with a spattering of white cotton balls dancing before the sun. I don't have a say in which way the wind will blow, how the sky will change, or what the future might bring, and I feel as though I'm left without a sense of gravity.

I shouldn't be staring out a window while I'm supposed to be clearing soot out of the fireplace in the grand salon, but I need a moment to straighten my thoughts because I'm due to leave the premises within the next hour. I'm not sure when Ben is planning to speak to his parents or if he already has, but I think I should return to the settlement again to see if my family has returned by chance. I dread how unfavorable the odds are as I don't recall a time when we've ever returned to the same place, but there also hasn't been a time when they left me behind either.

With the echo of footsteps along the wooden floors in the corridor, I return to the fireplace to finish what I started. My knees are sore as I kneel to brush the inky soot into a pile, but I manage to clean the last of the debris before anyone enters the room.

"Mila, may we have a word with you?"

I find Mister and Madam Bohdan standing beneath the arch opening of the room. Each side is decorated with tall palm plants which accent the overall art deco feel of the entertaining room. Seaweed green, indigo, and gold Aztec patterns cover each wall. High-end pieces of art are placed between framed mirrors with a set of blue-green suede chairs encircling an over-sized chestnut oval tea table. The crystal chandelier hanging from the center of the arched ceiling panels ties in the beauty of each piece of decor.

This is my favorite room in the chateau. While I'm in here, I feel like I'm visiting somewhere exotic where jungles surround the land and parties roar through the night.

"Of course," I reply, rising to my feet. My mouth becomes dryer than sand.

"Please have a seat," Mister Bohdan says, gesturing to the nearest sofa.

I must assume Ben has spoken to them and they're preparing to ask me to leave the property. If the news was good, I'm not sure Madam Bohdan would be accompanying her husband.

Alone on the sofa, I stare up at Mister and Madam Bohdan, feeling like a small child about to be scolded by my parents. I clasp my fingers together and rest them on my lap. They each take a seat in a set of armchairs across from me on the other side of a short coffee table. Madam Bohdan isn't making eye contact. Her nose is somewhat pointed up toward the chandelier. Mister Bohdan is looking straight at me though.

"Benedikt informed us of what happened to your family."

I'm not sure what to reply with because Ben may have only shared a small portion of the story. I know he's at the university now, so I assume they waited until he left the property to speak to me.

"Yes, sir."

"I'm very sorry this has happened to you. I can't imagine what you must have felt like last night."

I'm not sure he could imagine, even if he tried. This family seems to have everything waiting for them at their fingertips. Life may be more challenging now with the state of the world and the economy, but they are still living much better than most.

"I'd like to help you find your family, but until we do, we'd be happy to make up a room for you to stay with us," he says.

My breath hitches in my throat and my muscles tense, leaving me feeling speechless.

Madam Bohdan clears her throat, still holding her gaze upward. "But—" she says.

Mister Bohdan glances at her from the corner of his eye. "We'd like to get to know you a little better."

Madam Bohdan scoffs at her husband then shifts her glare toward me. "Are you a Gypsy? I need the truth," she says.

My eyes dart between the two of them. "Do you mean to ask if I'm a thief, liar, or a fortune-teller, as your youngest sons have asked me multiple times?"

Madam Bohdan places her palms down on her knees. She straightens her shoulders and finally lowers her stare, making it clear she is offended by the question.

"I didn't ask any such thing. How dare you put words into my mouth?"

"Please accept my apologies, Madam Bohdan. Perhaps you might clarify what you consider to be a 'Gypsy'? There seems to be a certain assumption tied to the race of people you are asking about."

She swallows hard, loud enough for me to hear across the

table. "Are you a nomad who believes she doesn't need money to live?"

I lower my head for a moment, collecting my thoughts before I speak out too abruptly. "With all due respect, madam, I wouldn't be working for pocket change if I didn't believe money was a necessity in life. If you are wondering if I have moved around my entire life with my family after my ancestors migrated here from India, then yes, I am Romani."

"Might I ask why your family sees the need to move around so much?" she continues. I'm not sure she's digested a word of what I've said so far as she seems to be focused on the list of questions she must have built-up in her head.

"Much like yourself, many locals do not want our kind present in their villages due to the fear of behaviors many nomads are known for. However, not all Gypsies are thieves or beggars. I also believe the unfair treatment of Jewish people across German occupied countries is unfair and unjust as I don't believe you are the monsters Hitler would like the world to believe you are."

"It seems we have more in common than we might have originally thought," Mister Bohdan responds rather quickly, and I assume it's to stop his wife from saying anything more. "Which is why we would like to offer you residence here in our estate," he says affirmatively. "You've become invaluable to our family over the last couple of months, and we'll do right by you in return."

I'm pinching my fingers together so firmly, my knuckles are turning white. There is just one question I must ask: "Thank you, I'm very grateful for your offer. Do you mind if I ask what your plans will be if Hitler gains control of Czechoslovakia? I hear of the damages being brought upon Jewish families in Germany and Austria. They're being forced to emigrate. Do you see that as a possibility here?" I realize I have no other option but to move from one bad situation to another, and it's anything but comforting.

"I assure you, there's nothing to worry about here. You have my word," Mister Bohdan says.

I appreciate his confidence, but I don't believe he's as powerful as he may think.

"That's a relief to hear."

"Good, now that this is all settled," Madam Bohdan says, "I have one last question for you, dear." Whenever she calls me dear, it's usually followed by an insult delivered in a cheerful intonation.

"Yes, madam."

Her eyes are like daggers, staring at me, after doing whatever she could to avoid eye contact prior to this question. "My son seems smitten by you—lovesick, really. There isn't anything I should be concerned about, is there?"

I can't control the heat flushing through my cheeks. I can only hope they don't notice. "I'm not sure what you..."

My heart pounds and my stomach burns. It's impossible they would know anything, especially since there wasn't anything until earlier today. Not anything more than friendly chatter. "I see. Well, I suppose I should believe Ben when he gives me his word that there is, and never will be, anything between the two of you. 'Never the maid, Mother. You know I'm better than that,' I believe were his exact words. I just needed to confirm so, myself."

Her words are like small knives, each slicing through me slowly, one at a time. "I'm sure you should take your son's word over mine anyway," I manage to say without faltering in tone.

"Well then. Now that this is all settled, I assume you know where to find a spare set of bedding to make up one of our guest rooms for yourself. You are welcome to whichever room you choose downstairs." I'm not surprised by her need to keep me away from the family, beneath ground level, and I won't dare complain about the heat or lack of electricity because I gather it's what she expects to hear.

"Darling, I thought we had decided on—" Mister Bohdan tries to intervene.

"We hadn't decided on anything other than allowing this young woman to stay here so she isn't considered a Gyp—nomad," she says.

Mister Bohdan releases a throaty grumble and stands from his seat. He checks his wristwatch and looks over at me. "There are only a few minutes left in the workday. Why don't you go out for a walk? The weather is lovely."

"Yes, sir. Thank you. I will."

I don't hesitate to make my way out of the salon as fast as my worn feet will carry me. In fact, I don't take a minute to breathe before bursting through the back door of the laundry room. The fresh air feels like the simple dose of oxygen I've needed for the last half hour. My chest aches like I've been punched. My organs feel like they may be in knots, tangled up together. I want to convince myself Ben wouldn't say such a crude thing to his mother, but everyone seems so afraid of her too, and I'm not sure what to believe. Either way, she believes she has the power to determine who will feel what.

Despite the exhaustion catching up to me, I jog down the hill, placing as much space between me and my new place of residence. I run until I reach the fork in the road and turn down the next street. It doesn't take me as long as it did yesterday to reach the dirt road, but then I wasn't worried that I was about to face abandonment.

My heels sting as they rub against the borrowed shoes that are slightly too small for my feet. I've been able to ignore the pain while waiting for my skin to toughen but running seems to exacerbate the tender area. My heart plummets when I arrive. It was all for nothing. The settlement is still starkly empty, not a vardo, caravan, or horse in sight. There is only an empty field of grass and several ashen spots where fires were burning just two nights ago. Someone must have enforced the evacuation. They wouldn't all leave at once. In the past, we've been given a warning to leave, but there was always time to tie up loose ends. I'm a loose end. Something must be keeping them from me.

I drop to my knees, feeling like my body is too heavy to carry. They must be okay. I can't assume the worst. It won't do me any good. But I'm not sure if my optimism is masking ignorance. I press my hands into the cool grass, clutching my fingers into my palms until the roots pluck from the soil like threads torn from fabric. Fragments of dry dirt sprinkle over my lap; life, as I've known it, is this dirt. "Will you find me?" I ask, knowing only the trees and wind are listening.

Without even a mild breeze in response, I stare down at the peppering of dirt and release the handfuls of grass. It takes every bit of energy I have left to push myself back up to my feet. "I won't give up hope, I promise you." The words catch in my throat, and I can't bear another moment in this open space.

I return to the main road and walk until I pass the turn I would take to the chateau. Instead, I continue straight, knowing the village is all that awaits me at the end.

I hardly recall what the village looked like from the one and only time I passed through, sitting in the front of the vardo with Papa. My eyes fill with tears, as I recall how the local people were pointing at us, and whispering lies. But I had Papa, and the rest of my family—that should have been all that mattered.

Entering the village, people appear happy as they walk around in pairs or groups, most caught up in chit-chat or laughter. Children are playing with a ball in the square, and shopkeepers are sweeping their front stoops. No one pays much attention to me since I'm not parading through in a vardo. Though it's nice to be overlooked, I also feel quite invisible to society. This world has shown my family nothing but loneliness, and I feel it now more than ever before.

A small courtyard comes into view. It's enclosed with only a pergola covering, vines woven neatly across the top, both horizontally and vertically. Tables are scattered between the wooden posts and people my age are sitting around each table, enjoying one another's company. Any friend I've ever had has been left behind or has left me behind. I'm not sure what it feels like to make plans and have something to look forward to without the looming threat of leaving a village in the middle of the night, never to return.

"Mila!"

I'm just about past the courtyard when I consider who would know me well enough to shout my name here. I continue walking, acting as if I didn't hear anything, but it doesn't seem to matter. The voice calling my name follows. "Mila, wait. I didn't expect to see you down here."

His voice is enough to make me stop for a moment, but I'm not sure I have much to say to him, not after the earful I just received. I turn around, finding Ben in his university attire, a suit, tie, and shined shoes. From what I can see, he fits in well with the others here. I assume he's out with some of his fellow collegiate peers.

"I wasn't expecting to see you down here either." Of course, he isn't a prisoner of his racial defining looks, so it shouldn't be a surprise to see him. I'm not sure where these thoughts came from. I've never felt sorry for myself. It's as if I've lost the strength to be proud of who I am—who I was. I'm not sure who I am now. Just a maid, I suppose.

"Come join us for a beer."

"I don't think that would be a wise idea."

"Why not?" He genuinely doesn't seem to understand the difference between the two of us, which adds to the confusion I was already feeling.

"Your mother doesn't want us socializing on anything but

on a professional level, and your friends... I'm sure I'm not anyone they would want to spend time with."

Ben furrows his eyebrows like I'm speaking nonsense, but before I can argue any further, his hand clasps around my wrist. The unexpected gesture causes goosebumps to shoot along my arm. He pulls me toward the covered courtyard. "Ben..."

"Everyone, this is Mila," he says, introducing me to a group of silent people sitting around the table.

There is a moment of silence as I pull up a seat to squeeze in beside mine, muddying my thoughts and making me fear saying something wrong.

"I'm the maid. I work at his estate," Mila says, smiling at the six others I was sitting with.

I don't know the other students well enough to predict what they might be thinking. We share the same classes, and we fraternize after hours once a week or so, but our conversations hop around between the weather and economics, sometimes overheard stories about our professors. We're all studying economics, so we banter more than anything else. They weren't aware of where I live, at least I assumed so.

"A maid," Durko says. He's the most outspoken of the bunch, the one most likely to start a diplomatic argument over insignificant movements that might cause a financial crisis twenty years from now. "We didn't know you live so lavishly." I'm glad the response is directed toward me rather than Mila.

"She's only biding her time as a— Mila is a wonder with horses, in fact, and she's been rehabilitating two. It's brilliant to watch, really," I say.

"Ah, are you an equestrian?" Fiala asks. She's the quieter one of us. I often feel that she's a spy, taking in all our chatter. It's as if she takes notes with her eyes, and it makes me wonder.

"Not exactly. I know how to ride, but I don't do much of that anymore," Mila says.

From the corner of my eye, I notice her hands fidgeting with the material of her dress, crumpling it so tightly, her hands are blotchy.

"Are you originally from the area?" Fiala continues. "You look... I can't quite put my finger on it. You're certainly not as pale as the rest of us." Fiala's cheerful expression eases my concerns for a moment. She seems more intrigued than judgmental.

"Personally, yes, I've grown up in Czechoslovakia. My family originated in India, but several generations ago."

"How interesting," Fiala says, lifting her glass to take a swig of her drink.

"If you're going to stand out here, at least it's not as a Jew," Durko says through laughter. "Nobody wants to be one of them at the moment. We should drink to that!" He lifts his glass and holds it up to the center of the table.

I've been so concerned about what they think of Mila that it takes me a moment to realize what's happening. The others clink their glasses, each laughing alongside Durko.

I feel frozen in time, staring down at the wooden tabletop, at a wet ring left behind from a glass.

Mila takes me by surprise when her hand rests on my knee beneath the table where no one else can see.

"We should all be so lucky that we don't have to live in fear like the Jewish people of Germany," Mila says. "No one deserves the treatment they're receiving."

"In all fairness, Jews aren't exactly innocent. Some say they've had it coming," Jak speaks up. He'll follow the lead of whoever is guiding the conversation. I'm not sure he has any of his own opinions. He'd just rather fit in.

"I'm not sure I understand what you mean?" Mila continues.

"For one, they are the cause of our economic crises. Everyone knows this. Most Jews hold higher financial gain and assets over others in Germany. At a time when the world is running out of money, you don't see them doing anything about it, do you?"

"That seems somewhat absurd. A small race of people who occupy Germany should hand over their assets to support an entire country that's falling apart? I don't see how that would make a dent in the economy."

Mila's words leave me winded. I wasn't aware of her knowledge of economics or politics, but if it's possible to be even more attracted to her than I already was, I'm certain I am now.

"What are your thoughts, Ben?" Fiala falls onto her elbows, leaning across the table, proving she's had a bit too much to drink.

"I agree with Mila. I believe everyone should do more thinking for themselves and observe less of the bulletins slipping through Germany's cracks."

"You know that makes you Jew sympathizers. I'd be careful who you argue this point with," Durko says.

"Many would say it's better than being known as Nazi sympathizer," Mila says. She abruptly shoves her chair backward along the stone walk, causing a clattering which draws attention from every other table around us. She stands up as if she's triggered ammo, shooting out from a weapon. "It was lovely to meet you all, but I must be going."

"I'll join you," I say, following her lead.

Durko holds his glass up toward us without another word. Reality is a rude awakening; one I knew was coming but didn't realize was already on my doorstep.

Not one person says goodbye, and not one of them is any wiser to the gravity of their insults. I toss a Koruna onto the table to cover my portion of the tab and leave them with the same respect of silence.

Mila is a few steps ahead of me by the time I turn the corner from the pub's courtyard. "Wait," I call out. I speed up and wrap my hand around her elbow. "I'm so sorry you had to bear witness to that."

"I've seen worse," she says, refusing to comply with my hold. She won't look at me and I'm not sure what changed between this morning and now.

"Do you want to be caught in public holding the arm of your maid? You're better than that, aren't you?" Her words bite and she finally turns to look at me.

"Why would you say something like that?" I ask.

"Why would you?" She pulls her arm out of my hand and continues to walk in the direction of the estate.

I lose some of my speed when I recall the conversation I had with Mother and Father earlier today. I knew they planned to speak with her, but only to invite her to live with us. They promised me they wouldn't say another word outside of the topic of her living with us.

"Please, slow down. I don't understand your question," I say, calling out to her again. People on the curb are looking over at us and it must look odd to see a man in a suit chasing after a maid. That's the only view the world has of us, but only because they don't know I'm Jewish.

"You don't have to pretend, Benedikt," she says without stopping to take a breath.

"Pretend what?"

We reach the end of the curb, where a narrow alleyway branches off to the right. She takes me by the wrist and pulls us onto the unlit path. "You don't need to pretend that I'm not a maid or an assumed beggar, so far beneath your standards.

You're eighteen, almost nineteen, and you'll be looking for a wife soon. We both know that person cannot be me, so there's no use in pretending what happened this morning could ever go any further."

I wish I could see the look in her eyes, but I'm afraid it might ruin me too. "Why would you say any of this? I'm not my brother."

"Your mother said it all for you, so you don't have to," she snaps.

"Mila, I don't know what she said to you, but if it was an insult, it didn't come from me." I reach out for her, finding her shoulders and trying to pull her into my embrace, but she pushes her hands against my chest and backs away.

"I am the maid in your house and that's all," she hisses. Disappointment takes a hold of me as hot tears form on my bottom lashes. "Please let me be what I've been hired to be."

My eyes adjust to the darkness just in time to see her walk away, leaving me winded.

My car is parked across the road against the opposite curb. I make my way over and slide in, trying to spot her walking through the blinks of streetlights. I reach into my pocket for the key and ignite the engine. After a long moment of cruising down the road at a slow speed, I see her turning up the street in the direction of the estate.

Once I make the same turn, I pull up beside her. "I won't say a word to you if you please get into the car. If not, I'll drive beside you to make sure you get inside the estate safely. It will be much quicker if you comply."

Mila stops walking and folds her arms over her chest. The winds are picking up as the seasons begin to blend into one another. It isn't long before the frigid temperatures will be freezing us all to the core. She doesn't even have a coat.

I open the door, step out onto the curb, and remove my coat —something I wanted to do at the pub, but I knew she wouldn't have taken it in front of the others, given the way she introduced herself.

"I don't need your coat," she says, preparing to drop down onto the seat.

"Wonderful, well, you're taking it anyway." I place my coat over her shoulders just before she slides across the leather bench.

"You said you weren't going to say a word," she reminds me.

Rather than respond and give her more to become angry about, I try to hold up to my promise and quietly fold myself back into the car. I must bite my tongue the entire way up the hill toward the estate.

Once the car is parked beneath the back awning, I step out and stand back as she makes her way out. She removes my coat and reaches it out to me.

I take it and watch her walk off toward the stone steps that descend into the servants' hall. Mother agreed that she could occupy a room upstairs where the rest of us are. It's not hard to imagine she lied to me and directed Mila downstairs into the cold dark cavern beneath our home.

"Hold on for a moment. Where are you going?" I ask.

"To the servants' quarters, Ben," she says, continuing forward.

"Mother agreed to let you stay in a room upstairs."

Mila turns around to face me but continues to walk backward. "Has it occurred to you that some people tell you what you want to hear so you won't continue fighting to get your way?"

"You're not sleeping down there," I say sternly.

"Your mother made the decision, not me." Mila makes a run for the door, leaving me out here without the option of a last word.

Maybe she thinks I'm afraid of Mother and won't stand up

to her, but that isn't the case and I plan to rectify this situation immediately.

It's not late. I assume dinner will be served momentarily. I wonder if Mother even offered to feed her. It's the very least my parents can do while financially taking advantage of her.

I'm nearly out of breath by the time I reach the dining room. Everyone is seated around our long oval table, waiting on Marena as she prepares to serve the dishes. "Benedikt, don't you worry. I have a plate for you, as well," she says.

"We'll need another for Mila, and I think we should invite Marena to join us too. And if there isn't another, please set mine aside for them," I say.

"Benedikt," Mother snaps.

"How do you treat another person the way you fear people treating you? You sent Mila to live in the servants' quarters. There's no heat down there. The fireplaces haven't been cleaned in years and certainly won't be lit at any point tonight. The water hardly runs clear, and there isn't proper electricity."

"Ben, calm down," Tobias scolds me as if he's taking over for Father, who looks ashamed to be a part of this scene. I feel the same. "Maids don't sleep upstairs with the family. We've never had that."

"We haven't had a maid in sometime, and the quarters downstairs have not been maintained. She isn't an animal," I continue.

"Well," Tobias says, coughing into his fist.

"Enough already," Father interrupts. "Ben, make up a room for her upstairs, as we discussed with you this morning."

"Absolutely not," Mother interjects. "What would people think?"

"What people?" Father argues.

People don't come into our home. Anyone who knew us now sees us as a danger because of who we are.

Marena places dishes down in front of everyone, doing a

fine job of ignoring the arguments she's become used to around here. Marena goes home each night once she cleans up after dinner so Mila would be the only person working for the estate that would be staying on the premises. Times are not what they used to be, and I refuse to pretend otherwise.

"I'll do that, Father. Thank you." I turn to Mother. "I expect you won't say another word to her? And I would appreciate it if you didn't speak on my behalf again too."

Mother is glaring at me, a darkness is brewing in her eyes. "Have you been drinking?"

"Marena, is there any possibility you might bring up the two extra plates to the first guest room on the right side of the hall upstairs?"

"Of course," she says, pulling in a deep breath. I'm sure she's worried about being dragged into the middle of this dispute, but Father will defend her before he defends Mother. I've seen it happen before. I assume it's because Father has become tired of Mother's behavior, and he feels the need to protect innocent people.

"Thank you very much."

Tobias narrows his eyes at me as if I have personally offended him. Pavel and Filip are staring at each other with gawking gazes, likely trying to piece together the conversation. I only hope they begin to see the way Mother is treating others. I don't want my younger brothers to become part of the belligerence here.

FIFTEEN
AFFLUENT JEWISH MEN ARE THE FIRST TO GO

MILA, NOVEMBER 1938

To be silent is painful when I have so much to say, but the less I'm heard, the better off I'll be. I'm grateful Ben convinced his parents to allow me a room upstairs in the estate, but in turn, I've done what I can to stay away from him. It may be my only chance of longevity in the estate, as well as protecting his integrity among his family. However, Ben doesn't see eye-to-eye with my concerns. Daily, he has been trying to tempt me to sneak away with him. One thing I admire about Ben is his boundless determination. Though it pains me to force a distance between us, there's comfort in knowing I'm worth a fight to one person—to him.

I continue to wonder if my family has endured the same exertion to reconnect with me. It's been over a month since they disappeared. Each night I return to the barren land with hope that they have returned, but each night I'm sorely disappointed. I feel like I've been left at a cliff with nothing more than a ledge to cling onto.

Madam Bohdan has asked me to go into the village for a loaf of challah bread and a bottle of wine for their Shabbat dinner tomorrow night. With the comfort of knowing I'm not as suspecting as I once was of being Romani, I don't fear walking through town like I did at first, but the curbs are packed full of people. It's never this busy down here in the morning. I wonder what all the fuss is about.

The closer I get to the crowd, the more I speculate. Everyone has their eyes locked on a newspaper. Many people have one in their hands. Others are gawking over the shoulders of those holding one.

The street becomes narrower as I set my sight on a boy holding a pile of newspapers in one hand and the front page of one up in the air with his other.

The headline is clear as day.

Jews Are Ordered To Leave Munich
Synagogues Set On Fire

There are so many different conversations filling the air around me, it's hard to focus on any one person speaking. The commotion echoes: —*shop windows of Jewish-owned businesses were smashed then looted...* —*synagogues, burned to ashes...* —*thousands of homes and schools of Jewish people, destroyed...* Through it all, I clearly hear: "It was retaliation on the Jewish people for their assassination of Ernst vom Rath."

I stand frozen on the spot, picking up snippets of conversation, and all I can think about is Ben. If he were a citizen of Germany, a short distance from here, this could have happened to him for the simple fact that he is Jewish.

He isn't safe here. None of them are.

The village seems to be spinning around me. The road leading back to the estate becomes blurry and I'm unsure how I'll be able to deliver this unthinkable news.

With another shout from someone describing the incident, the haze around me dissipates. "'Demonstrations in the Reich have resulted in the destruction of more than seven thousand properties in Germany.' It also says here, '—they are currently arresting Jewish men, particularly the affluent.'"

"But this was premeditated?"

The questions and answers grow louder.

"It seems it was somewhat unexpected, but it's hard to tell."

"One young Jewish man is responsible for the assassination. I'm not sure an entire race should be punished—"

"Everyone knows the Jews are just trying to antagonize a revolt between European countries."

"What would the purpose of that be?" I shout, the words spilling off my tongue without thought. "Aren't *they* the ones being forced out of Germany?"

It feels as though every set of eyes on this road is on me. In truth, I'm aware no one knows the answers, leaving the conversations to continue with speculation, whooshing around like a balloon floating along a breeze.

A man dumps his newspaper into a metal rubbish receptacle with haste and shakes his head before walking away. The newspaper is draped over the top, still in a neat pile, so I snatch it up before anyone sees. I fold it under my arm and continue to the bakery for the challah.

When I reach the front door to the shop, a sign blocks the window's view. "*Zavřeno.*" I wonder if the shop owner closed of his own free will or did so out of fear. The Third Reich is a form of mold, growing across the border of Germany and into Czechoslovakia. I'm not sure there is anything that will prevent the mold from growing out of control. I wonder if the Bohdans are aware of what took place last night. I should warn them. The question of what will happen next is one that feels as though it will forever be present in our lives.

Once I'm halfway up the hill to the estate, I realize I forgot to pick up a bottle of wine, but they prefer kosher, and I should only imagine I won't find any now.

Madam Bohdan is going to be a mess if she doesn't know

anything about what happened last night. I pull the paper out from beneath my arm and search for more information before I say anything.

I flip to the second page of the paper where the copy continues, filling up nearly an entire full-page spread. I scan through each word. My eyes burn from the brisk wind and not blinking. My heart aches for every person who is either suffering or grieving a loss. How could anyone blame the Jewish people for what happened in Germany? It wasn't even just Germany. Austria and the Sudetenland border too. We're only an hour east of where this took place.

According to the article, Jewish homes, schools, hospitals, and synagogues suffered severe destruction from the use of sledgehammers. How could anyone do this? Hospitals? This is inhumane. Thirty thousand Jewish men have already been arrested, but it seems obvious that the Jewish people wouldn't destroy their own homes and businesses, which means this must be under Hitler's command, not a random act of destruction.

I close the newspaper and refold it just as I approach the tall double doors at the front entrance of the estate. The right-side door moans and creaks as I slip through a slight opening. No one appears to be in the vicinity of the foyer or the library off to my right.

I continue down the corridor, the cream-colored walls trimmed with ornate golden flourishes between several prodigious family portraits. My footsteps are silent against the old wooden floor panels as I reach the master stairwell where the ceiling blossoms up to the top level. Hanging there, a grandiose Empire crystal chandelier reflects light from the surrounding windows.

I poke my head into the quiet dining room to the left of the stairs, but thunderous footsteps startle me into spinning around, bringing me face to face with Tobias.

"Why do you have a newspaper? Mother sent you to fetch bread and wine. You must be confused," he says, eyes narrow.

"The bakery was closed. Have you seen the headlines?" I hate how hesitant I sound, but he brings a flare of fear out of me, one I've never felt before.

"I don't read the newspaper."

I lower my head and take the paper out from beneath my arm again. "Perhaps you should today." I hold the paper up, allowing him to easily see the main headline about the Jews being forced to leave Germany.

"What is it?" he asks.

"Can't you see the headline?"

Tobias tugs the paper from my hand and brings it to his right side, scanning it from an odd angle. "My God. Why didn't you say so?"

Despite feeling perplexed by his behavior and the assumption he may not be able to see out of his left eye, I'm taken aback at his reaction.

"I just found out."

"Mother, Father," he shouts, walking toward the center foyer. "Come see this. It's important. Come right away."

Mister and Madam Bohdan trample out of the grand salon, meeting Tobias and me. We are no sooner joined by Filip and Pavel clomping down the stairs to likely find out what all the excitement is about.

"Son, you're reading the newspaper?" Mister Bohdan says with a proud smile. "Good for you."

"Father, take the paper," Tobias snaps.

Mister Bohdan narrows an eye and glances over at Madam Bohdan. The look of concern across both of their faces is of wonder and not knowledge yet. I can't imagine how they will feel in a moment.

Mister Bohdan grabs the paper, reading all the headlines first.

Madam Bohdan does the same. She has a handkerchief crumpled in her hand and places it over her mouth. "What is happening? Has the world gone mad?" she cries out.

I feel as though I shouldn't be standing among the family while they read what will likely scare them more than anything has before. Even worse, Ben isn't home, and yet, I'm revealing this unworldly news to his family. I would have waited, had Tobias not cornered me. Ben's fears are coming to fruition, and knowing how it will affect him, pains me deeply.

Mister Bohdan's complexion becomes pale. "It's only a matter of time before this happens here. We can't assume there's time or that the conflicts will end before they reach us. We must protect ourselves and I'm not sure how exactly."

"What do you mean, you don't know how, Father?" spits Tobias. "We've known Hitler has been pushing through Sude- tenland. We aren't that far from there. Of course, we certainly won't be giving in to this bullish behavior. We should hire an attorney."

"Tobias," Madam Bohdan scolds him. "Don't be a fool. There isn't an attorney in all of Europe who can stop Hitler from what he's doing. It would have been done by now."

"Well, there must be something we can do. We are armed and we'll protect our property at whatever cost that may be," Tobias says.

"They are taking assets and wealth away from Jewish people. We won't be an exception to this radical law, not when the rest of our country is pulled into the German Reich. We won't have a foot to stand on," Mister Bohdan says.

My fingers are tightly woven together, hanging in front of my apron, and I find it best to keep my focus set on the wooden floors rather than the eyes of everyone around me.

The front door opens and closes with a loud thrust and dress shoes stomp through the house with urgency. It must be Ben. He's the only one missing, but he should be in class.

"I see you have a paper," he says, anger lacing through each word. "Well, good. I was just told to leave the university at once. Jews are not wanted there at this time, not with everything that occurred in Germany and Austria last night. Since we are registered Jews in the country, they had no problem tracking me down today. Who would have thought we were walking into a trap when filling out simple paperwork like every other citizen of this country?"

"Wait a minute. They told you to leave the university?" Madam Bohdan questions, her eyes bulging, mouth ajar, and brows arching with appall.

"Does that mean we won't have to go to school anymore?" Pavel asks with a bit too much enthusiasm for the subject matter.

"Pavel," Filip scolds him. "Shush."

"Yes. I was escorted off the property as a matter of fact. It was deliberately humiliating. My scores have all been in the top level of each class, and this is how they treat me. I'm—I don't have words to explain the rage I feel now. If you'll excuse me, I need to be alone," Ben says, pressing his fingertips against his temples and closing his eyes. I've never seen him so distraught.

When he pulls in a lungful of air and opens his eyes, I try to catch his attention before he walks away. For the briefest of moments, he peers over at me. The lump in his throat lowers and he nods at me before brushing past, toward the stairwell. He's tried to steal so much time with me over the last few weeks, but I would do anything for some time with him now.

"Mila, maybe you could go speak with him," Mister Bohdan says.

"Josef, is that necessary? We're capable of handling our son, don't you think?" Madam Bohdan replies.

Mister Bohdan gives his wife a long hard stare and shakes his head. "Please, Mila. I would appreciate it."

Rather than seek approval from Madam Bohdan too, I jump at the opportunity and follow in Ben's path up the stairs.

"Boys, go into the library. We'll join you there shortly. I need to have a word with your mother," I hear Mister Bohdan say as I reach the top of the stairwell.

I tap the backs of my knuckles on Ben's door, keeping quiet as I'm already worried about disturbing him. "What is it?" he calls out.

"May I come in?"

He doesn't respond, but I hear him walking across his bedroom. The door opens and I'm toe to toe with a man who looks utterly destroyed. His eyes are glossy, and his hair is a mess, no longer greased down as it always is. His jacket has been strewn onto his four-poster bed and his tie is hanging from a loosened loop. "Your father asked that I come upstairs in case you wanted to talk."

"He should know I don't need to be checked on as if I'm a child. I'm a grown man."

"A grown man who just had his life stripped away from him. I know something about that. Maybe your father thought I might understand something of what you're going through."

Ben's shoulders fall and he lowers his head. "Come in," he says, opening his arm toward his bedroom.

He closes the door behind me as I turn to face him. "When I read the headlines, you came to my mind first," I admit.

"I wasn't aware you even cared to remember who I am. We're passing strangers in the night now, are we not?"

I deserve his words, but not the anger he's feeling from something I have no control over. "I've been terrified to take a risk that could result in losing a place to sleep and work. Consequently, our friendship has been the casualty to bear."

"Friendship?" He huffs through a laugh full of aggravation.

"We are both destined to get hurt, one way or another, Ben.

There's no one way around it. You know this just as well as I do."

He shrugs. "Maybe you care, but I don't. Only God knows what tomorrow will bring and I need today to make me feel alive. Right now, I only feel as though I've just lost everything I had been working for. I'm nothing, no one. I'm a Jew—left to be exactly what the Germans want, and they haven't even made their way to Prague yet."

"Nothing?" I question.

He tugs at his tie and paces back and forth. "That's how I feel, and you can't tell me otherwise."

My chest aches as I take in heavy breaths to keep up with my racing heart. "Don't say that again. You are so much more than you are giving yourself credit for."

"How are you one to give advice when you look in the mirror every morning and tell yourself you're just a maid and that you aren't worthy of anything more than what a beggar has? Do you honestly think I don't know of the thoughts that go through your head, Mila? You are no better. You are far crueler to yourself than I've ever been to myself, and you're right, I was a casualty of that, and it wasn't fair. I didn't have a say in the decision." Ben throws his hands up in the air and slams his fists against the wall. "It was all for nothing. Every damn day."

My hand trembles as I reach for his wrist, hoping to calm him down from the anger reeling through him. "It wasn't," I mutter. "Everything we experience in life leads us somewhere new, and maybe the new place isn't always better than where we were before, but it's part of our journey."

He twists his head and lowers his gaze to me. "I'm not sure I'm capable of thinking that way."

I close my eyes for a moment, garnering the strength I need to take some of his pain away. I swing under his arm as his fist is still pinned to the wall. "I'll help you think that way. Every day is something new you're meant to experience, a lesson, or just a step forward. Trust me."

Ben lowers his eyelids, a downcast stare pinning me to the wall beneath his fists. "Trust you when you won't trust me?"

"I trust you."

He lowers his hands and drapes them around my waist, pulling me in against him. His lips crash into mine and I can taste his pain, the heat and torment rippling through his veins. He seems to use every ounce of strength he has to hold on to me, and I know I understand his agony in more ways than I can explain.

My body becomes numb and weak in his hold, and I can only hear the struggling breaths between the two of us as we dance around in circles, trying to steal each other's air, feel each other's woes, and heal one another's hearts.

SIXTEEN

WHO CAN BE CONSIDERED A FRIEND?

BENEDIKT, JANUARY 1939

I'm likely the only fool in this country standing outside in chilly temperatures without a coat, while working on the motorbike that is still in dozens of pieces months after beginning this project. I've had plenty of time to work on it, but a few of the parts were almost impossible to come by and I've had to find junkyards and mine through abandoned vehicles and motorbikes to find what I need. I believe I have the remaining missing parts now, but I still need to put it all back together. It shouldn't be long now though.

After struggling with stripped screws all morning, I've worked up a sweat and no longer feel the cold against my skin. Though I'm aware of how cold it is when I spot Mila ambling through freshly fallen snow, through the shimmering white frosted pines. She folds her arms across her chest, bearing the wind as it blows a dusting of snow off the stable's roof. The stark footprints against the smooth blanket of untouched powder strikes me with a new type of guilt I seem to feel whenever I'm around her. There should be two sets of footprints. I should be helping her, not standing here working on a pile of metal. Though she's asked me several times to allow her to do the job she's been hired for, I still don't feel right about watching from afar.

At least I know she isn't as cold as she was before I found one of Mother's old coats in the attic. I forced her to accept it so she wouldn't freeze whenever leaving the estate. With whatever I have given Mila for the purpose of basic survival, I receive Mother's wrath, and I'm not sure why she is still bothering to be irate about so many insignificant issues, but I figure it's a self-centered distraction. She's changed so much over the last few years that she feels unfamiliar to me, entirely different from the woman who raised me. She hasn't smiled or laughed or said much of anything pleasant, and she's painted her misery across every wall inside, which casts a dark shadow over all of us.

I place down my tools and clean the grease from my hands on a rag. She may not want help with her work, but it's hard to stop myself from spending time with Mila, especially since I'm home all the time now. It's almost a tease to watch her stroll by so many times a day. I've promised to keep our public interactions to a minimum. Though, speculation about our relationship has been brought to my attention by Filip and Pavel during our family dinners. Mother simply narrows her eyes and clears her throat to change the subject. I'm sure she's more than aware that something is brewing between us, but it's best left unspoken.

No one else in my family seems to care much about visiting the horses when it's this cold outside, so it seems to be a safe opportunity to meet Mila.

Before entering the stable, I'm struck in awe at the beautiful scene before me as I admire Mila working with Twister and Nova. I'm struck by the cloud-like puffs of fog billowing from her cherry-red lips as she whispers sweet words to the horses while stroking their muzzles as they fight for her attention. The sun breaks through the clouds for a moment and a reflection from the wet snow strikes her long wavy hair with an amber tint, highlighting the rosy hue of her cheeks. There's something so angelic about her and yet she hides pain in a way the rest of us aren't capable.

"I know you're watching me, and I've told you before I'm not a painting on display," Mila says without turning away from Nova.

"I would be bored if you were only a painting. I'm very glad you aren't."

"Then I'm flattered to know I keep you entertained."

"How do you say such a thing without so much as hinting a smile?" I ask.

"Years of practice," she says. She answers everything I say much faster than I could offer her if she was the one asking the questions.

"How's Twister today?"

She's moved from Nova to Twister and is brushing her coat. It seems it's the only time of day Twister feels well enough to nuzzle her muzzle against Mila's chest. "She seems all right. I'm sure she won't find much relief until the foal is born."

"You said that won't be until May or June though. There's nothing we can do to help her feel better?"

"She enjoys being brushed. Whatever I can do to make her happy is what's best."

I walk closer to Twister's pen, taking a good look at her. She's just starting to show some swelling around her belly. "I'm surprised my mother and father haven't asked about Twister since I brought up her pregnancy. I suppose I should take that as a good thing. Plus, they have more to worry about than a horse, I guess."

Mila gives me the same look she does every time we have this conversation. Two lines deepen across her forehead, and she purses her lips. "I'm still waiting for the day they say the horses must go. It's not practical to have them here when there is, as you say, more to worry about."

"Let's try not to fret just yet. We're all okay for the moment and should focus on that."

I hold my gaze on Mila's profile, waiting for her to find some comfort in my statement. I know I can't force her to block out what she fears, but we all need moments of peace.

"Well then," she says with a sigh. "Nova is becoming much better at following me and trotting at a steady pace. Even our walks are becoming smoother. She follows my guide very well. That's good news, isn't it?"

"That's wonderful news," I say. "Do you think she might be able to take us both for a walk? I haven't ridden in longer than I can remember."

Mila turns her attention to Nova and angles her head to the side. "What do you think, sweet girl?" Nova snorts. "I suppose the snow is powdery enough that it won't bother her. Plus, it seems your motorbike still isn't going to take you very far." Mila's teasing smirk forces a rush of heat to flourish through my cheeks.

"Not yet, but soon. I should be done with it in the next week or two, and then I'll take you for a ride."

"I'll pass," she says. "I'm content with a horse's four legs."

She doesn't know what she's missing. There's something about the rush of excitement while traveling at a high speed on only two wheels. "Hmm. Well, you might change your mind, but for now, there's a perfectly suitable horse for us."

With a subtle shake of her head and a smile she's trying to hide, she turns to face Nova and strokes her hand down the length of her nose.

I spot the saddle hanging from the far wall and lift it off the rusty hook. Mila opens the gate and I sweep my hand along Nova's mane before placing the saddle over her back. As soon as I step away, Nova picks up on the cue and clomps out of the gate, then meanders outside of the stable. "I think she's ready," I say.

Mila follows Nova and reaches her hands up to the saddle as if she's offering her a warning. Without much thought, I place my hands around Mila's waist to help her up.

Before lifting her foot into the stirrup, she glances at me over her shoulder and pinches her lip between her teeth. The shy, yet inviting, look in her eyes ignites every nerve running through my body.

I give her a boost then follow, pulling myself up behind Mila on the saddle. With the reins in her hand, I loop my arms around her waist. I'm reeling in the comfort and warmth of her body against mine.

"Aren't you going to be cold without a coat?" Mila asks, peeking back at me.

"Not a chance."

With Mila's aid, Nova sets out for a path into the woods behind the stables. I haven't been down here since I was Pavel's age. "I used to build forts out here when I was younger," I say, resting my chin on her shoulder to whisper in her ear.

"I'll bet you climbed every one of these trees too, didn't you?" she replies.

"That's where the best views are, and it's always the place to pen out thoughts."

"You write?"

"Secretly," I confess. She's so easy to talk to, I have no idea when I begin spilling secrets. "Mostly poetry, but I'm not that good."

"Said by every true artist," she laments. "Maybe I should be the judge of that."

The thought of showing anyone my words makes my throat tighten. I'm not sure I could bare my soul to that extent. "Perhaps, someday."

We've traveled to an opening in the woods and Nova must know she's in new territory as she veers off the path to acquaint herself with the nearby trees. Mila finds her behavior amusing and laughs while stroking her neck.

"You really love her and Twister," I say.

"I think I might understand them more than people. Being blind in one eye gives Nova this disadvantage in life. She must find her way differently than other horses, and her future might not be as bright as a horse with two good eyes. It's like me, left behind without my family to fend for myself in an unfamiliar place. I'm not blind in one eye, but I feel like I can't see much of anything too clearly now. Nova doesn't know there are more trees to her left. At least, not yet. I don't know if my family has been imprisoned, or worse. At least, not yet."

My heart aches for the truth she keeps to herself, despite how many times I ask her what she's thinking, feeling, and how she's coping. I know I can't take the pain away but I want her to know I'm here for her to lean on.

I loosen my arms from around her and place my hands on hers, taking a moment to kiss her cheek. "If Nova can find some light in the darkness, I hope you can too," I whisper.

Mila rests her head back against my chest. "You're my light."

"You're my escape," I reply.

Nova circles around the open area once more and decides to head back in the direction of the estate but picks up the pace. "Oh my," Mila yelps. "Easy, girl."

She pulls back on the reins, but Nova isn't interested in following her aid. I encircle my arms around Mila and wrap my hands around hers to keep us steady as Nova gallops through the woods.

The cold air against my face and the internal rush from the speed ignites my pulse and revitalizes me. It's a moment of freedom.

Nova stops just before the estate's property line. "That was unexpected," I say, sighing with relief. "Are you okay?"

Mila falls into a bout of laughter, a beautiful sound I've rarely heard from her. "That was incredible."

"So are you, Mila."

She shakes her head then tips it to the side. "I'm not sure why you care about me so much, but some might say you should have your head examined."

I press my forehead down to her shoulder, trying not to grin in response to her daily routine of insulting me. Her ability to be on her own page and no one else's is what I find most striking about her. It's hard not to assume most women in her situation would jump at a chance to be with a former aristocrat, but she doesn't see me the way Tobias sees himself, and I'm grateful for that. I'm more than my family's lineage and assets. All those breadcrumbs could be destroyed in less than a night as we've seen, and if I have nothing else to rely on, I'll have nothing at all. "I know you think about us more than you lead me to believe."

"Your confidence is going to land you in trouble someday, Benedikt," she says with a coy grin.

I want to tell her the same, but I wouldn't be correct. Her confidence is raw, built from life experience, hardship, and pain. Mine is self-taught from a book. Wealth doesn't always complement confidence, not like many might think.

"Or it will take me where I want to be; somewhere with you. Nova understands," I say with a chuckle.

Mila doesn't respond, and I notice she's craning her neck to the side. "Do you recognize that car pulling around to the side of the estate?" she asks.

I stare out at the vehicle for a long minute, trying to get a better look. "I believe that's Mister and Misses Becker," I reply. "They're friends of the family, but we haven't spoken to them in some time. Father didn't mention he was expecting a visit from them, so I'm not sure why they would be here."

"Are they a Jewish family as well?" Mila asks.

I tap my heel against Nova's side to get her to continue to

the stables. Thankfully, she follows and does so promptly. I demount first and swiftly help Mila down. She seems a bit flustered by my reaction to having visitors, but I'm anxious to find out why the Beckers are here.

"No. Elias and Julia Becker are not Jewish, thankfully for them, since they live in the Sudetenland region," I answer.

"Maybe you should go find out why they're here. It seems like it's troubling you."

"I might. At least, I'll go and say hello."

"Good," she says.

"Don't stay out here much longer. It's bitterly cold."

"I'm supposed to listen to a man who is dressed for a summer day while snow is covering the ground?"

"Yes," I reply with a grin, reaching out for Mila's hand. Her dimples deepen and she complies with my tug. Her arms loop around my neck and she rises onto her toes in search of my lips. "One kiss from you can easily make me believe it's summer at any time of the year."

She reaches up and tugs on my tweed cap, pulling it down over my eyes. "Let me know what you find out," she says.

By the time I make my way inside, Mother, Father, and the Beckers are in the library making themselves comfortable as Marena sets up cups and saucers for tea. The door is partially closed. I assume it's to let the rest of us know that they are conversing privately, which entices me to lurk and eavesdrop.

"Truly, Josef, I don't know what to tell you," Misses Becker says, sighing with grief.

"That you will do us this favor," Father follows. *A favor?* What could Father possibly need from them?

"Josef, you know you are like a brother to me, but think about what you're asking of us," Mister Becker says.

"I'm asking you to ensure our estate isn't seized by the regime," Father snaps. "God knows, I would do the same for you if the circumstances were different. It's simply a piece of paper." My stomach tightens and I cup my hand around my throat, coming to terms with the level of desperation I didn't know we were at.

"It's a title, Josef. If we put it under our name, the records will show the truth and we will be jeopardizing our safety too. It isn't a decision we can make so quickly, not without thinking through every possible scenario," Mister Becker continues. I lean back against the wall to the side of the door, trying to wrap my head around this ridiculous proposition. How could we trust anyone with the title to our estate right now? Lifelong friends or not—where have they been while Jewish people have been receiving unthinkable treatment? They basically acted as if they were strangers.

"I'm quite uncomfortable having this conversation," Misses Becker says. "In fact, I'm uncomfortable being here at all. It's nothing personal to either of you. I care about you both so dearly, just as I always have, but times are different, and everyone must do what's best for themselves." Misses Becker makes us sound like we're a sort of plague, rather than a Jewish family. Of everyone we've ever known, I wish I didn't have to overhear this truth from them.

"You're uncomfortable here because of what reason?" Mother asks her dearest friend.

"Hana, everyone in Germany has been explicitly told not to converse with any Jews. We wanted to do right by you and come over here as requested but being here makes us feel very uneasy. Surely, you must understand where we are coming from as well." It takes everything I have not to storm into the room and hand Mister and Misses Becker a piece of my mind. The nerve they have sitting in our home, speaking this way, is despicable.

The sudden silence is startling and I step away from the door. I imagine it won't be long before Father escorts them from the estate.

I cross through the foyer and head toward the salon, knowing there is a pillar large enough to hide behind. "I beg you to think about this," Father pleads, following Mister and Misses Becker to the front door. "We're former comrades. We promised to always be like family. I've never seen you as anything less." I haven't heard Father plead with anyone the way he is with Mister Becker.

"Please, Josef. Allow us time to think this through. Hana, it's so lovely to see you after such a long time," Misses Becker says.

"Julia," Mother says, sighing before cupping her hand over her mouth. She clearly has nothing else to say as she scampers away, clutching her chest. She's about to cry and likely doesn't want Misses Becker to see. From the little I heard, I can't say I blame Mother for hurting the way she must be. I only wish it would make her see more clearly out of her own eyes and realize that she makes others feel the same awful way.

Once the Beckers are out the door, I step out from behind the pillar. "Father, I couldn't help but overhear some of your conversation. Please tell me what the meaning is. Are we losing the estate?"

SEVENTEEN

SHADES OF COMPLEXION
MILA, JANUARY 1939

I've been trying my best to avoid the array of family discussions happening throughout the day, but the arguments have only gone from bad to worse. Whatever is going on has caused quite a bit of turmoil. Though, I would take a good family argument over the unthinkable situation I'm experiencing with mine. I regret feeling such frustration every time I tried to create peace between Mama and Papa during an argument. Sometimes, their disagreements came with warning. Or so it seemed. Perhaps I just became so intuitive to the changes in their daily mood that I could feel the tension brewing. For reasons I still don't understand, I was able to stop impending quarrels before they grew into something larger. The last one I broke up felt effortless. I was proud of the peacekeeper I had become.

Papa wakes before the rest of us to check the borders of the settlement. It's something we've become accustomed to over the years. No day is a safe day, but it's another day, nonetheless. Sometimes, I follow him, wanting the quiet alone time that's sometimes hard to come by with either him or Mama. "Papa, wait for me."

He stops between the row of vardos and turns toward me with a smile. "You're here to keep me company again, are you?" he asks.

"Of course, Papa." When I catch up, I notice red veins tinting the whites of his eyes. Just as I suspected by the heaviness of his steps, either he didn't sleep much or he's worried. "Something is wrong." It's not a question.

Papa runs his hand down the side of his face and stretches his neck to the side. "Your intuition is quite strong, my dordi." We continue walking toward the enclosure of trees and Papa takes in a deep inhale before saying anything more. "Your mama is upset with me, and your brothers as well."

Papa never does anything to stir up trouble but being on the run as often as we are, disagreements are bound to happen every now and again. I hate when they argue. It seems pointless to me. "What for?"

"Your mother and brothers would like to remain here in the southern region near the lake. I understand it's easier for food procurement but from what I predict, the border of Austria is not somewhere we should be now. I may be wrong, but I might be right." I'm not sure there is a right or wrong. We're always being chased by someone or something.

"Mama has always said I must get my intuitive nature from you. Perhaps, we should remind her of such."

"Maybe, but I do understand her points. I don't enjoy taking risks, not when our family's well-being is on the line, but what other choice do I have?"

"You must follow your heart's advice," I tell him, the same as he tells me all of the time.

Papa wraps his arm around my shoulders and pulls me into his side. He kisses the top of my head. "We are one of a kind, you and I."

"At least the area is clear of officials," I say as we step out on the other side of the woods toward the foothills of the nearby village.

"For today, we should be all right, so maybe we can talk this out as a family."

"I'll see if I can explain my reasons to your mother and brothers more. I would rather us all be united than arguing."

"We are stronger as a unit. Isn't that what you always say?"

Papa takes my hand in his and squeezes. "I must have done something right with the way you've turned out, Mila."

From what I inadvertently overheard, Mister Bohdan is concerned about the estate's title, and is hoping a friend will take it off his hands. I'm not sure how any of that works, but I can't imagine it would be a simple transaction. I don't think I blame him for his concern though, not after the uptick in demolition to Jewish businesses and homes occurring not far from here.

The Germans have also made their presence known here, creating a corridor for military traveling purposes between Poland and Austria, crossing through Czechoslovakia. Each time I make my way into the village, I notice more and more men in German uniform roaming the streets. We aren't near their claimed corridor, yet they seem to be everywhere, with a demeanor of superiority as if they know something we don't.

After noticing the guests had left rather quickly following what sounded like outrage, I don't think anything has gone over well today.

"Why wouldn't you have spoken to me about this first?" Tobias hollers. It might be the tenth time I've heard these words spew from his mouth today.

"Again, I don't have to consult with you before deciding on behalf of our family. It's clear you don't understand the complexity or danger of what is looming ahead of us."

I don't understand how anyone in this family has the patience they do for Tobias. He seems so ignorant to the truth, or maybe it's denial. Either way, it's a dangerous way to live.

The foyer is the last place to dust and polish before my work is complete for the day. I feel like I'm eavesdropping, standing so close to the door of the library where the conversation is continuing.

The telephone outside the library chimes, the sound of the hollow bell clashing against the wall, bouncing from one corner to the next. I jump at the surprising interruption. The telephone has only rung a few times since I've been here. It acts more as a piece of decor than a functioning object in the estate. I dust it daily, careful not to knock the receiver off the brass hook.

I stare at the telephone as if it's going to answer itself, but I've never been told to answer an incoming call and I don't think it's my place to do so.

The door swings open from the library and Mister Bohdan storms out, so I spin around to dust the gold-plated picture frame.

"Bohdan residence." Mister Bohdan answers the call.

From the corner of my eye, I peer toward him, curious to see the expression on his face. Mister Bohdan seems to be overly expressive when conversing with anyone and I've found it easy to determine what he might be saying just from the look on his face or his hand gestures.

He presses his hand to his chest and hunches forward. "Elias Becker, my good man. I'm at a loss for words. I'm not sure how I could ever repay you for the help you are giving my family."

Mister Bohdan straightens his posture as if he's regaining a small sense of pride he must have been missing before the phone call. "I will have the papers drafted so we can settle on this as soon as possible."

The small smile along Mister Bohdan's face fades into a straight line, taking in the last of whatever the caller has to say. "Of course, I understand the risks involved, but please know I would do the very same for you if you were in our situation." Mister Bohdan holds the receiver to his ear, listening intently and pressing his hand to his forehead. "I understand. Thank you, Elias. Thank you."

After placing the receiver back onto the hooks, Mister Bohdan takes a minute to breathe before turning to return to the library. He spots me in the corner and forces a small, uncomfortable smile in my direction before entering.

The conversation becomes much quieter than it was before, and I can't hear anything. It's best if I finish up the dusting now while I have the chance to make my way out of this area, so no one thinks I was out here listening the entire time. I know Mister Bohdan saw me, but I don't think he was focusing on what I was doing.

Thankfully, I'm able to complete the task before anyone steps out of the library, but I don't make it all the way up the stairs before the family spills out into the foyer. I continue toward my bedroom and secure myself inside, wishing I could piece together whatever is happening.

I take a moment to change out of my uniform, trading it for one of the long-pleated skirts Ben was kind enough to buy me, along with some new blouses. I argued against his kind gesture, but he assured me he has more money than necessary thanks to the trust he will "likely never make a dent in," or so he says. For a man with a wealthy lifestyle, he truly seems to despise the thought of money altogether. Even though I was given some necessities upon learning that my family was missing, I was saving up to purchase new clothes to wear when not working, but he bought some before I could. We've so seamlessly fallen into a kinship that makes me feel as if I've always belonged to him, and he has forever been mine. But, at the same time, there doesn't seem to be a place where we can be open about our adoration. While we're in the presence of his family, I am the maid. Nothing more.

A soft knock on the door causes my fingers to swiftly clasp the remaining buttons on the blouse. "Just a minute," I call out.

With a glance in the mirror, I notice I'm still a bit of a mess. My hair has fallen loose from my braid, and I appear tired after a long day. I suppose it's no different than how I usually look though.

I sweep some of the loose strands of hair away from my face and open the door, finding Ben looking as worn as I feel. He's in his typical attire; an undershirt and tweed pants. His smile isn't what it once was though, at least I don't see it as often as I did. He seems worried more often than not and it's like his mind is spinning with revolving thoughts.

"Care to go for a walk?" he asks.

"Actually, I was going to walk to a couple of wooded areas around the village. I spotted some on a map and wondered if there might be other Romani settlements. If I find one with inhabitants, there's a chance they may have seen my family, perhaps. It will likely be a lot of walking though, so if that's not what you had in mind, I'm perfectly fine to go on my own."

Ben's gaze drops to the space between us, and he folds his arms before leaning against the threshold of the door. "It upsets me to no end that you spend so many nights searching for your family without ever finding a clue. I wouldn't give up either, but I wish I could do something more than just keep you company."

I shrug and drop my hands into the pockets of my skirt. "I enjoy the company, and there's nothing anyone can do. I only wish I knew if they were okay."

"I understand," he says. "Would you rather I drive, or do you prefer to walk? The weather is mild today."

I enjoy the fresh air, even if it's frigid. The air has been too cold these last couple of weeks, and I haven't been able to go far without worrying about possible frostbite. The temperatures are above freezing tonight at least.

"Are you comfortable walking through the village?" I ask

him. I've noticed he's been avoiding it after being pushed out of the university and the visit with his friends at the pub.

"I'm all right. It will be dark soon anyway. We can walk," he says. "I'll get my coat."

I have yet to ask Ben about what happened between his family today, but I assume he'll tell me if he wants to talk about it. I try my best to keep boundaries between us, knowing in any other circumstance, I wouldn't be living in his house or be privy to information I shouldn't. With my lack of questions, we've spoken less than usual as we walk side by side down the narrow road lined with bowing trees blocking out the last of the sunlight. Snowflakes blow off branches as we walk by, dancing through the swells of wind before melting into the gravel ahead of us.

"Do you feel all right?" I ask. "You look a bit pale."

"I'm sure I always look this pale in the dead of winter," he jokes. "We can't all have a natural tan like you're lucky enough to have."

I've never considered the difference in skin color to be lucky. If anything, my olive skin has betrayed me, allowing people to make false assumptions about who I am. I refuse to let the quiet, or sometimes loud, thoughts of others bother me much, but they often play in my head like a broken record.

"My father has decided on behalf of our family to sell the title and deed of our estate to family friends, the people you saw waiting at the front door this morning," he says. "He thinks it's best if we don't have our name on this property for the time being."

His news is somewhat startling, though it shouldn't be. I would be rightfully concerned if I were his parents too. To assume what Hitler will do next is as foolish as grouping people based on their skin color.

"I heard some of the frustration carrying through the foyer today," I say.

Ben stretches his neck to the side and wraps his gloved hand above the collar of his coat. "No one is fond of Father's plan. The Beckers were hesitant to help us and knowing that, we're all a bit uneasy about how this will unravel. When we can safely reclaim the title to the estate, we can only hope the Beckers do right by whatever agreement Father has drafted up."

"I thought they were friends of the family?" I ask, wondering why they wouldn't trust them of all people.

Ben squints into the distance, seemingly searching for an answer to my question rather than looking to see what's ahead. "Friends aren't what they used to be. I wouldn't want to compare my life to yours in any way as I haven't suffered through the hardships you have told me about, but it seems most people are choosing to believe the lies Hitler spreads. Everyone needs someone to blame for conflicts and economic crises. Each person will protect themselves before others, and in this case, even family friends will do the same."

"I understand what you mean," I reply.

"In any case, the Beckers have decided to comply with Father's request, but Mother and Tobias are not in agreement and think it's a mistake that could cost us everything."

"What do you think?" Ben is never short of opinions so it's surprising to hear him speak of his mother's and Tobias's thoughts before his own.

Ben moves his hand from the back of his neck and takes a hold of mine, squeezing gently. "I think there's a difference between wanting to believe everything will turn out for the best and weighing the chances of it happening. I'm not sure the odds are in our favor whichever direction we go. It doesn't matter now anyway. Father has made the decision and we're going to hope for the best."

I wonder what changes this will bring about, if any? It's not the right time to ask when I'm sure he's already thinking the same, but selfishly, every route scares me now.

We walk through the village, filled with gothic-style houses of contrasting yellow, pink, and green façades. The rows of windows above the shops are framed with thin overhangs, salted with a thin layer of snow. The cobblestones of the square are wet and dark with scattered puddles stealing reflections from the glow of streetlamps. Ben becomes quiet again and I find myself playing a guessing game about what he's stirring over now. Though, I might be able to answer my own questions as we pass several shops that look to have been abandoned.

"Jewish people are beginning to leave the area," he says. "That's why these shops are closed. I know a lot of the owners or their families."

"Do you blame them?" I ask, curious about how he feels.

"No. In fact, I wish I could sweep you away from here and go somewhere safer, but I'm not entirely sure where that would be now. There are so many changes happening every day, I wouldn't have the confidence to form a decision like that."

"Sweep me away?" I ask.

"Is that such a terrible idea?" He peers down at me, waiting for me to look up.

I smile, wanting him to know I don't think it's a terrible idea at all. Perhaps if I left the area, I wouldn't feel obligated to go searching for my family so often. I wouldn't have to bear the guilt of being angry with them for leaving me no choice but to flee the area like they must have done. "I would be okay with running away with you."

"I'm glad to know we're on the same page," he says, squeezing my hand a little tighter. I lean my face against his arm, holding on to him.

I point toward a road veering off the main one we're on, knowing I saw the open spot of land just north from here.

Once we arrive at the dimly lit snow-covered meadow, my gaze falls to the sprigs of brown and yellow grass poking through the white covering around my feet. The silence makes me feel like one of the lonely ice crystals falling from the sky.

"Is that—" Ben begins to ask.

"No."

My fists are clenched by my sides as I walk toward the circle of vardos and caravans. Not one of them looks familiar, but worse, not one of them looks to be occupied. Pain sears through my chest as I peek inside the back opening of the nearest caravan. It's not only abandoned but the belongings look to have been thrown around. Drawers are unhinged and hanging, cupboards are open, and the shelves are bare. Clothes and bedding cover the floor, and handmade dolls are torn at the seams with the cotton stuffing escaping through the loose threads.

"Do you know who lives here?" Ben asks, his brows pulling in. His reaction is subdued, almost as if he's having trouble understanding what he's seeing.

"No, and whoever was here doesn't live here any longer."

I continue to the next wagon, finding the same scene. Then again, seven more times as I walk around the ring of horseless caravans. "People like us don't desert our homes."

Ben has his hand splayed across his chest. "They were chased away. Is that what you're insinuating?"

"There's no other explanation." I sound calmer than I feel. I'm not sure where travelers were taken or sent—or where they went if free to run. I haven't heard of any change of laws, but I question now whether I ever knew the truth about the existing laws. Mama and Papa tried their best to normalize life for us and I always felt there was more to our story than I've been told. Papa made us feel safe, and Mama seemed free of worry. I didn't question the reality of what the world looked like through the eyes of an adult rather than a child.

I feel so foolish for being unaware of the questions I should have been asking all along.

"Mila," Ben says, reaching for my elbow as I pace through the flattened snow.

"I don't understand," I say. "None of this makes sense."

"Nothing in this country makes much sense right now," he says.

"I always thought we were running away from villagers who didn't want beggars to inhabit their region. They weren't strong enough to force us away without our lifelines—these vardos and caravans. These are our homes."

"Romani people are forced to carry IDs around, aren't they?"

"Yes, I've had one since I was fourteen, but Papa told me it was simply for identification since we moved around a lot."

Ben shakes his head and clutches his hand around his opposite wrist. "I think there's more to it than just having it for the purpose of location. Are there laws you're supposed to abide by? I embarrassingly haven't paid much attention to the scrutiny Romani endure while I've been so concerned about being Jewish."

"I don't know..." I admit.

I only realize how dark it has become when a moving spot of light captures my attention from the surrounding trees, distracting me. I'm watching the flare bounce around. "We should go," I whisper.

Ben turns to where I'm staring and takes my hand. We run as quietly as we can, unable to avoid the crunching of snow beneath each footstep.

I look back to where I saw the light, spotting two more bouncing flashes.

"*Zastavte se tam!*" They are shouting at us to stop. "What are we going to do?" I cry out through ragged breaths.

"We're not stopping. Keep running, Mila," Ben says, pulling me to run so fast, my feet are barely touching the snow.

The beams are to the right of us, still much too close for us to take a moment to catch our breath.

"Follow my lead," Ben says, turning around to face the lights to see who is following us, but I'm worried we'll trip if he doesn't turn back around.

"We must go faster," I tell him.

"Trust me, Mila." He pulls me into a thick settlement of trees and throws his back against the trunk of a tall pine. His arms swing around my midsection, and he pulls me in against him. "Kiss me. That's all you need to do, okay?"

Ben lifts his hands to my face before I can answer. The leather of his gloves is cold against my cheeks, but I do as he says and press up on my toes to reach his lips. He holds me still, our mouths frozen in place until a moving flash of light grazes my closed eyelids. They've found us. Ben lowers a hand to my waist and holds me firmly against him as his lips move rigidly against mine. My nerves are caught between panic and a fervor of passion. I hardly realize I'm clutching the sleeves of his coat in my fists, trying my hardest to focus on his warm lips against the cold I feel on the rest of my body.

Heavy breaths grow louder, but they aren't coming from either of us. "What are the two of you doing here?"

Our lips both part and I stare up into Ben's eyes, watching his expression as he faces whoever is behind us. "We were just out—"

"Yeah, yeah. We've heard it all before. Maybe you didn't see the chain and sign you stepped over upon entering the territory, but it says *do not enter*."

Ben's heart is beating so hard, I feel it against my chest.

"I apologize, sir. This was my idea. I shouldn't have stepped over the chain. We'll leave," Ben says. He shouldn't have to take the blame when it was my idea. I open my mouth to speak but Ben glances down at me and widens his eyes. I take it as a warning not to say anything more.

"Do your parents know what you are doing out here, Mister

Bohdan?" As we're being questioned, it becomes clear the men know Ben. I should feel relief, but their condescending tone doesn't give me a sense of hope. I remain standing with my back to them, fearful of what they might think if they see my complexion beneath the bright lights from their torches.

"No, sir. We were just out for a walk."

"Is the girl Jewish too?" he asks.

"No, sir," Ben replies submissively.

"I suggest you get her home immediately and then see yourself home as well."

Ben swallows hard, and I can only assume it's his pride he's trying not to choke on. "We're leaving."

The group of men mutter between themselves, one chuckling as if this is a joke. "Go on, get out of here before I write you up for trespassing."

Ben takes my hand again and swings me behind him, hiding me from who I assume to be authorities of the village. He pins me close to his back and I bury the side of my face beneath his shoulder, facing away from the torches. We don't run, but walk swiftly, passing by the men as we step back onto the main dirt path we followed into the settlement. "Keep looking straight ahead," Ben whispers as we create some distance between us and the trouble we escaped.

Until we're back on the main road, I'm not sure I'll be comfortable enough to breathe normally.

"Are you okay?" Ben asks.

"I shouldn't have dragged you there," I say. "I saw the sign when we entered and I ignored it, thinking nothing of it."

"Mila, if my parents vanished, I would be looking for them too. I wouldn't stop until I had answers. I'm worried along with you. No one should have to live like this, wondering whether their family is okay and safe."

Ben turns the corner back onto the main village road where a streetlight greets us at the curb. People are talking and walking about, carrying on with their lives as usual. It's as if we stepped out of a nightmare, but I'm afraid we won't be able to shake the feeling away as easily as we would if we'd just woken up. He releases my hand to catch his breath, and I lean my cheek against the brick edifice of the shop we're standing in front of. The harsh texture of the cold surface seems to shock me out of my dizzying haze. "For a moment, I didn't know who they were looking for—Gypsies, Jewish people, or just trespassers."

"Likely any of the three. Teenage trespassers will receive less wrath than the other two options, I'm sure."

"This is why you don't leave the estate much anymore, isn't it? There isn't a rule that you can't be a resident here just because you're Jewish," I say, cupping my hand around the back of his head.

"No, but some of the police are of German descent and they have been given rank, uniform, and permission to act according to German law. From what I know, extramarital relations between a Jew and non-Jew aren't allowed in Nazi Germany. The 'laws' are just slowly leaking into our country."

"That man knew you?" I ask.

"He's been an officer in the village for as long as I can remember. He's just wearing a different uniform now."

"Just because they have German blood shouldn't mean we have to abide by their laws. We aren't in Germany, and we aren't Germans," I argue. "How dare he tell you to take me home?" I'm speaking with a great deal of haste. My anger is getting the better of me, and I don't know how to make it stop. "What if I want to stay out with you a little longer?" I'm aware Ben isn't the one laying the foundation of these groundless rules, but I can't help but share my dismay.

Ben's eyes soften and he loops his arms around my waist. "I'm standing here with the most beautiful woman I've ever had the privilege of knowing. You must not know what I would sacrifice to stay out with you all night," he says, sweeping his gloved fingers down the side of my cheek. "I don't want to be away from you, even if that means staying right here, just like this, while I stare into your soulful eyes beneath the lonely streetlight behind us."

Everything he says mirrors my feelings for him, ones I can't seem to put into words. "I wish we could freeze time, hold on to this moment, and never let go," I utter. "I've never had such a consuming connection to anyone before you. I'm not sure I could go back to having anything less."

Ben tugs me in closer to him and lowers his lips to mine. The cold sensation between our mouths sends sparks through every bit of my body. I clench my hands around his neck, wishing my strength was all that was needed to make this moment last.

I'm not sure when I gave up control over this unsuspecting pursuit between us, but I can't deny that I have become help-lessly enraptured by this man.

When we run out of shared breaths, our lips part. He appears so pensive as he stares into my eyes and I wish I could hear his every thought. I loosen my hold around his neck and skim my finger along the scar stretching from his eyebrow down and across to his opposite side cheek. "What hurt you?" I ask.

His arms loosen and the corners of his lips shift to one side. A huff of laughter follows, but I don't think he's going to answer my question. "It doesn't matter."

"It does to me."

"Does the mark take away from my good looks?" he jests with a perfect grin.

"The opposite, really. It makes you rare, like an exquisite gem with perfectly unique flaws—one of a kind."

Ben's smile fades as he glances over my shoulder toward the corner we came around. "We should keep walking."

I try to turn in the direction of his gaze, but he takes my hand and guides me across the road toward the estate.

"I'm sorry to cut our time short tonight. I despise that we are in the dark when it comes to our rights, and I don't want to be caught off guard when someone shines a light on either of us." His honesty is raw, and I understand why he feels the way he does.

"Is this how life is always going to be now?" I ask, though I can guess the answer by the speed of our pace. Ben might read more than I do and follow the headlines I'd rather not see every day, but I thought we were safe outside of the Sudetenland counties.

"The gates have been left open for the Germans, and everyone in our country is feeling the threat and the need to comply to keep the peace for as long as possible. We have no other choice when it comes to protecting ourselves."

"This is why your father has been so apprehensive," I say. I'm sure he's aware, but it's all hitting me at once, because I was blind to what I didn't want to see.

"Let's just get back to the estate," Ben says, not responding to my statement.

I can hardly feel my legs by the time we reach the top of the hill. They're numb from the cold and sore from walking and running. "I'm sorry for the trouble," I offer as we head through the back entrance into the laundry room.

Ben closes the door behind us and turns the bolted lock. I can't see much inside the dark room aside from what falls beneath the glow from the full moon. "There is nothing you can say or do to cause trouble. We are living in troubling times, but we'll adapt."

"If there's anything I'm good at doing, it's that. I've spent my entire life adapting, always having to keep a look out for whatever might be happening behind me." For a moment, I convinced myself I had left that life behind, but now I see there's no escape. "Each in our own way, we're prisoners of a world we didn't create."

Ben finds my hands in the darkness. "Listen to me. I know I can't promise you that anything will become easier for either of us. In fact, I'm quite sure there's a steep hill ahead, one we can't see past the current horizon. But no matter what falls from the sky and lands at our feet, I'm here. You're here. That makes it so neither of us must face the unknown alone."

I lean in and rest my cheek on his chest, feeling his arms wrap around me as he rests his chin on the top of my head. "No one has been able to distract me from fears, not like you do. You make me feel like we're living in our little world sometimes, and it's a blessing. Aside from having my family, I've always thought of myself as alone in life, but you've changed that, and I'm grateful," I say.

"Mila," he says. "I love you, and nothing will change that for me."

My mouth becomes dry and my hands tremor as I come to terms with his confession. "It wasn't long ago that I questioned what this type of love is supposed to feel like, but when I'm with you, there's no doubt in my mind that what I feel is love for you too."

Ben holds me a little tighter and I wish we never had to let go. When he releases me, it will feel like I'm back out in the cold again.

"Why don't you go upstairs first so we don't draw attention to ourselves by going up together?" he suggests. I can only hope that if we don't cross any lines, we'll be okay.

"Good night," I whisper, reaching up to leave a lingering kiss on his cheek.

He sighs and I leave through the narrow opening of the laundry room door, removing my boots before tiptoeing up the stairs.

For the length of each kiss, I can convince myself life will somehow turn out all right in the end.

EIGHTEEN

A LIST LIKE NO OTHER

I knew there wasn't an end in sight for the conflicts surrounding our country, but it's taken a sharp turn that I shouldn't find shocking. At the same time, I can't wrap my mind around the announcements Hitler has publicly made. The headline is so large, Father couldn't hide it when he opened the fold at the table. We can all see what the words say:

Hitler Will Annihilate the Jewish Race

I was hoping I'd read the words wrong, but I don't think this could be much clearer. One man would like to kill off an entire race and that's something to be celebrated?

"What does that mean?" Filip asks. "Are we all going to die?"

"We are not going to die. There is nothing for you to worry about," Mother tells him with a smile that doesn't express happiness. "He's just making threats, dear. That man lives to terrorize people."

Father is still reading the article from one end of the page to the other. He must be in denial like me. It's hard to believe those words could be printed.

"Hitler said this during a speech at the celebratory sixth-year anniversary of him coming into power. I'm sure he was trying to excite the crowd sitting before him," Father adds. I don't believe my parents can honestly think the headline is something we should look past, but I suppose there's a chance they may be trying to avoid hysteria between us all.

In any case, I can't think that way or act as if those words aren't plastered across the newspaper.

I've lost my appetite again. I don't remember the last time I felt hungry enough to crave a meal. Every morsel of food that touches my tongue makes my stomach tense up, even my favorite sweet cake that Marena prepared.

"How would one man even go about annihilating an entire race of people?" Tobias asks, shoving his mouth full of the soft pastry. "To make a threat like that seems absurd."

Hitler has proven time and time again that he won't let much stand in his way. We should all fear the worst.

"Ben, have you seen Mila around this morning?" Father asks me, dabbing his napkin across his lips. His question evokes a flutter in my stomach. "I have a question for her." I haven't denied their speculation or confirmed what they think is happening between Mila and me. Mother's eye rolls are enough of a warning to stay away from the topic. We all feel seemingly trapped in the estate, and it's hard for any of us to hide our emotions and feelings from one another.

"She was helping me in the kitchen," Marena speaks up. "Would you like me to bring her in here?"

"No, no. It's not important. Not yet anyway."

I'm desperate to ask Father what he's thinking of that may involve Mila, but the less I speak of her, the easier it is to maintain peace here.

"Have you heard back from Elias?" Mother continues with

her morning list of questions, taking a sip from her steaming cup of tea.

Lost in thought, I hold my focus on the red lipstick stain left behind on the rim of her cup, wondering why she continues to wear makeup when no one ever sees her. I have thoughts that she might be suffering from melancholia according to what I've read in one of Sigmund Freud's books. While I could guess that she's simply in denial, I don't think it's the case. Freud states that a drastic psychological disorder could appear when a person's worldly ideals are no longer accompanied by incentive or reward. In Mother's case this is true as she must feel like she is no longer seen as a high-society woman.

"I'm afraid I haven't heard a word from him. It's been nearly two weeks since we finalized the paperwork. Perhaps I shouldn't worry and rather feel relief that the title is safe in his hands."

"He took the title and has written you off like I said he would," Tobias says.

These conversations make me feel like an insignificant fly on the wall. I assume Filip must feel the same, judging by the empty look in his eyes as he chews the last morsel of his breakfast. Pavel is the only one of us lucky enough to benefit from his age. He's too young and unknowing of what's happening around us.

"He made it clear we should keep contact to a minimum. There were just a couple of loose ends I wanted to tie up that slipped my mind during our last conversation."

"Maybe we should pay him a visit," Tobias suggests.

"It might not be the worst idea," Mother agrees.

Father places the newspaper on the table and shoves his chair out to stand up. "Enough. I'm not concerned so you shouldn't be either. When I feel it's time to worry, I will let you all know."

The stress of so many opinions is getting to Father. It's

evident by the building veins running along the sides of his fore-head and the maroon hue of his neck. He leaves the dining room without another word, but Tobias and Mother find it best to follow him.

Filip and Pavel follow their lead, but not for the same reason. I'm sure they'll be outside looking for trouble among the growing snowbanks outside the horse stable.

I rise from my chair to reach across the table for the newspaper, curious to see what Father was reading before asking for Mila's whereabouts.

Military Reorganization Indicates an Imminent Change in Czechoslovakia

It doesn't take long to skim through the article, finding the headline to be hinting at trouble rising soon and what it could mean for our country. If Czechoslovakia becomes occupied by Germany, all Czechs will be forced to live under German law. There's a list of what changes could occur if the worst was to happen.

- Jews will be forbidden from changing their names
- All assets belonging to Jewish people will require a report on all property above five thousand reichsmarks
- Mixed marriages between a Jew and a non-Jew are prohibited
- All properties belonging to Jews are to be confiscated, and a transfer of any assets will be regulated between Jews and non-Jews
- All Jewish children will be expelled from public schools

- Jews will be forced to surrender their passports, and
  these will be invalid until a "J" has been stamped
  on them

Never have I felt like my life might be flashing before my eyes. These rules will be the end of all rights for us. If we don't prepare now, we may never have the chance again.

I drop the paper onto the table and leave the dining room, burning from thoughts brewing in my head. Father made the right decision by handing off the title of our estate to the Beckers. He knows this is all coming too. We must hide our gold and silver. I wonder if Father has said this to Mother. We can't put this off. We can't put anything off.

If we can't look toward a future with stability, it's time to live in the present and hold on to whatever we can't afford to lose. And I know exactly how I intend to do this.

While looking for my parents in every room, I run into Mila, who has snuck into the dining room. "How do you manage to move around and go unnoticed?" I ask. "I've been running laps around the estate for the last half hour and didn't see you once."

She smirks in response and folds up the newspaper I left behind. I wonder if she saw the article I was reading. "Did you or your father want to save the paper?"

"I'll take it. I didn't mean to leave it sprawled out on the table." I race over to where I was poking at my breakfast and take the plate and teacup too. "Sorry for the mess."

"It's my job to clean up the mess. Put it back down, Ben."

I pull the stacked china against my chest. "No. I'm capable of carrying my dishes."

"If your parents see you carrying dishes, they will think I'm not doing my job. Or, worse, they'll assume you're helping me. Hand it over."

It pains me to watch her clean up after me. I would never

ask this of her. I steady the teacup and saucer on top of my breakfast plate and reach it over to her waiting hands. "You won't have to do this forever," I whisper.

A small smile frames her cheeks. "Until then, stop worrying so much."

Until then. Then must be now. I shouldn't have said what I did, knowing there's a slim chance of either of us becoming free from the German shadows growing closer each day, but she gives me hope and perhaps the two of us together are stronger than either of us alone.

Mila leaves me standing alone in the dining room, watching as she gracefully walks away, balancing dirty dishes in each hand. I take the newspaper out from beneath my arm and again peer down at the list of laws we may become subjected to.

Mother and Father walk by the dining room, still in discussion from wherever they were hiding moments ago. "Mother, Father, may I have a word with you?" I call out.

They stop just outside the room and Father notices the paper in my hand. He inhales sharply and tosses his head back. "Ben, it's not time to worry just yet," he says.

I feel like we must have read two different articles. "What could you possibly mean by that? We need to prepare for the worst," I insist.

"I understand and it's something I have been handling for some time now. I'm sure the transfer of the estate's title makes more sense now," he continues.

"Of course, but we must go through our belongings and hide our valuables. We don't know when this could happen."

"Or, if," Mother says.

"I don't think it's safe to make assumptions that would be in our favor," I argue.

Mother looks at Father, waiting for a reaction. "You're right, son," he says. "I'll inform your brothers to collect their silver and gold items and bring them to me at once. I plan to hide our valuables in the safe behind the false wall downstairs. Please keep that to yourself, of course." Father hasn't mentioned the false wall since we were children. We would play down there sometimes, but for the life of me, I can't remember what we found enjoyable about the coldest and darkest corner of the cellar beneath the estate. Tobias and I convinced Filip the dark hallway was a home for the ghosts of everyone who once lived here. It was enough of a story to keep us all out of the hiding space after that.

"Are you sure it's safe enough down there? I can't help but feel as though eyes are on our estate with a value easy to assume."

"We don't have many options, son."

"As long as it's not with the Becker family," Mother states.

Father holds his hands up to both of us. "Please, give me a moment and have some faith in the decisions I make."

I don't envy him, having to make these kinds of decisions on behalf of the family, and Mother can't seem to take a breath long enough to give him time to think.

"Of course," I say, twisting on my heels to leave them to their conversation.

"Every investment I have ever made needs to be handled immediately, Hana. I'm doing the very best I can, and your impatience is wearing very thin on me," Father says as I reach the stairwell.

"We're about to lose everything. How am I supposed to feel?" she replies, a breathy hitch catching in her throat.

I take the stairs up, two at a time, wanting nothing more than to distance myself from their dreadful conversation because I have something more important to focus on for the moment. Mila is at the top, polishing the long golden-framed mirror to the right of the washroom.

"I need to talk to you tonight. It's important," I say,

sounding as if I've just ran up and down the stairs a dozen times.

She seems taken aback, her eyebrows creasing. "We talk every night. Should I expect a different type of talk?" Mila keeps her sights set on the mirror, avoiding my gaze as I stare at her reflection. When she worries, she fixates on whatever is in front of her. I get the feeling she disappears to a place inside her head.

"It's nothing you need to worry about if that's what you're asking," I say, feeling guilty for causing her apprehension, but my nerves are currently fraying enough for the both of us.

"Well, of course, we'll talk tonight. It's the best part of my day, Mister Bohdan," she says, finally finding my gaze in the mirror. The moment our eyes meet, I'm surer than ever that I live for these brief instances every day. I need to ensure the moments never end.

"Mine, as well." I gently take her elbow and lean in to kiss her cheek before leaving. "By the way, you know I hate when you call me that—" I murmur near her ear.

"Which is precisely why I do it," she says, smirking again.

NINETEEN
MY WORDS AND GLOVES ARE MISSING

MILA, FEBRUARY 1939

The arguments between the Bohdans and the tension radiating from Ben leave me feeling uneasy. He says he needs to talk to me. He could tell me that he cares deeply for me but it's time I left the estate, that this isn't safe for anyone. I would understand. Despite the secrets I've tried to keep, there isn't much I can do to change the fact that I am registered as a Romani woman. Every bit of information the country would want about me is listed in official records. I hold the weaker hand of cards. We both know it's the case.

If there's a measure of hope to reach for, it would be the times he's mentioned running away from here, but it only takes a moment to realize there are equal amounts of danger at every border. We're surrounded by terror.

I should offer to go and make it easier on Ben. He must choose his family if it comes down to a choice. I wouldn't allow for anything else.

Or maybe, whatever it is he has to say has nothing to do with us at all. I should put it all out of my head before I drive myself bananas.

Over the last several hours, I've felt as though I'm watching a parade as each member of the family paces back and forth or marches up and down the stairs as if they have no clue of where they're going. I saw the newspaper. I understand their concerns.

Their worry is causing me hysteria. I know well enough that I shouldn't think that way, and no matter what, I must continue to act as if nothing is wrong, but while they are troubled about losing their wealth, I'm afraid of being chased off to wherever my family might be, if they're even still alive.

I should be ashamed to feel so much selfishness.

I finished my work a few minutes early so decide to go to the stables to check on Twister and Nova to make sure the cold temperatures aren't bothering them too much. I make my way out of the grand salon and to the right beneath the staircase, toward the rusty-red colored walls of the gallery hall. Each time I walk through this corridor, I feel as though each person in the line of framed portraits is staring at me.

The laundry room is cold as usual, which doesn't help the hanging clothes dry any quicker, but I've gladly gotten used to having a machine aid me in wringing water. It saves a good amount of time. Plus, the fresh scent of lavender soap is a benefit of walking through the room.

Upon crossing the frozen grass landscape to the stables, I find Twister and Nova to be content, thankfully, after I found horse blankets in the storage shed. From what I recall learning from Papa, I believe pregnant horses have a harder time controlling their fluctuating temperatures, so I've been checking on Twister more often lately.

"How are you already out of water?" I ask Twister, lifting the metal bucket up to release the hook. I don't usually have to replace their water more than twice a day, but it looks like that might be changing for the mother-to-be. "I'll be right back with more."

I step out into the snow, feeling the slushy ice under the thin leather of my boots and the metal handle of the bucket roll back and forth between my tight grip. It takes me a long moment to make my way over to the well off by the corner edge before the line trees. The wind is making the air much colder and my face stings as I crank the rope wielding bucket down into the ground.

"Where are your gloves?" says a voice.

It isn't a surprise to hear Ben out here. The stables are one of the few places we can be alone unless Filip or Pavel decide it's a good time to visit. Although, I'm not sure I'm much of an incentive to brave this arctic air.

"They were in my bedroom and—"

"Mother and Father were still arguing in the hallway," he says, completing my thought.

He comes around to the side of me and takes the lever from my hand. "Put your hands in your pockets," he commands, leaning over the side of the well to see how much farther to drop the bucket.

He's quicker than I am when it comes to retrieving the full bucket, which I'm grateful for now with the relentless wind.

I follow him into the stables, where he reattaches the bucket, proving he knows far more about caring for these two horses than I thought. It's clear he's been watching my every move.

"Have you been wondering about what I wanted to talk to you about?" he asks, with a teasing lilt. All my concerns seem less heavy now, but it wouldn't be the first time he's used a light-hearted introduction to lead into a serious topic.

"I had nearly forgotten until you brought it up just now. What was it you wanted to talk about?"

I can't help but notice how tightly he's clasping his hands together, pulling the brown leather of his gloves taut across his knuckles. "I'm sure you have a lot on your mind," he says. "I don't want to add any more uncertainties."

"We all have a lot on our mind," I retort.

"That's why I wanted to talk to you."

Maybe he is trying to fray my nerves. I won't tell him he's doing a fine job.

"You have my attention, but I hope you weren't about to ask me to go for another test ride on your motorbike in the snow because my answer is still no." He hasn't had the chance to ride it after working on it for so long, but he's joked about testing it out despite the ferocious weather. He'll break his neck and he is aware of this, so I think he just enjoys getting a rise out of me until I tell him not to even think about doing something so ridiculous.

"I promised you I'd wait until spring after the last time I asked," he says, smirking into his dimples. "There's something more important than the motorbike that I want to talk to you about. I've been trying to think of a proper way to say what's on my mind but I'm afraid no matter how I present the thought, you might throw something at me, or perhaps slap me."

Out of instinct, I press my hands against my chest as if I need more proof of how fast my heart is pounding. "What is it?"

There's silence where I thought there might be a joke or another silly question before he spills whatever it is he needs to say.

"Mila—" his voice deepens. "I hope you will truly think this through before answering the question I'm about to ask because it's quite serious and very important to me. And I didn't think it would be so hard to gather my words right now, but I'm—I just want to know, or I'd like to ask you if—Mila, you know how much I care about you, and you know I've fallen for you quite hard. In fact, I've more than fallen for you—I physically can't bear to be away from you, and I worry about you as if you're the most valuable object in the world. I've tried to put my feelings into words several times, but there's no way to adequately describe the longing and desire I feel through every fiber of my being for you. I love you, every single part of you, and the thought of this world having any measure of chance to come between us isn't something I can fathom."

My heart pounds so hard, I feel a bit lightheaded, but I force out a chuckle despite my apprehension. "Ben, what are you trying to say?"

A small smile curls into his lips as he pulls in a long, deep breath. "Mila, I want to ask you if you will marry me?"

He's breathing hard and heavy, or maybe it's me who can't catch my breath.

I've never felt my heart beat so rigidly and so wild, then suddenly stop for a lifeless second. "Ben..."

For a moment I consider whether he's fooling around. It wasn't long ago that I firmly believed someone like him wouldn't want to be with someone like me, no matter how much enjoyment we've gotten from being with each other these last six months.

"I'm quite serious and hopeful you won't turn me down." He takes a step toward me and lifts my hands out of my pockets to envelop in his. "I've thought this through and it's something I truly desire."

"You couldn't possibly want that. Why now when every-thing feels as though it's spiraling out of our control? I would only cause harm to your life." I know the German laws regarding intermixed marriages. They're prohibited and have been so for quite some time.

"You know that's not true, Mila." His eyes are pleading. "I know this seems quicker than if times were typical, but the thought of running out of time, it's not something I can consider."

I know I should say something more but all I can do is stare into his glossy eyes. I don't know how it's possible to see so much feeling in those amber hues, but I can't question his reason, not as the truth feels to be piercing through my soul. "There are so many reasons for you to deny me. I understand this," he carries on, "but if I didn't ask, I would regret not doing so for the rest of my life."

If I could see through the thick heavy fog of what looms ahead, I'd easily be swept away in this reverie. A life with stability, roots, promises of tomorrow, it's not what defines me, and it's not how I was raised. I've never stood at a fork in the road debating which direction will be the lesser of two evils.

This might be my last chance at happiness before the world granulates into a million fighting arms. The question of whether the gift of temporary elation is worth the risk of a grief-stricken burdens weighs me down, locks my lips tightly together—prevents me from responding.

"Say something, please! We're running out of time."

TWENTY
FOREVER ISN'T MEASURED BY TIME
BENEDIKT, FEBRUARY 1939

While I stand here in contemplation, in agony from waiting, I wonder what I've done to make her hesitate. I tried to be clear about how much I love her, and perhaps it's all happening so fast that she needs a minute to place her thoughts in order.

She pulls her hands from mine, and I feel like I'm slipping off a ledge. Mila paces for a moment and stops in front of me, staring up with a look of wonder in her eyes. "I don't even know how you earned that scar on your face," Mila says, clearly still running through a list of overwhelming thoughts. "Shouldn't I know such a thing before agreeing to spend the rest of my life with you?"

A question about my scar doesn't seem important enough to weigh on her answer. She must be stalling for other reasons. I don't want to ruin this moment with a story about my scar as it represents a time where I lost all respect for my brother and it's something that pains me to talk about.

On the other hand, she's right. Mila deserves answers to whatever she would like to know, and I realize it's not fair to keep secrets from her. It's just not the right time. I know she will despise Tobias more than she could imagine, and for reasons I'm ashamed to share. If I could, I would do anything to forget that night. "It's a story I prefer to save for my wife," I say with a sigh.

"Are you bribing me?" she asks with soft laughter, smiling in a way that gives me hope.

"No, no, of course not. This stupid scar has nothing to do with my love for you. That's all."

Mila bites down on her bottom lip and her cheeks glow with a bright blush. "Yes. My answer is undeniably yes, Ben. I want to be with you more than I've ever wanted anything else. In our world of two, I know I'll never be alone—we'll never be alone."

I'm at a loss for words. I thought she would need more time, have more questions, worry about what everyone or anyone else might think. I cup my hands around her cheeks and lean down to brush my lips against hers. "I love you so much," I mutter into her mouth.

"I love you. I will always love you," she replies.

I hold her tightly against me, reeling from gratitude and hope. I lift her up and swing her around, hearing a squeal of delight spiral around us.

"When will we marry?" she asks, eagerly. "When will—uh —will we tell your family first?" Her second question is filled with apprehension. I can only imagine what she might be thinking.

I put her down and place my hands on her cheeks, looking directly into her eyes. "No, my love. This doesn't concern them, and I don't want their influence. I am a man who knows what I want and what I want is a life with you by my side." I know we would be breaking traditions and going against society's expectations of intermingling our faiths, but I'm tired of letting the world decide who we should or shouldn't fall in love with.

"When would we tell them then?" she questions, knowing it will be a hard truth to keep from them as we all live here.

"When we are both ready. Is that fair?"

"Very," she says, pleasingly, wrapping her arms around my

waist. "I want to continue working for the estate. Will you be okay with that?" she asks.

As much as I despise the thought, I realize there is no other option if we are to keep this information to ourselves for the time being. "Only until I secure a new place for us to live. Once I do so, we can leave here. With my inheritance, I have the means to care for us both and you won't need to spend your days taking care of the estate. Instead, we can relish in the endeavors we've both dreamed about and share them together."

Unlike Tobias, who has found every imaginable reason to spend large amounts of his inheritance on absurd items over the last two years since turning eighteen, I've been frugal. Enough so that we won't have anything to worry about for an indefinite amount of time.

"I love that *forever* isn't measured by time, and yet, it still defines how long I have with you," she says, gazing up at me through her dark lashes.

"Beyond forever and whatever that may be," I say.

A warm smile stretches across Mila's lips and she bounces on her toes then swings her arms around my neck. "Who will marry us?" she squeals with delight.

"We'll go down to the registry office first thing in the morning before my mother will come looking for you. I know someone down there who will take care of us."

Mila lowers her arms, allowing them to hang by her waist. Her fists clench and her shoulders straighten. "Tomorrow then," she says. "Let's start our *forever* tomorrow."

"Tomorrow?" I question.

"Yes, tomorrow!"

I scoop her up and spin her around again—this time until we're dizzy and topple into a pile of hay. "I'm going to make you happier than you could ever imagine. I promise you. I promise you a wonderful life." I pray I can keep this promise despite the evolving crisis in our country. I will do everything humanly possible to give her what she deserves.

"And I promise you the same," she says.

I wrap my arms around her shivering body, pinning her bare hands between our chests. "I'm so unbelievably happy," I utter before kissing the lips I dream about each night. I close my eyes, feeling relief and excitement crash together, knowing she's mine and I can hold her like this for as long as she'll let me and for every day after today. She's the warmth I long for and the sun after so many endless nights.

I kiss her again, silently thanking her for starting the journey of this life that I've always wanted.

I didn't sleep. Instead, I counted the seconds until dawn, then until I met Mila out by the stables, and once more until I reached the moment where I could refer to this beautiful woman as my wife. A civil service isn't something I would have imagined, but nothing else quite matters to me now. Time isn't always on our side and to me, making a legal commitment is all I want until there is time for more.

I lead her to my car around the side of the house, noticing the cream-colored hem poking up from beneath the bottom of her coat. Her hair is in a neat braid, and her skin is glowing beneath the early morning sun.

The ride downtown is both short and long. She's had her cheek resting on my shoulder since we pulled away from the estate. She smells like vanilla and apricots. I don't want to wait another minute to make her my wife.

There aren't many other cars on the road, which means there hopefully won't be much of a wait at this hour.

The registry office is just a couple of blocks beyond the main area of the village. When we arrive, the arched opening before us stands beneath a tower tall enough to reach the clouds

on a gloomy day. I open the worn wooden door and gesture for
Mila to step in ahead of me.

I check my coat pocket for the third time since I've left the
estate, making sure I have all the necessary paperwork. As I'm
doing so, Mila hands me hers as well. "I'm ready," she says,
beaming with radiance.

There aren't many people inside except a few older
gentlemen sitting on a bench, smoking cigars. I recognize one of
the men. I believe Father used to work with him on an investment project. He notices me at the same moment and tips his
hat in my direction. "Benedikt, it's nice to see you, young man."

"You as well, sir," I reply, pulling Mila ahead to avoid
unnecessary questions.

We approach the registrar's desk, finding a middle-aged
woman wearing a sky-blue dress buttoned up to her collarbone
with her dark hair in tight curls, a ruby red stain along her lips.
She's busy typing, each clack of a key matching the quick pace
of my pulse. When the typewriter dings, she pulls the sheet of
paper out and reaches for a stamp. The paper takes a wallop
from the ink covered rubber and she adds the sheet to a pile.
"Pardon the wait. How may I help you?"

"We'd like to get married right away," Mila says before I can
speak. Her eagerness is apparent through each high-pitched
word.

"Right now?" the woman asks.

"Yes, ma'am," I reply.

She glances over her shoulder toward a gentleman filing
paperwork behind her. "Mister Markee, this young couple is
requesting a marital ordinance. Are you available?"

The gentleman looks in our direction and grins. "Ah, young
love. Why not? Do you have all the necessary paperwork?"

"Yes, sir," I reply.

"How about witnesses?"

Mila and I look at each other. Despair tugs at her eyes,

reflecting the way I feel. The thought didn't cross my mind. "We don't have any," she tells the man.

The memory of the three men we noticed in the entryway strikes an idea. "One minute," I say, racing toward the door. The men are still gathered on a bench, smoking their cigars. "Might I borrow you for a few minutes?" I ask without any explanation.

It's clear from their raised eyebrows that they are confused. "We need witnesses for our nuptials. Would you do us the honor?"

They scoff and chuckle. "Why not, son?"

A melody of moans and groans follow as they push themselves up to their feet to follow me.

"All set," I announce upon returning to the registrar's desk.

Mila's eyes widen and she clasps her hands below her waist. "Always thinking on your toes," she says, placing her hand along my cheek.

I take a deep breath, hoping we have endured the last hurdle. The paperwork and preparation take a bit of time, making the minutes feel like hours as they pass.

"I'll take your coat, miss," the woman at the desk says.

Mila unbuttons her coat, exposing a lovely cream-colored daytime dress, lined with navy blue buttons. It was one of the first dresses I bought for her, but I haven't seen her wear it until now. Little did I know, it would become my favorite of all her dresses. "You look exquisite," I tell her.

"Your dapper appearances are hard to keep up with, but I thought I might try," she says, her dimples deepening.

The clerk finally gestures for us to follow him. He leads us into a small, secluded area behind a row of filing cabinets, where a podium and a book awaits along the white walls surrounding us. The three men follow and stand a few feet away, keeping their silence.

Without wasting any more time, the clerk opens his book and begins to read a declaration of marriage, words I can hardly focus on while standing face to face with Mila—the woman about to become my wife.

"Benedikt, please repeat after me," the clergy says.

My nerves get the best of me while listening to the words, hoping I'll remember what to repeat. When the clergy becomes silent and points his gaze to me, the words seem to pour out on their own.

"'—To have and to hold from this day forward, for better for worse, for richer for poorer, in sickness and in health, to love and to cherish, till death us do part.'"

"And the same for you, Mila," he says.

She repeats the words lyrically with emotion. Her gaze becomes lost in mine and I realize I'm staring into the only future I've ever wanted—eyes glistening, rosy cheeks, and a smile brighter than the sun.

"Do you have a ring, Benedikt?"

"Yes, sir," I say, reaching into my pocket. I pull out a gold band and hold it up in front of Mila. "Father's mother left this for me. When I was just a young boy, she told me I would find the love of my life at a time when nothing seems to make sense. She said the woman I meet will be the answer to my every unanswered question."

A tear falls from Mila's long lashes and beads down her cheek. "It's beautiful. I hope to be the answer to all your questions and to make your grandmother proud."

"You already have, my love." I place the ring on her jittery finger.

"I now pronounce you husband and wife, Mister and Misses Bohdan."

I wrap my arm around Mila's waist and pull her into me, kissing her with every ounce of love and passion I have in my soul. I smile against her lips, feeling like the luckiest man alive.

The gentlemen behind us applaud and hoot and holler,

making a much bigger spectacle than I was expecting from them.

"Always say, 'Yes dear,'" the gentleman I recognize says.

"Be the one to apologize first," one of the other two says.

"Remember this moment for as long as you live," the third says.

"You've done this before, haven't you?" I ask with laughter.

"They don't just sit out there by the door for no reason," the clergy says.

"You never know when you might need a witness," the woman at the front desk shouts over, nodding her head and joining in with the laughter.

"Miss Simona will help you with the paperwork up front. God bless you both," the clergy says.

"Thank you, sir," I say, reaching out to shake his hand.

Mila takes my free hand and squeezes it between hers, pulling me away as she gawks at the golden band on the third finger of her left hand. "This is the best day of my life," Mila coos.

"The best is yet to come, I promise."

I place my hands down on the front desk, watching the woman place all the paperwork into an envelope. "We're expecting our first foal this spring," I say.

Mila playfully slaps her hand down on mine and pulls it away from the counter. "Ben, let the woman finish with the paperwork," she mutters, holding her smile in place. "We shouldn't distract her."

"Yes, dear," I say with a chuckle. "I can say that now."

"You're a natural, son," one of the men says as they pass by behind us.

"However," the woman says, "I do believe newborn people are called babies, not foals."

"Oh, no, miss, it's true, our horse, Twister, she's expecting."

The woman laughs along with us and hands us the closed

envelope. "Congratulations, Mister and Misses Benedikt Bohdan. I wish you a lifetime of joy and happiness, and to your horse as well."

I pull Mila's hand up to my mouth and kiss her knuckles. Then I pull her out of the office as quickly as I can manage, staring out into the daylight as if it's a new world waiting to pick us up and carry us away.

"I'm not sure how we're going to pretend like this didn't happen," she says, sounding as giddy as I feel inside.

"We'll make do," I say, leading her across the road toward the village shops.

We pass a set of windows with large displays of artwork taped up from one corner of the pane to the other. It's colorful and vibrant, so we both stop to look.

Upon a closer look, I find a depiction of a blonde housewife donning an apron and her lookalike child dressed in brown knickers and a forest green coat. With straw baskets in hand and a tall tree offering them shade, they are cheerfully plucking mushrooms from an assorted variety poking up from the grassy green forest grounds.

"Oh my—" Mila says with a gasp. "Let's go right now." She tugs me past the window, but I pull my hand from hers.

"Wait a minute. I didn't get to read the words."

"You don't want to, Ben. Please, let's go."

"Jews are like toadstools, hard to decipher from a criminal just like a bad mushroom from a good one," I read out loud.

I reach up to slip my fingers between the poster and the window, ready to tear the horrific cartoon down, but Mila pulls my hand harder than she has before. "Don't do it. Please. Let's go," she pleads.

"Why would I leave that up, in our own village?"

"Don't draw attention to yourself, please." I'm distracted by the sun reflecting off her icy blue eyes. The smile she had just moments ago is gone and in its place is pain and despair among the arch of her brows and the downward curve of her lips. "Please." I just promised to protect and keep her safe, and for that I will let my shame burn like a fire inside my chest. "Who-ever put it up there wants the attention you are giving it right now. Believe me. I understand what you're feeling, and I know fighting it will feel like a battle of one against a million. Let them laugh, Ben. You know the truth. I know the truth, and nothing else matters. Not now."

I squeeze my wife's hand, feeling more for her and what she must have been through than I feel for myself at this moment. I'm bewildered by how terrible people can be to others and to know this is nothing in comparison to what's happening in Germany or Austria terrifies me.

"We have each other," I reply. "For always. No one else matters."

"Please don't ever forget this, Ben. Promise me?"

I force her to stop walking and twist her around to face me. "I promise you with all my heart."

TWENTY-ONE

OUR COUNTRY IS NO MORE

I roll over onto one of the two cots we have pushed together, wondering what time it is. Without windows in our little secret hiding space in the cellar, it's hard to tell the time of day. My internal clock is usually spot on, though.

There are a few errands I need to run in the village this morning, but Ben is still fast asleep, and I hate to wake him when he looks so peaceful. I hold my hair behind my shoulders, careful not to let a strand brush against his bare skin, and lean over to place a soft kiss on his cheek. "I'll be back in just a bit," I whisper. "I love you."

My maid's uniform is in a pile on the floor, but I must feel around in the dark until I blindly find it so I can slip it on over my head. Two hairpins tumble to the ground after my dress unravels down to my knees. I reach down and find the pins quicker than I thought I would and twist my hair up into a knot at the bottom of my neck. Lastly, I slip my ring off my finger and tuck it into a small pocket on the side of my uniform. I hate that I can't wear it proudly, not yet anyway.

I'm quiet when slipping into the servants' quarters through the false wall, posed to be a bookshelf. The night after our wedding nuptials, Ben was eager to show me what has quickly become our new favorite place in the estate. So far, our little getaway has worked out quite nicely.

I make my way out the back door of the cellar and stay away from the windows on the side of the estate. Before heading down the hill toward the village, I peek toward the front entrance, checking for the daily paper. The newsboy hasn't been coming on a regular schedule lately and Mister Bohdan gets upset if he doesn't have his morning paper, so I tend to grab one while tending to the other errands in town. My main ambition is to do what I can to keep everyone from finding more reasons to dislike me seeing as they aren't aware of the nuptial agreements between Ben and myself. We both know we can't go on living in secrecy forever, but he has been relentlessly searching for work, and to no avail. His classmates might not have known of his religion, but it seems everyone in the vicinity is aware. Not even the pub will give him a chance to convince them he's worthy of work. It doesn't help that his family is well known for their money, but most might not consider the truth behind the wealth. Almost all of the Bohdans' valuables are where they hope the Germans won't find them if the worst occurs.

The crowd in the village is much louder than usual at this early hour, which means there is likely a headline plastered across the newspaper that is making everyone gasp. It seems the typeset is a bit larger every morning and I can't understand if it's for the purpose of warning people or terrifying them with the breaking news.

As I turn the corner, expecting to face a gathering of people surrounding the newspaper cart, I'm flabbergasted by the sight in front of me. I press the back of my hand against my mouth, feeling my stomach twist and turn. The blood in my body rushes to my head, leaving me cold everywhere else.

I'm frozen beneath the heavy wet snow crying from the sky

as I stand still on the curb watching a mob of soldiers with the bottoms of their rifles cupped in their left hands, the barrels resting against their left shoulders, as several hundred bayonets point sharply into the air. All of them are in brown uniforms aligned in perfect rows. They're marching down the center of the road, in my direction. The clap of their boots hitting the rubble is in sync, drumming louder than my racing heart. They aren't Czechoslovakia's army.

German announcements pipe through their bullhorns. The message is clearer than I wish.

"People of Czechoslovakia, as of six o'clock this morning, German soldiers will be occupying your land. You can best serve your land by abiding to regulations and continue working to best serve this nation, and by showing respect to the swastikas you will frequently notice across the country. Resistance will result in serious consequences."

Mama and Papa always laughed when they saw me reading a book in a different language or trying to learn the basics of German and Czech. As a race, we've done our best to stick to our native Romani language, but no one outside of our community understands us and most Romani don't understand them. From a young age I knew I wanted to be able to communicate with others around me, and I'm glad I learned what I did.

I could do without the German fluency now, though.

Residents of Bohemia are lining the curbs, watching with wide eyes and mouths hanging open. Some are saluting the Germans while others have their hand over their heart. Fear is evident but respect seems instant, and I don't understand what I'm witnessing even after hearing their words.

A sensation finds my toes, allowing my feet to move once again, and I spin around, nearly slipping on a thin ice patch as I run back up the hill to the estate. The brutal temperature in the air burns my lungs while I gasp for more air than I can take in. I must warn them. Yet, there is no more time for a warning.

My hair falls out of my braid and the loose strands are wet from the snow, sticking to my cheeks and forehead. I feel like I'm drowning in a frozen lake by the time I burst through the front doors of the estate.

"The Germans are here! They are marching through the village, claiming their new territory!" I shout at the top of my lungs, hoping everyone in their bedrooms can hear me.

Their doors open one at a time but in a succession of seconds. Each of them is pale as they descend the stairwell to face me and the truth—their worst fear. Ben rushes past all of them, taking my arm. "Why are you soaking wet?"

"I went down to the village to pick up a few items and I saw hundreds of them marching, shouting announcements."

"Shh, shh. You need to take a breath, Mila." Ben runs his hands across my cheeks, sweeping the wet hair away. He doesn't realize the affection he's showing me in front of his family, or maybe he doesn't care. I'm not sure they would even notice with the thoughts that must be flying through their minds. Ben pulls me in against his warm chest and holds me tightly. "It's okay. We have a plan. Right?"

A plan. It's what the family has been calling their ideas of how to handle this situation if or when it arises. In truth, every resident of Bohemia is blind to what is happening at this very second. Once the dust from the Nazis' marching feet settles, it will all be much clearer, but we know enough to have the right to be afraid.

"Lock all the doors," Mister Bohdan commands. "Draw the curtains."

I'm not sure either measure of safety will help but it seems like the right thing to do, I suppose.

Madam Bohdan seems stuck in the middle of the stairwell. Her hands are cupping her mouth and her eyes are filling with tears.

"Mother, why are you crying?" Pavel asks. He's staring up at her with eyes that seem larger than the moon.

Pavel's words seem to strike a chord with Madam Bohdan. She drops her hands down by her sides, clenching her fingers into fists before peering down at her son. "Oh, darling, you know how Mother doesn't like change. Everything will be fine. There is nothing for you to worry about," she says, placing a kiss on the top of his head. "Filip, please take your brother back upstairs until breakfast is ready."

Filip is quick to do what his mother says and marches back up the stairs, taking Pavel under his arm. "Come on, brother. Let's go build some of those paper airplanes we were working on yesterday."

"What happens next?" Tobias questions Mister Bohdan. He seems calmer than everyone else, but I'm not surprised with how unaffected he always seems to be when there's something serious occurring.

Mister Bohdan is staring toward the front entrance of the estate as if he can see through the solid door. "Well, we either comply with German law or suffer the consequences of disobedience." His statement is so simple, yet entirely too heavy to comprehend all at once.

"Meaning?" Tobias continues.

Ben and Madam Bohdan remain silent, allowing Mister Bohdan to clarify what appears to be confusing Tobias. "We as Jews have very few rights available to us now and though life has already been challenging as of late, we're about to experience an even darker side to what we've been witnessing."

Mister Bohdan's words sound rehearsed. He must have

been preparing for this day, knowing he would have to keep the family calm, especially Tobias.

"Because of the Germans?" Tobias responds, fury punctuating each word.

"Well, yes, son."

"I refuse to submit to their foreign laws. We don't live in Germany," Tobias says.

"We don't live in Czechoslovakia either," Ben says. "Not anymore we don't."

"This is laughable. You're all going to act as though you've been hypnotized? For what? So, they can add more unhinged laws to their list? No one is going to pay them any attention. Our country is strong enough to stand on its own. You'll see." It's clear by the lack of concern on Tobias's face that he truly believes every daft word he's speaking.

"This is why you should have been reading the paper's headlines at the very least," Mister Bohdan says. "This is no joke, son. We either obey or they will see to it that we receive a consequence."

Mister Bohdan squeezes his hand over his forehead, pressing into his temples. "Hitler broke The Munich Agreement. No one should have believed he would halt his plans to push right through the Sudetenland region. He won't stop now that he's come this far. He's going to plow his way through our country. It was his plan all along. We all knew. Yet we could do nothing to prevent it."

"We're under the government's protection, aren't we?" Madam Bohdan asks as if the thought has just struck her.

"Of course, we are, but I'm not sure how much or how little that means now. The most important thing right now is that the title of our estate is not under our name. That would be the biggest concern if we hadn't already handled this."

"Until the Beckers kick us out of our home for being the Jews they suddenly can't bear to speak to," Tobias says.

I've been taking everything in, feeling guilty for being the only one in the estate who isn't Jewish. Though I'm married to a Jewish man and I'm of the Romani race, I'm settled and therefore not considered a *traveler*. The lines are blurry, and our marriage is a smudge within those lines.

"Mila, I'm afraid our residence isn't going to be a safe place for you," Madam Bohdan says. "You should feel lucky that you aren't a Jewish woman."

"Hana," Mister Bohdan interrupts his wife, "Mila has nowhere else to go. If you force her out, she will be considered a nomad, which is a direct violation of laws instituted by the Third Reich."

"What about our family, Josef? And I thought you said we wouldn't be held under the laws of the Third Reich. You said we would remain under the Protectorate of Bohemia and Moravia government."

"The Germans weren't supposed to move into our region at all. Our government has essentially caved and betrayed us all. And Mila isn't going anywhere," Ben says, his voice sharp and deep. "She will remain here with us, and that's the end of the conversation."

"Son, don't speak to your mother like that," Mister Bohdan says, though his words are weak, as if he struggled to release them from his tongue.

I'm staring at Ben, terrified of what he might say next.

"You can't protect our maid of all things, Benedikt. We have far more important issues to concern ourselves with right now," Madam Bohdan says, finally descending the last of the stairs. "We can't afford to pay you anymore, Mila."

My breath catches in my throat upon deciphering her words. She can't tell me to leave. I have nowhere to go. "You don't have to pay me to work." I reply with the first response I can conjure while my heart plunges into my stomach.

"I'm afraid we can't afford to spend much on any extras right now," Mister Bohdan responds, his face ashen.

"I'll work for free," I offer, knowing it's either that or we confess the truth.

Ben's cheeks are burning red, and his jaw is shifting back and forth. He's angry and the frustration is emanating off him. Everyone has a right to feel this way at the moment, but anger won't help.

"For free?" Mister Bohdan questions.

"No. Mila won't be working for free," Ben states.

A long pause creates a sensation of chaos in my chest, my body becoming cold then hot, my pulse hammering. I stare at Ben, wishing he would look at me. He must know how dangerous this could be. I reach for his arm, hoping to capture his attention, but he holds his stare firmly on his mother.

"Ben, I think this is something Mila should make a decision on," Mister Bohdan says, lifting his gaze from the floor to look at his son.

"Mila and I are married. She is my wife, and I'm her husband. We love each other very much and I will do whatever is necessary to protect her. Therefore, if you would like to remove us both from your home, I will understand."

A loud gasp following a shriek expels from Madam Bohdan's throat. "Dear God, what have you done?" The unmasked disgust written into the sharp angles of her eyebrows and the narrowing slits of her piercing stare aren't a surprise. I already know she despises me.

My attention swings over to Tobias, whose eyes look as though they might fall right out of his head. I can already sense the ugly words rearing to spill out of his downturned mouth. "You must be out of your damn mind," Tobias grunts. "What in God's name would possess you to make an unsound decision that could affect the well-being of our family, and this estate, for that matter?"

"Tobias, you sound like an utter fool. Hold your tongue," Mister Bohdan says, returning his focus on Madam Bohdan.

"Mother, please take a deep breath," Ben snaps at her. "We were married by a clerk at the registrar's office last month. For obvious reasons—" he shoots a raging look at his mother. "We kept the nuptials to ourselves."

"You wed without your family present," Madam Bohdan states rather than questions. "How could you do that to us?"

Mister Bohdan is staring through another wall, clearly lost in thought again. "This might have been the best decision Ben has ever made," he says.

"My marriage isn't a business transaction, Father."

"No, no, of course not, and while I'm distraught that you wouldn't want your parents by your side at a time like that, I understand why you chose to act as quickly as you have."

"I love her. That's why."

We didn't marry out of haste. Surely, they know their son better than that? With my hand on my chest, I'm tempted to speak up and say the words I have kept to myself for so long, but I fear nothing I say will help in the slightest.

"Of course, you do. Anyone could see that. We've all known for months. You knew mixed marriages would become illegal if the Germans were to occupy our country and you took your opportunity."

"It's true," I agree.

"Mila has an established residency, and you are in a mixed marriage. You might be better off than the rest of us, son. I need to—I have to do something," he says. "Hana, go have a cup of tea and calm down." Mister Bohdan leaves a salient Tobias, Madam Bohdan, Ben, and me standing in a sloppy circle at the bottom of the stairwell.

"How could you do that to me?" Madam Bohdan asks Ben, holding her hand up to her mouth before rushing away from us.

"I'm at a loss for words," Tobias says. "That was not an intelligent move. She'll be the one to get us deported or locked up. You just put your entire family in jeopardy because you finally developed feelings for a woman. You're a disgrace to all of us. You should take your bride and move out of the estate. Our home is for family only."

At a time when the sky is crying with despair from the cold depths of hell, it's hard to watch the dysfunction between Ben's family when they all need each other more than anything. My family had never fought and hated one another as much as this family.

TWENTY-TWO

THE TRUE THIEF

BENEDIKT, MARCH 1939

I lean down and place a kiss on Mila's cheek. "I try to be a gentleman at all times, so forgive me for what I'm about to do," I whisper in her ear.

As if instinctual, she wrenches her hand around my wrist, holding on to me tightly. "He's trying to push you. Don't let him win. You're above this."

Tobias is laughing. I don't care what he hears. I've had enough of him, even if he is related by blood.

"The irony of this scene is phenomenal," Tobias says, clapping his hands slowly as if we are nothing more than a performance to him.

"The irony?" I ask. "I feel almost unhinged to ask if you even know the definition of the word."

"Did your pot of gold ever tell you how he earned that scar across his face?" Tobias says to Mila.

Beads of sweat form on the back of my neck and the veins in my temples are pulsating as I do everything I can to control myself. "I don't see how this story will do you any favors, brother."

"When Ben would like to share his story with me, I'm sure

THE MAID'S SECRET 175

he will," Mila says. "I don't think it's appropriate to hear it from you."

Tobias takes a step closer to us, smiling against his beet red complexion. He rolls his right shoulder and stretches his neck, hinting at whatever pain he's enduring today—a reminder of why I'll never lay a hand on him, no matter how irate I am. It doesn't mean I won't do what I can to make him back off. Mila doesn't need to witness the behavior between two brothers who will never see eye to eye.

"Don't say something you might regret," I warn.

Tobias inhales deeply and clasps his hands together in front of his waist. "Regret? There isn't much I would undo in my life," he says.

After all these years, it's clear he hasn't learned anything from the past. I recall many private conversations with Mother and Father as a child because I was upset by the way Tobias was treating me, excluding me, or picking on me in general. They both assured me he would grow out of the behavior as most children do.

"It all started one night when we were wandering around on the outskirts of the village," Tobias begins. I know there isn't anything I can do to stop him, and the story will likely upset both Mila and me equally, but that's his intention, and an odd one to have at a moment like this. Outside our doors, our village and the rest of the country is about to suffer like a turtle on its back, and we're rehashing unfortunate memories. I can see Mila doesn't want to hear what he's about to say, but at the same time, I'm sure she's wondering what this mysterious story is that I've managed to avoid for so long. "We ended up at a fair or a gathering of beggars in what was typically a secluded field not far from here. Naturally, we wanted to know what all the excitement was about. There was music, fires, food, and laughter. Some might call the scene inviting."

My sights are set on Mila, watching as she weeds through

his words. I would expect her to show discomfort. Instead, I notice the muscles in her jaw tighten and she fights to swallow the lump that must be in her throat. She doesn't break eye contact with him, and I believe she's mentally prepared for whatever he will say next.

"There were wagons, all painted with vibrant colors and unusual designs. The closer we got to the gathering of people, many began to stare at us as if we were creatures that had crawled out of a cave. We weren't the ones dressed that way though. It was the oddest thing. The people there were dirty and ragged, but it was like they appreciated their dirt-covered style."

Mila averts her gaze and folds her arms over her chest. "Tobias, stop," I say, hissing with scorn.

"But I'm getting to the good part," he replies.

"It's fine, Ben. Let him finish the story," Mila says.

"The people were serving food at each wagon and my stomach was growling with excitement. I helped myself to some of the goodies in front of one wagon and you would have thought I was the devil himself, approaching with threats to kill everyone around me. The music faded into the night and the silence became deafening. Suddenly, a man came out of one of the wagons and began marching toward me with his finger pointing at my face. He was shouting in a language I've never heard before. I was sure the man was casting a spell over me and I asked him to stop because I couldn't understand what he was saying."

"You didn't ask him to stop," I say, interrupting the flattering version of his story. "You leaned past him and took more food from his family's plates."

Tobias chuckles, reigniting the anger I felt about this night. "It was clearly a party, brother. How can you still defend them with that horrible mark on your face?" Mila's head slowly turns and she studies the faded diagonal mark left on my face. "Anyhow, the man reached for a walking stick that was perched up against the wagon and he began swinging it at me, shouting more words I didn't understand. I told Ben we should leave, but instead, he wanted to fight back."

I laugh because he is the worst liar and I'm not sure I even have to worry about Mila believing what's coming out of his mouth. "Even when you could see out of both your eyes, you still couldn't see what was right in front of you," I say. The words are harsh and an insult I would never normally use against him but his belligerent rudeness and cruelty toward others deserves far worse than a truthful insult.

"An insult, coming from you. Now that's something new," Tobias says. "I left right away, knowing we had overstayed our welcome, but then I heard the whip of wind from the walking stick and, when I turned around, Ben had become the target of the man's anger. The moral of the story is: Gypsies can steal from others but if someone were to steal from them, well, they will ensure permanent damage is done to remind a person to fear them for the rest of their lives."

The memory flashes through my mind as if it happened yesterday. I told Tobias to leave. I stood back for a moment to apologize for my brother's inappropriate behavior, but I believe the language barrier was too strong and neither of us could understand one another. I reached my hands out to show I wasn't intending harm, but the man must have seen the gesture as a threat and took his strike at me. We never should have been there in the first place, and I'm sure nothing would have come of it if Tobias hadn't helped himself to food that wasn't offered to him.

Mila's eyes are as round as buttons as she stares at me with horror. She reaches her hand up to my face and traces the tip of her finger along the length of the scar. "It was a misunderstanding due to the language barrier," I explain. "I'm sure of it."

"You were trying to apologize for Tobias, weren't you?" Mila asks.

"Yes. I said, I'm sorry for my brother, but I don't think the word brother made it out of my mouth before I was trying to maintain my balance as the blurry world spun around my head."

"*To mi ja l`ito*," Mila says.

"You have nothing to be sorry about," I reply.

"No, '*to mi ja l`ito*' sounds like the words '*tu melalo*' or '*tu muj melalo*' in Romani, which means something entirely different to those of us who don't understand Czech."

"What does it mean?" I ask. I've wondered for years what it was I said to cause more anger than Tobias had caused.

"You likely called him dirt or his face dirt."

Tobias bursts into laughter, a guttural sound that will likely follow with a stream of tears running down his face from the sheer humor of his revelation. "You thought I was awful for taking food. You called the man dirt."

"Our greatest weakness as a race is our lack of ability to speak other languages, especially the older generations. I believe there has been a great deal of miscommunication between Romani and the people of Czechoslovakia purely due to a misuse of words."

I nod, understanding her explanation, wishing I could go back in time and apologize to the man. "Is that why your family dislike Gypsies as much as they do?" Mila asks, unconcerned about Tobias hearing her question.

"Of course not," Tobias laughs cynically. "We can't forget the stories every natural-born Czech shares about your kind. We could start with the common act of theft, lies, and whatever witchcraft you practice, but I'm sure there's more. Believe me. My parents will never move past their distaste for your kind."

My chest aches with turmoil, feeling rage like I've never felt before. The blood in my body may be boiling but I'm not sure how to calm myself.

"Ben," says Mila.

"*Ben*," Tobias mocks Mila in a high pitch.

"Ben, look at me," Mila says, reaching for my chin.

I can't look at her. I can only stare at my disgrace of a brother as I step to the side to create space between myself and Mila. There is very little room between the three of us but I step forward and take Tobias by the collar and shove him against the wall. The painting of our family, hung only by a small nail, crashes to the ground. I lean in, keeping less than a hair between my nose and my brother's. "Do not ever speak about Romani people again. Do not insult my wife or her race. Do not speak to me about that day. You are dirt, brother—the true definition of the word. Your mouth, your ignorance, your childish mood swings are what will be the end of our family, you mark my words. The time is now, it's no longer a world you are safe to live in. If you choose to protect this family, do so by keeping quiet and following the laws we must all obey in exchange for what freedom we have left."

Tobias doesn't struggle out of my grip. I'm not sure if it's because of the poor eyesight he developed from his case of leprosy or if it's because no one has ever dared to put him in his place, but I hope he heard every word I spoke.

I release his shirt and turn around to take Mila by the arm and escort her away from this humiliating display. I bring her up to my bedroom and lock the door, knowing it's the only place we can be alone. The truth is out, and no one can think anything of me for being in an enclosed space with my wife.

"How can I apologize for his behavior?" I ask Mila, releasing her arm.

"You shouldn't ever feel like you must apologize for something someone else has done. He is a grown man who makes his own decisions. They aren't ones you should pay for, ever."

The love I feel for Mila grows more each day. I wish the battle with my brother was the only one, but I fear we are at the bottom of a very tall mountain and there is nothing but ice before us. "I'm terrified, Mila. Not of Tobias. Of what exists outside of this home. I've always been a believer that intelligence can pave a path to a promising future, but I'm no longer allowed to think that way, and I'm questioning my ability to protect you and care for you the way you deserve."

Mila lifts her chin and swallows sharply. I know she tries to appear unaffected by what she must constantly put up with here, but there's a hint of sadness in her eyes. "Neither of us knows what's to come, but for now, let's be grateful we don't have to look in a mirror and hate what we see because of your brother—that's his life and his misery, and I feel sorry for him."

Why do I feel sorry for Mila then? If she had left with her family, maybe she would be safe now. Though I'm not the one who hired her to work here, I take the blame for what she's lost. She was busy serving us while unknowingly losing everything she's ever known. I hold her against me, pressing her head into the crook between my chin and shoulder. "I hope we are always the good even when surrounded by nothing but evil," I say. I close my eyes to relish the moment, but a second doesn't pass before a succession of loud pops in the distance zing through the air outside the windows.

Mila gasps and her body jolts against me. I clutch her tightly and hold my breath while glancing around.

"This is a reality we must face, but we'll do it together."

"I think those were gunshots," I say.

"I'm nearly certain you're correct. From what I saw this morning, to anyone unwilling to comply with the new laws, action will be taken."

TWENTY-THREE

LOOPHOLES

The budding days of spring are among us, with dew dusting the fresh grass sprouts poking through the plush soil—a much-desired change from the soggy days of winter. The air is cool but not cold, and Twister is the first to inform me of the change. She has no desire for the blankets I've kept her and Nova warm with these last few months. With her growing belly though, she must be so uncomfortable. "It shouldn't be much longer now," I tell her, stroking her neck.

Whenever I'm out here, I wonder what Mister Bohdan must be thinking about the two horses. I fear he might be thinking about selling them after what I've seen over the last several weeks since the Germans invaded.

With all the family's assets now hidden underground, beneath the estate, they have managed to acquire faux jewelry, gold, and silver. If the home were to be searched, the Germans would confiscate it all. At least, this is what Mister Bohdan has learned from other Jewish residents around the village. Everything we know seems to come from a source of hearsay. It seems the region was given no notice upon the changing laws affecting Jewish rights of owning businesses and property, attending public schools, and traveling over country lines. They are seen as a lower class of humanity—a class that has nothing to do with wealth, work, or knowledge. Everyone is forced to agree with these laws, and without complaint. What's worse is that Mister Bohdan isn't one to sit back and wait for the next official announcement. He is assuming the worst is to come and tries to act accordingly to protect his family.

I'm not sure the man sleeps much anymore, understandably so. I don't find myself very rested in the mornings either.

"Mila, are you out here?" Madam Bohdan is calling for me from the front door. I can already tell by the tart tone of her voice she's hoping to convince me to run an errand for her. I've offered daily, but it seems she has come to recognize her role when it comes to me. I'm not receiving or asking for pay. Everything I do is out of kindness. I'm part of her family now whether she likes it or not. I still treat her the way I always have, with dignity and respect. I do it for her, not myself. I can't imagine going from a life with status to something along the lines of what I'm familiar with.

"Yes, Madam Bohdan. I'm just checking on Twister," I say, leaning out of the stable.

"Could I bother you for a favor?" she asks.

"Of course, madam. I'll be right over."

I return to the stalls and place Twister's blanket over the gate. "I'll be back soon, girls," I tell them.

While trailing up the wet grass to the front door, I spot Madam Bohdan fanning her hand in front of her face. "Is everything all right?" I ask.

She closes the door to the estate, stepping outside to join me. "It's much cooler out here than it is inside." She's not wearing a coat and the temperatures certainly aren't high enough to be comfortable here without layers. "I've been putting this off all week, but Josef—Mister Bohdan has informed me that we needed to let Marena go. Like you, we can't—"

"Pay her?" I ask, completing her sentence. I believe Marena had been expecting this news, but that was only whispers between the two of us in the kitchen. I asked her if she would consider staying without pay like me, but she has a husband at home who isn't able to work due to an injury from the war, so she's been seeking other means of employment. The thought of leaving the family behind seems to be very upsetting to her, which makes me wonder what everyone must have been like years ago. Madam Bohdan and Tobias have certainly cast a dark shadow over this family, and I imagine it's greatly affected Marena.

"It's not that we can't afford—Josef is being strict about what we spend now. He wants us to be cautious with our assets."

"I understand, madam. You don't have to explain yourself. What is it I can do to help you?"

Madam Bohdan clamps her hands together and presses them against her chest. "I'm embarrassed to say that I don't know how to cook a meal, and now that I've broken the news to Marena, I'm worried we might all starve."

"I see," I reply, waiting for her to find the rest of her words.

"Marena mentioned you were quite skilled in the kitchen and even taught her a few tricks."

She can't possibly be suggesting I add more responsibilities to my list of free labor. "Would you by chance be willing to offer me some guidance so I can take over and cook for the family?"

I'm baffled to the point of my mouth falling open. To hear Madam Bohdan asking for help is something I never thought I'd witness.

"Of course, madam. I'm happy to give you some pointers. When did you inform Marena?"

"Just before I came outside. She's collecting her things."

I look into Madam Bohdan's eyes, finding a hint of pain I haven't seen before. There is something in the look that makes her seem more human than she's proven to be. "I know she's been with you for many years. I'm so sorry you must part ways with her."

"Yes," Madam Bohdan says, staring over my shoulder toward the stables. "She's been with us since Filip was born. She's like family."

Part of me would like to ask her if she would treat her family like paid help, but I've seen more than I need to around here to know the unfortunate answer. In all technicalities, I'm family, and until today, she's never treated me as anything more than a servant. "I'm sure you will all be sad to see her go."

"For certain."

"Well, I might go offer her a hand if that's okay with you? Then, perhaps I can help you with dinner tonight."

Madam Bohdan's gaze falls to the stone steps we're standing on. "Yes, and Mister Bohdan and I are hoping for you and Benedikt to join us for dinner. I know the two of you have been eating in another room most evenings, but it would be nice if you would join us tonight."

"I'll check with Ben," I say, knowing he has been unforgiving of his mother and Tobias. His anger toward them hasn't subsided one iota since the day we confessed to our nuptials.

Madam Bohdan shivers against a chill and takes the moment of silence as a cue to step back inside the estate. I follow with the intention of finding Marena to see how she is getting along. "Mila, one more thing," Madam Bohdan says.

"Yes, madam."

"Have you seen Benedikt today?"

"I believe he's in the servant quarters using the old workshop to repair an old clock he found." *Yes, Madam Bohdan, your son would rather be downstairs without heat or properly functioning electricity than on the same floor of this grand estate with you.* By the sullen look in her eyes, it's clear she must hear the same words in her head.

"Thank you," she says, walking tentatively toward the back stairwell.

Marena is filling a straw basket on the long counter stretching from the oven to the sink beneath a row of windows that look out on to the side courtyard. I'm not surprised to see she's left the space immaculate. The white countertop is sparkling with a fresh sheen and the black and white checkered floor is swept clean of any crumbs. Her personal cooking utensils are stacked in the basket and her small pile of dish rags are the last to be placed on top of the pile. She mentioned she preferred to use her own seasoned tools to perfect her recipes. "I just heard the news," I offer, watching as she unties the apron slung around her neck. She folds the fabric and drapes it over her arm. When she turns toward me, I'm faced with a despairing sight. Her eyelids are puffy and pink, red webs of veins shroud the whites of her eyes, and her makeup looks to have been wiped off her face completely. She usually wears a white handkerchief over her head, and this is the first time I've seen her with her hair down. I never knew she had beautiful long golden blonde hair that splays into big smooth waves.

I open my arms and lunge at her, knowing she must need an embrace. She seems taken aback at first as we've always carried on with respect for our positions here, but she concedes and throws her arms around me as well. "I'm going to miss you, Mila," she says.

"Believe me. I will be missing you more," I argue.

"Take care of Ben. He's a good man, that one. I couldn't be happier to know his heart is safe with you. Follow your heart with how far you choose to go for Mister and Madam Bohdan. And Filip and Pavel—you already know the way to their hearts."

"Sweet cake, I know. Same for Ben," I say, pressing my finger to my smiling lips.

"Of course, you know this," she sighs.

"As for Tobias," she says, "well, I can't make excuses for the boy, but I still believe there is good in everyone. Unfortunately, with some, it seems the good is buried too deep. I'm sure he'll see the light at some point. Keep a distance but don't give up hope on his soul."

"I feel the same," I reply.

"Take care of you, Mila. Promise me."

"I promise."

"Okay, dear. I'm going to go find the young men and start my goodbyes there."

I follow Marena out into the foyer as she leaves with her basket. A round of shouts in a distant hallway greets us and grows louder by the second. A door slams and stomps follow.

"This act isn't going to work on me, Mother. I've already been clear."

It's unusual to hear Ben shouting, especially at his mother, but he's been so upset with her that I could only assume it was a matter of time before he burst with the words he's been stirring over.

"I just want you and Mila to join us for dinner tonight. I hardly think I'm asking too much of you." I shouldn't be listening to this conversation, but they're both so loud, it's hard to avoid.

"Your actions have proven that everything you ask for comes with a high price to pay."

"Mila already agreed to join us for dinner," Madam Bohdan says, using me as a weapon against her son. Ben knows I wouldn't do anything of the sort without speaking to him first, not with how raw the tension has been here.

"No, she didn't," he argues. "Don't act as if you know my wife better than I do."

Madam Bohdan hisses. "For God's sake, stop calling her that," she utters, likely assuming I'm not within hearing range. I should feel some sort of pain upon hearing her true feelings, but I feel sadness for her that she doesn't realize her words mimic those of the Germans marching around this village. Her finger is just figuratively pointing in a different direction. Those who hate others feel hated the most. I pity her.

There is quiet between them, and I'm worried about what might happen next. Beyond my better judgment, I walk out into the hallway, finding a hot-blooded glare in Ben's eyes, and spite written across Madam Bohdan's face.

"Are you ready for me to help you, Madam Bohdan?" I ask, interrupting their silence.

"This is a private conversation, Mila. I will meet you in the kitchen."

"You will not," Ben lashes back. "I suppose I can assume well enough that you convinced Mila to help you cook now that you've been forced to relieve Marena. God forbid you ever lift a finger for yourself."

"Stop!" I shout at both. "Madam Bohdan, I'm sure this is not what you would like to hear, but it's going to take a lot more than your cross words to put a knife through the love Ben and I share for each other. I could apologize for not being the person you might have imagined your son with, but I won't do that because I have done nothing more than show this family and estate the utmost respect despite every secret and truth, I have acted blind since the day I began working here. I agreed to help you in the kitchen, hoping you were turning a corner from the spite you have for me. I was wrong."

"Mila and I are going to be seeking another place to live," Ben says. It's a topic we have discussed, and know the plan would not be feasible. Homes are being taken away from Jewish families. Neither of us has a source of income. It's impossible to do what he is ultimately using as a threat.

"You can't leave," Mister Bohdan shouts from the stairwell. "Hana, go for a walk. Do something other than start yet another argument in our home. We are all tired of the fighting, and it will get us nowhere in the end. So, for the sake of our sanity, please go take a walk or draw yourself a bath."

"How dare you speak to me that way!" Madam Bohdan retorts at her husband.

"How are you able to bawl your eyes out about Marena leaving, and in the same hour, speak the way you are about Mila? I'm not sure when you became this person, but you are not the woman I married. We are all terrified of the conditions we are living in, but hurting others around you is not the answer, and you know this. Not one of us knows what tomorrow will bring and the regret you are inviting into your life will cause more damage than any antisemitic law rooting in this country."

"I am not in agreement with you or your plan to live life like we are impoverished, Josef," Madam Bohdan seethes. "If you want to educate me on regret, take a moment to rethink the abhorrent ideas you've come up with."

"What plan?" Ben asks.

"It's nothing," Mister Bohdan replies. "It's not the right time to discuss some thoughts I've had."

"It will never be the right time, and I refuse to have any part of this absurd idea," Madame Bohdan says. "I'll be upstairs until you decide to come to your senses, Josef."

TWENTY-FOUR

YOU HAVE MORE RIGHTS THAN US
BENEDIKT, APRIL 1939

The doors are always slamming. It's as if we've been left with no other way to punctuate the end of a sentence. Someone is always angry, and that someone is usually Mother. It's hard to remember back to when there was more happiness than the grief now filling this house with dark shadows. I would do anything for a moment of that peace and contentment I must have taken for granted. Mother changed due to no fault of anyone in our home, but we have all been left to pick up the endless amounts of pieces since that solemn day.

"Mother, you have a post," I shout through the foyer, listening to my voice echo and bounce off the walls.
"Benedikt, you need not shout through the halls. I'm right here. Goodness, at thirteen, your voice really does carry. I think the portraits upstairs might be rattling against the walls," she says, walking out of the library. "You could poke your head into the two rooms I'm usually found in." Mother smiles at me and ruffles her fingers through my hair.
"Sorry, Mother," I say, handing her the post.
Her eyebrows draw together and she tilts her head to the side

*while slipping her finger beneath the sealed flap. "It looks like it's
from your Uncle Bigham and Aunt Rose."*

*"Maybe they're coming out for a visit," I say, clamping my fingers
together with hope. Uncle Bigham is Mother's only brother and
when he comes to stay with us, there is always laughter and
games. He's a former soldier who fought in the World War, but he
doesn't say much about what he did when he was fighting. We
just know he's a very strong and brave man, something I strive to
be someday. Mother even said he was awarded honorable medals
for his heroic accomplishments. I can't imagine that honor.*

*Lost in my fond memories, I didn't notice Mother had turned
away from me. I take a couple of steps around her, curious, but
it's immediately clear that the letter contains bad news. Tears are
falling down her cheeks and her hand is pressed against her
mouth.*

*By the looks of her shaking hands, I believe something is very
wrong. I run down to Father's office and push open the door
without knocking as I might usually do. Father has his elbows
pinned to his desk, but he pops his head up with a look of shock. I
must have startled him. He holds his fountain pen still, pressing
it to paper as ink bleeds out. "Benedikt, I asked you to knock
before barging in here. I'm trying to draft a paper to bring to the
bank."*

*"I believe something is wrong with Mother. She's reading a post
from Uncle Bigham and she's crying."*

*"How odd. He just wrote to us a week ago. I wonder what could
have happened?" Father pushes his green leather chair away
from his desk and walks past me to find Mother in the hallway.*

*"Darling, is everything all right?" I step out behind Father,
witnessing their silent conversation from a few steps away.
Mother continues to cry, and her hands tremble harder than they
were before. She hands the letter to Father, allowing him to read
whatever has made her so upset.*

"Dear God," Father says after a long moment. "I don't understand."

"Why would they destroy their home? He would never cause issues to result in such hate and destruction."

"Mother," I utter. "Is Uncle Bigham okay?"

"No, darling. I'm afraid not." She can hardly form words well enough for me to understand, but her tears say enough.

"A traitor?" Father questions, still reviewing the letter. "Jewish Veterans who reside in Germany are being sought out for punishment under accusation of being a traitor to foreign interests, thus being the cause of Germany's defeat in the war."

Mother hasn't blinked in a long minute. She's staring through Father as if he's a window. "He was killed, and the police stood by and watched," she croaks out.

Father loops his arms around Mother, holding her tightly as her tears become heavy sobs. Tobias and Filip step up from behind me. "What happened? Is Mother okay?" Tobias asks.

"Is she going to be okay?" Filip follows.

"It's because he's Jewish. He fought in that war, braver than any one of us. He volunteered to stand before his country, sacrificing everything when he had more than most could wish for in a lifetime. And what was it all for?" Mother cries out. "How are Jewish people still being blamed for the loss of a war that ended fifteen years ago?"

"Darling, you know why. It's the very reason you have been pleading with Bigham for the last several months to move out here with us."

"The country I was born in has betrayed us," she says in a hoarse whisper.

"Not the country, the Chancellor is responsible for this betrayal. The headlines have been quite clear."

Hitler. Uncle Bigham is gone because of Hitler. Why would anyone want to hurt a war hero?

*My heart aches and I can hardly swallow against the dryness in
my throat.*

*"Mother, please don't cry," Tobias says, tearing up as he makes
his way to her side. "Uncle Bigham would want you to be strong
for him. He would want that from all of us." He takes Mother's
hand into his and squeezes.*

*"The world is made up of terrible people," Mother hisses. "Those
who will take from others for their own selfish good will destroy
the beauty of this world. I believe you will always know who to
trust when you follow your heart."*

"Darling, I don't think that's exactly right," Father says.

*"It is precisely right. He was killed without reason. He likely
invited whoever did this to him into his home and offered them
tea. How could we ever trust anyone now?"*

*Father glances over at me and Filip, seemingly worried for what
we might be thinking.*

*"You are right, Mother. Uncle Bigham would want this to be a
lesson to us. We shall never trust anyone who is not like us. It's
for our own good, to protect what we should be grateful to have,"
Tobias adds.*

Though I've done my best to block out that terrible day, it
marks the moment our mother stopped viewing life the way I
do. She became cold, bitter, quiet, and spiteful. I might also
argue that she took Tobias down with her.

"How long will your parents keep having the same argument over and over?" Mila asks. "There's never a resolution."

I take Mila's hand and bring her into the kitchen where we
can be alone, or at least away from Tobias now that Mother has
seen herself upstairs. "My mother doesn't deserve an explanation for her behavior, and I will never defend her, but six years
ago when my uncle died, she found strength in anger rather
than grief. She hasn't been the mother I remember her once
being since then, and it's left me, my father, Filip, and Pavel to

grieve the loss of the woman we knew better than the one here now."

Mila seems to understand what I'm trying to say. Empathy tugs her shoulders forward as if she can relate to Mother in some way. Perhaps she can, but Mila hasn't chosen the path of disgrace against others to pay the price of her personal losses.

"There's nothing worse than feeling hated for no good reason," she says. "No apology will do, and time won't heal the pain."

With every word or offering of wisdom Mila gifts me, I fall more in love with her. She's taken the feeling of hatred and used it as a shield. I envy her strength.

When the hallway outside of the kitchen becomes quiet again, I wonder if the argument has moved elsewhere or has ended for now. I hardly remember life before there was constant bickering and squabbles every other hour of the day.

"Absolutely not. Have you gone entirely mad?" Tobias shouts. "Father, come back here right now."

The heavy footsteps warn that there is no room far enough away to hide.

Father turns the corner into the kitchen where Mila and I are waiting for another round of whatever comes next.

"Ben, Mila, I would prefer for this impending conversation to be more intimate, just the three of us, but it seems I can't manage for that to happen with Tobias home," Father says.

"What is it, Father?"

"I've spent some time at City Hall and at the registrar's office, hoping to find a reliable source of information regarding some questions I have. It took a bit, but I finally have the information I need to present this idea to the two of you."

Tobias is opposing whatever this might be and by the scowl on his face, I assume Father's request has something to do with the property Tobias has already lost a hold of to the Beckers.

"What could we possibly do to help right now?" I ask,

curious as to how either of us could be of any relief to the family.

Father's collar is loose, his cheeks are flushed, and his eyes look like he hasn't slept in a week. I worry about the toll this family takes on his health, yet there's never anything I can do to stop any of this from happening.

"Now that the two of you are wed, Mila's last name is legally Bohdan, as you are aware, and she is registered as having a permanent address. With this all said, her updated paperwork will not have her marked as—forgive me, dear—a 'Gypsy,' as the SS have stated, due to her status here with you. However, you are a Jewish man, which is unfortunately not in any of our favor right now." Father takes a few short breaths as if he's been running in circles. Sweat is forming on his forehead. "Though you are both considered to be a part of a mixed marriage, which I commend you for doing before it became too late here in our country, Mila has more rights than you do. It may not be much considering a non-Jewish woman in a mixed marriage doesn't offer much of a break from German laws, not in the same way it would have helped if the tables were turned, and she was Jewish, and Ben wasn't. Still, she is not a Jewish civilian, so she can technically hold the title to the estate and keep it safe for our family for the time being. Thus, removing the Beckers from this situation, which has caused this family an insurmountable amount of stress."

Mila looks at me, like a scared animal caught in the light of a flare. "I'm not sure that's a responsibility I should be taking on," she argues.

"I agree. Look, Mila, see, we finally agree on something," Tobias says abruptly. "If she doesn't think it's a good idea, Father, then let's drop it, and continue with our original plan."

Father takes in a deep breath. "Mila, I have never doubted your authenticity, not since the moment you arrived here. I feel that I'm a good judge of people, but that has all changed in the last several years. Those I have trusted have greatly disappointed me. However, it's clear to see your genuine perspective on others and the world around us. I am overjoyed to have you as a part of our family, and I believe family should always be trusted over friends. I would rest easy at night, knowing this estate is safe in your hands."

Mila's gaze has fallen to the black and white tiles.

"This is a lot to ask," I say.

"There. See, Father, four of us agree this offer is out of haste," Tobias says.

"I didn't say such a thing," I argue. "I wouldn't want to ask this of Mila unless it's something that will not keep her awake at night. She's been through quite enough already in the past year and the last thing I want to do is add any burdens to her life."

"And that is why you married the girl, right?" Tobias says. "Certainly, the thought of a Jewish man marrying a gyp—traveler—wouldn't equate to any sort of burdens. How could it?" Tobias laughs sardonically and makes my blood boil.

"If I were to agree and say yes to holding the title of the estate, I fear for the worry of your eldest son and wife. The thought of causing more distress here isn't something I can assume lightly."

"She will make us her servants," Tobias adds.

"Why do you feel the need to continuously open your mouth when it is unnecessary to do so? What indication have I given you that if given the opportunity, I would treat you the way you have treated me?" Mila responds to Tobias. "You have been rude and cruel to me since we met, and I have done nothing to ask for that treatment, but the person I am is able to see far beyond your existence. You are not one of my concerns, Tobias. So, rest assured, if I was to help your entire family, and not just Ben, it would be done to help, not to steal something that you are biologically entitled to. This regime we are living under has not caused me to think differently of others. I know what belongs to me and what doesn't, and if you were to think the same, the laws we are living under right now wouldn't madden you as much as they are. We may all be gone tomorrow, and then you will have wasted so much energy on what you could lose rather than what you may have already had."

Mila has always been one with her words and she never ceases to disappoint me. She can knock the wind out of a man without lifting a finger, and I find that incredibly attractive.

"Mister Bohdan, if securing the title under my name will bring you peace of mind, then yes, I will do so for you and the family. When we are no longer living under these terrible laws, the title will be returned to whom it·belongs. It seems simple to me."

"Are you sure you don't want more time to think this through?" I ask her.

She looks me square in the eyes and nods her head. "Ben, I love you, and I would do anything to help your family, in spite of how some of them may feel about me."

Father launches in Mila's direction and scoops her up into his burly arms. "You may not be my daughter by blood, but you are the daughter I have always wanted." I wasn't aware Father wanted a daughter, but it's heartwarming to hear him treating Mila this way.

Mila squeaks as Father squeezes the air out of her lungs. "You've given me a roof over my head and though I sorely miss my family and think about them every minute of the day, I'm beyond grateful for the safety you offered me these last eight months. Helping you and Madam Bohdan would be a way for me to repay you with my gratitude."

"Ben, do you remember the day you told me you didn't think you'd ever find a woman suitable to be your wife? It must have been two years ago now."

I place my hand over my eyes, embarrassed to be rehashing the private conversation we once had. "Yes, Father."

"I told you: when you least expect it, the wonderful woman you deserve, and who deserves you in return, will no doubt find a way into your life, or you to hers, and when it happens, there will be no question of whether she is the one you've been waiting for. You will know, and you will never let her go. I think I'd like to collect interest on that advice and request a *thank-you* now."

"I'm very grateful for your wise words, Father. Thank you for giving me hope that Mila was out there somewhere. She's already the best thing that's happened to me, and I know if everyone allows her to be, she will be the same for the rest of the family too."

"I couldn't agree more, son. Mila, with your blessing, I'm going to make my way to the Becker residence to handle this matter. Would you like more time to think this through first?"

Mila shakes her head before answering. "No, sir. I've heard all I need to hear. This is what I want to do for you and the family. Thank you for trusting me. I won't ever let you down."

Father gently pinches Mila's chin. "I have no doubt, darling."

"Father," Tobias says, gritting his teeth and chasing Father out of the kitchen. "A word, please."

TWENTY-FIVE

MYTHS OF TRUTH

MILA, APRIL 1939

Ben is slipping on his coat and securing his boots. "I wish you didn't have to go," I say.

He takes my hand and guides me to the laundry room, a place we can often buy a minute of solitude. "I must go with Father. If Tobias is joining him, there's no telling what will happen when we arrive at the Becker residence."

These uphill battles seem never-ending, but I remember Mama always telling me that before we can win a fight, we must experience the hardship first. I can only hope her words stay true throughout my life.

"Why is it we allow people to decide whether we stay or leave?" I ask Mama as she weaves a tight braid into my hair.
She tugs on the braid. "Keep your head straight, dear," she says, taking a moment to answer my question. "We prefer to stay only where we are not an annoyance to society."
"We keep to ourselves, though. Why would anyone consider us to be a bother?"
Mama takes a deep breath, sounding frustrated by my question. "Mila, I think it's time you know the truth. I've done my best to

keep the darkness of this world out of the lives of you and your siblings, but you're almost fourteen and it's time you know the truth." Despite the braid she's working on, I twist my head to look at her. Mama's hands travel with my braid. "Mila!"

"Tell me, Mama. Many thoughts have crossed my mind over the years, but I thought much of what I've witnessed was part of my imagination. It's hard to accept a world that seems to be so cold and cruel to people."

Mama sighs. "Well, as you know our family originated in India, but many, many years ago."

"Why would our family leave India if that's where we are from?"

"No one quite knows for certain. It seems there is a debate as to whether we were forced out by the military of Ghanzi or if the skills of our people were needed elsewhere. We as a race have become who we were ultimately intended to be: skillful, peace-makers, unified, and strong. We don't need what others believe they must have to survive, but rather use the God-given land for why it was created."

Mama makes us sound like innocent bystanders to a cruel society that has developed around us, but it's hard to understand that so many would feel the need to hate when so few choose to show love. "Why do people who are different from us dislike our kind as much as they do?"

I straighten my head again so Mama can finish the braid. "Our roots are not from Europe, and many believe we are here to steal from their land."

"But why?"

"It was less acceptable then to inhabit land where people did not originate. Therefore, when Romani first arrived in Europe, we were enslaved since it was all we could offer the country. Unfor-tunately, the view of our kind didn't change and only grew worse."

I try to make sense of everything Mama is saying, but all I can gather is, "We weren't wanted in the country where we origi-

nated, but also, we aren't wanted anywhere else either. Is that right?"

"To our misfortune, yes. That is correct."

"Why don't we stand up for ourselves and prove we are no different than others? Why must we continue to shy away from what people believe about us?"

"Because we are peacekeepers. Kindness will always be the end to every battle, no matter how hard or long one must fight. And if we die trying, we have accomplished our life's challenge and will be rewarded in our next life."

"Can't we prove to be better than what people see us as and still accomplish our life's endeavors?"

Mama laughs as if she's heard this question many times before. "Darling, if you are the one to accomplish such a thing, the pride will be yours, knowing you have made a difference."

With my braid secure and my scarf slung over my head, I twist around on the log I'm resting on and face Mama's pretty eyes. "Why do people call us thieves and beggars?"

Mama takes my chin in her hand. "People see what they want to see. Anyone, of any race, can be accused of this behavior. If a person has little to offer and must find alternative resources to survive, theft becomes an easy answer. Someday, people will come to see the difference between a person who works hard for everything they have versus a person who may feel sorry for having nothing and has given up their pursuit for more. Desperation can make a person do unthinkable things, but desperation comes after a person has submitted to a struggle."

"Hatred makes the world feel like a lonely place," I reply.

"Mila, remember that the myths and folklore of our people and it will guide you to where you need to be. All you must know is cruelty is cured with love, wealth is appreciated with hardship, and with privilege comes sacrifice. Therefore, we show love first, endure necessary hardships, and offer sacrifices before all else. Then, we will find peace."

"Why can't your father tell Tobias to stay here?" I question him. His brother doesn't need to add to the uphill journey. I realize Tobias is a grown man, but the title of this estate should still be under the care of Mister Bohdan. Someone should stand up to him. I don't understand why no one chooses to stop him.

"Father will not argue with Tobias. He lives with guilt since Tobias lives in pain from the leprosy. Father's guilt has added a layer of misfortune to our family over the last several years. He takes the blame for Tobias contracting an illness when he was under his personal care."

Tobias has both his mother and father under his power and neither of them see what that has caused.

"I understand," I say, though I don't. My family would never allow such disrespect from any of us at any age. It is not who we are or who we were raised to be.

"The drive will take no more than an hour. We should be back by dinnertime."

"And if you're not?" I shouldn't ask a question that could cause him more distress than I'm sure he already feels, but the thought of him chasing down a man who has refused all phone calls and letters from Mister Bohdan doesn't leave a comforting feeling in my stomach.

"I will be back tonight, I promise." Ben takes my hands in his and holds them against his heart. "Nothing will keep me away from you." He feeds my heart the words I want to hear, but the truth darkens his eyes, overshadowing the bright golden hue.

"Please be careful. If anything was to happen, I would take blame for assuming this responsibility."

"You are offering our family a brilliant gift. You are not allowed to think otherwise. Do you hear me?" His eyes mesmerize me when he's determined to prove his point and I can't help but comply with a slight nod. He leans down and claims my lips with longing and desire, something we both constantly feel while living within a home full of watchful eyes. My heart pounds against his chest as cool air fills the space between our mouths. I'm left with the taste of tea lingering on my tongue as he places his hand on my cheek and leaves one last kiss on my forehead. "I love you."

"I love you, Ben. I do. So much."

TWENTY-SIX

OUR PASSPORTS ARE NO GOOD

"What roads do you plan to take, Father?" I ask from the narrow bench in the back seat of the car. My knees are nearly pinned against my chest, but I learned long ago not to argue for the front seat when Tobias is with us. He would claim that his precious custom-tailored coat trimmed with golden thread would wrinkle, and since I don't dress up to par with the rest of our family, I shouldn't have an issue with sitting in the back.

"The least traveled ones," he replies, handing me a marked-up map. "I think it's best we travel north to Chbany, staying just east of the border. Elias's estate is in Havraň, which is approximately ninety kilometers from here." Father traces along the outer edge of the thick tree line separating farmlands between here and there.

Property laws have not been mentioned in an official statement under the Protectorate of Bohemia and Moravia, but under the laws of the Third Reich, Jewish people are no longer allowed permits to drive and every district within the claimed Sudetenland region is under German law now.

"Are we going to risk driving across the border from Chbany to Havraň? Because once we hit any district within the Sudetenland region, we'll be greeted by the Germans, asking for identification," I continue.

Father's shoulders continue rising, proving the tension he must be feeling.

"I plan to leave the car on the outskirts of the lake near Chbany, just a short distance from the border," he confirms. "We'll continue northeast on foot for ten kilometers and reach the outskirts of the village just behind the Beckers' estate."

"You can't be serious," Tobias argues. "The Becker estate is ten kilometers from the border? That's at least a ninety-minute walk from there if we're moving at a quick pace."

"And you don't think there will be border patrol checking passports?" I snap back, shoving my knee into the back of his seat.

Father has a hand clamped around the back of his neck, pressing his fingers into his skin. "We will cross the border by foot," he says. "That's final."

We'll be trekking through the woods. It would have been best if we made this trip at night rather than in broad daylight.

"If we are caught and asked to present our passports or identification, what is our plan?" I ask.

Father clears his throat and Tobias leans back forcefully into his seat, pushing my knees in closer to my chest. "Then we will not cross the border and will have to come up with another plan," Father says. His plan doesn't account for a situation where we have already crossed the border and we're spotted.

The ride takes a bit more than an hour since we've been traveling through unmarked dirt roads, relying on nothing more than the number on the odometer and a compass to ensure we're heading in the proper direction.

"According to the number of kilometers we've traveled, it's time we stop and walk from here," Father says finally.

With another childish groan, Tobias continues his slew of

complaints. "You could have warned me that I would be walking so far."

"I asked you to stay home. You argued, and made sure to come along. I don't want to hear any more remarks. If you're in pain, we'll take a rest."

Tobias rarely mentions the nerve and joint pain he suffers with. Instead, he takes his anger out on the family. Sometimes I wonder if he uses the pain as an excuse to treat us all so horribly.

Father has hidden the car between a mess of trees we can only hope will conceal it well enough not to attract unwanted attention. I've made a mark on the map he's given so we won't have trouble locating the vehicle later.

"Thank you, Ben. Good thinking, son," Father says.

Father leans over my shoulder to take another glance at the map and traces his finger along the line he drew. "We'll just continue northwest now and we should end up at the edge of the woods near the Becker estate."

The cool April climate hasn't done much to encourage the trees to fully bud, but there are enough pines to conceal us and the car, especially with a wide pond to our right. There hasn't been much rain in the last several days, leaving only a scattering of small puddles to avoid. The thought of trudging through mud didn't dawn on me before now, especially since we seem to be on unchartered territory due to the lack of beaten paths. I'm hopeful officials won't be lurking in the nearby vicinity. At least the chirping and singing among the birds seems to drown out most of the sound from our footsteps crunching over twigs and rocks.

A half hour passes and a glow from the sun splinters through the trees ahead. It must be the edge of the woods. We will recognize where we are when we make it to the clearing.

"Your navigation is spot on," Father says as the brightening distance comes into view. "We're just a hill away from their estate." The narrow roads are lined with Bavarian-style houses with dark crosshatch woodwork. Each window is adorned with a flower basket, filled with sunflowers, daisies, and tulips. However, there aren't enough beautiful flowers in the world to mask the truth of what each foundation is built upon.

Judging by the lack of commentary from Tobias, it's safe to assume he may be in pain and choosing to silently suffer so he doesn't hold this process up. If he's so entirely against this plan, I don't see what the difference is, whether he is here or at home. Maybe he would like to share his scowl with Mister Becker or perhaps he is going to attempt an intervention at the last moment.

Father pulls a handkerchief out of his pocket and blots the sheen of sweat off his forehead. "It's April. I shouldn't be working up such a sweat."

This walk is more than the three of us have physically done in a while. I'm sure it's reason enough to sweat.

"Finally, here we are," Father says. "Tobias, not a word."

The community here is much different than ours since we have much more land sprawling between neighboring properties. Here, some houses sit on top of shops while others break up the scene with a luxurious front entrance and golden finishes. Though the entire community is quite small, it's clear everyone lives lavishly.

Father straightens his coat before we approach one of the impressive front entrances in a row of buildings, framed with yellowing stone pillars to match the same pastel tone of the stucco façade. Above us is a protruding awning, encased by embellished iron gates which offer only a slight view of the upper deck patio Mister and Misses Becker have used for many parties over the years. The overhang casts a deep shadow beneath, masquerading the worn hand-carved wooden door. I follow Father's lead, but Tobias uses one of the surrounding pillars to hold himself up.

Father rings the bell and we wait in silence. I believe Mister Becker still employs a full staff, which means he will not be the one to greet us. We will likely have to convince the person to let us speak with Mister Becker.

A heavy-chested man with a narrow waist opens the door. He recognizes Father. "Mister Bohdan, we weren't expecting your company today," the man says.

"Yes, yes, of course. I've been wanting to pay my old friend a surprise visit. I hope that's all right with you, Charles."

"Would you mind waiting here until I fetch Mister Becker?" the man named Charles asks.

"We are happy to wait here, yes." Father pulls at his necktie and blots his handkerchief against the back of his neck.

Minutes feel like an hour before Mister Becker greets us at the front door. "I wasn't expecting you," he says, taking a moment to look at all three of us individually.

"Yes, well, you haven't been returning my calls or posts. Good friend, I know you have done us an honorable service, and I am very thankful for that, but I'm here to re-collect what belongs to me. It seems we have other means of handling our business and I don't want to put you out any more than I already have. The paperwork is already drafted," Father says, pulling an envelope from the inner pocket of his coat.

Mister Becker scans the area as if worried about who might be witness to this exchange. "I'm glad you have found other means of safety," he says in a hush. "If anything changes—" Mister Becker looks over his shoulder this time. "You know where to find me."

"Why haven't you returned my calls?" Father asks bluntly.

"It would be a risk to the both of us, Josef. It is a risk that you are here at all right now. Please understand this has no relevance to my feelings about our friendship."

Father hands Mister Becker the envelope. "I understand."

"I'll just need a moment with the paperwork," Mister Becker says, before heading off.

"Thank God," Father says when the door closes.

"Why are you being so kind to him?" Tobias asks. "He has blatantly disregarded your friendship and held the title to our estate without feeling the need to return one phone call. I suppose it's much easier to hide within these walls than it is to face the harsh reality we're living through."

"It doesn't matter now," Father hisses.

Tobias isn't necessarily wrong, but this is certainly not the time to remind Mister Becker of what he's done wrong.

What matters is that he has made good on his promise. He returns within minutes, signed paperwork and title in hand. "I wish you nothing but the best, Josef. Truly."

"How dare you?" Tobias says, pointing his finger toward Mister Becker's chest. He grunts like an angry animal. "You should be ashamed of yourself."

"Tobias, please stop," Father says.

I try to take a deep breath, but I feel like my lungs have fallen flat.

"No, if you're not going to say anything, I will. Never did I think you would become a Nazi sympathizer. Never." Tobias's voice is much louder than he must realize, and I yank the back of his coat, hoping he will stop speaking.

"Son, I understand what this looks like to you, and I hate what you are going through," Mister Becker says.

"No. You hate that we are Jewish," Tobias says. "I can see it written all over your ugly face."

From the corner of my eye, I see Tobias's volume has attracted unwanted attention. "Father," I utter. "People are watching."

Father takes the papers from Mister Becker's hand and gives them to me. "Put those in your pocket at once. You must keep those safe at all cost. Can you promise me you'll protect this?"

"The title?" I question.

"Yes, Ben. Please. I need you to hold on to this."

Sweat is beading along the sides of Tobias's face and his mouth is agape, staring at Father with bewilderment. "Unbelievable," Tobias shouts.

"Please, I beg you to keep your voice down, Tobias," Mister Becker warns. "There are Nazis everywhere, all of the time."

Father takes Tobias's arm and pulls him back from the front door. "Again, thank you, Elias. You've been a true friend."

Tobias takes this opportunity to spit at Mister Becker. "You are nothing but a coward."

Father and I are desperately trying to force Tobias to stop without causing a scene, but I discern the clamor of boots marching not far from where we are.

"They will check on a disturbance. They've likely already heard the commotion," Mister Becker hisses. "You must go at once."

"Not until you apologize for the way you've treated us," Tobias says, pulling his arm out of Father's grip.

"Tobias, we need to leave. You are placing us in grave danger. Do you hear me?" Father seethes.

"All he has to do is apologize," Tobias says, folding his arms across his chest.

Mister Becker is staring at Father with anguish.

"You don't owe us anything," Father says. "We're leaving. I apologize for this trouble."

Mister Becker steps back in through the front door, his figure blending into the dark shadows. "Goodbye," he says.

"No, I'm not leaving," Tobias says, making his point louder.

"I'm leaving," Father says. "You are my son, and I don't want to leave you here at the hands of the Nazis, who are seconds away from turning a corner to find us—to find a disturbance demanding of an identification check. We will be punished for not only crossing a border illegally, but for being Jewish and starting an argument with a German citizen."

"You're overreacting," Tobias states. The vile irony makes me want to grab Father and drag him away, leaving Tobias to fend for himself.

Father's face becomes pale, damp with sweat as he looks between me and Tobias. The stampede of heavy boots has come far too close.

"Fine," Father says, turning to leave. His hand is on my back, and he nudges me forward.

Part of me assumes Tobias will drop the act and storm after us, but after a few steps, Father and I glance back, watching the stubborn fool stand guard before Mister Becker's door.

"You're both my sons. I can't leave him here, knowing what will likely happen," Father says.

"This is his choice," I argue. "I don't want you in the face of those soldiers."

Father slaps his hands down on my shoulders and squeezes tensely. "I agree with you, son. I do. But I need you to leave now before it's too late. You have the title to the estate. Bring it home. Go find the car, and don't come back to look for us. God willing, we will take the train home. We will be fine."

"You'll have to walk quite a way to reach the train station over the border," I tell him, pleading quietly through my unblinking glare. "This is senseless, Father."

"Ben, I need you to go. Do you hear me?" My chest aches, knowing I'm obeying Father by abandoning him and Tobias, even if he is unhinged. I stumble forward, watching over my shoulder, hoping the boots pivot toward another direction. "I love you, son. Go, now. Run and don't stop."

"I love you, Father. Please come home."

The sound of a fist beating against a door startles me into moving faster. Tobias shouts, "Do you know my father has stayed up all night several times, sitting by the phone in the foyer, waiting for it to ring, hoping you would come to your senses?"

"Tobias, please stop!" Father cries out.

"I love you, Father. Please come right home," I whisper to myself, knowing he cannot hear me anymore.

"I'm not through talking," Tobias growls, the sound of his voice echoing down the road. "Come back at once, Mister Becker!"

As I reach the end of the block, I wish I was imagining the moment when several Nazis step out from the shadow of another awning down the road. "Halt! What is it you think you're doing?" They spot Father and Tobias. *No, no. Please no.* The head-to-toe camel brown uniforms and red bands wrapped around their upper left arms, doting the swastika, are the last I see before forcing myself to do what Father said to do, and run. I'm out of breath within seconds, gasping for air as I clutch my aching chest.

I will never forgive my brother. I knew his mouth would someday bring us more trouble than we could handle. I look over my shoulder just as I'm turning the corner and I spot a group of SS officers walking toward Mister Becker's front door, toward Father and Tobias.

TWENTY-SEVEN

STAMPED WITH A J
MILA, APRIL 1939

I've dusted every vase and picture frame three times in the hours Ben has been gone. Madam Bohdan has been pacing back and forth through the foyer, checking her watch, then matching the time up with the grandfather clock.

"They've been gone longer than I assumed they would," she says for the dozenth time.

"I'm sure they're all right, just taking extra precautions, if I had to guess." I'm not sure what these precautions would be, but I assume Mister Bohdan thought everything through before sliding into his vehicle with Ben and Tobias.

"I don't know," she says with a groan. "Something doesn't feel right."

I hate to agree with her but I'm fearing the worst too.

"Why don't I fix Filip and Pavel something for dinner? I'm sure they're hungry," I offer.

Madam Bohdan stops mid-pace and shoots a crestfallen glance in my direction. "You don't have to do that. I can find something for them."

"It's no burden, madam."

She blinks slowly and nods in agreement. "I appreciate your help."

I amble off to the kitchen and rummage through the pantry to see what I can put together for the boys. Weeks ago, there was so much food on these shelves, it was hard to find what I was looking for. Now, there's only cans, a few cloth bags full of vegetables and fruit, and canisters of grains. Barley and mushrooms it is tonight. We've been mindful of the produce, fish, and meat consumption after finding many bare shelves at the store.

I set up a pot of water on the stovetop and fire up the gas burner. While slicing the mushrooms and lone carrot stick left over from the night before, I fall into a rhythmic daze, wondering what will happen if we're no longer allowed to purchase fuel. The appliances in the kitchen are fairly new and I'm not sure there's a way to use coal or wood if we need a different source of heat. At the very least, I know I can survive off a wood-burning fire outdoors, but I'm not sure I can picture the family complying to such unthinkable ways of living.

Just as I pour the barley and chopped vegetables into the water, I hear a faint rumbling in the distance.

I dry my hands on a dish rag and step closer to the kitchen's door, listening. The back door swings open and the thud of boots clunk against the floorboards.

Ben turns the corner and my heart falls to the pit of my stomach, making me clutch the apron and press it into my ribcage. He's pale, covered in sweat, and his hair is everywhere. "Ben," I utter, stopping him from walking by the kitchen. He didn't even notice me standing here. He stops short and turns to me, and I see that his eyes are stained red beneath his thick lashes. He drapes his arms around me, pulling me into him, but he appears unsteady on his feet, wobbling from side to side as he holds on to me.

"Are you okay?" I ask.

"What's going on?" Madam Bohdan calls out. Her heels

sound like hammers against the wood floors as she makes her way down to us. She stops a few steps away and her eyes widen as if someone has stolen her breath. "Benedikt, where are your father and brother? Are they getting the car settled?"

"No, Mother. They will be taking the train home."

"What? Why?" I ask, still pinned in his arms.

Ben holds himself up against the wall while keeping me secure beneath his free arm.

I glance up, worried to see the expression on his face. He's shaking his head as if in disbelief. "Everything was going as well as possible. Mister Becker had signed the new papers and handed the title back to us without any hesitation. He even said if we change our minds, we know where to find him. He had been avoiding calls and posts because of the scrutiny they are under beneath the regime."

"Then why on earth would your father and Tobias decide to take the train back here?" Madam Bohdan asks. The look of shock in her unblinking eyes turns to horror.

"Tobias—he—he uh—he couldn't keep his thoughts to himself," Ben says, breathlessly before swallowing hard. "His anger got the best of him, and he wanted Mister Becker to know exactly how we have been feeling about his silence. Father tried to make him stop, but with every plea, Tobias became louder. It got to the point where people in the village were staring at us."

Madam Bohdan grapples her hand around her neck, squeezing so tightly her skin reddens. "What happened?"

"Father told me to leave with the title, obtain the car we parked in the woods before the border, and to go home with the title."

"How will we know if they made it to the train station?" Madam Bohdan shouts at Ben as if this is his fault.

"We won't," he says, dropping his head forward. He takes a shuttered breath before speaking again. "As I was running off, I saw a group of soldiers address them."

"What would that mean?" Madam Bohdan cries out. Her lips fall into a sharp grimace.

"What do you think they would do? The Germans, I mean," I ask. I'm sure Madam Bohdan is wondering the same.

Ben shrugs, pinching me beneath his arm as he does. "They could ask for their identification. Then they'd find out that we're Jewish and unlawfully over the border." Ben tosses his head back against the wall. "Tobias did this. It's his fault, entirely. If the worst did happen, not even my nightmares can conjure up what form of hell they could be facing while I'm here, home safely. I shouldn't have left, but there was just no reasoning with him, Mother. I'm sorry," he says, wheezing through each breath. "Maybe—just maybe, the soldiers didn't ask for identification. They could have walked away after asking if there was a problem. In that case, Father and Tobias would be on their way home now. I'm sure that's what happened. That's what we must believe."

Ben is either lying for the sake of his mother, or his sanity. Every muscle in his body is tensing harder and harder. We see the headlines. We know the Germans of the Reich do not give second chances, nor do they have understanding. I can't imagine they let Mister Bohdan and Tobias go after approaching them. I'm sure Ben knows this. I don't want to steal hope away, but the Nazis are ruthless and heartless.

Madam Bohdan is staring between us, unblinking, with a look of horror darkening her eyes. "Yes, we must assume they are okay. Your father is a smart man, Ben. He'll make sure the two of them make it out of there." Her breath shudders deep within her chest and she wraps her arms around her stomach as if she may keel over in pain. "Do—uh—Do, do you know how far away the train station is from the Becker estate? I can call up for a schedule, so we know what time the train is coming in. That way we'll have a better idea of when they will be home, won't we?" Madam Bohdan asks, dropping her arms by her side.

"I'm not certain, but Father said it wasn't too far over the border."

"Did he seem worried?" she continues, lifting her gaze to Ben's. Her eyes fill with tears and her chin quivers.

I'm not sure what type of response she's seeking from Ben. Maybe she's hoping he'll tell her lies so she can breathe a bit easier.

"It all happened so quickly. I'm not sure how he seemed," Ben says.

I smell the starch steaming from the barley, and I almost forgot I left a boiling pot on the stovetop. I slip out from beneath Ben's arm and return to the kitchen to take the pot off the burner.

"She's cooking dinner again?" Ben asks Madam Bohdan.

"She offered, Ben. We were worried sick about you three and she wanted to make sure Filip and Pavel had something to eat. I can't think about Mila right this second. Your father and Tobias—" she bawls, sounding as if she's struggling for air.

"Damn it," Ben grunts before seeking me out in the kitchen.

"You don't have to worry about me," I tell him as he charges toward the sink next to where I'm standing. He whips a dish rag from the counter and drops his hands to the rim of the enamel basin.

"Mila, please go sit down," he says.

"I'm fine. You've had a long day. I made enough of the barley and mushrooms if you're hungry too."

Ben takes the wooden spoon I had laid out on the counter and stirs the contents in the pot. "Mila, I'm in agony—my chest is searing with pain and worry."

"What are you imagining?" I ask.

He continues stirring for another moment before answering my question. He must be hypnotizing himself by focusing so intently on the swirling starch-stained water. "Their passports are stamped with a 'J' and they aren't from the Sudetenland region. There was a public dispute and I think it's less likely they'll let them go with a slap on the wrist versus possibly arresting them. They've done far worse here in the village for minor acts of resistance."

"They weren't resisting though, right?"

"It's hard to assume Tobias would have suddenly come to his senses. If he tried to fight the Nazis off, then yes, he would be considered resisting."

I rest my head against the side of his shoulder. "I would take your pain away if I could."

Ben releases the wooden spoon from his grip and turns to face me. "I wouldn't want that. How much pain do you think one person should go through in a lifetime?"

"I've been in pain for so long that I feel as though I'm becoming numb to the reality of losing everything. I question whether I'm truly here some days, and if everything that's happened between us is real. I wonder if, perhaps, I've gone mad and merely imagined a life better than the one I was living. There's no resolution to this undying torment and I can't bear the thought of watching you go through the same."

"I don't know what I did to deserve you," he says, placing a kiss on my forehead. "Thank you for stepping up to take care of my brothers. I'm afraid Mother won't be of much help until we know what's happened to Father and Tobias." I must stop myself from cracking a smile, knowing Madam Bohdan wouldn't offer to help even if everything was perfect here. "I know, I know... She didn't need an excuse."

I retrieve a stack of bowls from the cupboard and watch as Ben ladles the barley and vegetable mix into each. "I'll take these to the dining room."

"I can handle it. Why don't you go see where Filip and Pavel are? I'm sure they're eavesdropping from a room upstairs and trying to piece together what's happened. I'll explain everything to them when they come down here. I don't want you to have to be put in that position."

"If you don't let me help, it's only going to make matters harder on you. I'm right here, ready to help carry the burden of whatever may come. I want to be your partner in all things good or bad."

"I can't steal hope from them until I know more."

I sweep my hand across his back as I leave the kitchen and make my way up the stairs. I knock on Filip's door first. Pavel whips the door open, smiling at me with pure innocence. "We weren't doing anything wrong, I promise."

Filip is sitting on the edge of his bed with his head in his hands and elbows pressed into his knees. "Are you okay?" I ask.

"I'm just tired. It's been a long day."

"I made something for you to eat if you're hungry. Ben is bringing it into the dining room."

"Ben?" Filip asks.

"Yes," I say, ready to turn around and leave before there are any more questions.

"Where are Father and Tobias?" Pavel asks.

"I'm sure your brother knows. Why don't you come down for dinner?"

"I'm sure you know what my brother knows. Please tell me," Filip begs.

"I don't—please." Before there are any more questions, I take the opportunity to lead them down the stairs, hoping that they follow.

TWENTY-EIGHT
A HAWK'S CRY
BENEDIKT, APRIL 1939

They were supposed to return yesterday. There's no way to convince myself that my fears aren't true. I couldn't sleep last night. I didn't even try. Mila and I sat at the dining room table and stirred our spoons around dinner bowls until Filip and Pavel became restless and returned upstairs. Mother didn't even say a word for the hours she sat across the table from us. It must have been the middle of the night when she finally stood up and excused herself from our presence.

"Is there anything we can do?" Mila asks, placing her hand on top of mine. I'm not sure I've lifted my arm off the table since we sat down last night, not moving since. Every bone in my body feels heavy and worn.

"I will phone Mister Becker with hope he might have insight as to their whereabouts. He must know if they were escorted away by the gestapo or if they at least left freely to find their way to the train station."

"Do you think he would have phoned you, had he known something happened to your father and Tobias?" she asks, curling her fingers around my hand.

I sniffle through the dry air that feels stale in this room. "I don't believe he will, nor do I think he might accept a call from us, but I must at least try. He mentioned the dangers involved. I assume the Germans are monitoring every signal and note coming and going from their claimed territories."

The only true option beyond an attempt to contact Mister Becker is to wait. But with every minute that passes, the chances they are okay diminishes.

The sound of tires crunching over rocks pulls my attention toward the windows I can't see out of from where I'm sitting. Perplexity is tugging at Mila's eyebrows, telling me she heard the same sound. Father wouldn't be in a car. They would have walked from the train station. Fearful of what I might find, I use more strength than necessary to push my chair away from the table. I stand, feeling an ache in my thighs and the joints behind my knees. I walk around to the wall of windows. The sun is above the horizon but not the tree line. The road outside the estate is barren and I don't see another car beneath the side overhang where I parked last night.

"It must have been someone passing by," I mutter through a sigh.

I turn back to face Mila, noting the discomfort on display across every inch of her body. Her fingers are tangled together, her shoulders are hunched forward, and her half-lidded eyes seem to be struggling to stay open. "Why don't you go rest?" I say. "There's no need for us both to be sitting here like this."

"I don't need rest. I'm not leaving you to sit here alone and wait."

I take a different seat at the table, one across from Mila rather than the one beside her where I sat all night. "This doesn't feel like an appropriate time, but in the same regard, I'm not sure when a moment might seem proper."

Mila tilts her head to the side, something I don't think she's aware she does when curious. I reach into my coat pocket, realizing I haven't taken it off since I left the estate with Father and

Tobias yesterday. The papers Father handed me are still neatly folded and crisp. It takes me a moment to set out the documents along the table. The newly signed release papers between Father and Mister Becker are among the paperwork for the estate title. I wonder if Father drafted paperwork for Mila to sign. He seemed to move so quickly on the plan, I'm not sure what he had prearranged, but knowing Father, everything was thoroughly prepared.

"I'm going to check Father's office to see if he has papers drafted for you to sign so I can put the title in your name."

Mila is silent but agrees with a slight nod. I imagine she must feel overwhelmingly unsettled and the thought of piling this responsibility onto her shoulders is tearing my heart into pieces.

At the same moment I step out into the hall, a strong fist pounds against the main front door. Shock stills me as if my feet are stuck to the floor. There are no windows around the front door. Father wouldn't come in that way and wouldn't knock.

From the corner of my eye, I spot Mila standing from her seat in the dining room then gliding toward me as if sensing my fear. "I can answer the door if you'd prefer," she offers.

I understand Mila is trying to protect me because I'm Jewish and she isn't, but I've explained to her that nothing is going to change between us. As her husband, I promised to protect her. "I'd rather you stay in the dining room, if you wouldn't mind," I suggest.

"Ben," she huffs with frustration.

"Please," I beg.

She doesn't return to the table but doesn't step out into the foyer either.

I pull in a lungful of air and straighten my posture before heading for the door. Halfway to the entrance, another knock makes me want to leap out of my skin. I can barely swallow the lump forming in my throat as I reach for the lock and handle.

This is my home. I shouldn't be afraid. This is my home. I shouldn't be afraid.

I open the door enough to see who's standing out front and though there's a sense of relief at recognizing the face I'm staring at, it doesn't take more than a second or two for my stomach to tighten with pain.

A look of shock overwhelms the man's face and his mouth parts before speaking. "Oh, thank God you're okay," he says, holding his hand against his chest. Mister Becker is the last person I thought would be at the front door.

"Sir, to what do I owe this visit?" The words hardly form on my tongue. "I didn't notice a vehicle outside."

"I parked my car up the road just beyond the estate," he says, clearing his throat. He doesn't want to be seen conversing with the Jews who live in this house. I understand. "And, son, I know I've told you many times throughout your life to call me Elias. Julia and I would rather you feel like family to us. May I come inside?" He checks over his shoulder as if someone might be watching.

"Yes—yes, sir. Elias, yes, please come inside." I take a step back and wave my trembling arm out to the side. He's quick about stepping over the threshold and into the foyer.

I close the door, feeling sweat creep down my back. "I'm afraid to know why you appear to be so pale," I say, waiting for him to start talking. "Could I offer you some tea?" I hope he doesn't accept. I can't possibly wait any longer to know what he's here to say.

He holds his hand up. "No, no, thank you," he says, taking a deep breath. "Ben, I'm afraid I'm not here with the best news." He places his heavy hand on my shoulder.

"I assumed not," I reply, clenching my wrists behind my back.

"I'm not sure how much you saw or didn't see yesterday

when you left, but I went looking for you and I was praying you made it back here safely."

Gentle footsteps creep up behind me and I already know it's Mila. I should stop asking her to stay behind when I must handle something because I know she won't listen. She never does. I've never had someone worry about me the way I worry about them.

"You must be Mila," Elias says, removing his hand from my shoulder and reaching it out to shake hers. "I'm Elias Becker, a friend of the Bohdan family."

Mila seems hesitant to take his hand but does so out of respect. "It's a pleasure to meet you, sir."

Elias looks back and forth between Mila and me, maybe wondering if it's safe to continue the conversation with her by my side. I take Mila's hand and slip my fingers between hers, needing the feeling of her tight grip. "Should I find my mother?" I ask.

"Ben, your father and Tobias were escorted away by a group of Nazis. They questioned them after receiving complaints about a disturbance."

"Did Tobias continue speaking the way he was to you?" *Please, tell me he knew better. Please.*

"No, no. The Gestapo seemed confused at first. Tobias went quiet the moment they turned the corner, but rather the Gestapo approached them, looking for identification. It didn't matter what they had heard. They didn't need much of a reason above a complaint to take them away. I don't know where they brought them too. I'm afraid there isn't a way to find out either. Anyone working under the regime is tight-lipped."

Breathing should be an instinctive human function, but I can't remember how to inhale. Mila's hand slips from mine and she clasps her arm around my waist. "What does this mean... How are they treating the Jewish people in your village?" I ask.

Elias removes his cap, resting it on his chest. "I don't think I would be doing you any good by withholding the truth, Ben. They've executed Jews for less than what they assumed was going on at my front door. It doesn't mean that's what happened, but—"

Again, I can't manage to take a full breath. Mila is now running her fingers from side to side between my shoulder blades but I can hardly feel her touch. I'm not even sure I feel my heart beating in my chest. "We're supposed to just wonder? Every day from here on out we'll have to question whether Father and Tobias have been executed."

Elias takes a hold of my wrist and pulls me toward him, wrapping his arms around me. "I'm sorry, Ben. I don't know how to make this better and I feel responsible for not taking his calls, but if I had, I might have gotten you all in trouble. No one knows what to expect from those mongrels. Things are changing every day and it's terrifying for everyone, but I can't imagine being Jewish and being in their direct path." Elias's chest bucks in and out as if he's having trouble breathing also. "I don't know what else to do. I didn't know what to do. I spent the night walking the village streets looking for where they may have been taken but there wasn't a hint of them anywhere. That's why I drove here first thing this morning."

"I must tell Mother," I say, my face still pressed into his shoulder. Colorful dots swirl around in the darkness of my closed eyes, and I wish I didn't have to open them to face the gray clouded world.

"Mila," Elias says with a sniffle. I lift my head, surprised to hear him address my wife. "Josef spent half of his last letter to me talking about how wonderful you are. He mentioned the elopement and said though he was sorry he couldn't bear witness to his son finding everlasting happiness, he was grateful you were here to stay and become the daughter he's never had. He mentioned he had been thinking about you, regarding the title and wondered about my opinion. I wanted to respond, but the chance of the post being intercepted felt too great."

"It's kind of you to share that with me, sir," Mila says. "I'm very fond of Mister Bohdan."

Mila sounds distraught, more so than I would have expected when it comes to my family. Her heart holds too much for any one person to carry around.

"Ben, is your mother still asleep?"

"I'm—I don't know. We stayed up quite late."

"I'm not asleep. I'm here, Elias," comes Madam Bohdan's voice. "I hope you know where my husband and son are," she says, descending the stairs, one at a time and very tentatively. "I wasn't expecting to see you. Where is Julia?"

The moment Mother sees the look in my eyes she's going to know the truth of what we all have been fearing. I keep my gaze set on the ground, hoping the distance between us buys her another few seconds of peace before the misery sets in.

"I'll talk to her," Elias says, stepping away from me. "I've had all night to think of the least jarring of words," he mutters as he walks toward Mother. "Misses Becker had a bit of a headache so I told her it would be best if she stayed home and got some rest."

She pulls her robe tightly over her chest and then folds her arms as if she's trying to embrace herself.

Mila takes my hand. "Perhaps we should give them a minute and go check on Nova and Twister," she says.

I debate if I should be standing beside my mother to support her, but I might only make the moment worse. My chest feels like it's on fire and I may combust from the pain searing through every nerve of my body.

The moment we step out the front door, a devastating sound, like a hawk's cry, pierces my soul.

TWENTY-NINE
FRIEND OR FOE?
MILA, APRIL 1939

Mister Becker has been here for the greater part of the day. The discussions between he, Ben, and Madam Bohdan have been emotional and perplexing as they discuss matters of the estate. I feel like no more than a witness, but I'm not sure I have helpful input either.

"Would you have said all of this to my husband if he was sitting here with us?" Madam Bohdan questions Elias once again.

We've taken up most of the furniture in the grand salon. Ben and I are on one sofa, Madam Bohdan is across from us, and Mister Becker is in the stud-lined leather reading chair by the tea table. The sun's rays have slipped behind the thick clouds, casting a grim chill throughout the room. "What I know is hearsay, Hana, but I would be remiss to exclude any information I know, whether it be true or false."

"What you're saying is mixed marriages are not exempt from brutality against the Jews despite what the law dictates," Ben says. "I don't understand why you didn't say this to my father before signing the paperwork and handing the title back to our family."

I'm aware Ben must be drowning in heavy emotions ranging from one extreme to the other, but it sounds as if he's interrogating Mister Becker. I place my hand on Ben's knee, wishing he would calm down or at least take a breath. Madam Bohdan's glare strikes my hand as if I'm committing a sin by touching my husband's knee. For the first time since being married to Ben, I decide to keep my hand where it is rather than comply with her silent dismay.

"The title belongs to your family, Ben. He came to collect the papers. I had no intention of taking part in a discussion on the matter on my front stoop. To be frank, I'm not certain on the legalities of myself holding the title. The law under the Reich states that titles are to be handed over to German occupants in Sudetenland, but here the law might be different with the Protectorate of Bohemia and Moravia. The title might need to be held by a citizen of this region."

"You do realize you are contradicting every word you speak, Elias," Madam Bohdan says, stretching her shoulders back from sitting upright for so long.

"I'm aware, Hana. The truth of the matter is many of the laws contradict themselves and many seem to be changing by the day."

"All I'm hearing from you is that the title is not safe in any set of hands between us," Madam Bohdan continues.

Mister Becker leans into his chair, resting his head against the high back. The leather crinkles below him, stretching against the moving pressure. "I'm not here to tell you what's best because I don't have a proper answer. I can offer to continue holding the title in the case you are concerned for what may happen to those in mixed marriages. I'm also happy to assist Mila in filling out the paperwork to claim the title under her name."

Ben and Madam Bohdan are staring at one another as if trying to have a conversation with their eyes. I'm not sure I know what either of them are thinking. "Will either you or Mila be in danger while holding the title?" Ben asks Mister Becker.

"If I may be honest, no one in any German occupied country is safe at the moment."

"Elias, could I refill your teacup?" Madam Bohdan offers.

Elias leans forward to check what's left in his cup. "No, thank you."

"Very well. I hope you don't mind but I'd like to speak to Ben privately for a moment. If you'll excuse us, we'll just be a few moments."

Ben glances over at me and his nostrils flare. "You're coming with us," he whispers.

He takes my hand from his knee and gently tugs me to my tired feet. We follow Madam Bohdan out of the salon and down toward the foyer, where she closes us in the library for privacy. I'm somewhat surprised at her lack of commentary about me joining them in this family discussion. Perhaps she's come to realize there are more important matters than her disapproval of her son's marriage.

"I'm not sure what's best," she says.

"I'm wondering if it might be safer for us if he continues to hold the title," Ben says. I'm taken aback to hear him considering this option. He was very questioning about everything Mister Becker spoke about.

Curious to see what Madam Bohdan thinks, I glance to the side to examine her expression. "Are you sure this is what's best?" she says to Ben. Her rigid eyebrows are sharply pointing toward one another and the creases on her forehead deepen with concern.

"You heard what he said, Mother. If mixed marriages are not being treated the way they have been intended, we are putting ourselves in jeopardy."

"And if the estate's title needs to be in the hands of someone in the protectorate region, the title will be taken from him and handed to God knows who."

"God knows where it may be safer than us being persecuted for disobeying a law," Ben argues.

Madam Bohdan shakes her head and clenches her fists by her side. "I don't agree. Elias had no qualms about disregarding your father's phone calls and posts, ultimately forcing him to cross the Sudetenland border to pay him a visit. A friend wouldn't do that to another."

"A friend wouldn't come to a Jewish family's home at this time and offer to help," Ben argues.

"I realize this may not be my place to insert my opinion," I say, "but it seems there is a question regarding the trust of Mister Becker. Maybe a hasty decision isn't wise."

"There isn't time to think on this matter," Ben replies. "Otherwise, yes, of course. I agree hasty decisions are never a good choice."

Madam Bohdan begins to pace from the closed door, past the wall of books, to the window, and then pivots for another lap. The tip of her thumb is pinched between her teeth and her eyes are bulging as she seemingly stares through the floorboards. "I don't trust that man."

"It would be easy for you to jeopardize Mila's safety though," Ben says, "am I correct?"

Madam Bohdan halts her steps and shoots a glare at Ben. "I am thinking of the estate, our home, not whom I like better. Regardless of who holds the title, there is a risk."

It was an easy opportunity for Madam Bohdan to say something nasty about me and I'm somewhat shocked she didn't come up with anything more impressive. "Ben, if there is risk either way, it might be best if we keep it here rather than across a border you aren't allowed to cross," I say, unbelievably agreeing with Madam Bohdan for the first time since I met her.

Ben takes a step back, recoiling as if dodging a blow to the head. "You're siding with her now?"

I expected him to be upset, but if I don't speak my mind, I wouldn't forgive myself. Ben has told me many times before that he loves me because I am my own person with a unique mind and I'm unafraid to speak up when I disagree. It just so happens I haven't felt the need to disagree with him before.

"I'm stating my opinion. The thought of you having to cross the border to his village after what has already happened feels like an unnecessary risk. And while I trust he's speaking the truth about his reasons for being unresponsive to your father's attempts at communication, it's all a bit unsettling."

Ben runs his fingers through his already messy hair. "If the Germans try to obtain the title from you by means of trickery or lies, I can't fathom what could happen to you. Ultimately, this comes down to us risking Mister Becker's well-being or yours, Mila. I will not put you at risk."

I reach forward to take one of Ben's swinging arms. He's agitated, pressing his fists against the wall, then his hips, and back to his head. He's obviously livid, understandably. Yet emotion can't be involved in the answer, and I'm not sure I can explain this to him. I wouldn't want to be in his shoes deciding on behalf of his safety or my family's home.

"Ben, I think we should keep the title. Allow Elias to help with the paperwork so we can place the title in Mila's name, and if we need to re-transfer it back to him at some point, we will," says his mother.

I'm nearly dizzy from the role reversal Ben and Madam Bohdan are taking but I believe she's correct.

"How do we know he's telling the truth about your father and Tobias?" Madam Bohdan adds.

"What could he be telling stories about? I watched all of it happen up until the Gestapo turned the corner. Either they took Father and Tobias away or let them go, and if they let them go, they would surely be home by now."

The door to the library swings open. Elias is standing in the doorway with a handkerchief held to the side of his head. "I must go at once."

"What is it?" Madam Bohdan asks.

"From the salon, I spotted German soldiers stopping by my vehicle up the hill. They will be looking for identification unless I make my way out there at once."

"You mustn't be seen leaving the estate," Ben scolds him. "There's nowhere else for you to go until they leave."

"I can't stay here. If they find me in here—"

"You'll be as terrified as a Jew, I assume," Mila says, arching her brow and pressing her lips into a flat line.

"Mila, you need to go with Elias. They are bound to come to the door, and I need to handle this."

"I would be best off answering the door, Ben," I argue.

"Absolutely not. I need you to take Elias downstairs to the servant quarters and bring him into the storage unit behind the false wall. You know where I'm talking about."

"Of course," I say. "But—"

"Are we in danger?" Madam Bohdan cries out.

"Yes, Mother," Ben says, matter of fact. "Go upstairs to your room or somewhere else, please."

"What if they take you away?" I ask Ben. My chest feels like it's caving in.

"They have no reason to take me away. I don't know a thing about the vehicle parked down the street."

"If they ask for the title of the estate?" Madam Bohdan adds. "Then what?"

"Then—you show them your confidence. They'll wonder why you seem so sure of yourself. It's better than appearing weak."

My mama always said so.

"I don't want to go into that shop with you. They'll call us names and throw things at us," I complain to Mama, tugging her arm before she reaches for the door handle.

She shakes her head. "No, Mila. You have it all wrong. You see, as a Romani traveler, we are known to be deft, astute, unpredictable, and wise enough to fool a scholar. That's why others are afraid of us. We can outsmart all of them quite easily and with little effort. You, your siblings, your father, and me—we use our traits for good. And for that, we can accomplish anything. Come with me and watch the way I carry myself. Do the same, and you'll see—those with gawking stares will be quick to stop looking."

Mama was always right.

I run past Mister Becker and down the hallway toward Mister Bohdan's office. I scuffle through the paperwork on his desk, sure he had the papers already prepared for me to sign upon his return.

A faded yellow envelope pokes up from beneath a stack of papers and I slide it out, finding my name scribbled in small print along the top left edge. I dump the contents of the envelope onto the desk and spread them out, scanning the words. On the last paper in the pile, I find a line with an x beneath Mister Bohdan's signature. I scan the desk for a pen, finding one secure in a decorative case at the front and center of his desk. I remove the cap, hoping there is still ink left on the tip and press the pen's tip to the line. Ink bleeds, and I drag the pen across the space, signing my name and adding a date to the end.

I shuffle the papers into a neat pile and slide them back into the envelope, then place it in the desk drawer. By time I look up from what I'm doing, Ben, Madam Bohdan, and Mister Becker are staring into the office with ghostly complexions.

"The papers are signed. Your father had them prepared.

The title is in my name. If anyone asks, your wife is out of town," I say.

With a racing heart, I charge forward and take Mister Becker by the sleeve, pulling him down the hallway to the door that leads down into the servants' quarters. Madam Bohdan scurries up to her bedroom as Ben suggested though I think she should be by Ben's side as an owner of this estate. I shouldn't be surprised by the cowardly action on her part.

THIRTY
I MUST SPEAK THE LANGUAGE
BENEDIKT, APRIL 1939

"Go find Filip and Pavel. Tell them if anyone comes to the door to keep quiet. They aren't to speak a word about Father or Tobias being missing, nor Mila or Elias. Tell them it's okay to be afraid if there is an unknown man or men in our house and that showing their fear will keep them safer."

Mother releases her hold from my arm. "I shouldn't terrify the boys. What good will that do?"

"We can no longer hide the reality of what is happening outside of this house. They aren't even aware that they may not see their father and brother again. This isn't an alarm, Mother. This is happening."

Judging by the lost look in her eyes, she seems confused. With her hand on her chest, it's easy to see she's having difficulty breathing. "This is going to destroy them," she says. I'm not sure how this thought hadn't crossed her mind until now.

"This is going to destroy all of us and if we don't prepare them—they must know the truth."

Mother crosses her arms, grappling her fingers around her ribcage. She turns and solemnly makes her way to the stairwell.

I step in through the entrance of the great salon, peeking out the back window from a distance. The German vehicle is still parked along the side of the road behind Mister Becker's car. They're going to search this house thoroughly before believing a man has abandoned his property.

When I step into the dining room, I hear the hum of chatter coming from outside. My throat tightens and my body turns cold.

In the foyer, I drop back against the wall and press my head back, wishing I had time for a prayer to be answered. *Please, let us be. Please, God. Help us. Help all of us.*

The knock on the door startles me like a riptide pulling my feet out from beneath me. I'm not sure what Father would do but I know he would open the door and do everything in his power to appear unaffected by the presence of the German Gestapo.

I take a few deep breaths before releasing the lock on the door.

Three men stand beneath the short overhang. Each of them in sharply pressed brown uniforms, the rims from their caps casting shadows over their eyes. "*Guten morgen, Herr...*" he speaks with a pompous inflection enforcing his superiority as though his words should bring me to my knees.

"Bohdan," I reply.

"Do you know who owns the stranded vehicle on the side of the road?"

I'm grateful to have learned German over the last several years. It became a mandatory study in school. Though we don't use it often enough to be fluent, I likely understand more than I'm able to speak.

"A vehicle?" It may be best to play ignorant.

"*Ja,*" one responds, pointing toward the road.

Normally I would step out of the estate to look at what they are referencing but I cannot give them free access to the doorway.

"My car is here. I'm not sure," I say, pointing toward the side of the house where our two cars are parked beneath the awning. I then peek out between their shoulders, attempting to make an effort to see what they are talking about.

"Herr Bohdan, do you own this property?" It takes me a moment to piece their words together, though only with hope that I misunderstood the question.

My pulse pelts in my ears like hail on a tin roof, my blood boils, and though I'm quivering from the inside, I tighten every muscle in my body and hold my shoulders back. "No, Herr. My wife holds the title." At least my words aren't a lie.

"Papers," one demands. "And your wife. Is she here?" Not one of them appears affected by what they are doing, invading privacy, demanding identification of an innocent man in his own home.

Tell them your wife is out of town, Mila's words ring in my head.

I pull my passport out of my pocket, holding it firmly between my fingers to prevent my hand from trembling. "My wife is out of town, visiting family in Germany." Mila wouldn't be visiting family in Germany if she was Jewish. Therefore, I hope my explanation of her whereabouts answers enough of the questions they might gather upon opening the flap of my passport.

The man holding my open passport nudges the one to his right, holding it up for the three of them to see the large "J" stamped inside. Laughter follows because that is what every Jewish man and woman deserve, according to their thinking.

"She's a stupid woman to marry a Jew, ja?"

They expect me to agree with them. "Yes, Herr. Very foolish," I reply. The words pain me, even in a foreign language. *My wife is brilliant.*

Their laughter continues. The rotten cigar-laced breath assaults my nostrils and I would do anything to slam this door in their faces. They stall, standing still, staring at me. It's obvious they are doing what they can to intimidate me. The man standing slightly in front of the other two leans around me to look past my shoulder. "It's very quiet here and it smells like horse manure." They glance around until they spot the stables off in the distance. "You still have horses. What for?" The German soldiers seem to become more intrusive by the day. We aren't allowed privacy and it isn't hard to imagine they will continue to become more aggressive until they have everything that belongs to us and every other Jewish family here.

"They belong to our family," I reply, not knowing what else to say in response to an absurd question. I'm more concerned that they are suspecting something isn't right by the lack of noise. I'm sure they find silence to be their biggest clue when searching for their enemies. "It is usually quiet when my wife is out of town."

"Ja, I'm sure," he agrees, but stifles another laugh.

The main Gestapo peers over at the other two and juts his head toward the road. Without further salutation or regard for the abandoned vehicle, they leave, chatting among themselves with humor I can't make out as the distance between us grows.

I gently close the door and secure the lock before pressing the back of my head against the rich mahogany slab. Terror bleeds out of my body through a cold sweat as a wave of over-whelming dizziness forces my body to the ground. I pull my knees up to my chest, allowing my head to fall forward.

"Benedikt, what is it?" Mother's voice whispers from the top of the stairwell.

"It's—I—"

"Why are you on the ground?"

"Never mind that. I'm going to check on Mila and Elias."

"Well, what did they want?" Mother continues.

"What do you think? They want the estate. We're Jewish and have no right to the title now—they are seeking proof that it doesn't belong to us. Aside from that, it's a large property and an asset the Germans can utilize as they continue to take over this country. With so many of them moving in, I'm sure they've run out resources for residency. They won't think twice about occupying space for themselves wherever possible. It's the precise reason we were worried about holding on to the title."

"You didn't tell them who the vehicle belongs to, did you?" How can a woman of this status, one who appeared so affluent and intelligent while I was growing up, become this person I don't know today? The vehicle should be the least of our worries now.

Disregarding her questions, I make my way to the servants' quarters, hoping they are hidden where I advised them to. The number of nooks and crannies carved out of the thousand-year-old cement offer many frightening games of hide-and-seek for children, but only a few spaces are in areas most wouldn't think to look.

The irony of searching for the only two non-Jewish people inside the estate is not lost on me.

"Mila, Elias," I call out, keeping my voice low as I enter the hidden room behind the false wall. This hideaway has been a retreat for Mila and me, but now it will be forever stained. The bookcase with only a few dusty books piled up on each shelf swivels with ease, exposing the dark path that leads through the walls. "Are you all right?"

"Ben?" Mila calls out, sounding as if she's at the complete opposite end of the narrow way.

"Yes, you can come out. They're gone for now."

Tentative footsteps echo between the walls, one after another for longer than my patience can tolerate. When I see a glow from outside the false wall flicker over Mila's face, I lunge toward her and scoop her into my arms. "I'm so sorry."

"Why are you apologizing?" Mila asks.

"You're down here in the dark without any idea of what's happening upstairs."

"I'm the one who should be apologizing," Elias says, his voice hoarse and forlorn. "It seems I've done nothing but cause your family more harm than good. Every assumption I've made has been with hope of keeping you safe, but I see now, it's nearly impossible."

"We appreciate everything you have done to help us," I offer. Though we've all had our questions and wondered what Elias was truly thinking, I believe he is the man I've known my entire life—a good man with a big heart, but also suffering from the same riveting fear every person in our country is living with.

"Just as soon as the road is clear, I will leave at once. I've given Mila my telephone number and address in case something was to happen to any of you."

"I thought you wouldn't answer a call from this residence?" I ask.

"I wish I had thought of this idea sooner so I could have had a better way of communicating safely with your father, but after having time to think during the car ride here today, I've come up with a way for you to reach me if need be. Place a call three times in a row. Wait for me to pick up, then end the call immediately. After the third time, I will know it's you and will seek a private location to return the call."

"I'm glad to know the option exists," I say.

Upon returning to the main level of the estate, I'm thankful to see the Nazis have left with their vehicle, leaving the road clear for Elias to depart. "Give my regards to Misses Becker," I say. My goodbye and thank-you aren't coming easily to my lips, and I can see the effect my disposition is having on Elias. He appears ashamed and full of sorrow. Yet, all I can think is, it must be nice to only feel that little.

THIRTY-ONE

THERE ARE NO BOUNDS
MILA, JUNE 1939

Over the last two months, Madam Bohdan has made a strong commitment to the act of silence. It's easy to see the turmoil she is living with, but she has three sons here who are watching her shut the world out and it isn't healthy for anyone, especially Filip and Pavel. They were sent home from school in March and told to find private education, but I know they have been hoping to return to their classrooms and friends this coming fall. I don't see much hope of that happening.

Ben and I have done what we can to keep the jarring headlines from them, but we've been honest about what it means to have the Germans annexing our country just as they did in Austria.

The Jewish people must abide by the German Nuremberg Laws—all of which are hard to remember, but all so unfathomable. I continue to run errands on their behalf, knowing what the other Jewish families are going through in the village. The segregation is brutal, and I suspect mostly out of fear for being grouped with the Jews. Anyone who is not of the Jewish faith seems to keep their distance as if to avoid contracting the religion, like some sort of a virus. Because of this, it's easier to determine who is Jewish just from the way they walk through town, with their heads hanging low, shoulders slouching forward, and utter terror pooling in their eyes as they enter a shop to utilize their allotment of food rations.

Filip and Pavel ask about their father daily, and even Tobias. The only answer we can give them is the truth: we don't know.

"Eat up your bread and jam," I say to Filip and Pavel, who both pick the crumbs from the darkened ends of their bread slices. "After breakfast, I must tend to Nova and Twister, but after, I thought we could go over some of the arithmetic we were working on a few days ago."

Filip's elbows fall to the table. "Why are you doing this?"

"Doing what?" I ask, already aware of what he's going to say. I'm doing what I can to help them while Madam Bohdan lies in bed all day.

"Mila, what is the purpose of going through these old dusty schoolbooks if Mother won't even allow us to attend the Jewish school down the street? She thinks we're going to be taken from her in the middle of learning about mathematical factors. I'd rather go outside and help you with the horses than stay locked in this house all day. It isn't fair that you get to go riding and we don't."

It was a rash decision Madam Bohdan made just after Ben returned without Mister Bohdan and Tobias. She won't allow the boys to leave the house, not even to play outside. Filip is becoming rebellious and I'm not sure I blame him for the way he feels. They are hurting too and rather than find distractions to help pass the time, they are forced to sit inside and stare at curtain-draped windows while Ben spends his days thumbing through his father's paperwork to make sure all business endeavors he had his hands in have been tied up in some way.

"What will happen if you go back to school a year from now and you're the only one who can't multiply by eight?" I shouldn't make comments like this when there is very little hope, and the thought of taking care of Nova and Twister didn't strike me as a source of freedom until now.

Filip's head shifts to the side and he leans back in his chair, his collar rising above his mouth. Neither of the boys put much effort into the way they dress anymore and since Madam Bohdan isn't speaking, no one is going to argue with their unbuttoned and unkempt attire. I certainly couldn't care less.

"We both know these dumb rules won't end within a year," Filip says. He's small for his age and I often forget he's a few years older than Pavel.

"Would you rather I teach you more German?" I offer.

"No, no more German," Pavel speaks up. "Why should we have to speak their language just because they made the decision to move into our country?"

While I know he understands more than he often lets on, many of his questions don't have an answer I can respond with.

"Did you hear that?" Ben pokes his head into the dining room with an arching eyebrow. "It sounded like a scream of some sort."

"It wasn't us," Pavel responds.

Ben stomps through the foyer, likely checking between all the drawn curtains in each room before becoming desperate enough to open the front door.

I didn't hear a noise. Perhaps a swarm of birds have found something good for breakfast in the wooded area behind the estate.

"Mila, come quick!" Ben shouts. He sounds far enough away for me to assume he's about to step out the front door.

"Stay here and finish your breakfast," I tell the boys.

I run to follow Ben, seeing he's left the front entrance wide open and close the door behind me. Just as I reach the round table with the empty vase that used to contain fresh flowers, a shrilling moan carries on the wind.

Twister.

My feet move faster than they have in a long time, bringing me to the stables breathlessly. I don't see Twister or Ben, only Nova, who seems to be nervous as she swings her neck from side to side.

Taking a few steps inside the stable, I see Ben is on his knees kneeling beside Twister. She's on her side.

"Is she okay?" Ben asks, stroking the back of her head. I reach for the work gloves I use when tending to the stables and try to calm myself before moving any closer. If she senses my nerves, it will cause her more pain. "Mila?" Ben asks again, his voice in a hush this time.

I hold a finger up to my mouth. "One minute," I whisper.

As I reach Twister's back side, I find confirmation of my assumption. "Ben, you need to take Nova and go outside. She'll become nervous and panic, wondering what's happening with Twister, who needs a calm environment."

"I'm not leaving her—she's in pain," he argues.

"If we stay here while she's trying to give birth, it may delay the process, which could hurt the foal. She knows what she's doing." I remove the gloves and pull Ben up to his feet. "We'll know when it's over."

I struggle to force Ben up, but he complies after I tug harder. He releases Nova from her stall and leads her out of the stables, glancing over his shoulder as he passes, as I rub Twister's muzzle. "I'm not going far, sweet girl." As much as I don't want to leave either, I know what's right and follow Ben and Nova.

"We've known this was coming, but we are completely unprepared to care for a foal," Ben says, tying Nova's rope to the tree beside the stables.

"Twister can care for her foal for now. Let's not worry just yet."

"You can't always be the voice of reason," Ben utters. "You're making me look bad." I know he doesn't mean what he's saying, but I also know the capture of his father and Tobias is taking a toll on him, making him suffer. Madam Bohdan's behavior is not helping him cope any better.

I watch him a lot and wonder how I'm able to control my emotions so well in comparison to him. He either has a positive outlook or he fears the worst, and lately there's been more fear. It seems impossible for him to hide his thoughts even if he doesn't share them verbally. Maybe I'm more used to disappointment in life. Not having much in the first place, losing what I did have doesn't feel like a big loss. Though not knowing where my family is keeps my mind reeling with questions night after night. I wonder if I'll ever see them again, if I'll ever find out why they left me behind—whether it was a decision they opted to make or were forced to make. Wandering down the path of endless questions never brings me anything more than a sleepless night so I continue to tell myself, there's a reason for every event no matter how big or small, and the act of patience is the only path that will lead us to a resolution.

The crackling sound of rubber against rubble pulls my attention toward the road. I can barely see just over the hill that leads to the front of the estate but it's clear a vehicle has come to a stop.

"Again," Ben says. "You should go inside quickly."

"You can't continue to tell them I'm not home. They will keep showing up until they see that I exist. They want the estate, and one of these times, they will do whatever they feel is necessary to acquire what they want if I'm not here to prove you're being truthful."

Ben drops his head back against the stable. "Damn it."

"*Guten morgen,*" two Nazis address us as they appear over

the peak of the shallow hill. "We heard an awful shrilling sound while driving up the hill."

"It's our horse," Ben says. "She's giving birth."

The number of Nazis in this village must be multiplying by the day. They're seemingly everywhere all at once, never missing a sound or disturbance. "Oh, how nice," the other Nazi says. "Let us have a look."

"I wouldn't disturb her. It can be detrimental to the health of the mare and foal," I say, hoping they won't go any further past us.

The men share a laugh and walk past us as if I didn't say a word. They're cooing at Twister. "The baby horse is already born, ja?"

"Oh look, there it is," the other, with additional laughter.

I hate to watch what they're doing and I wish they would leave us alone. "You must be the non-Jewish wife with the title to this estate, ja?"

I debate whether to answer, hoping they'll leave Twister alone and come back outside to question me here. Ben and I share a look and I don't think either of us knows what to do.

"You shouldn't touch the foal," one of them says to the other.

I'm imagining the worst. If either of them steps in too close, Twister is going to panic.

"Yes, I'm the owner of the estate," I speak up.

I can't see what's happening in the stable because I refuse to look, but I don't have to guess much when I hear Twister neigh and grunt like she used to when she first arrived here. I hear her hoofs clomp against the hay-dusted cement. She shouldn't be standing up just yet.

"Oh, what's the matter, poor horse?" one of them continues to verbally poke at Twister. "Do you want a carrot?"

Ben is biting his cheek, and breathing heavily. I know he's

doing everything in his power not to react, and I'm grateful he's capable of restraint. Another grunt from Twister, a warning to the men that they should back away.

The stable shakes as the sound of a heavy thud followed by cracking wood travels between the inner walls. *"Was zur Hölle machst du?"* one of them shouts. I twist my head slightly to peer inside the stables, finding one of the Nazis on the ground, against the wooden wall by Twister's gate. The other Nazi is clearly smarter as he's standing in front of Nova's closed gate.

The Nazi brings himself to his feet. "I should kill this dangerous creature," he says, spitting on her.

As if Twister can understand the words the soldier is speaking, she squeals out in what sounds like horrific pain. I'm petrified of looking at her. Nova is groaning, likely upset from the noises coming from Twister. The Nazis bolt out of the stables as if their pants are on fire, staring inside like the horses are the threat.

"What is wrong with that horse?"

"She just gave birth to a foal," the other Nazi responds.

"That's not what I mean, you imbecile." The Nazi who was thrown against the wall pulls a pistol out from a holster on his hip and points it directly at Twister.

"Please don't shoot her," I wail, running into the stable.

"Mila!" Ben shouts after me.

"I will have no qualms about shooting you too if you don't get out of the way," the man continues. With one look at Twister, I see what's happening. "Why are you just standing there, stupid girl?"

"Mila," Ben snaps my name out again.

"She's dying. You don't need to shoot her," I hiss in response.

"How do you know this? Are you an animal doctor?"

"She is bleeding to death," I groan, feeling my insides twist and turn, forcing me to buckle over. Tears flood down my cheeks and I block out the sight of the Nazis, no longer caring about what they threaten. This is their fault. They are to blame. I open Twister's gate and run my hand along her muzzle. "It's okay. We'll take care of her, your sweet baby." Krása, it's the name Ben and I came up with because it means beauty. She's unfurling from the fetal position she's been in for so long, stretching out each limb while she figures out how to use them.

The hemorrhaging seems to cease, but I'm not sure if it's too late, especially since Twister's knees buckle from beneath her, forcing her to fall onto her side. She's breathing heavily and I'm not sure how much longer she has or if Krása will be able to nurse before it's too late.

"I demand to see the title of this estate and your identification immediately." The one who had been shoved by Twister steps into the stables, brushing the hay off his backside. He's staring at me with fury, waiting for me to jump.

Ben appears to be in shock, seemingly staring through the soldier as if he's a piece of clear glass.

"I'll be right back, darling. I'll go collect the title to prove ownership of the estate," I say to Ben.

"Okay," he replies in a breathy whisper.

"I find it odd you own this entire property all on your own," the denser of the two Nazis says.

"Why is that?" I ask before walking toward the front door.

"It's obvious you aren't a born Czech, are you?"

"I was, in fact, born in this country."

"I don't believe you."

I decide to continue walking toward the estate, hoping they stop talking, but I'm afraid of what they will do to Ben while I'm gone.

With a few more steps to contemplate how this might go, I come to a quick realization that I'm the one who should be afraid. The proximity of their footsteps in the shadows of mine give me a horrible inclination of what's to come.

"Stop!" Ben shouts at the Nazis.

I can't breathe.

My ears are ringing. My vision is blurry. My hands tingle with sweat. And I fear one of us might not walk away from this encounter.

I'm scared to turn around and witness the look upon the soldiers' faces in response to Ben's shout. I know they have no tolerance for insubordination, and they will do whatever they feel necessary to resolve such an issue. My heart is in my throat, my head feels disconnected, but I turn to peek over my shoulder, finding Ben walking in my direction. "I'd like to go with my wife."

I wish he would keep an eye on Twister to ensure they don't harm her more. She may be dying and I'm tending to the demands of enemy occupants.

"Either she goes in, or you do," one says to Ben. His teeth grit together and his jaw muscles clench.

"I'll be quick," I say.

Only one of the soldiers follows me inside. I don't say a word as I make my way to Mister Bohdan's office, being quick to prevent the Nazi from having much time to look around.

I lift the envelope from the desk drawer and turn to find the placid soulless look in the Nazi's gray eyes. Is there even a human left in that body? How can anyone find it within themselves to act with such hatred for others who have done nothing deserving of this behavior?

The man yanks the envelope from my hand and takes a step backward. "I'll follow you back out," he says.

My face burns as I take long strides toward the door, feeling as though I'm walking toward an execution. We've tried so hard to be compliant, but nothing is good enough for them.

I'm not sure how long I've gone without taking in a breath, but it isn't until I see Ben still standing outside that I'm able to fill my lungs with enough air to hold me upright.

The two soldiers inspect the paperwork, finding the truth of our words to match what is inked on paper. The two speak under their breath and I can't hear a word of what they're saying. They stare up at me for a moment, hinting at what they may be discussing. My stomach threatens to purge as terror takes a hold of my every nerve.

"Very tricky," one says before making a tsk-tsk sound. "You must think we are fools, ja?" The man tosses the papers and envelope in my direction. The sheets drift in the wind before scattering across the lawn.

"No, sir," Ben replies before I do.

"Very well. Carry on and take care of that godforsaken horse."

Both Ben and I stand frozen as if our feet are anchored to a stone walkway, waiting for them to slip back into their vehicle and leave the property.

It feels like an hour passes before Ben lunges for me, wrapping me up in his arms, and pressing his face into my shoulder. "I'm so sorry, Mila. What have I done?"

"Enough," I say. "We're okay. They're gone. We still have the estate."

He's holding me so tight, it's hard to breathe but he's trembling and the awareness of the weakness running through him causes my chest to ache.

Ben releases his grip and retrieves the scattered papers from the lawn, slipping them back into the envelope. "Twister," he says through a gasp.

I step ahead of him and run to the stables, praying she is okay. I close my eyes before turning the corner and pull in a deep breath to hold as I inspect the stall, expecting the worst.

Krása is curled up against Twister's side as she cleans her foal's head. She's still alive. "Ben! I think she's going to be all right," I cry out in a breathy shrill.

Ben's footsteps grow louder as he runs across the grass to

find us, giving Nova a rub down as he passes her. The moment he steps into the stable, Twister pulls herself up and we watch as Krása does the same to nurse from her mother. Ben huffs with a sigh of relief. "Does this mean they're going to be okay?"

"I think so." How does so much beauty still exist in the world that's teetering on the brink of destruction?

THIRTY-TWO

THE CATATONIC WORLD AWAKENS
BENEDIKT, SEPTEMBER 1939

Nothing has changed, but nothing is the same. Life has felt stale for the past six months and we've had the watchful eyes of hawk-like men circling our perimeter day after day—desperately trying to see in through our windows and finding reasons to force us to open the doors at their beck and call. Everything I've read says the wealthy are in sight above all others. We are their golden geese. Part of me would like to think they would have done something to us by now if we were of such value, but the other part of me thinks they are maliciously instilling the fear of God into us with every word they speak and each step they take in our direction.

There's nowhere to hide outside of the estate. Getting fresh air feels like nothing more than a risk. I can't even ride my motorbike. I only got the chance to enjoy it a few times before we were told vehicles were being taken away from Jews.

All we can do is sit here and think about what lies ahead.

Mila says she believes other Jewish people are out and about in the village, but the only way she can determine the difference between a Jew and a non-Jew is by the look of fear they desperately try to hide when anyone looks in their direction.

I fear leaving the estate, thinking the Nazis are waiting for the moment I'm not here to invade our home. Perhaps I'm giving myself too much credit, but with Mother barely coexisting with the rest of us, I feel responsible for Filip and Pavel, as well as Mila's well-being.

With the feeling of pins beneath my feet, I pace the foyer whenever Mila walks down to the village to collect food or other necessities for us. She has been our eyes and ears, and though I'm grateful for the insight, I'm uncomfortable with her walking around alone, knowing she looks different than all other Czechs just by the slightly darker shade of her skin. Assumptions are easy to make, and easier when the *animal* has a certain radar for its prey. Gypsies and Jews—the demise of Nazi Germany, that is what the enemy sees us as—nothing more than labels.

She promises to keep her scarf over her head and around her neck with the collar of her coat as high as it can go. I hope this is enough for her to blend in, but I'm aware anything can happen at any time. Despite our allies, it doesn't seem a good change is imminent in any way. Hitler has proven to be too strong to fight against.

"Why are you pacing again?" Filip asks, walking down the staircase, still in his pajamas at ten in the morning. None of us cares to dress properly and Mother doesn't have the energy to argue, nor be a part of our family. She cries morning, noon, and night, weeping for Father to return. The constant reminder of what we're missing feels like a sword dredged into my chest. If I pull it out, I might bleed to death. Therefore, pain is the only way to live now.

"I'm waiting for Mila to return from the village."

"Is she shopping for food?" Filip asks.

"Yes," I answer simply.

"Brother, if we have hidden all our assets, where is the

money coming from? You don't have a source of income and we don't have Father. How—"

"I have access to what we need. It's nothing you need to worry about."

"Are you using the fake gold to—"

"No. It's nothing you need to concern yourself with. Do you understand?"

The less Filip knows, the less Pavel knows, and the less I need to worry about a potential interrogation going sideways. Father, Tobias, and I each split enough of our funds to keep us afloat without having to unearth what we buried. I have found the small amount of currency from what they kept aside in their rooms and have re-hidden it in loose boards, wall panels, and socks. Still, the Nazis won't be foolish enough to think we are living in this estate as poor citizens. Hiding what we have should be impossible, and may very well be, but all we can do is try our best to win at a potential game of hide-and-seek.

"Pavel said you've hidden money all around the estate. Is that true?" I understand Filip wants to be in the know alongside me. I felt this way growing up in Tobias's shadow, but I'm doing something Tobias never did for me—I am selflessly protecting my brother.

"Are we through with this conversation?" I ask.

Filip shakes his head and continues down the steps and into the kitchen, likely to rummage through the empty pantry for something we don't have. "When will Mila be back?"

"Soon, I hope."

"If she's the only one who is safe to walk downtown in the village, why are you always so uptight when she leaves?"

Maybe he's trying to convince himself that the world isn't what it is said to be beyond these doors. I'm not one to pull the wool over his eyes, but at the same time, I feel there is a thin line between what he must know and what could give him night terrors.

"Nothing is as it was down there, and it worries me. That's all," I say. "You don't need to feel the same."

Filip drops his hands into the back pockets of his pajama pants and his head drops forward to look away from me. He's struggling between childhood and manhood and it's hard to see how much it's bothering him. "I know the well-being of our family has fallen on your shoulders, and I'm aware you don't see me as old enough or mature enough to help in any way, but it's very diffi-cult being treated like a child. You don't have to do this all alone."

I place my hands on Filip's shoulders, failing to have real-ized he's grown a couple inches in the last few months. The top of his head reaches my chin, and I don't have to look down at him as much as I used to. "I'm sorry. My intention wasn't to make you feel this way. I've been trying to do what Father would expect of me."

"You mean Tobias," he replies with a sharp tongue. I'm aware we've all lived in our brother's dark shadow for many years.

"Yes, but I've taken on the responsibility, so it doesn't weigh on you or Pavel."

"Mother should be helping you, and she can't do so. Mila is pulling more than her own weight, and I'm sitting twiddling my thumbs for hours a day. Allow me to help you, please."

He must think I'm much busier than I am. I spend a lot of time in Father's office, going through his paperwork so I know what we have, what he's sold, given away, borrowed. I know enough to put us in danger, but not enough to keep us safe, not yet. That's not something I'm willing to share with anyone at the moment.

The back door swishes open and slaps shut with what must have been a heavy thrust. "Mila?" I call out, walking toward the ruckus.

"Yes, it's me." She has a basket with food and a rolled-up

piece of paper poking out of her pocket. "There were Nazis everywhere, more so than usual, which is hard to imagine. I didn't want them following me, so I went through the woods."

"What's on the paper?" I ask.

Mila makes her way into the kitchen to place the basket down and the two of us follow her inside. She's been angry and less optimistic every time she returns from the village. "We knew it was coming," she mumbles. "By the way, we need to see if the farmer up the road has more vegetables for Twister. The hay isn't enough while she's expelling all of her nutrients to nurse Krása."

"We'll find food for Twister and you said Krása should be about ready to start foraging now too, right?"

Mila looks at me with despondence. "I'm not sure if it's too soon, but perhaps she's ready. However, there are other issues to concern ourselves with now."

"What do you mean?"

She pulls the scarf off her head and unwinds it from her neck, then pulls out the paper and hands it to me. "The bulletin was posted on every window and lamppost. I couldn't even see the headlines of the papers. The crowds around the newsstand swelled into the roads."

I unroll the paper and skim through the lines, finding everything I need to know at the very top:

Great Britain and France have declared war on Germany after Hitler's invasion of Poland, thus marking the start of another world war

My stomach aches, thinking back on the horrible stories I heard about the First World War. We've spent so much time learning about those days to ensure it wouldn't happen again, yet here we are.

"We're on the wrong side of the war," I state, forgetting that Filip is listening to my every word.

"War?" he questions me.

There's no use in hiding this information from him. Life is going to change yet again and I'm not sure how or when that will be. It's just a fact.

I hand him the bulletin, watching as his eyes bulge as he reads every line. "We're not Germans. Why are we on the wrong side?" he asks.

"Our country has been seized by Germany. Therefore, we either take their side or die fighting them."

"Ben, hold on," Mila says pointedly before turning her attention to Filip. "We don't know what this means just yet, and until we know more, let's assume everything will remain the same for now." She has a better way of talking to Filip than I do. He listens to her. Once she turns her cold, worry-stricken stare back to me, she says, "You may want to share the news with your mother."

I inadvertently shake my head, disagreeing before thinking through her suggestion. "It will only make things worse with her catatonic condition."

Mila sweeps a loose strand of hair behind her ear and fills her lungs with air as her posture stiffens. She reacts the same way every time we discuss Mother. We don't know what's wrong with her because there are no Jewish doctors left in practice, and German doctors are no longer allowed to treat Jewish patients. From a few medical books I found in our library, all of her symptoms point to a catatonic depressive state. Aside from taking her to a hospital and hoping someone will take pity on her, there aren't many options.

"We need to find a professional. I'm sure there are Jewish doctors living in the area. They may not have a license to practice now, but perhaps some of them are still working privately for other Jewish families. At least someone with knowledge could offer more than just assumptions," Mila says.

"She was speaking to me yesterday and sat up for a bit," I say, knowing these minor details won't change Mila's thoughts on the matter. It's all too much to think about at once.

Life is blazing through uncharted territories at a speed neither of us can keep up with. I love Mila with everything I have, but I wish we could have a moment to ourselves to indulge the lifestyle of newlyweds without the emerging ruins of war. I would give anything to hide from the truth and forget about what is happening outside of this estate. I can't see how the future might turn out. I'm not even sure what to hope for now. Whatever comes next, I'm sure it's going to be much worse than what we're currently experiencing.

THIRTY-THREE

A LINK OF SAUSAGE

MILA, NOVEMBER 1939

I must have slept in somehow. It's rare when I don't snap upright at six in the morning. The emotional distress must be taking a bigger toll on me than I'll admit to out loud. Ben is already up and about, and I'm not surprised he didn't wake me before leaving. He's been asking me to take a step back and stop assuming so many responsibilities in this house, but with Madam Bohdan in the fragile state she's in, I don't see any other choice.

I poke my head into the kitchen. The sizzling crackles and snaps from the oil in frying pans takes me by surprise as I find Ben juggling a spatula and tongs to cook a breakfast of sausage and eggs. The aroma of herbs and spices tickles the inside of my nose and my mouth waters upon eyeing the dishes he's filling with food. "You made breakfast?" The words against my throat sound as rusty as it feels to speak. I'm parched from the recent spell of dry weather.

"You finally listened and slept in past six. I stole the opportunity to beat you to the kitchen and whip up something so you didn't need to sweat over the stove at this hour."

Ben hands me two plates and places one on a bed tray next

to a cup of coffee and a slice of toast. "Why don't you bring those to the boys, and I'll be in with ours in just a moment after I bring this to my mother?"

We're only allowed to experience small moments of what life could be like for us if we were traveling down a common path. But since we aren't heading in that direction, along with the rest of Europe, I'm grateful for the small gestures that feel much grander. "Thank you for making us breakfast," I say, admiring the way his unkempt hair falls across his forehead. I still feel the need to pinch myself some days as I wonder how I was lucky enough to end up with a kind-hearted man who is also blessed with a charming appearance. I always assumed it would be rare to find a person with so many wonderful traits, never mind finding a person who cares for me as much as Ben does.

My heels echo along the quiet hallway floors as I make my way to the dining room, finding Filip and Pavel sitting patiently with prepared place settings for four. "Did you two set the table?"

"Ben told us he would hang us upside down by our underwear outside for the day if we didn't straighten up the dining room and set the table for breakfast."

Filip drops his head into his hand as Pavel rats Ben out. "What's the purpose of adhering to our brother's threats if we're just going to make him look bad after?" Filip asks Pavel through a sneer.

I try my best not to giggle. "My lips are sealed. I appreciate you both helping him."

"I'm starving," Pavel whines. "Is that for us? Where is Ben?"

"Yes, these are your plates. Ben is just bringing a plate up to your mother," I say, placing one down in front of each of them.

"She doesn't even eat the food," Pavel says, sighing as he throws himself against the back of his chair.

"Well, we can't just starve her," Filip argues. "She does eat some of it, sometimes."

It isn't hard to sense their frustration with Madam Bohdan's condition, but she's suffering from heartbreak and, like myself, she is desperate for answers about our families that we have no means of obtaining. "She's going through a lot. It's all quite unthinkable. You are all going through so much right now. Everyone handles their pain and emotions differently," I explain.

"You lost your family too. You didn't lock yourself in a room and refuse to exist," Pavel says.

Ben walks in with our two breakfast plates and I'm thankful for his impeccable timing. There are only so many excuses I can continue to make for Madam Bohdan.

"Where did you find sausage?" Filip asks, eyeing his plate.

"Mila was one of the first in line at the butcher's yesterday and luckily got a share before they ran out as they have been each morning."

"I'm going back down to the village after breakfast to see if they replenished any of the canned goods they were out of yesterday," I tell them. "I know it's been challenging to give up the meals you've always enjoyed so much, but with so many German soldiers living in the area now, there doesn't seem to be enough food to go around."

"You mean the Nazis," Pavel corrects me.

"Yes," Filip grunts.

"Just appreciate what you have on your plate and let's stop complaining for a moment, shall we?" Ben asks, shoveling the food into his mouth as if he's been starving for a week. It pains me to see how hungry they all are. They haven't gotten used to the shortage of food and I can see the difference in their faces—their cheekbones are more prominent now. I wish there was something more I could do, but the Germans have made it impossible to live comfortably now.

All three of them polish off their plates within a few short minutes so I split up one of my sausage links to share with them.

"No, you need to eat that," Ben says as I plop a slice down on Pavel's plate across the table.

"I'm fine," I tell him.

After placing another slice onto Filip's plate, I stab my fork into the last bit and reach for Ben's plate. "No. I want you to eat your breakfast. We all need food, not just the three of us."

"Why are we fighting over one link of sausage when Mother likely won't even touch her portion?" Pavel asks.

Ben's cheeks redden as he drops his fork onto his empty plate. "Mila, please eat. Please," he begs.

The tension is palpable, and I wasn't trying to cause more anguish. I slice through the last bit of meat and feel my throat tighten upon swallowing the food. It's agonizing to hear how much spite they feel. "I found the name of another doctor we can try to contact," I tell Ben. "He practiced from his house before the occupation so I think there's a good chance we can reach him by phone."

We've gone through a list of contacts Mister Bohdan had kept in a book, but not one of the doctors he had contact information for has returned our calls. There's a part of me that wonders if they know Madam Bohdan too personally to want to return our inquiry. I haven't seen her act pleasant toward anyone in the time I've been here.

"No, no more phone calls," Ben says.

"Why wouldn't you want to help Mother?" Filip argues.

"It's complicated," Ben snaps with haste.

Filip shoves his plate and pushes himself away from the table, the chair legs scraping against the wooden floors, piercing the sudden silence. He scoops up his plate and place setting and storms out of the dining room.

"May I be excused too?" Pavel asks.

"Yes, yes, go on," Ben says.

Pavel is much quieter about leaving, but also takes his plate and setting before walking out.

I twist in my chair to face Ben, wondering what's troubling him so much. His elbow is anchored to the table and the side of his face rests over his closed fist. "Do you know they're deporting Jewish people from Poland? They're just forcing them out of their homes and sending them to—God only knows where. It's obvious we'll be next on their list here."

Ben is a realist and while I appreciate the necessity of not being close-minded, living from minute to minute in terror isn't going to help anyone under this roof. "You don't know what's going to happen next. None of us do."

"And my brothers are right. My mother's behavior is appalling. She's wasting food and acting as though she has no responsibility to her children here. Quite frankly, I'm tired of the act. She needs to pull herself together and handle this situation like the rest of us are."

I reach for Ben's plate and place it on top of mine. "She might be truly ill, and you will feel very remorseful if you find this out and it's too late."

With the plates in my hand, I stand from the table, but Ben takes a hold of my free hand. "Mila," he says with a sigh, dropping his gaze to the table, "if she is truly sick and we find someone to diagnose her with whatever ailment she's suffering with, she could be marked down on a list of 'mental defectives' and killed by one of the SS. There are clippings in the paper about this happening in Poland. No one can know that she might have a notable issue."

I wasn't aware of this news. The explanation lodges in my throat as I try to digest what he's just said. "Killing them?"

"Yes."

"Then we must get her help now, Ben. If we wait longer, there may be no turning back for her and all hope will be lost. A Jewish doctor isn't going to report her illness, and it's our only chance to give her any possibility of recovering from whatever she's going through." Even if it is just a broken heart. Some aren't built as strong as others, especially when life's foundation has been made of thin glass.

Ben takes the plates from my hand then pulls me onto his lap. He pulls me into his arms, and I drop my head against his chest. "I'm sorry if I've been hard to live with. This isn't who I am."

I draw back and twist to look him straight in the eyes. "Do not apologize for picking up all the broken pieces in this house. This is who you are. You are the strongest man I've ever met. Your love is unconditional for everyone in your family, and that's what I love most about you."

THIRTY-FOUR

THERE'S ONLY ONE RAT HERE

When the only option I have left is to sort through newspaper clippings hoping to connect the dots to determine where Father and Tobias may have been taken, the outcome remains dim. Day after day for ten months, and I've had no further inkling of where to look for them. Articles in the paper touch upon local arrests due to resistance. Prisons are overflowing with Jewish "criminals." Some are held at bail. Others are being kept for harsher punishments. I've placed phone calls to local prisons and those near the Becker estate, but I've been told multiple times if the arraigned men are being held at the location, we will be notified if paying bail money is an option to release them. From word of mouth, it's been said that some prisoners are allowed to send postcards to their family, but we haven't received anything. My only other option aside from continuing my search is to assume they were executed because that, too, isn't uncommon with any form of Jewish belligerence. The insufferable thought pushes the parabolic knife in deeper toward my already severed heart.

The private Jewish administration building in the village sometimes receives updates on missing residents, but even they aren't privy to reliable sources of news. They answer questions and supply us with changes pertaining to Jewish law, and if we have issues with ration cards or identification cards, they can assist with that as well. Many days, I have the urge to stand in line outside of that small building among other Jewish citizens just to feel less lonely in this hostile environment. Though, Nazis line the streets on horses, guard each corner, and seemingly have two pairs of eyes for every one of ours.

I stack the articles into a pile and place them back into an envelope and set it to the side, leaving me with a clear space on the desk. Faint scratches emboss the wood from years of use, and I run my fingers over the divots, wondering who pressed too firmly with their pen or pencil. Father was always careful when writing, padding his paperwork to protect the wood. But I would sneak in here at night and sit by candlelight and compose poetry for hours, scouring my mind for uncommon words and unlikely metaphors. Hours would pass like minutes, and I wasn't as careful with a pen and paper as Father.

I pull open the desk drawer and retrieve the leather-bound notebook I've been leaving in here after the many restless nights I've struggled to sleep. The scent of newspaper-ink, and the rich vanilla and moss from Father's smoking pipe make me feel like he hasn't been gone so long. This comfort allows me to write, which clears my mind well enough that I'm able to return to bed and find a few hours of sleep before morning. When I open to the last written page, I'm reminded that my words are somewhat unfamiliar, as if someone else has written them. The stanzas are constructed from somewhere deep within me, a subconscious voice that can tap into the hidden corners of my mind.

"Ben," Mila calls for me from outside the office, "I have to go down to the village to pick up our rations." She appears in the doorway already in her long wool coat, gloves, and scarf wrapped around her head and neck. I glance out the window, noticing the gray sky sinking toward the wet dark road.

"I'm going to join you. I just need a moment," I say, pulling the drawer open to replace my notebook.

"Are you writing?" she asks, placing her hand over her chest. She's the one who has been insistent on me writing at night when I can't sleep.

"Not this morning. I was reading what I wrote last night."

"Is it worthy of reading?" she asks with a smirk, knowing I'd rather burn the notebook than show her my nonsense.

"Absolutely not. It's hardly legible and nothing but a mess of words that don't form intelligible sentences."

"Someday, when I see the proof, I'm going to disagree."

"If you outlive me, the words are yours to keep. Fair?"

She steps in closer toward the desk. "You aren't going anywhere without me, mister."

"My beautiful, stubborn wife—if you ever need these incoherent words, they are yours to keep."

A smile forms along her ruby lips as she clasps her hands in front of her waist. "Are you sure you want to join me in the village?"

"Yes. Would you mind if we stop by the administration building before returning home?"

Mila seems to struggle as she swallows an apparent lump in her throat. Her gaze falls and her thumbs swivel around each other as they often do when she has something to say but doesn't want to hurt my feelings.

"I have no expectations of any new information."

"I know," she says.

She hates to see the disappointment I try very hard to hide. I already know her thoughts quite well.

. . .

The wind is bitter and the fog whispers against my face. "It looks like it may snow again tonight," Mila says, gripping my hand as we make our way down the road.

"I'll place down bales of hay in front of the stables to keep the snow away from the horses. I wish we had a blanket light enough for Krása. Do you think she's faring the cold well enough?"

"She squeezes in between Twister and the stall wall at night. I'm sure she's just fine."

"Sounds like you, stealing all the space in our bed so you can use me for warmth," I tease Mila.

"It's not my fault you enjoy sleeping on the very edge of the bed," she retorts.

As we turn the corner into the village, thick flakes of snow slowly float down on us. If only the snow was heavy enough to shield our view entirely. Our village is no longer the property of the residents who have lived here their entire lives. The Germans have made it clear the property and land belongs to them as they watch us walk.

The line to the small market is out the door, wrapping around the arch of the curb. Jewish families are only allowed to shop at this hour of the day, every third day. Mila no longer has additional rights since she married me. Yet, she has more rights than the other Romani had before being forced out of the area. Anyone who isn't Aryan, blonde hair, blue eyes, built to be German is a misfortune to the world in accordance with their irrational theories.

There are so many of us and we are their puppets.

"Benedikt Bohdan, is that you, young man?" Mila and I both turn around in the line, to face whoever knows me.

Age has not been kind to this familiar face. His navy cap doesn't do much to conceal his chapped, bald head, or the tired sagging skin beneath his eyes. I never knew the man to be unshaven or to stand hunched over in the shape of a question mark. He was untouchable, a hero of sorts to our family. "Doctor Adel. How are you, sir?" I say, offering my hand to the family practitioner who used to care for all of us Bohdan boys before he retired a few years back. I haven't seen him around town and wasn't sure he was still in the area.

"Same as you, I'm afraid. Is your family well?" He tries to stand a bit taller, but cringes through the attempt. *Poor man.*

"Half of us—oh—pardon me. Doctor Adel, this is my wife, Mila. Mila, this is Doctor Adel. He used to care for my brothers and me years ago."

Mila reaches out her slim gloved hand to greet him. "It's a pleasure to meet you, Doctor." A second barely passes when Mila's elbow presses into my side as a not-so-subtle hint that we are desperately searching for a doctor to check on Mother.

"The pleasure is all mine, Misses Bohdan." Doctor Adel returns his solemn icy stare to mine. "Only half of your family is doing well? What about the other half?" His sincerity is unquestionable, and so is the look of concern tugging his lips into a grimace. I've never met a more caring man than he, and nothing has changed in all these years.

My eyes feel heavy as I try to maintain my composure. "Father and Tobias were detained almost a year ago. We're unsure of their whereabouts and have had a terrible time tracking them down. Mother seems to be suffering from a severe bout of melancholia, or so I assume. Filip, Pavel, and I are well with thanks to my darling wife for taking such wonderful care of the three of us all the time." I glance at Mila, wishing I could end the conversation and only focus on her.

"My dear boy, what tragedy you are dealing with, and on top of this hellish life we're living. My thoughts are with you and your family. If there is anything I can do to support you, please do say so."

I clear my throat and drop my hands into my pockets. "I

appreciate the kind offer, Doctor. I'm afraid there isn't much you can do to help me find my father or Tobias, of course."

"But, perhaps, if you had any free time, you might come check in on Madam Bohdan?" Mila adds. "We would be ever so grateful."

While listening to Mila's plea, I can't help but again wonder how she has such empathy for someone who has been shown very little kindness. I hope her benevolence will someday rub off on me.

"I would be happy to stop by." Doctor Adel glances around and over each shoulder as if looking for prying eyes and ears. "Are you still at the estate?"

"Yes, sir," I reply.

"Very well. I will see about a visit this week."

"We would be so grateful. Thank you for your kindness," Mila says.

"*Aufstehen du Ratte!* Get up right now, you old rat!" The shout forces us to turn in the direction the line is facing, but I lean to the side and see the cause of the Nazi's vulgar shouting.

An elderly woman is sitting on the curb, cowering in fear of the whip held above the Nazi's head. The people around her lift her up to her feet and pull her into the line.

Silence rolls down the curb. Everyone in front of us straightens their posture and holds their sights ahead as if each has a pistol aimed at them. I squeeze Mila's hand. She squeezes back and inhales a quick shivering breath.

I hate wondering if she may have been safer with her family than with me on this dark road to purgatory.

THIRTY-FIVE
GIVE HIM A LITTLE KISS
MILA, JUNE 1940

I sometimes wish I could sleep in just a bit later than Ben. There are too many mornings where I find myself staring at the side of his face, memorizing faded freckles, admiring how complacent his expression is when the daily terrors aren't reeling through his mind. His hair falls into short loose waves and glistens beneath the sun leaking through the draped curtains. I hold myself back from running my fingers through his silky hair, knowing it would wake him, but there's nothing I want more than to be asleep, curled up in his arms.

"Go back to sleep," he mumbles. I'm not sure how he senses me staring at him, but he does it every morning, just a few minutes after I've woken up.

"If I could, I would," I whisper.

He pulls his arm out from beneath his pillow and curls it around my shoulders, pulling me in closer. My head rests on his chest and the calm rhythm of his heartbeat and the warmth of his skin convince me to try and sleep a bit longer.

I never want to take our intimate moments for granted, knowing they were once hard to come by. It makes no difference whether we share a bed in Ben's bedroom, the guest room, or in the cellar. Madam Bohdan wouldn't know any different.

While her mental health has mildly improved over the last year with thanks to some natural remedial treatments from Doctor Adel, the melancholy seems to have become a part of her overall being. She acts like a shell of the person she once was, suffering from constant grief and despair. It's as if her existence is almost ghostly. Doctor Adel explained to us that heartbreak can be severe enough to end a person's life, and unless she can find it within herself to see through some of the pain, she will feel weighed down by sorrow like a coffin beneath dirt.

My thoughts blur as I relish the moment, the thread of sunlight spilling over my face.

Ben snaps upright, startling me to follow. "What's wrong?"

"A knock on the door. Did you hear it too?"

"No," I say, peering over at the clock on the nightstand. An hour slipped by while I was in the comfort of his arms. It felt like a mere minute.

The muffling disturbance of knuckles against the door captures my attention this time. "There. I'm not crazy," Ben says.

"It's so early in the morning," I mutter. We both know who would be at the door at this hour, which brings us nothing but anguish. "I wish they would leave us alone."

Within seconds, Ben is out of bed, pulling on a pair of trousers then slipping his arms through the sleeves of his shirt. I do the same, knowing neither of us want the other facing whoever is outside, alone.

The banging continues even as we reach the foyer. I can hardly pull in a deep enough breath to keep me from feeling light-headed as we open the door. It's no surprise to see two

Nazis standing before us, again. It seems like it's a weekly occurrence now.

They spout off their usual German dictations, requesting our identification and title to the estate. They've requested this of us several times and yet they act as if they've never been by to check.

I keep the title in my nightstand drawer so I have it close by whenever we are summoned to provide proof of ownership and residence.

My hand always trembles before handing over the paperwork, but I tighten every muscle in my arm and do as I'm told.

"The title is not valid," one of them says. They have tried this comment before.

"Yes, it is valid, sir," I reply.

The Nazi stares me in the eyes and I can feel the heat radiating off Ben. "You are calling me a liar, ja?"

"No, sir." We've learned to keep our responses simple, our expressions blank, and any hint of fear hidden.

"We have records stating that your surname prior to your marriage is Leon, daughter of Doran and Rebecca Leon, ja?"

My heart falls to the pit of my stomach like a brick falling onto a pavement. "What does it matter if we are legally bound?" Ben asks, keeping his tone complacent.

"You were married shortly before we came to your country," the same Nazi continues to play on his every word as if this is comical.

"I'm not sure I understand the correlation," Ben says.

"Some might suspect it was an arranged plan to keep the estate, which was formerly in the Bohdans' name, and switched once before finding its way into the hands of the new Frau. Bohdan, a woman of non-Jewish descent, but also a woman formerly registered as a 'Gypsy'—it all seems very convenient for both of you and your family, Herr Bohdan, does it not?"

I may faint. A cold sweat is crawling up every one of my

limbs and my throat feels tight. They've gone above and beyond with their research to find this information and they wouldn't have done so without the intention of it serving a consequence.

"We have been together a while and though the story you are portraying might appear suspicious, we wed out of love," Ben says, keeping his words soft and calm—a way I'm not sure I would be capable of at the moment.

Both Nazis share a look and the one speaking places his hands on his hips. "Gypsies have a reputation for lying, stealing, and trickery. Has it occurred to you that you may be the victim, Herr Bohdan? Why choose a Gypsy of all women to save you from the German laws?"

Whatever it is they plan to do, I wish they would get to it.

"This was no ploy on either behalf."

The Nazi pulls out an envelope from his coat pocket and removes a set of folded papers. "When was it you said you were wed?"

"The law states that a Jewish man shall not marry a German woman. My wife is not German," Ben says, passing over the question.

The other soldier shifts his weight from side to side, seemingly uncomfortable with the length of this conversation. I wonder if everything he does for a living makes him this uncomfortable or maybe he is just a bad actor.

"The law states that a Jewish man can marry an ethnic Czech woman. Your wife is not an ethnic Czech. Her records state she was born in Waidhaus, Germany."

"That is untrue. I was born in Rozavadov, Czechoslovakia," I correct him.

"You call me a liar again, ja?" The talkative one turns the papers he is staring at to show me the truth they have smudged out and written over. "What does that read?"

Ben looks at me, wondering if they have the truth or if I have given him the truth. Regardless, where I was born wouldn't have influenced our relationship. He must know I've only been truthful to him.

"That is not where I was born," I argue.

"Your family are Romani Gypsies. They have been deported and imprisoned, as I'm sure you are aware."

I cover my mouth to stop the pain in my chest from becoming audible. The assumption was difficult enough to bear. To know is unbearable. My breath shudders as I try to inhale. *My sisters and brothers—they are prisoners. They wouldn't even understand why.*

"She hasn't spoken to her family nor seen them in almost a year," Ben says. "The papers reflect inaccurate information and are falsely accusing my wife of violating a law she didn't break, even if she was a German-born."

I want Ben to stop talking to them. Every word will only antagonize them more.

"This paper states you were married on the twentieth of March this year, just five days after we obtained control here. Do you see the date?" He takes a paper from the bottom of the thin stack and places it on the top, pointing to the false date.

"This isn't true," Ben argues. "We have the paperwork with the original date and location."

"But it is a Jew's words against ours. That won't work in your favor." He grins maliciously.

"Either your wife is a liar, as we suspect, or you are, Herr Bohdan. And lying to the government is a crime."

I can't look at Ben, knowing what I'm about to do—I don't know if it's right or if it will cause more harm to him. "I am—"

"I am the liar," Ben interrupts me.

"No, no, no, it's me. I am responsible," I cry out, trying to step in front of Ben as if I'm capable of physically protecting him from these awful beings.

"You also hurt an innocent horse, ja?" the Nazi asks me.

"I did not hurt a horse," I say through gritted teeth. "She

was terrorized just after giving birth and almost hemorrhaged to death because of—"

"That was also my fault," Ben says, placing his hands on my shoulders and moving me to the side so he can step forward.

"Why can't you leave us alone? We have done nothing to you. We have done nothing wrong," I hiss, trying to keep choking sobs from erupting in my throat.

"We will leave now, but Herr Bohdan is under arrest for breaking the law."

"He has not broken a law," I growl, pleading through each word so they don't take him away.

The Nazis grab Ben, each holding an arm, spinning him around to face me. His jaw trembles and his lips crinkle as he presses them together so tightly, they turn white. "Please don't take my husband," I say.

"Why don't you give him a little kiss goodbye, ja?" I launch toward Ben, wishing I was strong enough to pull him from their tight grips, but they pull him back, causing me to almost fall. "Never mind." They laugh in succession—the monsters revealing their black souls.

"I love you, Mila," Ben says, hoarsely. "So much. Forever."

"Ben!" I shout as they drag him away. My heart thuds faster than it's ever done before, as if I've just run the fastest and farthest to save my life. "I love you. I love you so much. Please, come back. I'll take the blame. Please, let me take the blame." I'm screaming at the top of my lungs as the world turns black around me. "Please!" He looks helpless, pale, and terrified. He's left without a voice, without control, without me, and I am without him. This must be a nightmare.

The sound of bare feet slapping against the wooden floor on the other side of the front door should force me into looking away. I can barely breathe. I'm not sure my throat is strong enough to form sound. All I can do is watch my life, my future, bleed into the distance.

"Mila, Mila!" Madam Bohdan shouts breathlessly as she reaches the door. "What is happening?" The urgency in her voice is something I haven't heard in a very long time. "Where are they taking Ben?"

"I don't know," I shriek.

Madam Bohdan tries to rush past me, about to run toward the Nazis taking Ben away, but I grab her by the arm, knowing Ben would not want her to intervene. "I tried to take his place. I offered to go instead of him. They said he's under arrest for breaking the law, but we didn't break any laws. They have forged papers and they said our proof would be invalid."

"Come back, please!" I cry out, my voice hoarse from shouting.

Madam Bohdan falls to her knees, horror in her eyes, her mouth agape. She heaves through wailing howls, loud enough to be heard up and down the road in both directions. "My son. Give me my son back!"

Filip and Pavel appear in the open doorway, and I shake my head, whispering, "Go back to your rooms at once. Go, now." They are both staring at me as if they have been hypnotized. "Please go," I cry through a raspy whisper.

Filip pulls Pavel away from the door and they disappear into the shadows of the foyer.

The tires crushing against rocks in the distance fade, inform us that the vehicle the Nazis arrived in is gone, along with my husband.

"We must find out where they are taking him. I will go to the registrar's office and find out any information I can. We'll hand the title back to Mister Becker in case they return here. I'll keep you and the boys safe. We'll get Ben back. Then we'll find Mister Bohdan and Tobias too." I'm blubbering words that may not become a reality—words that are likely not to have merit.

"They can't take him too," she squawks, reaching out as if

he were close enough to touch. "Please God, give me my men back."

I wrap my tired arms around Madam Bohdan's waist and pull her up so I can bring her back inside. I'm unable to make it more than a few steps in before she drops all her weight onto me. I'm forced to lower her down before she collapses. "We all need you right now," I say to her. "Please. I will do whatever I can to help find Ben, but I need you to stay upright."

"I want to die," she grunts. "Just let me die."

"I will do no such thing. You are stronger than this, Madam. Get up," I demand.

My authoritative way of speaking to her does nothing. It's as if she can shut her mind off with as little effort as it takes to flip a light switch.

THIRTY-SIX

A PRISONER OF MY MIND

I can't form a thought and my stomach feels like it's full of bricks. My entire body aches with fear, and heartbreak—I'd take any other form of punishment than what I'm feeling as I'm shuttled from one vehicle to a larger police wagon. Others are already inside the metal container. Some have belongings in their hands, others like me have nothing more than what's in my pockets. I might be the last to step into the back of the wagon. No one is behind me, and the vehicle is surrounded by Nazis. I step inside, finding the temperature within the metal confines much hotter than the outside. Men line the parallel benches, not an inch to spare except for a small spot for me to squeeze into. No one is speaking. Every man has his head down as if living in shame. Most are dressed in business attire, others in casual slacks and shirts like me.

The wagon door closes and a succession of German shouts start up, informing their comrades that the wagon is secure and ready to go. *"Wagen ist gesichert! Mach weiter."* The instructions seem rehearsed, as if we aren't the first to be taken away. No one has told us where we are going, but after switching vehicles in the village, I assume it isn't the local prison.

The temperature inside the wagon rises quicker than I would have thought. Each of us is covered in sweat, and the accompanying foul odor sits among us, stale and unmoving. Each bump along the road feels like a slap against our rears or a thwack along our backs. I'm trying not to look at each man individually, but I'm curious what they did or didn't do to end up in the same place I'm in.

Mila must be making herself crazy trying to figure out how to find me, and of all the times Mother could find her way to the front door, I wish it didn't have to be at that moment. I stare at the metal seal at the back of the wagon, wondering how hard it would be to kick it open. They would shoot me if I was successful. They would murder me if I wasn't. I was the only one left to care for them all and now they've been abandoned again. I promised I wouldn't leave Mila. I said the same to Filip and Pavel. I should never have given my word when I knew it was an impossible promise. I wanted to give them comfort and now I've left them in more grief. Mila, I made more than just a commitment to her. I vowed we would never part until death found one of us. Is that what this is? The end of me?

The man sitting across from me is holding a small notebook, thumbing through each page slowly. The gentleman beside him has a piece of wool in his hand, a torn piece from a blanket, perhaps. He's sweeping his thumb back and forth over the material as if it's helping him at this moment.

There are two small square windows above each bench, a few feet above our heads. It's the only source of light, but I'm not sure any of us needs a better look at our surroundings, though I don't want to be alone with my dark thoughts either.

The rumbling trek feels like we've been traveling for hours, but I'm not sure more than a couple of hours have passed when the vehicle comes to a sudden stop and the engine's hum is silenced.

A dry swallow from every man in this wagon can be heard

among the melody of ragged breaths. Our shirts are soaked from sweat and those wearing light colored slacks have sweat patches behind their knees. Laughter floats around the outside of the wagon and minutes pass before the back door opens to allow us out.

I feel weak upon standing. My muscles are tight and shaking from the position I was sat in for too long, and there's nothing to grab a hold of as we step down onto the pavement. I haven't a clue as to where we are, but the sights around us are dreary, run-down, and abandoned. The greenery is overgrown, and the trees are thick, making it seem like we are in an enclosed area surrounded by medieval-looking brick buildings, all which are collapsing from disrepair.

A stretch of cobblestone sprawls out in front of us, leading to an arched opening that's framed with black and white stripes, matching two windows on each side. Beneath the arch appears to be a tunnel, appearing dark as night from here, leading to what I can only assume to be another nightmare.

We're led through the tunnel and out into a cement court-yard surrounded by more buildings, all with a faded yellow textured façade. Across from the tunnel is another archway, leading to what looks to be another set of run-down buildings.

"You are to follow every instruction given. You will turn in your civilian clothing here," a Nazi shouts at the line of us standing to his attention. He points to the building on the right. "You will receive prisoner attire, a blanket, clogs, and a metal bowl with a spoon in exchange. You will receive a work assign-ment, which you are to tend to daily. When you are not work-ing, you will reside in the cell block we show you to. You are all criminals of this war and will be punished as we see fit for the consequence of your actions."

I didn't commit a crime. I wonder how many others standing with me are also innocent. How many people have they made up stories about?

We shuffle along, following one another in the mindless action of stating personal information for them to add to their records, following the next direction into the clothing warehouse, where we are told to strip out of our clothes in exchange for an old Czech Army uniform. Upon changing our clothing, some of the men I traveled with are taken across the courtyard to another rugged building. Others remain with me.

The grounds aren't filled with other prisoners like I would expect. It's almost as if we're one of the first groups to be taken here, but why me—a man who has not committed a crime? I wonder if what I'm being punished for is notated anywhere, or if there is a blank spot next to my name.

We are escorted into yet another dirt courtyard. "You will be living here," a soldier yells unnecessarily when we are all quiet and listening. He guides us into a small dreary building with metal grated doors. Dust-covered cement tiles cover the floors, and five wooden doors surround us, each hinged by metal. The white walls are stained with water marks, arching up to a rounded ceiling.

Our group is split again. Another Nazi leads one group through an opposite door on the other side of the contained area, while me and several others are guided into an enclosed space with stacked wooden planks lining one wall and tall thin cubbies along the other. A narrow table resides between the stacked planks and cubbies on the far end. There are already men living here, being imprisoned here, but for crimes they may not know of either. By their appearances, they have been neglected, with no food or the ability to clean themselves. They're rotting as I'm about to. Every shuffling foot or closing door causes me to flinch. Sweat is spilling down the center of my back. I'm light-headed and weak, and only from this mere preview of what to expect. I'm not built to withstand these conditions. How can anyone survive this? I'm not sure there is even enough space for those of us who have just walked in.

The air is musty, and the space is enclosing like a tunnel with two thin scratched windows that allow minimal sunlight in. A sink adorns the wall between them.

The other prisoners don't make eye contact. They are either leaning against a wooden plank or lying in between them like they are bunk beds. I suppose that's where we will sleep. A punishment like this for doing nothing but following the ridiculous laws bestowed upon us over the last year is inhumane.

I've never gotten myself into trouble. I always avoided it all cost.

"You are to stay within these confines unless told otherwise," we are told just before the heavy wooden door closes us inside the tight space.

Minutes pass before someone speaks. A man who was here when we arrived pushes himself away from one of the stacked wooden planks. "What are you all in here for?" he asks. "Resistance, I assume?"

Some remain quiet. Others agree with a nod. One says, "I didn't follow their ignorant laws and I was caught crossing a border through a wooded path."

All I can think of is Father and Tobias. Were they brought here too?

"How long has this location been in use as a prison? Where are we?" I ask.

"I'm not sure if you would like an award for being one of the first groups of prisoners to begin filling these cement holes, but they've run out of space in local prisons and have decided to start using these former Czechoslovakian Army barracks for overflow. We're in Terezín."

We're on the other side of Prague, from where the estate is. It explains why it took so long to arrive here. "Is this the only building with prisoners?" I continue.

"This block and the block next to us. A and B. Some are in solitary confinement, depending on what they are being imprisoned for. Others are in cells like ours, crammed in like sardines."

The man speaks in a monotone, not inflicted by his surroundings. Perhaps he was transferred from another prison and this life is nothing unusual to him.

"What are you in for, son?" The man walks closer to me. He appears to be around Father's age, but he could be much older by the wear and tear he looks to have experienced.

"I'm not exactly sure. They amended our so-called records, for me and my wife, and told me I broke laws. I hadn't broken a law of any sort. It was all a ploy to either take my wife or me away. I made sure it was me, but now I fear for her safety."

The man appears perplexed by my story. "What purpose would they have?"

My gaze drops to the rubble-covered stone tiles. "I've been privileged, living in an estate my entire life. I know the Germans have been doing whatever possible to obtain the titles to properties like my family's. We put the title in my wife's name because she isn't Jewish, before the occupation. It didn't matter, I suppose."

The man steps closer again and places his hand on my shoulder. "You're damned if you stand up for yourself, try to protect your loved ones, and do what is necessary to avoid where you are standing now. Most of us are here for similar reasons. You're not alone."

The man is kind to say so but his appearance, odor, and sunken cheeks bring out the worst thoughts of what will happen to us here. "I refused to surrender my jewelry shop," he continues. "It had been in my family for decades, and I couldn't let my family down. At least I know I did everything I could to try and stop them from taking my business. You should think the same way."

I reach my hand out to shake his, appreciating his sentiment. "Thank you, sir."

"Call me Slav," he says.

"I'm Ben."

"Choose a spot on one of the beds now before they are filled up entirely. You don't want to be sleeping on the floor," he says. "I suggest the top row. The air flow is better."

I turn around, seeking a spot on the top row. The platform next to the windows is taken, but the next one over is still free. I place the wooden clogs, blanket, and a metal bowl with a spoon on the plank I'm claiming.

I'm stuck wondering how long I will live. Every minute that passes comes and goes with me questioning whether I will ever hear that Mila is safe or if I will ever see anyone I love again. Is this my end, or the beginning of a new life I won't want to survive? There isn't even a scrap of paper or a pencil in sight to release my words onto paper. I'm not only a prisoner within these walls, but one of my mind, too. The only thing I'm sure about now is that there isn't a way out.

THIRTY-SEVEN

WE ARE PUPPETS

MILA, OCTOBER 1940

Months have passed and the world seems blind to the horrors that the innocent people of German-occupied countries face every day. Are the hands of all world leaders bound as they learn of Hitler's destruction? Or does everyone believe the lies being fed to them? We're just a small dot on a map, but every dot should matter. I fear the worst is still to come and I'm not sure I'm capable of imagining what that might entail. It's like we all know there will be another gunshot, but all we can do is sit and wait until we are startled out of our seats and curled up on the ground with our hands over our heads.

The four of us still living in this estate walk around like corpses that have risen from the dead. If I didn't check for my own pulse, I might question if my heart is beating. The weight I bear, and the heartache, is unbearable. It's excruciating. I want to tear my limbs off and scream at the top of my lungs to make this nightmare end, but the horror only grows worse by the day. My imagination grows stronger, and I think the worst, finding myself in dark corners of my mind that I never knew existed. It's clear, nothing is impossible now. Every horrid thought could become a reality, and there's nothing more frightening than knowing I cannot wake up or catch my breath long enough to convince myself everything will be okay.

It's been nearly five months since Ben was ripped away—since he sacrificed his well-being for mine. The thought of his chivalry brings me to tears each night while I try to avoid thoughts of his living conditions. I pray he's alive and not suffering, but all I can do is hope and wonder, which is just another form of punishment for anyone not of the Aryan race. We aren't entitled to information regarding our loved ones. We are undeserving of basic humanity, and unrecognized by society—hardly human, it feels.

I want to search for Ben. I want to question every man in uniform, knowing it will likely bring me to the same outcome as Ben. To sit in this estate and do nothing makes me feel like a traitor, a horrible wife, and someone unworthy of the sacrifice Ben made for me. All I have left of him is the notebook he left in Mister Bohdan's desk drawer. All of the poems he couldn't bear to share with anyone, even me—unless I'm ever to be without him. I keep the worn leather notebook closed, worried if I peer into its pages, it will mean the future is determined and I will forever be without him. It's a superstitious thought preventing me from feeling Ben's words—the only form of comfort I can acquire, but for now, I must hold on to the hope that we will not be apart for long.

Just like Mister Bohdan and Tobias, not a post has been received, and no information is available to tell us where they have been taken. I feel like I'm being chased and surviving for the sake of entertaining those who may be watching—knowing what our fate will eventually be. We are no more than puppets in this country and there doesn't seem to be any help in sight.

We spend much of the day in the servants' hall, whenever we are not caring for the horses or preparing food, we remain down here. Knowing the Nazis can stop in whenever they wish has left us with no choice but to stay close to a spot where we can hide if necessary. We can't allow them to take another one of us for false reasons they shamefully create.

The walls don't provide much heat and the lack of lighting creates a fog of confusion between the daytime and nighttime hours when we're down here for consecutive hours. I believe it adds to our trouble sleeping. My thoughts keep me awake more than anything, but I'm grateful for the flimsy cots left behind from the days servants lived down here.

"We're married—man and wife. We should be allowed to share each other's company at night," Ben whispers, pulling me down the long dark hallway in the middle of the night.

"I have yet to disagree with you," I reply. Ben tugs my arm, curling me into his arm, then cradles his hand around the back of my head. His lips graze mine like a feather against silk, as if he's testing the waters before diving in headfirst. "We're married. Why are you hesitating?" I ask.

"I'm not hesitating. I want to memorize the moment, reel from the longing of your touch. With darkness around us, we can be anywhere we want to be, and I'm imagining a lush garden surrounded by candlelight, a babbling creek nearby with frogs humming and crickets chirping. A summer night, with dew coating our hot skin, and a gentle breeze toting the fragrant scents of plumeria."

"You have quite the imagination."

"I like to dream. Don't you?"

"Only when I feel like I'm not living inside of one as I am right now," I say.

The gentle touch of his hand behind my neck tightens and his other arm loops around my back. The featherlike kiss fills me with passion as he carefully presses me into the wall behind us. His lips explore mine before peppering marks down the length of my neck. "I love you so much," he says.

*"A feeling doesn't require words. I would never question such a
thing, and I hope you never question my love for you."
The last of my words spin us into a dizzying motion of breathless
whispers against each other's lips. Ben scoops me up into his
arms and carries me to the end of the hall. "It isn't much, but
there are cots we can push together."
"I'd sleep on the floor if it meant being with you," I say.
The chilly temperatures in the cellar walls no longer matter as
we're intertwined in every possible way. The bed could be made
of springs or feathers, and I'd still feel the same while relishing
every touch, every rush of warmth, every soaring sensation.
To be held in his arms removes every worry and disappointment
from the reality we wish didn't exist. I could lie like this forever
and forget all the rest.*

"I feel terrible to have ever expected someone to sleep on
one of these cots," Madam Bohdan says, tossing and turning like
she does every night down here. Even with a blanket and a
pillow, she's unable to find a comfortable position. Though she
has stopped complaining about our current situation for the
most part, she seems more remorseful of her past doings.

Anytime I wrap myself up in a blanket in this spot, I
imagine being held in Ben's arms. It helps me sleep. "The cots
aren't so bad. I don't mind them all." It may only be because of
the memories I have with Ben, but a cot is better than sharing a
hard bed with all my siblings. Though, now, I would give
anything to have that to complain about again.

Filip and Pavel opt for the floor most nights, claiming it feels
more like camping when they are beneath a set of cots. They've
become much closer, and the age gap seems to have little
meaning to Filip now that he is the eldest one left of his brothers. I'm grateful they have each other.

"What if this goes on for years?" Madam Bohdan asks. She
asks this a lot, and though she knows I don't have an answer, she

still wants to hear whatever response I'm able to conjure at the time.

"Like I've said before, it's something we should consider. Finding another place to stay might be in our best interest."

She disagrees. She always has and always will. "I cannot just abandon the estate, Mila, even if it's under your name. This house is all I have left of Josef, Tobias, and Ben. Leaving our home would feel like I'm leaving them too."

She isn't wrong in the way she feels, but I do feel like there must be another option. I'm less emotionally attached to the property and more concerned for our well-being. If it's the estate the Nazis want, as they have led us to believe by faking information on our records, I feel it's only a matter of time before there are unwanted houseguests upstairs.

THIRTY-EIGHT
TASTING THE WORDS
BENEDIKT, FEBRUARY 1941

In the dead of winter, I should be frozen to the core with nothing but flimsy linen threads to shield my body. Yet after months of being trapped here like a moth between the pages of a thick book, only more pages have been added—more prisoners have been shoved into this dark fold. There are more than sixty of us in this cell block suitable for one or two people. We haven't been allowed to shower in almost a month and though the stench has become all we know, it's still noticeable, nauseating, and inescapable.

We lean against each other's backs if there isn't an open spot against a wall or a wooden plank post. Tonight, I've been fortunate enough to find a spot against the wall.

Some days we share stories of our loved ones. Other times, we dream up an imaginary future that doesn't seem plausible. Silence outweighs chatter because it takes energy we don't have to talk.

I sometimes drag my fingernail over the dirt-covered cement floors, tracing words. *I love you* is the message I wish to send Mila. The sensation of scribing letters makes me wonder if she can feel it too somehow. I spend too much time thinking of a way to connect with her, craving her wisdom and positive outlook. There is only a small part of me that has hope for survival. The intelligence left inside of me says we have been left here to rot and die. Some have already perished, and all the guards did was replace the lifeless bodies with living ones.

We aren't privy to war updates, so we sit in our tomb, left to wonder nothing more than what will happen to us after we die.

"What do you think those pigs are eating for supper tonight?" Peter grumbles from beside me. He's one of the few I've bonded with here. He's only a year older, also married, but has a one-year-old daughter to add to his list of estranging torment. He was arrested on account of resistance while caught trying to purchase an extra loaf a bread from a private vendor on the street. The Germans have formed their own definition of resistance. I'm sure the act of blinking too many times in one minute is a motive to argue their right way of living. He didn't have the chance to say goodbye to his wife or daughter. I'm not sure which is worse: to see the agony on your wife's face as you're pulled away, or to wonder how she must have felt when realizing her husband isn't coming home again. I should be grateful that Mila and I didn't have the chance to discuss starting a family. It would have been twice as much torture, knowing what I've left behind. I don't envy Peter for having the opportunity to start a family. I pity him.

"Succulent duck legs, glistening with a golden complexion over the freckles of black peppercorn. Scarlet ripe cranberries bursting with tangy juice strewn over a lush bed of evergreen sage, and translucent shallots with thick starch-coated potatoes roasted in sizzling Schmaltz," I answer, feeling the familiar gnaw in my hollow stomach. The agony is worth the moments of imagining each flavor and how it would feel to experience sparks of pleasure along the insides of my cheeks at first taste.

"Paired with an aged Bordeaux," Peter adds. "I can taste it."

I close my eyes and picture the dish sitting before me,

steaming, with a blurry view of Mila sitting across the table as she stares at me with the same sense of fervor that burns through me every day. "Wine would be a perfect complement."

"Did you ever write poetry about food? After listening to your depiction of food, I bet you could make a brick loaf of bread sound appealing too," Peter asks.

I try to chuckle at the question but a cough barks through my throat. "The thought never crossed my mind. I only wrote about the parts of life I didn't take for granted—the wants and desires, not what I already had." Maybe that's why I'm being punished now.

THIRTY-NINE

MARK THE PAGE

MILA, SEPTEMBER 1941

I play the part of living a pretentious life just as well as Hana does. The teacup on the low art deco table in front of me is full of liquid no warmer than room temperature. The book in my hand appears to have been enjoyed by the reader—me, but I've merely been flipping pages every minute or so. I'm not sure I know the title of this book, and this is a typical day here now.

I'm hard-pressed to think Hana knows the title of the book in her hands too. It's easier to act as if our minds are busy with common activity than it is to stare at a wall, providing proof of our lost and dark thoughts. Filip and Pavel often join us in the grand salon, playing along with the theatrics of reading for the sake of portraying leisurely pleasure.

Hana isn't the same woman she was two years ago. Over a year ago, just after Ben was taken, she kindly asked me to stop referring to her as Madam Bohdan and speak to her as an equal rather than the maid I once was for the family. Her request shocked me and it took me a while to switch my mindset from never taking the wrong step over the eggshells I felt I had to cross before her day and night.

"Mother," Filip's voice carries into the room from the open

area around the stairwell. "Did you know there was a poster nailed to the doorframe in front of the estate?"

Hana's lack of energy is still prevalent as she always appears to pause before responding to anyone. She lowers her book and folds the page corner down to save her place. "What poster?" she replies, twisting her head to peer over to the opening of the salon.

Filip glances at me first. Concern is obvious by the ridged brow lines along his forehead. "I was checking for the newspaper—"

"The newspaper?" I argue, knowing we are all aware we don't receive a newspaper at the door any longer. It's a privilege we aren't entitled to.

"I stepped outside for a breath of fresh air. The sun is warm, and the sky is clear. It would normally be what we would call a pleasant day," he says, correcting his story. My vision clears and I focus on the poster he's holding up in front of his face.

Reichsbürgergesetz

"What now?" Hana whines, as if someone's asking her to simply clean another dirty dish.

"There is a new law pertaining to Jewish people," Filip says.

"Of course," Hana continues with a huff of frustration as she tosses her book onto the table between us. "Let me see."

"Prior to tomorrow's date, we must tend to the—Das Näherin—in the village and purchase yellow star badges. All Jews are required to sew the fabric pieces to every article of clothing we own," Filip says upon handing Hana the poster. "Just another way to humiliate us."

"The former seamstress shop—that's where we must go," Hana says, translating the German Filip read.

Jewish families are struggling to survive off rations and are living without most human rights, and now I'm to be treated the same because I'm married to a Jewish man—one whose where-abouts I have no knowledge of, nor whether he is alive, or at the very least, surviving. I sit here day and night, empty, alone, parched of life. I foolishly check the post multiple times a day, thinking, praying, and hoping there will be something from Ben —anything, even a postcard with only his signature. It would be a sign that he's alive. Everything inside of me feels rotten, moldy, and sour. I've lost my family and for a greater reason than I can ever understand, I was blessed with a man who became family at a time when I needed someone—anyone. Now he's gone too, and I sit here in his shadow, trying to step up in his place. Yet, all I can do is watch the terror continue to rain down over this estate.

The foundation here is gone. It's only a matter of time before the roof crumbles over us too.

But even with nothing left, without an ounce of hope, or a glow of light in the grim, opaque world ahead of us, I would still marry Ben again without question, and for that, I will hold up this family to the best of my ability.

"We have to purchase these badges we are being forced to wear?" Hana questions while re-reading the poster. "They want to leave us with nothing, strip us bare."

The money left behind by Mister Bohdan and what Ben gave me access to is dwindling, and through no fault of our own. We aren't sure where Mister Bohdan has hidden other assets on behalf of the family, but we don't have the option to go searching either. He kept enough out to keep his family afloat, but I'm not sure he imagined it would need to sustain anyone for this long.

"There's probably a long line in the village. We should at least try to acquire the badges today. If we reach curfew, we'll return in the morning," I say.

"Must we all go?" Hana asks. The thought of walking into the village is at the top of her list of nightmares. The embarrassment she feels when others look at us like we've crawled out of a cave makes her fall back into a dark place—one we still haven't fully pulled her from.

"I will go," I offer.

"I'll join you," Filip says. "Pavel will come with us too."

"Go where?" Pavel steps into the room. I assume he was listening in as he usually does. No one keeps much from him, but I believe he thinks there are secrets still being kept from him. There's no sense in hiding the reality we all must face now, though.

The disappointment on Filip's face as he stares at Hana is a gesture grander than one he's dealt her before. "You aren't an exception to this law," he tells her.

Hana holds her gaze on the book she tossed down on the table. "Very well. I'll fetch my sweater and scarf."

The line is as assumed, long, winding, filled with irate Jewish residents who are doing their best to keep their thoughts to themselves. People walk past us from the direction we're facing, their hands filled with yellow stars. I fiddle with the coins in my sweater pocket, wondering how much they will ask us to pay for each star. The German soldiers are scattered along the road, doing little to hide their laughter as they watch every Jewish man and woman exchange precious currency for tangible forms of embarrassment.

I check the time too frequently; worried nightfall will arrive sooner than we're expecting. From the speed at which we've moved along the curb, I suspect another hour will pass before we reach the shop. Curfew begins in ninety minutes. The soldiers won't be kind enough to warn us of the time. They will switch modes and begin shouting orders, demanding proof of identification to ensure no Jew is on the street past sundown.

Hana is watching each person walk by, just as I am. "How will we manage to sew these onto all of our clothes?"

"I will teach you how to sew," I offer.

"I know how to sew," she argues.

"No, you don't, Mother," Filip adds.

"We'll get it taken care of—it's nothing to worry about at the moment," I say.

"At least we don't have to wear a swastika like the awful soldiers," Pavel says.

The three of us tell him to hush at the same moment, hoping no one heard his comment. "You can't speak like that outside," I warn him. "You know this."

He stares at me with a clueless gaze. He understands well enough, but denial is common, especially for a young man.

I wonder if my family has been badged with the word "Gypsy"? I suppose I should only hope they are well enough to wear a badge at all.

Somehow, we make it out of the shop with a half hour to spare before curfew. Each of our hands are full and my pocket is empty. I have no coins left, and I took more than I thought we would need.

"Jude," Hana says, reading the one word marked on the black outlined Star of David. "What's the purpose of labeling the badge? The Jewish star is enough to know who we are, is it not?"

I'm sure she knows I don't have an answer to her question. There is no reason or logic for any of the laws bestowed upon us. "By the length of the line, it's clear we won't be the only ones wearing these stars," I say.

"We're targets now. They won't have to ask for our identification anymore, will they?" Filip asks.

I can't help but wonder how many Jewish residents will try

to get away with not wearing the badges, or what will happen to them if they're caught. The soldiers seem to enjoy teaching lessons by demonstration. "Maybe we won't have to come face to face so often with the soldiers who are always asking for identification. That, in and of itself, would be worth the sacrifice."

"I disagree," Hana says. "This is degrading in every human way."

She's correct, but we are still choosing from our pick of poison, and there is no end in sight to this way of life. We can either survive with heartache and humiliation or find ourselves at the other end of a gun's barrel.

FORTY

YOUR ROOM ELDER

"Block A, line up with your belongings!" I'm not sure it's dawn when the voice startles me, forcing my eyes open. I push myself up from the wooden plank, my arms trembling through weakness. "Peter, wake up," I say, nudging my elbow into his shoulder. "Peter." My throat is dry and I'm not sure my words are very loud. "They must be doing roll calls early this morning." I press my elbow into his shoulder again, noticing a chill between his skin and mine. *No. Not him. Please, no.* "Peter!" I pull my knees in to give me more leverage and reach over to yank him onto his side. Before seeing his face, I know... His body is lifeless. The whites of his eyes are all I see at first. His mouth is ajar. "No, Peter. Wake up." I beg and shake his lifeless body to no avail. Bile rises from my stomach, and I straighten my torso to prevent myself from becoming ill. Why him? I only had one real friend here.

I stifle a sob in my throat and reach over his eyes to close his lids. "Rest peacefully, friend. You're in a better place now."

"May His great Name be blessed forever and to all eternity, blessed. Amen."

I tremble and shake as I climb over his body to reach the unsteady wooden ladder. Up until a few weeks ago, I was able to hop down from the top plank, but my knees aren't strong enough now to support my weight. According to my fingernail scratch marks along my plank, I've been here seventeen months. Though I feel as if I perished a year ago. They're starving us slowly, working us to the bone, and forcing us to sleep like diseased rats.

I scoop up my metal bowl and blanket and rush to the courtyard. I'm not the last to make it outside for roll call, but I'm also not one of the first. An SS guard stands tall before rows of men from our block. "The list of names I call are to step forward and form a line over there."

Those I arrived with look the way I feel, which is an indication of how I must look: emaciated, spineless, fragile, and dead. It's a struggle to hold my lips together. I never knew there were so many muscles controlling basic functions of my body, but now everything is difficult.

My body sways back and forth like a thin branch. My hands are like weightless leaves, useless.

The prisoner beside me shoves his elbow into my chest. "Your number was called."

I'm not sure how I didn't hear him call me, but the wind is howling below the white blanket of clouds hiding away the blue sky I often dream of. It's as if the sun refuses to shine over this place.

I step forward and toward the other line, trying to see my way through the grim fog blocking out any hope of sunlight that may be creeping over the horizon. A pile of clothes is thrown against my chest. I'm not sure if they were once mine or someone else's. *Am I leaving?*

The voices around me are bouncing off one another and I can't tell who is saying what or what directions I'm to follow. The queue I'm in moves forward, everyone shuffling one in front of the other as we're brought to a line of wagons waiting for us to step inside. I haven't been in a wagon since we arrived here. Others have, depending on the labor work assigned to them, but I've been assigned to laying bricks for a project we know nothing about. I wonder if they are forcing us into labor just for the sake of watching us work to the bone.

The memory of being in the wagon feels distant, yet also like it was just yesterday. I wonder if there is even a world outside of the prison gates. We can only see so far and for all I know, everything else could have been flattened. I haven't even seen a bird glide past the small window of the cell block.

No man can hold his head up in the wagon. Our bodies all fluctuate and bounce with every movement, as if we're wind-blown paper bags.

We should all be so thankful that the ride isn't long, but every one of my muscles pulsates uncontrollably as I fear where we could be taken. It's easiest to assume wherever we are is where I will inevitably meet my end.

We're unloaded just moments after the vehicle comes to a stop, dumped onto a cobblestone road covered in rubble between rows of short buildings. It looks like some kind of village. There is a cold eerie feeling among the people lining the streets. Many look as though they have been suffering much like myself, but perhaps somewhere else, or maybe they've always been here—wherever here might be. By the looks of others, confusion and chaos seem to be the common feelings we all encompass.

I stand on a curb for what seems like hours, staring at the cracks between the stones, each packed with shattered fragments of rocks. They're flattened to a smooth surface, showing the wear and tear from thousands of feet, hooves, and vehicles over the years. The village is by no means new, only new to the people who live here perhaps.

Whistles blow in the distance and shouts congest the air. It seems as if voices are coming from every direction, and no one knows who to listen to or what information to ingest.

Lines of people begin to form, and I walk toward them, knowing I should likely be in one. I continue to listen for direction, but nothing is audibly clear. Looking closer at those who are shouting instructions, I come to see the men are Czech Gendarmes, civilian police, taking on a different task than serving and protecting. I'm not sure if we are better off with them rather than SS soldiers at this point. It seems so many have become traitors. What lies are left to punish us with?

I go through the motions, supplying details in response to questions asked, and I'm handed a paper with confusing information, including a prisoner number, then given a yellow star and a red triangle patch to adhere to my clothing. "You are to meet with this Gendarme Haymen for more information on your impending duties," one of the Gendarmes declares.

"Where do I find him?"

"Long Street at the SS Headquarters," he states affirmatively before shoving me to the side to speak to the next person waiting. Would he shoot me right here, standing before him? Or would he force me to walk in my weak state to torture me first? I have more minutes to consider what it will feel like to be executed or worse. I pray it's quick, but there's no fun in that for the bored soldiers, living to watch us suffer.

I don't want to die. I don't want to feel this way. I also don't want to live. I want everything and nothing, and it makes no sense.

I don't know where Long Street is so I begin walking down blocks of similar-looking row buildings, finding people lining the streets with sullen looks upon their faces. I pass two roads before finding Long Street, and again must take a guess at which direction to travel to find the SS Headquarters.

It isn't a surprise to find I've walked several blocks in the wrong direction before turning around to travel the opposite way. There are no clear signs, only guards who don't want to answer the question from Jews or others who look as if they're decaying by the moment.

The burden of finding the SS Headquarters drains me of all my strength, but the last Gendarme points me in the proper direction to find Gendarme Haymen. I can hardly breathe when I spot the entrance to the building. Nature could have its way with me right this moment and spare me of whatever comes next, but then I would be giving up and not fighting for the life I promised Mila. How do I want to go? Is it even up to me? My knees threaten to collapse as I cross the threshold and find myself in a small room with other faces I recognize from the prison cell. Haymen doesn't hesitate before spitting off instructions that make no sense to me after just stepping into the room.

He spots me and doesn't ask for the number I was given or my name. "You are all assigned to be Room Elders," he explains. "Responsible for each person living in the barrack cell listed on your registration form. This is where you will reside as well. You are to report any violations and illnesses. You are also responsible for dictating bulletins to the inhabitants in your cell, making them all aware of policies and expectations. You are not on their side. You are not to help them in any way, despite your similarities in beliefs or lifestyles. As a prisoner, we trust you can withdraw from your emotional ties to the others living beneath your rule and will do whatever is necessary to keep yourself alive and well. After all, that is what brought you all here much sooner than the rest. This ghetto is a transient location, not a permanent place for anyone passing through. You will have people coming and going from your barrack on a regular basis." No one asks a question. No one lifts an eyebrow. "You will receive an extra daily food ration and the means to keep yourself on your feet while seeing to these orders."

I can't understand if I was just given a gift or a larger punishment. Is this hope or am I reaching another end?

After a bowl of cold soup and bread, I'm able to at least lift my shoulders enough to stand up straight before stepping into my assigned barrack. If I don't follow the instructions given to me, I'm sure it's safe to assume the worst outcome will be my fate. Though when I step into the barrack and see the same decomposing conditions in each person here, I'm not sure how I can act as if I am above them. Who am I to act superior after being a prisoner for almost two years? I am supposed to be a scare tactic to them, if I was to assume correctly.

People continue to shuffle in throughout the day. I assume this enclosed village-like area must be another overflow for wherever these people were previously kept.

The barrack looks like the space I was living in, but there are fewer plank beds and much less room. I drop my pile of clothes, blanket, spoon, and bowl onto an open space in the center row of planks and take the clipboard I was handed at headquarters, pressing it against my chest.

I clear my throat, hoping the chatter will lessen, but the commotion is filled with a sense of panic, and I don't blame anyone for ignoring my cue, especially since they don't know who I am.

"Attention!" I'm speaking in German and the foreign word on my tongue makes me feel like vomiting. "I am your Room Elder, responsible for whatever happens in this space." I suspect everyone might feel a form of hatred toward me, but possibly pity too. None of us want to be seen as superior. Most of the men before me stare with sullen, tired glares. Many have their heads tipped to the side, proving their continued irritation. Others seem to be holding their gaze on me for the sake of doing what they are told, and likely aren't listening to a word I'm saying. "I will be supplying the daily bulletins and submitting daily reports to the SS. If you are unsure about a policy, check in with me." I don't have any more knowledge than these men do, yet I'm supposed to be their source of information. The bulletins are to be memorized upon receipt as nothing will be marked down on paper, yet I can hardly recall the moments of yesterday. They must not know I'm as blind as they are, and it's my job to ensure they don't find out. I'm not sure what village we are in, what region we are even in. I can only be sure we're still on Czech territory due to the Czech Gendarmes.

As we approach the time of evening bread distribution, the men in the barracks pile out into a line, walking along the same path as others spilling out from their assigned barracks.

I remain behind the line to watch and make sure they arrive where they intend to be, which I hope is the same direction everyone else seems sure about as we walk.

A crowd billows out of a building, all men waiting with their bowls and spoons in hand. Everyone is filthy, staring off into the distance with their shoulders hunched forward. We must all look the same. The wait feels never-ending and I'm sure those who are new to this dreadful life must be in turmoil from hunger.

As the lines loop around each other, I'm given the opportunity to study each person we pass until we come to another stop. I notice two men with sunken faces, hollow figures, and ashen skin standing still with no movement in their eyes. This life isn't new to them. Something familiar strikes me about them. The coat. The man is wearing a coat similar to one that Tobias often wore. It was unique with red silk lining the inside seam with gold-colored thread, hemmed to perfection. It was custom made, fitted him like a glove. The coat I see across the way looks the same but it's large and dirty, loose on the frail, pale man wearing it. We all look alike, with very few differences in height, skin tone, and bodily markings. Like many of us, his mouth and eyelids hang low as if his skin has no elasticity left. The other gentleman, similar in disposition, but hunched forward with bowed shoulders and equally emaciated, must catch me staring as he glances in my direction. He also looks faintly familiar. "Benedikt?" he says, loud enough for me to hear, but quiet enough so his voice doesn't travel farther than necessary.

I step out of line toward him, finding more details along his face as I come closer. His nose has a slight bump at the bridge, and his hairline, though shaven close to his scalp, forms the outline of an uneven ocean wave. "Father?" I choke out in nothing more than an audible exhale. *How is it even possible?*

"Dear God, it's you." He stumbles toward me with his arms dangling outward, reaching for me.

I can't move. My feet are solidly glued to the ground. *Am I imagining this?* The moment his arms wrap around me, I know the sensation is not one I could conjure in my mind unless I've become utterly insane.

"Ben?" My eyes are closed but Tobias's voice is unmistakable. His arms, though bony and limp, feel familiar in an unexplainable way.

My chest heaves in and out and the thrust of my lungs throws me off balance. I cave forward, my palms blocking my fall as they scrape against the unforgiving shards of gravel. Hot tears sting my eyes as I struggle to lift myself back upright. They each grab one of my arms and we fall into each other, holding on as hard as we can.

"We were just transported here from a prison in Prague," Father says.

"I've been in a prison here, or somewhere close by."

"For what?" Father asks, shocked and appalled, knowing I had gotten away from them that day.

"They falsified our registry papers, changed dates and locations. They tried to take Mila, but I told them it was me who lied about the paperwork."

"You didn't lie, though," Tobias says.

"It was my say against theirs."

"Do you know if Mila, your mother, and brothers are all right?" Father asks, horror lacing each word.

"It's been nearly two years. I've had no way to communicate with them. I pray they are and think about them every minute of the day, but I'm as desperate as you for information."

I don't want to tell him the state of Mother's mental health. I fear the worst has come of her since I've been gone. I'm capable of forming a sense of hope but not for miracles.

"What barrack have you been assigned?"

"E3B-10."

"We're in D3-7," Father says.

"You're together?" I question, assuming everyone had been assigned random barracks.

"We weren't separated," he says.

I see the line moving along without me and I know I must take my duties seriously for fear of what will happen if I don't. "I must go," I tell them. "I'm a Room Elder. I'm not sure why, but I am."

"Good," Father says. "That can only be a good thing." He grips my head between his hands and presses his lips to my forehead. "Dear God, I'm thankful you are alive. Thank you, God. Thank you."

"Brother," Tobias says with a groan of grief, "I know there is no time to say what I want to say, but I have been dreadfully remorseful of the way I treated you and the rest of our family, including Mila, and I will pay a consequence of knowing how terrible I was for the rest of my days. I wish I had been a better brother. You deserved much more than what I was to you."

His words sound like a goodbye even though we have just,

by odd luck, found each other here in this unfamiliar village. "Thank you for your words," I say.

"I wish I could fix all I have done wrong." As do I, but my thoughts will not be helpful to anyone now.

"We all have regrets. Now, we must do what we can to survive this to the end," I tell them.

FORTY-ONE

BEN'S GETAWAY

MILA, JANUARY 1942

Why must hope be everlasting? It isn't a measure of relief. It's everlasting misery and sorrow. With each day that passes, it doesn't feel as though any time has passed at all. The pain still spirals like a record without a needle—nothing exists outside the non-stop motion of us racing toward an end no one can seem to find.

I collect the post for the day on my way back from peering into the horse stables, knowing Jewish families aren't allowed horses per the list of laws. I'm not sure why they haven't been taken from us, but I pray it's because I'm the title holder of the estate and still considered a loophole of sorts.

One post looks to be official, from the Third Reich. Whatever is inside will not be bringing good news, I'm sure.

When I step back into the estate, I find Hana preparing food in the kitchen and the boys trading out books from the library. We all come upstairs and return down to the cellar together. The Nazis haven't been swarming the perimeter like they were a year ago, but we have yet to let our guard down after what happened with Ben. The war has only evolved and safety for any person of Jewish or Romani descent is not shielded from the torments other countries are already facing.

I step into the kitchen, finding Hana ladling out soup into bowls. "Is there important post?" she asks, glancing at me with fading hope.

"There's a post from the Third Reich," I say, handing her the envelope.

Her eyes bulge as she stares at me with a questioning look, likely wishing I already knew what was written inside.

She cups her hand around her throat and fans herself with the envelope. "Did something happen? You look ill," she says.

"No, I'm as worried as you are," I explain, my eyes unblinking, my breath not flowing.

Hana's hands quiver as she tears open the envelope and pulls out the neatly folded papers. and begins to read. She immediately places her free hand over her chest.

After a long moment, she nods her head as if understanding what she's reading. "We're being deported," she whimpers. "There will be several transports of Jewish citizens departing the area throughout the month. We're being taken to Terezín, it says. We're no longer allowed here in our village. Because we are Jewish. It also says we are to bring enough food to sustain us for three days, bedding, and dishes. The documentation included needs to be filled out prior to deportation." She thumbs through the following sheets of paper and her eyes fill with tears. "After all this, we are left with no choice. We are being forced to leave our home."

"That can't be possible," I argue, stepping in beside her to read over her shoulder. "The title is in my name. You shouldn't have to leave. That was the whole reason we did what we did."

"I'm not arguing those facts, Mila," Hana says, staring through a clearing in the ice-frosted kitchen window.

"Where will we go? Does it say why or how?" I don't panic. I'm supposed to be the voice of reason, the calm one with a positive outlook. I'm failing and falling. I'm shattering because I will have let Ben down after he sacrificed himself for us and this generational heirloom estate.

I've been living in a fog. How could I be so naïve, thinking this wouldn't happen to us after my entire family was pushed out of the country, or worse? That should have been enough of a warning for me, but I've been living in a glass house as if it's underground and surrounded by steel. No one is safe. "Does the notification have a date for the transports?" I press up on my toes again to read more over her shoulder, but I can't see the bottom fine print.

"No, nothing," she says, handing the paper over to me to read.

With the paper pinched between my fingers, it doesn't take me long to notice there isn't much more to read aside from what Hana already said. The only part she left out was that my name is not included with the three of theirs.

"My name isn't listed," I utter.

"I know," she cries. "I'm so grateful you aren't included. You've already been through so much, dear."

I'm not sure what to be grateful for now. Being left with the responsibility of the estate doesn't feel like a positive gain to me.

"What would you like me to do?" I ask, speaking to her as a parental figure rather than the equal she has asked to be.

"I would like you to find a place to hide and keep safe. It's not going to be this estate. I'm not sure if there is a clerical error on their part, or purposeful, but in the case that it's purposeful, you need to get as far away from here as you can."

The pain in my chest never ceases but now I feel like there are a ton of bricks weighing me down in addition. "I have nowhere to go."

"Stay here with Filip and Pavel. I must go into town to take care of something. I will return within the hour. Don't leave the house, okay?"

"Of course. Whatever you need." Hana hasn't left the estate alone. She's terrified of the village. We can only be considered weak prey to those living a higher status in life.

"If there is even one of us that is capable of keeping herself safe and possibly bringing us back together at the end of this nightmare, I have faith it will be you, and shame on me for ever doubting this," she says, cupping my chin. "No apology will ever be enough for what you are owed, but I am grateful for you in every human way because you have given me a source of strength I didn't think I would ever be capable of embracing."

I'm at a loss for words. She has shown me kindness after her initial cold-hearted ways, but I didn't think she cared as much as she's claiming to right now.

"Bring the soup downstairs. I'll tell the boys to join you. An hour, I won't be any longer." She takes her coat from the counter and slips her arms through. I stare at the yellow star she was forced to sew onto the chest of her coat, feeling vacant inside as I wonder how the world has allowed humanity to progress to this point.

"Of course," I reply.

Hana slips her gloves on and places her hands on my shoulders before kissing my cheek. "Thank you, Mila."

In a trance, I take the bowls of soup downstairs and set them on an old narrow folding table we've placed between the cots. One of the bowls tips just slightly, enough that broth spills over the side. I stare at the reflecting droplets of liquid within the dim light from the gas-lit lamp we keep down here. I'm trying to understand why I've been spared the deportation list and the rest of them haven't.

We spent the majority of last night and today cleaning up the cellar, voiding traces of our existence even though the Germans know people will have been living here until given notice to leave. We don't know how much time we'll be given, if we're given any at all. I've helped Hana, Filip, and Pavel pack up the few belongings they're allowed to take, and they are ready for when called upon.

"I can stay until you receive the next notice," I tell Hana, offering to keep them company up until I can't.

Hana pulls in a sharp breath and closes her suitcase, clipping each clasp. The low pings of metal bring a chill to my spine, knowing or not knowing what she is packing for. They are being deported from their lives, from their legacy.

"I don't want you to wait. There will only be more eyes on us, and you, if they summon us to leave. It won't be a good time for you to leave in a different direction."

"Are you sure Mister and Misses Becker are willing to take me in? I don't want to cause them any trouble."

Hana went to the village yesterday to use the telephone booth to call Mister Becker and explain their situation. He didn't hesitate to offer me a place to run to, if I make it there without any trouble. He gave Hana a route I should follow, explaining it should be the safest way. Ben explained the hazards they encountered crossing the border to visit Mister and Misses Becker's estate, and I fear I won't be as stealthy as he.

I plan to leave just after sundown and I'm taking Ben's trusty motorbike, praying it works the way it did when he last used it a few years ago. He taught me how to add air to the tires and fuel to the tank, and I rolled my eyes as he slowly walked me through the steps, thinking I would someday need to know the information. I couldn't imagine a time I would be desperate enough to climb onto the bike alone, without him.

I've tucked my belongings into a knapsack and I'm ready to say goodbye, wondering whether it will be goodbye forever.

Hana, Filip, and Pavel have been sitting in the library, waiting for this awful moment—for me to collect my strength and bravery to leave what has been my only source of safety for almost four years. My heart and soul have both lived and died in this very house and now I must put the memories aside and move forward, fearlessly, with hope of surviving. I'm not sure who or what I'm trying to survive for. I'm also not sure anyone would be waiting for me at the end of the war—if there is an end to this war.

I mustn't cry. It will only cause them more pain than they are already feeling.

Pavel looks so grown-up when he stands up first upon me entering the room. He's fourteen, and to think he was only ten when I first came here, it's heartbreaking to think I won't see how his life moves forward. And Filip, he's almost Ben's age when I first met him. He looks just like him, but quieter. He carries pain on his shoulders in the same way, and I hope he will step into Ben's shoes, much like he already has, and protect his family to the best of his ability. Filip stands up and Hana follows. She has tears in her eyes and a handkerchief crumpled in her fist. All I want to tell them is that everything will be okay, but it wouldn't be fair of me to say that. We've all seen how unlikely this is. Another link to Ben, my husband, my life in place of the one that left me behind. The hollowness in my stomach accompanies a sharp pain, one that matches the feeling deep in my chest. *I can't cry.*

I give Pavel an embrace first. He's taller than me now, and it makes him feel older and more mature. "Everything is going to be okay," he says, offering the lie I refuse to give them.

"You take care of your mother. She needs you to be the strong man you've become."

"Will you be back when this is over?"

"When this is over, I won't let anything on the face of this earth stop me from returning." *If. The question is: if.*

Filip is next. I reach up on my toes to wrap my arms around

his neck. "I know you have this all under control," I whisper. "I have faith in you."

He squeezes me tighter and his chest bucks, struggling against a threatening sob. "I wish you really did have a crystal ball. Then you could tell us everything that we're about to face." My heart seers with pain as I recall the memory.

"Me too. Believe me, I wish I knew." *I'm not sure I believe me.*

"I'll never see you as anyone but a sister to us. Not seeing you every day is unfathomable."

"We have our memories, and it will be enough to carry us through this time. You are braver than you give yourself credit for, and I want you to remember that, always."

"I love you, Mila," he whispers, squeezing me again.

"I love you. All of you."

Hana is verging on hysterics and it's hard to watch, knowing the ups and downs we have gone through to get to a place where I feel pain for leaving her side. She wasn't like a mother to me, and I didn't need that because I know my mama loves me wherever she may be, but Hana has taught me a lot and given me understanding for life outside of the one I grew up in. We've supported each other this past year, more than ever before, and I will never forget it. I place my hands on her shoulders and press my cheek against hers. "Promise me you'll be strong," I say.

"I can't, Mila."

"Be strong for your family, and I will be strong for you and the others too."

She nods her head against my shoulder. "I'm sorry for all the wrongs I haven't righted. I'll always be remorseful."

"Let's just start anew. Move forward with your chin up and know you are better than the Germans who think they have a right to what is yours. You must."

I kiss her on the cheek and turn away, unable to bear the

sight of the three of them anymore. "You know where I'll be," I say, praying I make it there.

My body jitters along with the motorbike as I perch myself on the seat. The lessons Ben gave me come back to me and I close my eyes for a moment, recalling the first time he convinced me to go for a short ride. The warmth between us, my arms around his chest, my cheek on the firm muscles of his back. It was a beautiful memory and if I could feel like that for just one moment right now, maybe I could convince myself I'll be okay too.

FORTY-TWO

RUBBLE BETWEEN STONE

Daily, the frost-covered grounds of the ghetto are flooded with incoming Jewish people. Each already has a yellow star sewn to their coats, leaving no purpose of questioning who these unfortunate people are. Amid the winter months, the frigid air doesn't spare the overwhelming number of people living in one block. We convulse as frequently as we breathe. The uncontrollable muscle spasms leave us sore without moments to recover. Regardless of the time of year, the weather is unforgiving and won't take pity on us. All we have is a wool blanket and the clothes on our back.

We're going to run out of space at the rate the trains come in and spill people out. It's hard to know who is coming from where and why they have been sent here. It's clear there is a system in place but the truth is kept from us.

With the masses of people arriving, it seems as many are being deported, but to where, no one quite knows. Rumors of deportees being sent to their death spread like wildfire, but there isn't a Jewish person here who knows what the Germans don't intend for us to find out. It seems most of those who arrive are from the Protectorate of Bohemia and Moravia, but I haven't recognized any more faces.

I see Father and Tobias at mealtimes, and I'm grateful for those sparse moments among the rigorous days of following orders and keeping our heads up while depleted from enforced starvation. We are living off so little and I'm not sure how any of us are able to keep upright and moving, and I know I receive more than others because I'm a watchdog over the innocent Jewish men living in the same barracks as me.

Half of the time I spend waiting in line for daily bread distribution, I'm inspecting each person before spotting a hint of Father and Tobias. Today, I've been standing here beneath dark clouds that have burst with squalls of rain and sleet, soaking through the thin layer of fabric retaining the last bit of natural warmth. Maybe the precipitation is fogging up my vision, but I never have this much trouble spotting them even though the grounds are overflowing with men in long black jackets.

The longer I stand and wait, I debate if I'm seeping into the stone beneath me like the forming puddles. There's an ache behind my knees, swelling around my ankles, and muscles strain along my neck and back. I don't have the strength to even stretch. Yet, I see newer imports of Jews trying to salvage their well-being through playing instruments in the roads, painting or drawing pictures from the edge of the curb. Others are reciting poetry with their eyes closed, likely imagining they are within their beautiful words and somewhere other than here. I wish I had the strength to write or do something to distract me from the misery I have become. I have my imagination and memories, both of which have kept me on my feet, praying I can someday create more wonderful memories, especially with Mila.

The Romani people have their own section in the ghetto. There aren't as many of them as there are common Jewish people, but it's clear they have been stripped from their lives and given no say on being here. When I walk by their barracks,

I wonder if any of them are related to Mila, but they keep to themselves. Understandably so. Still, I take the time to look through the crowds, wondering if she might have ended up here too. Even among similar-looking beings, dressed alike and covered from head to toe in dirt, I would still recognize her even with my mind hardly working the way it should. I know I would. I dream of her dazzling crystal blue eyes against her olive skin every night. Every single night, I depend on a dream that makes me wonder if my past was only a figment of my imagination. My mind isn't intact, and I'm in pieces. A person can't mend their mind with missing pieces. It would be like repairing shattered glass without all the fragments. It's impossible.

"Benedikt, Benedikt," my name faintly resonates in the nearby vicinity. I twist and turn, seeking the source, but a hand on my shoulder pulls me in the opposite direction before I can see whose voice is raspy and hoarse.

"Father," I say, recognizing him at once. How was he able to spot me when I couldn't find him? His jaw hangs open and the skin beneath his eyes is inflamed and red. He struggles to inhale and exhale, over and over, before conjuring a word. A dry swallow in his throat causes him to choke and his fingernails burrow deeper around my shoulder.

"I can't find Tobias."

I take his arms and lower my head to look into his eyes. "Father, what do you mean?" They've been living in the same block.

"When I woke up, he was gone. What if they deported him? They must have taken him in the middle of the night. I didn't wake up. He would have woken me if he left on his own." Father sobs and shivers in my grip.

"If they were deporting people from your block, you would have heard them," I say, shouting so he can hear me over the pelting rain. "Were others gone too?"

"I don't know," Father continues to weep.

"Stay here. For just a moment."

"Where are you going? Don't leave, please," he begs.

"I will be back," I say, holding my gaze on his as a promise.

I drag my heavy body along the gravel, making my way toward larger groups of prisoners gathering near the incoming arrivals registration lines. While I trudge along, I question my motivation, wondering why Tobias might be standing somewhere different or crowding with others. He wouldn't be hiding from Father. He mentioned he hadn't been sleeping at night but that doesn't explain any of this.

Rain is brimming on my eyebrows and lashes and welling over my top lip. The wind howls between the narrow openings of the blocks and I'm trapped in a turbulent downpour.

"Brother!"

People are scurrying to wherever they're trying to go, rushing past me, kicking up puddles against my legs, but I hear it—the simplest word.

His voice. I know this voice. I stare contemplatively at two men walking toward me, but like a strike of lightning coiling around my body, my heart stalls as I realize Filip and Pavel are standing before me, both grown so much. Filip is my height and Pavel is only a couple inches shorter. Their heads are freshly shaven, but there is flesh on their bones. They haven't been here long, thank God. They hesitate momentarily as they wrap their arms around me, using caution as if I was a thin piece of glass.

Tobias steps up behind them, and I shake my head to clear my vision, sure I must be seeing things at this point. "I found them," he says, breathlessly, placing his hands down, one on each shoulder. "Our brothers are here."

"How—" I question through a short breath.

Tobias shrugs and the bridge of his nose crinkles as if he's trying to piece the occurrence together. "I step outside some nights when I can't sleep, and as I backed into the nook between the blocks, a flashlight shone down over them in a line of new arrivals. I stared for a long second until I convinced myself it was them. Then, I followed the line without thought."

"Father is falling apart with worry over you," I say, directing my attention to Tobias. "Come with me." I take Filip and Pavel by the shoulders and guide them through the sheet of rain limiting our view.

It doesn't take long to return to the food line, and I find Father where I left him. "I found them," I say.

"Them?" Father croaks the question.

I stand to the side, allowing him to see the sons he has gone years without. Father's eyes widen and his lips part. He's seeing for the first time. It's as if he was blind until this very moment. "I found them, Father," Tobias says.

"We're so glad to see you," Pavel says. "You have no idea how worried we've been."

"Rightfully so," Filip adds, clearly having a hard time comprehending the sight of what he sees in the three of us.

We fall into each other's arms, all of us just about the same height, but only three of us worn to the bone. Pavel and Filip's clothes still smell like soap. I've forgotten the scent. They appear healthy and just a bit older than when I saw them last. I'm grateful they weren't subjected to this life as early as the rest of us.

"Where's Mother, and Mila? Please, tell me they are well."

The embrace between us all wanes. Filip takes a step back and runs his hands beneath his eyes. I can't tell whether he's wiping away tears or rain. The sky is crying on behalf of us all. "Mother was sent in a different direction when we stepped off the train. Mila wasn't on the transient list we received in the post," Filip says.

"Where is she?" I grunt more forcefully than necessary, but I haven't been this close to an answer in years, and I need to know right this second where my wife might be.

"Don't worry, please. It's not safe for us to say where she is, Ben. We said goodbye and went separate ways. Please, have faith, just a little faith if you can manage to do so," Filip says.

I grit my teeth, hard, painfully, and my body sways back and forth, threatening to topple onto an unforgiving dirt road. "Tell me," I choke out, heaving for more air. "Tell me, brother. Just tell me where she is!" I nearly fall against Filip and cup my hands around the sides of his neck. "Please, I beg." Air won't move in and out of my lungs. I'm suffocating against my closing throat.

"The SS are watching," Father says. "You need to calm yourself."

Filip swings his arm around my neck, pulling the side of my head toward his mouth. "We only know that she left on your motorbike to find her way to the Becker estate. Mother arranged the plan. She is well and you shouldn't worry about her right now, not when I see what you have been through. She would be far more worried about your state."

I want to think Mother would selflessly set up an escape for Mila, but she showed her so much grief during the time we were all together. It's hard to imagine. And she's my mother—my blood, a woman I am devastatingly praying for with hopes that she is also okay somewhere in the vicinity.

"Your mother is here somewhere?" Father questions as if the statement is just catching up to him now.

"Somewhere," Filip says. "We don't know where."

"I must find her," Father says. He hands me his food ration. "Split this among yourselves. I'll find her, and I'll return soon. Please keep an eye out for each other when you can."

He doesn't give us time to speak. He clutches my face between his hands and kisses my forehead. He then does the same to Filip, Pavel, and Tobias. "I must bring our family back together. It's my only job. I will do whatever I can, but if I can't, and if I don't find your mother, and you are reunited someday, please tell her I love her with my entire heart and I wish our lives could be what we had dreamt of them being. Please," he says through a whimper.

"We love you, Father."

A second shared hug is all we have left, and the seconds of warmth and comfort aren't nearly enough to hold on to. "I love you all."

Time turns to ice, much like an arctic blast hitting a thin puddle of water, leaving us no time to find warmth or protection. The solemn tune of a violin along with a baritone cello vibrates inside my chest, making me wonder if I might crumble into millions of pieces and fall between the cracks of cobblestones.

FORTY-THREE

THE ENEMY IS OUR SOLITUDE

MILA, JULY 1942

The heat is unbearable up here in the loft's alcove of the Becker estate. The small circular window, the only source of light, attracts the midday sun, heating the tight space as if I'm enclosed in a metal box. I can see through a few spots in the aging window, corroded by condensation, dust, and cracks. Aside from that bit of clarity, the rest of the glass offers a blur, hinting a hue of blue or white, depending on the weather each day. The colors are a better sight than the marching Nazis pacing up and down the street morning, noon, and night.

A paper fan is my only source of circulating air, but I won't dare say a word to Mister and Misses Becker as I'm grateful for the acceptance into their home. They were kind enough to open their door to me at the end of January—a door I wasn't sure I'd reach.

The map to their estate, left behind by Ben, was confusing with trails marked through mostly wooded areas. The last time he traveled to visit Mister Becker, he was in Mister Bohdan's car and there was no snow covering the ground.

When traveling here in the midst of winter, I had Ben's motorbike and though it was easy to maneuver on gravel, the rubber didn't take nicely to the patches of ice along the way. Some areas, I had to push the motorbike along and walk by foot. It took me almost two days to travel the distance that shouldn't have taken more than a couple hours in a car. Of course, I'm not new to sleeping outdoors in all varying temperatures, but I didn't have much for warmth other than what I was able to fit into a knapsack.

I spent the night fearing the thought of authorities at the invisible bordering line between the Protectorate of Bohemia and Moravia, and the Sudetenland region. I remember Ben mentioning the checkpoint being along the main road. With the extreme measures the Germans were taking to keep control, it wouldn't be a surprise to find guards along the wooded borders.

I may not be Jewish, and I was luckily left off the transport orders, but I am not Aryan, as I do not resemble the typical blonde-haired, blue-eyed race. The entire trip to Havraň, I felt watched as if there were binoculars centered on the back of my head.

Beyond all measures of luck, I made it the doorstep of the Becker estate. It was just before midnight when I tapped my knuckles against their front door.

My heart pounded against my ribcage, and I could hardly catch my breath after walking the motorbike silently through the dark, quiet streets.

What felt like hours was likely only a minute or two before I heard a sound from the other side of the door. The ruffling of fabric against a wooden surface made me wonder if someone was checking the peephole to see who was outside at such a late hour. It was an opportunity for Mister Becker to see who was standing there and walk away as if he'd never heard a sound.

To my surprise, the door cracked open, just enough for Mister Becker to reach his arm and head out and grab me by the hand. He pulled me inside so quickly I felt like the candle-lit foyer was spinning around me. "I thought for sure something

happened," he said. "Hana telephoned me days ago, explaining
the situation. I thought you might show up a day ago, and since
then, I'd lost hope of your well-being with every passing hour."

Before I could answer his question, it was clear from the
faint glow from the candlestick on the center table, he knew the
exact reason why I was at his door at that hour.

"Per Hana's request, I've sent a friend—an Aryan farmer to
take care of the horses. He'll keep them safe. He's a good man.
I'll also bring Benedikt's motorbike into our storage unit around
the back of the building. Misses Becker and I have set up space
for you in the alcove off the loft upstairs. The enclosed space
offers a means of hiding, if necessary."

I had no right to question or wonder why I would need to be
in hiding if I wasn't a prime suspect the Nazis were searching
for. By birth, I'm seen as a "Gypsy" to the German soldiers, but
by marital law and Ben's last name, I'm simply a resident of
Czechoslovakia married to a deported Jewish man. The laws
have become so blurry and confusing, it's hard to know what's
allowed and what isn't. With Mister and Misses Becker being of
Aryan race and living in German territory, I wouldn't have
thought their estate would be a target for property raids. So far,
we've been lucky.

A sheet-covered mattress lines the wall beneath the
window, a quilt folded up at the foot of the bed. It's the only
portion of the room where I can stand up straight without
knocking my head against the angled ceiling. I must crouch
across to reach the old writing desk and chair. They make me
think of Ben. It would be all he would need up here. Although I
don't have much use for the desk other than a change of scenery
from one wall to another. My few belongings reside in my knapsack acting as a bureau next to the short door I duck in and out
of to use the washroom and toilet a few times a day.

Aside from the meals Misses Becker is kind enough to bring
upstairs to me, I sit in solitude with Ben's notebook of poetry

clenched between my arms and chest, wishing for the verses to be spoken out loud by the only voice I desire to hear. Every long day I'm away from him is another day closer I come to opening the book and reading what feels like forbidden words of hope.

With nothing but time to think, I imagine the unfathomable conditions of what my family must be enduring, or Ben and the rest of the Bohdans. I wonder if something inside of me would feel different if they were no longer alive. I long for whimsical signs—a hint that they are okay. Sometimes, I stare at the dark wooden paneling along the bare wall across from the window, and I convince myself the natural wooden cracks are shifting into shapes.

Solitude can make a person go mad.

FORTY-FOUR

THE OLD, WEAK, AND ILL

There's a fog holding on to last night's rain with a pocket of cold air. The sun is rising in the east but I'm walking toward the west, always seemingly walking to a darker location from the one I'm already in. If I don't pick up my pace, I'll be late to hear the morning bulletins, and therefore, will let the overfilled cell block go a day without any impending warnings of happenings in the ghetto. The news is always poor, no matter the day. I often wonder if anyone would care if I made any more morning announcements. Half of my block has been fighting off various ailments and we've had fleas taking over most of the beds. Many are covered with angry rashes of red bites, and we can't seem to find a way to rid ourselves of the pests. I assume we see the fleas much like the Nazis see us.

I've advised everyone to cloak their bodies as well as possible while in bed. I've gone as far as covering my neck, head, face, and hands with mud since it's the only part of my body I can't cover with clothing. Not everyone agrees with my method, which is why we can't seem to stop the infestation.

I approach the end of the block and wait for the block elder. As I lean against the wall of the block, my pants slip past my waist a little, reminding me it's time to puncture another hole into my belt. It seems like I'm tightening my belt far too often and I know the reality of how the progression will end.

Kral, the block elder, steps into sight, his head hanging between his shoulders as he scratches along the scruff of his shaven head. "Didn't sleep well last night?" I ask.

He steps up to me and lifts his head. His eyes look wild with concern, alert as if he's been shocked by an electrical current. "There's only one bulletin today," he says, shaking his head.

"What is it?" I ask, squinting as if I'm preparing for a swing at my head.

Kral curls his hands into fists by his side, his veins bulging from the thin skin stretched over his bones. "There's a plan to deport thousands of people from the ghetto. There are transports set to leave. Elders, weak, and ill, particularly those who came from the Protectorate of Bohemia and Moravia, who will be the first to go."

My lungs sever from incoming air and my throat tightens like I'm being strangled. We never know who is safe and who isn't. Now we're supposed to make this announcement and scare every living being in this block. "Where will they be taken?"

"The rumor I heard after we were dismissed was Auschwitz, a death camp in Poland," Kral says. "There's no more room here and they keep bringing in more and more people. I don't understand."

"Do we have any idea of who is on the initial list?" Father and Tobias hit two of the three check marks—elderly and weak. Tobias's nerve pain is getting the best of him and I'm not sure how much longer he'll be able to tolerate physical labor like he's been tending to.

"They mentioned more than half of the D barracks, 2A, 2B, and 3 are the most overcrowded with ill and elderly. They will likely start with them as soon as today."

A burn gargles in the pit of my stomach. "I'll pass on the information now." I twist around and walk back to my block, facing the sun spilling over the horizon, blinding me from what I used to think was a form of hope. The sun just leads to another day of misery now.

The bulletin escapes my mouth as mechanically as it was served to me. A wave of gasps and questions filter through the air, but the bulletin didn't include specifics as to which barracks would be first to go. Therefore, it's not my place to inform the others even though I feel it's only fair that they know what I do. Still, I do my job the way I'm told to, to maintain my well-being, or stature of just being.

No sooner than the barrage of incoming questions begin do I set my view on the doorway. I need to find Father and Tobias.

With each step I take, I try to imagine I'm somewhere else, somewhere with Mila, walking along the water's edge, feeling the sun beat down on the backs of our necks as we stroll hand in hand, doing nothing more than inhaling the crisp autumn air. Her hair would glow with hints of rouge only present under the early morning sun's rays, and her eyes would pierce through me, the translucent blue hue picking up extra tones from the sapphire lake. I'd tell her I love her just because I do, and she would smile and tell me the same. It's simple, but it's too easy, and it's all I want, and it's all I can't have.

The corner of the D block barracks are only a few steps away. The door to D3 is already open. They've likely heard the same bulletin I just gave my barrack.

I wait until people spill out the door, ready to stand in line for their morning bread, and I rush in to find Father and Tobias, both slowly moving along, buttoning their shirts and securing their pants.

"Father," I call out.

The sound of my voice claims his attention quicker than anything usually does. He finds me almost immediately among the crowd walking through the narrow walkway between the tiered planks. "Son, what is it?"

We normally meet along the food line, where we find Filip and Pavel as well. Their barracks are across the square, not in the D block like Father and Tobias.

"We need to talk somewhere else."

Father looks at Tobias as if he's wondering what he might know, but I'm positive neither of them have thought too far into whatever announcement they were given.

They follow me outside and I notice the clouds parting, exposing the blue we seem to rarely see. Parting clouds should be a foreshadowing of good, but it's not.

I sense their struggle to keep up with me as I hustle toward the food line. "Ben, slow down," Father says. I want to tell him we're running out of time, but I need to choose my words properly. I can't terrify them when this might possibly be their unfortunate reality.

Filip and Pavel spot us from ahead and walk toward us. Filip's stare meets mine and his head straightens as if he can read the thoughts looming in me. "What is it?" he asks as we reach each other.

I place my hands on my hips and fight for breaths that won't move through my lungs fast enough. "Bulk deportations are set to begin as soon as today due to the overflow of people in the ghetto." I debate whether to tell them the rumor of Auschwitz but if the gossip is true, it would be like lighting the fuse of a long wick attached to an explosive within their bodies. I can't do that to them. A wave of nausea sloshes through me as my family stares at me with questioning looks. "We were told this morning. There have been deportations clearly, seeing as Mother is gone already. Why do they seem so surprised by this news?" Tobias asks, his face pale beneath the abundance of sun.

"I was told," I whisper, "the elderly, sick, and weak from the

D block units, those particularly from the Protectorate of Bohemia and Moravia, will be the first to go."

Father's bottom lip falls. "Perhaps they will take us to your mother," is the first thought that escapes his mouth. We don't know where she was transported to, and I pray it wasn't a death camp. "I don't want to leave you boys." He's unsound with logic and reason, but who could blame him?

"I'm the weak, I assume?" Tobias asks, his eyes half-lidded. His shoulders hang forward, highlighting the appearance of the hunchback he's become over these last few months.

"I don't know more than what I've said," I admit, although lying at the same time, leaving out the part about the death camp.

"Will we have a warning?" Father asks.

"I'm not sure," I reply.

Pavel loops his arms around my neck and Father's. Filip does the same, bringing Tobias in closer to our huddle. "Please God, keep us together," Pavel says. "Please, I beg of you."

"I love you, my sons." A sob bucks through Father's chest. "I can't take much more of this pain. I am heartbroken without knowing where your mother is, and the thought of not knowing where you will all be—"

"Don't speak that way, Father," Filip says sternly. "We need to fight and be strong so that when this is over, we can be together again, no matter what happens."

Filip is always the one who has more hope than the rest of us, at least he has been that way since arriving at the ghetto.

"We love you, Father," I say.

"We do," Filip echoes.

"And Tobias too," Pavel says.

"We all love each other," Tobias says. "Even if any of you have questioned that—particularly about me. I know I'm not one to show much compassion—but—"

"We understand," Father says, patting Tobias on the shoulder. "Now, let's enjoy some bread together while we can," he adds. "I feel blessed to have had this time with you, even in these terrible conditions."

Tobias remains quiet, contemplative, and I can't begin to imagine what must be going through his head, but I would be angry, knowing I have been dealt a poor hand. I've never felt sorry for him due to the way he's treated us all, but now, I've never felt sorrier for anyone.

Father places his hand on my back and pulls me into his side. "Will you promise to watch over your brothers?"

"You don't need to ask for my promise, Father."

"I know," he says, releasing a heavy exhale. "I'm going to stay strong despite the pain in my chest. I will do whatever I can to stay alive and find your mother so we can reunite our family, I promise you."

None of us can make promises like this. We have no control over what happens next, or even what will happen an hour from now.

FORTY-FIVE
A SINGLE SNOWFLAKE

MILA, JANUARY 1943

From the peephole of my window, I've seen a change in the people passing down the road. No one can hold their heads up, and there isn't even anyone left wearing a yellow star badge. The Jewish people have all completely gone, taken to wherever Ben must be. Every person in this village seems to carry the weight of shame around.

Humanity has changed, and I've seen people at what I would have thought to be their worst. My family and I have been chased out of every place we've called home, purely because we were not wanted among other kinds. Where will the lack of acceptance for others end? I don't know if there are any Germans willing to stand up for the rights of non-Germans. Those headlines certainly aren't published anywhere. The Third Reich controls the papers, the news, the updates on what we should know. But is it the truth? Where is the other side of the argument? Who is left to defend the innocent? People like me, hiding in an alcove.

It isn't those who are walking around in shame, afraid to look another person in the eye without guilt of being witness to the ruination of the most basic human rights.

Mister Becker, Elias, as he has requested that I call him, says everyone is too afraid to react. I don't understand how an entire nation can be afraid of one man and his army. I'm not sure anyone walking down the road can answer this question either, but they continue to live with a type of freedom too many would die for.

A knock on the door causes my heart to leap into my throat, knowing I fear the day of a house raid exposing my existence with one quick look at my non-Aryan complexion. "Yes?" I question. There has been little talk of any Romani left in the area.

Elias opens the door with caution or hesitance, I'm not sure. "Are you all right, dear?" Whenever he comes upstairs to check on me, he asks the same question. I answer the same each time.

"No. Are you?"

He hangs his head just as the others do. "No." He clears his throat and peers back up at me. "There's quite a chill up here, yes? I've brought some extra blankets in case you become too cold."

I have a half-dozen quilts and blankets now. It seems like it's all they can offer at this point aside from small portions of food. The drought and economic depression are affecting everyone, not just those who aren't Aryan. "Thank you." I pinch Ben's notebook against my stomach and reach out with my other hand.

"You still haven't opened that book, have you?"

I stare at him as thoughts flash through my mind. If I do, I'm giving up. If I don't, I can't hear him. There is no benefit to holding this notebook aside from knowing that his hands touched it last before mine. "No."

"My horse handler is caring for Nova, Twister, and Krása at his farm. They're all thriving. I wanted you to know they're doing well." I miss the horses deeply and I know it's unsafe to visit or leave the estate, but I would do anything to spend time with them.

"It would be nice to see them again."

"Of course. I hope we can arrange something soon," he says. "Also, Julia is heating some tea. She will be up in a few moments."

Misses Becker has also requested that I address her by her first name. Maybe it makes them feel less guilty even though they are already going above and beyond by sacrificing their safety to keep me here. "That sounds lovely."

Elias pulls the wooden chair from the writing desk over to the center of the room where he can sit without hitting his head on the angled ceiling. "Mila, I read something rather unfortunate this morning and though I wish I could keep the news from you, I don't think it's the proper thing to do."

I place the short stack of blankets onto the mattress and lower myself down on top of it. I'm not sure what type of news he could receive that would affect any of us personally. Headlines are rather generalized.

A lump in my throat makes it hard for me to swallow, as if I've been parched for days. I place the notebook on my lap and clasp my fingers together, resting my hands on top. "Unfortunate," I repeat. "What isn't unfortunate these days?"

Elias places his left ankle over his right knee and folds his hands on his lap. "There has been word that any remaining —Romani—"

"Gypsies," I correct him with a hint of sarcasm, knowing the headlines or news sources don't refer to us as Romani.

"Yes. Well, it seems they have all been sent to extermination camps."

My blood runs cold as if the temperature in the room just seeped into my veins and took control. The room around me seems to sway as if I'm in a boat on choppy waters. "Extermination." The word isn't a question—it's confirmation. "All?"

"Apparently, per the news source."

"Meaning, if my family weren't already dead, they will be, imminently."

Elias can't seem to make eye contact now. He seems fascinated by the shine of his brown leather shoe. "We know news sources can't be fully reliable, but—"

"We don't have reason to believe otherwise," I say as I've been brainwashed to respond with those words.

"We will continue to pray. You said your father is a smart man and will do anything to protect your family. We have no reason to believe otherwise."

Elias believes they left me behind as a form of protection. I have no reason not to trust his suggestion to be the truth. "We may be beyond the hope of a prayer," I say.

"Perhaps, but it shouldn't stop us from still doing so."

A tear falls from my dry eyes. I shouldn't have any tears left after the number of nights I have spent crying myself to sleep. Yet, the tears return, reminding me I'm still alive, suffering with dread. "Thank you for informing me of what you know. I appreciate your honesty."

Elias nods his head and pulls in a shuttered breath. "Of course, dear. If you need anything, or would like to talk more, please let me know."

"Certainly," I reply, pressing my lips together to hold in the cries begging to pour out of me.

Elias stands and replaces the chair beneath the desk then leaves as silently as he entered.

I return to the window and squeeze the notebook tight against my stomach.

A large snowflake falls against the clear spot on the glass, and I lean in to take a closer look, finding it to be a perfect ice crystal, intricately carved with repeating patterns in each quadrant as if God designed the frozen droplet specifically for me. I stare at it, longing to recall my infatuation with snowflakes.

"It's snowing again. When will it ever give up this winter?" I ask Papa, watching the horses clomp through the freshly fallen snow, the sound of their rhythmic steps muffled from the thick sparkling white blanket covering the gravel. We've been on the road for a week trying to find a new settlement. The others have been complaining of the cold, so I've put on a few layers of clothes to last as long as I can up front with Papa. Unfortunately, we've had to stop many times due to visibility hindering the horses from moving in sync with one another.

He glances over at me with a quirky grin. "What if this is our eternal winter?"

"I'd prefer warm weather if we are to be stuck with one way over another for the rest of our lives," I argue.

"Oh, my dordi. You of all of us see details that no one else notices —the good in all evil, the beauty in the beastly, and hope within loss."

"I don't think so," I reply, confused by what he's saying.

"Look beside you on the black metal rail. Lean in closer so you can truly see it for what it is."

I do as Papa says and lower my face toward the metal rail, finding a perfect snowflake shaped just as we see them in illustrated books. I thought the beauty of an individual particle of snow was something designed in another's imagination. "It's beautiful. How does something so small offer so much to see, and yet, no one knows to look this closely?"

"Those who think God is simply watching us from above cannot understand such detail in superficial matters. The unique design in each snowflake is sent to remind us that we are being watched and that our lives are tailor-made from a labyrinthine blueprint just like this one droplet of frozen water."

My chin trembles at the sight of the snowflake. "Papa," I whisper.

FORTY-SIX

I NEED YOU

The turnover rate in my barrack makes me feel like the smallest target, but the one that a lucky shot will eventually hit. The only people who remain here now are those well enough to work. There are no exceptions. Failure to comply with commands is deportation or—much worse. There has been talk that those who are being deported are being sent to their death. The thought haunts me through every breath I take, especially knowing Father didn't return with news of finding Mother. Many families are enduring the same inhumanity as we are, and all we can do is watch the torment unfold before us. Men have been taking their lives in fear of what may or may not happen. We can only rely on the current moments, nothing that might follow.

When I wake each morning, my first thought is that I survived another night, and why have I been lucky enough over another? My second thought is to wonder whether a metal rod has been speared through my back, from top to bottom—the pain rivets through every nerve, but to feel an ache throughout my body rather than my chest and heart, is somewhat of a relief.

My third thought is wondering what I'll be required to

inform the men crowded onto wooden planks above and below me, each sleeping on their side to fit extra bodies. Will I have to add more terror to their already horrific lives?

My fourth thought forces my stomach to tumble and knot, knowing I must walk down to the barrack my brothers are living in, ensuring they are both still alive today.

Then, Mila—her kind smile, warm soul, the touch I can still feel—she encompasses me. I can feel her being, hear her words, embrace her thoughts. I wish I could write her a letter, and at least let her know I am alive. If I did, it would jeopardize her safety, and it's not a risk I'm willing to take. If I knew anything happened to her because of something I did, I would lose my will to carry on. I made a promise to Father that I wouldn't do that.

My last thought before climbing down from the plank is: should I assume Mother, Father, and Tobias have perished? I debate if I should hope they are no longer suffering or fear that they are miserable living like me. I exist in a world where wishing death upon loved ones is more common than praying for their longevity.

After setting my feet on the ground, I straighten my shirt, and clasp the buttons over my concave chest and stomach. I tighten my belt to the latest hole I have punctured into the leather strap, and I slip my feet into the wooden clogs that leave me feeling like there are nails piercing my skin with every step I take.

As I do each morning, I drag myself to the end of the row of barracks to wait on Kral for the morning bulletins.

Kral barely stops in front of me long enough to speak more than a few words. Another day of brief updates, which isn't surprising. I'm not sure what the point of the notices are most days since there is nothing we can do but fear the words. Yet I'm given no chance but to make the announcements.

I return next door to my barrack and call for attention. Each man pushes himself up to show me he is awake and listening.

"Today's bulletin includes further executions for misconduct, which will begin this afternoon. Typhus is on the rise once again, and there have been at least a hundred more deaths this past week."

The first bulletin reappears once a week. The second has been consistent since January. I'm not sure why they have medical staff treating those who are sick, but I'm sure there is a backward reason for that just as there is for every other abnormal form of treatment here. For those of us who survive, I wonder if we will ever find answers to our questions.

The grunts and groans commence as the deteriorating men struggle to make their way to the cold cement ground outside. Roll call is just a few minutes away and then we can carry on with waiting in line for our morning bread that will hardly sustain the work we are required to do today. Our barrack has been assigned to manual labor in the courtyard to create a finer-looking appearance for all the dying prisoners to view as they pass by. I'm not sure what other reason there is to make anything look delightful around here other than to give us false hope. Everything is a tease, a way to toy with our minds.

The mornings carry on smoothly when every man is in line for roll call. When someone is missing, we all pay dearly. Today is a lucky day. No one is missing from our block.

I roam down the road toward Filip and Pavel's block, prepared to wait for their roll call to conclude. Sometimes it's before mine. Others it's a minute or two later. Today, Pavel is running toward me, his face panic-stricken. "What's wrong, brother?"

"Come fast. It's Filip. I think he has Typhus. He's very sick. I can't get him to move. It happened so suddenly, maybe overnight. He told me he felt off last night, but I didn't think anything of it until I saw how pale he was this morning."

No one will come to our side to help. We either seek aid or give up hope. We're both running as fast as our legs can carry us, which doesn't feel very fast at all. My inside feels as if it's filled with boulders. "Did you tell your Barrack Elder?" I ask breathlessly as I approach his barrack.

"Yes, he is seeking assistance now."

I can hear my brother coughing before I step inside his barrack. He's the only one still on a wooden plank as the others have left for their morning rituals. I climb up to the top plank, where he's curled into a ball. "Filip, it's me. It's Ben." I place my hand on his head, feeling the heat scorch against my palm. He's sweating and it isn't overly hot in here, just humid. I pull him onto his back and he begins to cough again. "We're going to get you treatment. You don't need to worry."

"I didn't have lice," he groans.

"How are you sure?"

"How are you not sure?" Pavel argues with me.

"What else could this be?" I ask.

"It could be anything. We're malnourished, dehydrated, and worn down to skin and bones. We don't have much in our bodies protecting us from even the worst of diseases now." I still find it striking to have mature conversations with Pavel, even if we're both angry and distressed. I often think about how our lives would have turned out if we weren't victims of Hitler's crusade. Pavel was so young when this all began. His childhood was tainted, and Filip didn't have it much better.

The wait for word about medical aid seems to take forever by the time his barrack elder returns. "We need to bring him to the infirmary right away," the man says.

Pavel drops down to the floor, prepared to help me slide Filip off the top plank. He's nowhere near as heavy as he should be at eighteen, making me realize I can take him on my own. Once I'm steady on the ground, I gain a better hold of Filip's skeletal body and take him into my arms, carrying him tightly against my chest as my arms tremble from overuse. The world spins around me while Pavel shouts directions at me as we follow the barrack elder toward the courtyard.

Filip's cough sounds weaker and weaker each time he tries to expel the built-up phlegm in his throat. How could he become so sick in a matter of hours? I don't understand. I would have noticed something yesterday. I should have noticed. I didn't.

A Kapo, a fellow Jewish prisoner in charge of keeping records on the ill prisoners, reaches us in a long line of others waiting to be allowed into the infirmary. Most of the Kapos aren't trained in their assigned jobs, and we can only hope the one assisting us has a medical background from before Jewish people were stripped of their career rights.

"It's certainly Typhus," the woman says upon checking Filip's vitals.

"What can you do to help him?" I plead.

The woman looks ragged like we do, worn, tired, and weak from working for the enemy to help her own. "We can pray."

"What do you mean? There must be something you can do for him?" Pavel shouts. He scares the timid woman; she holds her hands to her heart and gives us both a somber glower that says she is being truthful.

"We need to bring his fever down," I tell her.

"I understand, but you must realize by the time his symptoms have reached this degree, the infection has been spreading through his system for nearly two weeks. It's typical not to experience an inkling of sickness until this point, but unfortunately, all we can do is watch and wait."

Daggers must be shooting out of my eyes by the way she reacts to my expression. "We've lost so many to this infection."

The Kapo moves on as if she was crossing out our name on a

list, leaving Pavel and I standing outside the infirmary with
Filip in my arms.

"It's going to be okay, brother," Pavel says to Filip, placing
his hand on his chest. "Stay strong. Right, Ben?"

I hear Pavel's encouraging words but all I can do is focus on
the walk ahead of us, down the few blocks back toward our
barracks. My arms are numb. I can't feel the weight of Filip's
body. I can only feel the weight of every beat of my aching
heart.

"We'll bring him to my barrack. I'm in charge. No one will
be in to check on us," I say.

"He won't be well in hours," Pavel says, walking sideways
next to me. "What are we supposed to do until then?"

"You're going to report to your labor duty before you are
spotted as missing today."

"I don't want to leave him," Pavel says, tears lacing his eyes.

"I don't care what you want. I want you to stay here and
alive. Do you understand me?" I reprimand him.

He seems taken aback by my raised voice. I didn't mean to
shout but I must focus on Filip and not worry about Pavel
finding trouble today.

By the time we reach my barrack, Filip seems to have fallen
unconscious. His weight has doubled in my arms and I'm struggling to make it to the bed planks. Pavel lifts Filip's feet and
helps me the rest of the way, then we settle him in my spot on
the planks.

"Go on. I'll watch over him," I say to Pavel.

The fear in his eyes matches the tension in my chest. He
takes Filip's hand and squeezes tightly. "Please don't go," he
says. "I love you, brother."

"Be strong," I tell Pavel.

"You sound like Mila." Maybe we should be thinking the
way Mila always had. Her positive outlook gave us a type of
hope we would never have found without her insightful

suggestions to try and see life through a different set of eyes once in a while. I wish I could see through hers at this moment. I need her now more than ever. I can't face this likely outcome.

Pavel shuffles out of the barracks, leaving the two of us here to wait out the infection we can't treat. It isn't uncommon for a barrack elder to arrive later than others to their duties, but I refuse to leave Filip here. It's a risk I must take.

Kral, thankfully, said he would cover for me and tend to my duties while I take care of Filip. Hours have passed and Filip's fever seems to have only gotten worse. His cough is more sporadic, but it seems as if his lungs are struggling to take in enough oxygen. He's been lethargic or asleep most of the day.

"Can you hear me?" I call out to him quietly. He doesn't respond but his hand shivers beneath mine. "Filip, can you open your eyes, brother?"

He's so pale, I'm not sure what I would be thinking if I didn't still feel a pulse. After a long moment, he struggles against his eyelids, parting them slightly. "I'm sorry," he mutters through a breath.

"No, no, you have nothing to be sorry about. Do you hear me?"

I recklessly stumble to climb up onto the plank and roll his limp body onto my lap. I tumble backward against a wooden beam and curl him into my chest. "Filip, stay with me. We can make it through this. I love you. Pavel loves you. We all love you." My chest convulses, searching for air I can't seem to move through my lungs. "Please. I'm begging you not to leave me—us. Please. We're brothers, forever. We're supposed to be together always, no matter what. You know? Filip, I can't do this without you. You have to be okay. We're going to get through this. We're going to go home. I know it. You do too, don't you? Remember Father always said we'd be each other's best friends for life, and we were lucky for that? We promised to look after each other, so we must do that now. I can't let you slip away. You're too young. You have a life ahead of you. We both do. I know you can hear me. I know you can. Filip?"

A tear forms in the corner of his eye and skates down his cheek. "I—you," he says through a weak rasp.

It takes energy to form tears, muscles to release them, strength I don't have, yet my organs all feel as if they are climbing up my throat as I collapse over Filip's body. *Why does it have to be this way? We have already suffered so greatly.* A gut-wrenching sob purges through my throat and I smother my face into Filip's boney shoulder. My body quakes against his. "I need you," I say, begging for him to fight harder for my selfish needs.

FORTY-SEVEN

TAKE COVER

World War I lasted four years. We've been living with World War II for almost five years and without an end in sight. There is no life outside of this war and I'm not sure what will become of our nation with the unforgiving and relentless fight. I want to run away. I've never been stuck in one place for so long and I have a much clearer understanding as to why we have always kept moving, at least when my family was with me. If we stay put, we become hostages. If we run, we have a chance of staying ahead of the battles, but this time, we were boxed in and left without an exit. Even the trees can't hide anyone now.

When the sun sets each night, we sit in the dark, often listening to the hum of fighter jets soaring through the skies, heading for their next planned attack. The United States and the Soviet Union are fighting against Germany, but we're in German occupied territory. The objective of war is to cut off supply from the enemy—hit them where it hurts the most.

I lay awake at night, wondering if the Soviets and the United States know there are people being held against their will here, people who can't step outside for fear of risking their lives. We can't fly white flags because we are property of the enemy—left without a voice.

I've asked Julia and Elias day after day if there's anywhere to go that's safer than where we are. Elias has made it clear there is no such place and all we can do is pray.

Nearby cities have been attacked, even flattened, but all we can do is sit with an apple on our heads, hoping the archer has a bad aim.

Elias and Julia's footsteps echo through the estate most nights even after the sun has set. I'm not sure what they're doing, but often, they sound frantic as if they're in a rush to accomplish something within these walls. I can't imagine what it could be.

The road outside is quieter than it was. People aren't walking around as often, and there are fewer Nazis parading around on guard. It seems many of the soldiers were needed for defense and offense roles within battles. I'm not sure if it's a good or bad sign of what's to come.

Gusts of wind cause my heart to race as I wonder if I'm hearing something other than natural elements.

I hear the growing volume of stomping feet up the stairs to the loft and I sit up on the mattress, clutching a quilt in my hands as I wait, waiting for whatever information they must have to share.

Neither of them knock, which sets me ablaze with anguish. They both rush in and close the door behind them as if they are being chased. Elias is covered in sweat, his eyes are bloodshot, and his shirt is unbuttoned down to his white ribbed tank top. "Fuel plants on the eastern border of Germany are being attacked by US bombers. The brief radio announcement mentioned hundreds of aircraft, even close to a thousand, are heading in our direction. We need to take cover."

"Where is the nearest fuel plant?" I ask, grabbing my over-coat, boots, and Ben's notebook.

"Only four kilometers from here," Julia wails as she secures her plum purple silk robe over her matching pajama set.

I realize we don't have time for questions, and from the way they're acting, I suspect they think we might feel the effect of the explosives. They don't have a cellar like the Bohdans, and I'm not sure where they think it's safe to take shelter.

My question is answered as we head for the front door. I haven't left this estate for almost a year and a half. The only light of day I have witnessed has been through the peepholes in the window in the alcove.

Air raid sirens moan in the distance and the moment we step outside, a much louder howl of sirens rings through our ears.

Elias takes me and Julia by the arms and runs toward the village square, where I spot a line of people in their bedtime attire, pushing and shoving one another to descend a stone stairwell that disappears beneath the row of shops and houses.

We must fight to make our way down into the shelter as well. No one wants to wait their turn, understandably so. With the sirens crying out, fear is injected into our nerves.

There isn't much space left underground and I don't know how many more people can fit. There are a few low-hanging lights, flickering, and beneath are people drenched in sweat, eyes bulging, and mouths open wide enough to catch flies.

Only a minute or two passes before I hear a door secure and bolt. Elias has his arms around Julia and me and I want to cower to the ground and curl into a ball.

In the small bit of space between our bodies, I manage to open Ben's notebook, finding his neat handwriting scrawled in perfect short lines.

"I'm not saying goodbye," I whisper. "I just need you."

It's hard to see well beneath the dim lights, especially with so many people around us, but my eyes adjust after a moment and I'm able to make out the words on the page I have cracked open:

> Unsure of the obscure unfamiliar—which direc-
>   tion do I go?
> The unjust cold wind in spring, like tears that
>   adorn a smile,
> A muddle of watercolors blur within a wavering
>   faint glow,
> And the hint that a heart will guide the mind
>   once in a while.
>
> Our eyes then draw to a speck with the faintest
>   flare,
> Toward the chance of escape to the next
>   passage.
> A place built on insight from which you're
>   already aware.
> Where lost things are found, hiding from a
>   savage.
>
> Though, if the opaque sky shatters with light,
> Seize a blink for a moment to see a rare
>   distraction,
> A hardship blocking our outlook and sight,
> Is resistant to our divine magnetic attraction.
> We still have time to reclaim a fair fate,
> So long as you are there waiting, it will never be
>   too late.

I slap the book closed and bury my chin against my chest. "I'm waiting, Ben."

The ground rumbles and we sway into one another just as a

vacuum of wind pulls the air from us. Gravity has let us down and may not allow us back up this time.

FORTY-EIGHT
A BEAUTIFUL WEED
BENEDIKT, MAY 1945

When there is an uproar in the courtyard or in the roads between the row of blocks, it signifies either an uprising or a change of laws that will inflict upon every prisoner within the confines of this ghetto-turned-concentration camp. I step out of my block to take in the scene of what we are likely about to face. There are so many men, half dressed, dragging their heavy feet along the dirt, that I can't see what they are moving toward. Everyone has their hands up above their heads, either surrendering or waving, and crying out or moaning to be seen.

There is never a good outcome following a commotion filled with emotional distress. There never has been a positive outlook following the shouts that have typically come from an order of execution, another large deportation, or a mob of resisting prisoners.

Until today.

The SS spent more time in the past year trying to fool the Red Cross into thinking the prisoners on this enclosed land were living a luxurious lifestyle. A group of prisoners were the recipients of more food, better amenities for hygiene and had access to the arts, healthy physical activity, education, and opportunities for enrichment. Those who were chosen to take part had no choice but to participate in the charade. Resistance would result in immediate deportation.

The production began when a Danish delegate of the Red Cross was sent to inspect the ghetto. The delegate was taken on a specific tour, routed through fake movie-like sets with pris-oner-turned-actors portraying a lifestyle completely opposite to the one we're living. The livelihoods of the actors depended on their job to ensure the delegate saw only what was intended for him to see. Following the in-person theatrics, the SS produced a film for the use of propaganda to share with a wider audience of the Red Cross. The final picture was proof to validate the passing inspection, confirming how well the Jewish people here are being treated. It was all a lie. The rest of us were hidden from the path of inspection and the cameras.

It was like a rescue squad finding a man lost and starving, fighting for his life in the middle of a mountain, but rather than see a man struggling to survive, they only saw a waving hand and a smile.

There was no need to think twice about what was happening here.

To know the inspector for the Red Cross left with only lies, our last bit of hope was stolen.

My eyes may be deceiving me, but they are hard to mistake in their white uniforms—like angels without wings.

The illusory sight of SS officers scampering in the dust as people in white coats make their way through the center of the buildings has me pinned to the side of the barrack, watching like a bystander rather than the victim.

Chatter grows within the walls of the barrack and among those who are lining the road watching with me. "They're here to save us."

With the Soviets battling the Germans around the perimeter of Terezín, the Jewish prisoners have become hostages of their fights. Therefore, I'm not sure how the Red Cross were able to return for another look at the truth of our situation, or why they even came back for us when it will take walking through hell to save the grim leftovers here.

As word quickly spreads like an oil-lit fire, bodies spill out of the doorways of the barracks to see if what they were hearing is true. Are we being rescued? It could be an illusion. People around me are still able to bear the semblance of a smile, many with rotting teeth. I'm not sure my facial muscles are capable of such a drastic change. I barely have the strength to push myself off the wooden façade I'm leaning against. All I can do is watch what seems like a parade.

Water, food, means of hygiene, and other basic human necessities have been dispersed to the remaining prisoners in the camp over the last few days. Many thought we would be free to run out of the confines at the very sight of the Red Cross, but the battles between the Germans and Soviets outside these camp walls have continued to escalate. The Soviet Union has plans to occupy this territory and they are fighting Germany to do so. I'm unsure if we, as Jewish prisoners, are in their way or if we're worth saving in the Soviet's eyes. The allies have been closing us in for over a year but no one has been able to predict how this will end for those of us caught in the middle.

With Soviet vehicles lining the roads and declaring their victory, we wait for a cue. We wait to see if the gates will open and set us all free.

Pavel places his elbow on my shoulder, leaning on me as if I can offer him support. "This is it. I can feel it, brother. Maybe, Father, Mother, and Tobias, wherever they are, have already been liberated by the Soviets. Do you think?"

"Why do you assume they are here to save us?" I ask.

"You don't see prisoners climbing into their vehicles up ahead? Don't you hear the shouting and cheering?"

It all sounds like muffles of explosions, not what I recall a cheer sounding like. Pavel slaps his hand on my shoulder. "I'm telling you those gates are open. We can leave."

Pavel doesn't wait for me to agree. He grabs my arm and pulls me behind him. "Wait, wait—" I say.

I turn around to face the long row of barracks. "We're leaving Filip here," I utter. My face burns, hot blood rushing through my cheeks. *How can I just leave him here?*

Pavel's boots scuffle along the road and he stops beside me. "We aren't leaving him here." He loops his arm around my neck and places his other hand on my chest. "He's here, Ben. He will always be a part of us and if we don't stay here, he won't be here. We should take that part of him—the part we hold on to, and bring him home, where he'd want to be."

"If we find Father, Mother, and Tobias, we'll have to—"

"Tell them we were lucky enough to survive like them, and we did everything we humanly could to save Filip, but it was out of our hands," Pavel says. I twist to study my brother's face, wondering when he became so mature and wise. He still has freckles across his cheekbones and the bridge of his nose—boy-like, but there's nothing boyish left about him. He arrived with innocence and will leave with leather skin and a heart made of steel.

Together, Pavel and I turn around and face the crowd waiting to push their way out of the gates. It seems surreal after all this time. We can just walk out as if we were never prisoners.

We pass the crossroads where we would wait in line for food and recall the memory of the times the Bohdan men shared just one more meal, regardless of how little we had to eat. We were together. No one was arguing. We just wanted to sit by each other's sides, knowing the moment was a gift.

"I hope we never see this godforsaken place ever again," I say.

"Never. These grounds don't deserve the grace of our footsteps," Pavel says.

Soviet soldiers, dressed in camel-brown uniforms, march across the grounds with their sights set on targets that aren't Jewish people. They have other objectives, it's clear. I don't even see a German guard in sight. They must have been tipped off and are preparing for backlash.

The crowd, though anxious, moves slowly as we all want to squeeze through the gates at the same moment. It's hard to ignore the fact that we are fragile, frail bones and weak muscle.

"Where are we going when we walk out of those gates? How will we get there?" I ask the question out loud, but don't expect Pavel to answer when this is all happening so suddenly. It seems more than impossible to fathom.

Pavel gives me a slight shove toward an opening in the crowd, bringing us a bit closer to the other side of the gates. "I overheard someone say the Red Cross is setting up transportation and family services. I'm not sure what it all means, but I think there's help. We just need to get home."

"Home?" I question. "Do we even still have a home?"

"Where else are we to go?"

"I don't know," I say.

My calves burn with each step and my knees crack over and over. It's almost as if I'm walking on stilts. When we reach the gate, and I step away from the grounds of hell, tears form in the corners of my eyes and a knot grows in my throat. *Am I dreaming? Is this real? I heave for air, holding my fists against my chest as I cower forward and fall to my knees. Thank you, God. Thank you. Thank you.*

Pavel stands in front of me, then kneels. "Come on, brother. Come on." He offers me his hand to help me up to my feet. I feel defeated in every human way.

Other men and women are crying as they cross the perimeter too. It's the freedom, the air is ours to breathe, and the road is there to travel for as far as we want to go. The sky is hazy, but blue, a beautiful robin egg blue, and the clouds are like fleece. A cool breeze chills the tears still falling down my cheeks, but I'm reveling in the moment of detachment. If I'm dreaming, I pray I never wake up.

"Over here," Pavel says. "They're going toward Plzeň."

"No, no," I argue. "Sudetenland—Havraň. We need to find the Beckers. Mila."

Pavel stops and pulls me around to face him then places his hands on my shoulders. "You're right. Let's go there. But, brother, I need you to promise me you won't have expectations. This war has taken its toll on everyone, and we don't know what to expect beyond the walls we just left."

He's telling me I should keep an open mind, not to expect Mila to be safely sitting inside the Becker estate. In my head, it's the only place I've imagined her being. I've convinced myself she's okay, well hidden, and protected. Though, the last time I spoke to Elias, I doubted his accountability. We all did.

"We just need to get there," I tell him.

Pavel circles around, looking toward the various Red Cross trucks offering transportation to cities in the nearby area. It takes him a few minutes without an ounce of assistance from me, but he finds one of the relief vehicles going to the central Sudetenland region, close enough to the town of Havraň.

There's a sharp ringing in my ears as I enter the back of a vehicle, prepared to sit on a metal bench along the walls of the metal interior.

Pavel and I sit shoulder to shoulder, and I stare at the steel bearings along the floor. A cold sweat strikes me like a firebolt, and I'm back in the seat I was in nearly five years ago. I'm in borrowed clothes now versus then when I was wearing my high-end tweed pants and button-down shirt. I was sweating through my clothes, unknowing of where we were being taken. I'm not sure I'm hydrated enough to sweat at this point. My lips are parched, and they crack every time I talk. My eyes feel like sand is embedded beneath my eyelids and the scraping sensation burns with each blink. I haven't taken much notice in what I physically feel because it's been important to avoid ruminating over the damages I've endured.

What if Mila isn't at the Becker estate? What will I have been living for all this time?

As if my questions require answers, we hit a hard bump and Pavel's shoulder thuds against my chest. I glance over, my neck stiff, not wanting to comply. A man, hardly old enough to call a man, with possibly no one left in this world but me now—he is who needs me, and that is why I'm still here.

Agony is what I'll endure if I don't find Mila, and I will forever grieve if the rest of our family is gone, but I won't abandon Pavel, which means living for as long as I can to be what he deserves in life.

The two-hour-long trip goes much quicker than the ride between our estate and Terezín years ago. Despite papers with information and announcements we should be listening to more carefully in the case that we need assistance following this trip, Pavel and I are more concerned with stepping out of this vehicle and never looking back. The last of what I hear is that we will be able to seek assistance with a family reconnection organization within a week's time and to keep a watch out for additional Red Cross support nearby.

We're dropped off in the center of a nearby village within walking distance of the Becker estate. The roads painted with an array of multi-colored stone of various heights and widths seem unscathed, but the once pristine buildings colored in gentle pastels are fading. Debris from edifices forms piles along the curb, dust covers all storefront windows. A handful of people walk along the curb but not with the appearance of leisure, just purpose.

"What do you think happened here?" Pavel asks, shuffling through a pile of rubble.

"It's hard to say, but I'm not sure the village took a direct hit. It seems we're on the outer perimeter of wherever was attacked though."

Some of the buildings have collapsed but they aren't charred. The destruction is surreal as I thought the only visible horrors were the ones we were facing within the enclosure of gates. The people of this village are or were mostly Aryan. The war closed in on Germany—the enemies and the innocent.

"It feels odd knowing the war is over and no one will be questioning us for papers on every corner," Pavel says.

I forgot that was a form of freedom before all this. Being allowed extra water feels like a novelty now, never mind showing papers.

An hour may have passed since we stepped out of the vehicle, but the Becker estate is now in our viewing range. Their road is no exception to the others we've walked along. Cracks in walls, exposed plaster beneath shattered windows. Some buildings appear abandoned. The Becker estate has taken significant damage. The iconic overhanging patio is missing the short pillars between the stone wall fixtures. It's hard to say if anyone is living here. The road is quiet, but there are birds chirping—something I don't think I've heard in years. Sprouts of deliciously green weeds between stones are reaching up toward the sky. What was once a form of irritation to any gardener is now a sign of new life—a beautiful weed.

The bronze knocker on the door is rusty, seemingly untouched with cobwebs laced between the door and handle. "It's desolate," I say.

"Is this the correct estate?" Pavel asks. He must have been no more than seven or eight last time he was here.

My heart flutters without rhythm, terrified of facing the truth on the other side of this door. I close my eyes and rap my knuckles beneath the knocker, feeling a stinging pain on contact. *I'm too frail to even knock on a door.*

Minutes seem to pass without a hint of movement from within the estate. Pavel rings the bell. I should have done that. We look at one another without thoughts to share because neither of us know what to expect.

The door flies open, a gust of air nearly knocks us both over, but Elias stands before us—his forehead engraved with rows of lines, his eyes bulging, and his hand resting over his heart. "Can I help—"

Elias stares at Pavel for a long moment, knowing he looks familiar but in a confusing sort of way. Then he shifts his gaze to me. His mouth falls open and he lifts his hand to his mouth. "My dear God, Benedikt."

"Elias," I utter.

He sputters through short breaths, in and out heavily, as if verging on hyperventilation. "I was sure—"

I nod, understanding what he's trying to say. He steps out from beneath the overhang and throws his arms around me, holding me far too tightly, which he must notice quickly as he removes his arms and pulls them behind his back. Elias looks over at Pavel, studying him for a moment. "Filip, you're so grown."

Pavel presses his lips together so tightly his mouth becomes white, matching the pigment of his skin. "I'm Pavel," he says.

Elias closes his eyes and clenches his jaw, his chin trembling. He holds his hand up, measuring the space between the ground and the middle of his chest. "You were just this tall last time—"

"We've all aged quite a bit," I add.

"Where are the rest—"

"We aren't entirely sure about our mother, father, and

Tobias—they were deported to other locations, but we fear the odds of their survival are not in our favor. We are only certain that Filip—" Thinking of the words before I speak feels like the reopening a fresh wound, the loss of my little brother—like salt infiltrating a deadly infection, agony. "He—uh—he perished from Typhus less than a year ago. We were by his side—" I can't find the next word with my tongue lodged in my throat.

"We were lucky to avoid contracting the disease. It was viral among many of the prisoners of Theresienstadt. The odds were not in any of our favors," Pavel says. "It was— It is devastating."

Elias is clutching the fabric over his chest, trying to ingest every response.

"Elias," I say, struggling to breathe. "Please— please tell me you know of Mila's whereabouts."

Elias leans toward me and takes me by the elbow. "Come inside, both of you."

He takes us into his home, where we find Misses Becker—Julia—standing with a look of horror and shock lining the deeper aging indents along her face. "Darling, get them food, water, everything," Elias says.

"Mila?" I say again.

Elias nods his head and continues pulling me down the long hallway until we reach one of their grand rooms, one I believe was once used as a smoking room. The door opens and he guides me inside, but all I see are empty seats. Why won't he answer me?

FORTY-NINE

DAY ONE

Hitler is dead. Prison camps are being liberated. Ben, his family, and mine could be anywhere within the German-occupied region. Where do I start looking? There have been thousands of concentration camps listed, most are sub-camps within a core of almost two dozen. From the mere resources we have access to, we know most of the Jews and Romani who were once settled in the Protectorate of Bohemia and Moravia were sent to the ghetto of Theresienstadt, which became a concentration camp. Although many had been deported from there almost as soon as they arrived.

"Vehicles are transporting survivors. There are family services becoming readily available to help members locate each other. While we plan to have more information in the days to come, I'm afraid our lists are scarce for the moment. We advise you to add your name and all forms of contact information to our list for assistance in reconnecting you with your missing loved ones," a nurse speaks through a megaphone.

The line zigzags beneath a pitched tent, a Red Cross badge affixed to every panel of fabric. The others in line aren't chatting much. Everyone must be afraid of what they'll learn. It seems that fear outweighs hope. Millions of Jewish people have died from disease and starvation, or they were murdered. It was all happening within miles, and no one knew the worst of what was occurring. We couldn't gather information. No one had answers. Everything was a secret—one we could feel but couldn't access.

I reach the white linen-covered table separating me, the line, and the Red Cross volunteers on the other side. "As mentioned, we don't have access to all missing people at this time, but we do have a brief list we can scan for you."

"Yes," I say, my clenched fists trembling by my sides. "I'm searching for two families. Doran Leon and wife, Rebecca, with two children, Lela, and Bula, and two other adult children by the names of Broni and Morti Leon. There would be six of them in total—all Romani. I'm also searching for Josef Bohdan and wife, Hana. They have one son under the age of eighteen, Pavel. The other adult sons are Benedikt, Tobias, and Filip Bohdan." I don't know if they would be listed together as a family or separate. I know I listed far more names than anyone could recollect while looking at the long list the young woman has in her hands.

It takes a moment for her to flip through the papers. "I do see a Bohdan family, the head of household by the name of Josef. I'm afraid I only have record of three members of the family, and they have unfortunately perished."

Without intention, I fall forward, catching myself against the white table. I take in short breaths, not great enough to fill my lungs. I might faint. A cold sweat cloaks every inch of my skin. "Josef, Hana, and Tobias Bohdan are the only family members I have records of at this time," the woman says. A sob thrusts out of my throat, and tears fill my eyes. "Those three family members are gone. Yes, I'm so very sorry for your loss."

"And the others? The Leons?" I cry out.

"You mentioned they are of Romani descent?" Her words form softly with gentle hesitation.

"Yes," I reply.

She searches through a second list. "Most from this area were sent to Theresienstadt and I'm afraid we don't have thorough records from that camp. Unfortunately, I don't see any Leons on this list. If you can return in a few days, we should have another update then."

I nod and mouth the words thank you as I stumble away, feeling as though the world is quaking beneath me.

I should be able to enjoy the fresh air, the ability to walk around without being stared at, or questioned. Freedom is among us, but I don't have any sense of being free. If anything, I feel more lost.

I thought the night of the explosions would be the end of my life. We were trapped underground for almost two days until we were located. Over the two days, the crowd sharing the tight space around us stared at me as if I was a murderer, scanning my surroundings for my next victim. Julia tried to stand in front of me, shielding me from the stares. My skin color was a few shades darker than everyone else's and that's all they needed to see to make assumptions. This war has only made people more blind, and I have always been one to believe in growth following grief, but I can't see through this grim fog now.

My heels clack against the stones on the curb. There's too much to fix, to clean, and I'm not sure there will ever be enough time left on earth to undo what has been done. I cut through the woods toward the farm where Elias has kept Nova, Twister, and Krása safe. They were spared from the explosions. It seems they were just outside of the tremor zone, unlike us.

I went more than two years without seeing them, but Elias felt it's been safe enough these last few days to visit them. They remembered me right away—as if no time had passed. The farmer took good care of them and I'm quite grateful. Perhaps he wasn't aware they belonged to a Jewish family, but they were spared, nonetheless.

By the time I reach the farm and spot the horses inside the stables, the heavy sense of desolation weighs me down and I'm desperate to take a rest. I visit with Nova first and she lowers her head so I can rest my forehead against hers. "Half of the Bohdan family has died," I whimper against her. "I don't know about Ben or Filip or Pavel, and nothing about my family. My heart hurts so much, Nova."

Twister cranes her neck over the stall and nudges me with her muzzle. "Hi, sweet one." I scratch my fingers through her mane and slide down against the back wall into a pile of hay. More tears steam down my cheeks. I lean my head back and close my eyes, reeling with the overbearing weight of emptiness.

"Still such a pretty girl." My eyes flash open, and I'm immediately angry for dreaming of the moment when Ben found me sleeping in the stables. "You are just as pretty, and you look like your mama, don't you?"

I nearly trip over my feet to stand up, holding on to the wall for support as I look over the stall walls. My legs feel like limp rags as I trudge to the gate in front of Nova, and as I wrap my fingers over the side, a hand rests on top of mine—a familiar sensation, one almost too hard to believe isn't part of my imagination.

He takes a step to the side, so he's directly in front of me with only the gate between us. He's pale, thin, tired, and if I hadn't memorized every freckle on his face, the specks of gold in his amber eyes, or the unique scar he hates, I might not have recognized him, but he's here, in front of me, in one piece.

I can't seem to find the latch as I blindly reach for it, desperate to step out of the stall. The metal bar won't budge once I find it, and I'm stuck. I shove it as hard as I can and finally force the latch open. "You're alive," I cry out through shallow breaths.

Ben gravitates toward me, reaching out his hand for me to take. I nuzzle into his open arms as his forehead falls to my shoulder, and I feel every bone of his body press against me. "Mila," he sighs through a hitch. "I can't believe it's you." His body bucks through silent sobs and I follow suit. "I didn't think I'd ever touch you again, or feel your warmth, your embrace. I didn't think I'd ever see my wife again—my everything."

FIFTY

A MILLION YEARS AGO
BENEDIKT, MAY 1945

"Ben—" her voice so sweet, sounding rich like honey with tea, though questioning as if she isn't sure of my name or me.

She must be wary of me—the reality of what life has done to me over the last five years. I'm not the man she once knew. I'm sure I hardly resemble him. But Mila, she's more beautiful than I can remember. Her eyes are luminous, gleaming, and intense while studying me to acknowledge what she sees in front of her.

She's wearing a light blue fitted dress. Her hair is in curls, neatly pinned back and adorned with a ribbon to match her outfit. I'm not sure what she's thinking, but we might both be in a long moment of shock, keeping us from shifting a foot. My heart throbs heavily against my sternum. I can feel my pulse buzzing through every artery, but I take a step back, giving her space because I need to know that what she sees in me isn't too much to bear, or even look at.

She places her hand over her mouth and tears barrel out of her eyes. "I can't believe it's really you," she says.

In response, my jaw quivers. "I came back for you."

Without the strength I once had, and a stature that resembles a corpse, I wait for her to collect her thoughts, hoping she didn't let me go for the sake of saving herself from undying pain.

With every ounce of vigor in her body, she closes the space between us and throw her arms around my neck, squeezing me with all her might. She isn't afraid that I might crumple or shatter into pieces. Her heart is pounding against my chest. She's breathing hard, as if she's just run up a hill, and her cheek is against mine. The warm silky skin that I could only dream about, and her long hair, fragrant with the scent of spring morning dew, is surreal, but it is real again. "I've prayed every minute of every hour of every day you have been gone, pleading with whatever higher power will listen to me, to bring you back," she cries softly into my ear. "How did you find me?"

"Elias drove me here. He's waiting along the road. I knew you were sent to live with him, but I didn't know if you made it, or—"

She leans back to look up into my eyes. I want to fall into her and ask her to hold me forever, but she places her gentle hands around my face and presses up on her toes to kiss my dry lips. I forget that I am made up of toothpicks and take her into my arms, cradling her head in my hand. I drink in the flavor of floral tea on her tongue and sweetener on her lips.

I wish the moment would last the rest of our lives because in these seconds I'm able to forget about the hell still falling like ashes to the ground around us.

My lungs tire too soon, and I want to force them to hold out a bit longer, but I gasp for air. She pulls away but a small smile finds the corners of her mouth. She sweeps her thumb across my lips and kisses me once more. "I love you more today than I did all those years ago and all I've been left with is our memories."

"You were my reason to fight," I reply.

She steps back and runs her palms down my arms, taking a hold of my hands. "I hope I don't wake up from this moment."

I shake my head. "No, you're awake, I promise. Come on,

Elias is waiting." I take her by the hand, and we walk in short strides across the farm and around the bend of the dirt road to where Elias is patiently waiting.

"How did you know where I was?" I ask Elias while slipping into the car.

"I didn't. Ben did. We searched in the village since I knew that's where you were heading, and he said if you were there, you'd be with the horses."

I take Mila's hand in mine and hold it against my mouth.

She takes in a sharp breath and twists to look at me. "Did you come back alone?" she asks.

I place our hands on my lap and my gaze falls to her, to the golden band around her finger. "Pavel is back at the estate," I say, trying to keep my voice steady.

"He is?" she asks, elation filling her voice.

"Yes, he's doing well considering the circumstances, of course. But Filip—he—well, he—" I can't say the words. Every time I try, I feel like there's a noose tightening around my neck.

"I understand," she says, cupping her free hand over our bound ones.

We sit in stillness, our heads against the leather seat, staring at each other with so many questions between us—ones neither of us likely want to ask.

I'm in a trance as we make our way back to the Becker estate, where I find Julia tending to Pavel, helping him clean up and eat. He's already making jokes, but she is shrouded by a type of horror she can't hide.

"Pavel." Mila sighs with relief as she makes her way over to him and folds him into a loving embrace.

"I'm so thankful you're all right," he says.

Mila takes a step back, her head easing to the side. "Look at you," she says. "All grown up."

Pavel takes a few steps back and lowers his head. "We all changed, I guess. Filip passed away, and we're quite sure

Mother, Father, and Tobias didn't make it. They were deported and we were told they likely ended up in a death camp."

Mila's brows furrow and the lines across her forehead deepen with grief. She nods with unfortunate understanding. "We heard there should be more information about locating family members soon."

"Have you heard anything about your family?" I ask.

"Not yet." I was afraid she would say that.

"Mila, why don't you take Ben upstairs to help him freshen up?" Elias says.

Mila takes my hand and guides me out of the smoking room. Julia is still standing between us all with a look of shock that hasn't faded a bit since we walked into their home. She places her hand on my back. "Anything you need, sweetheart, we're here."

"Thank you," I say. Julia has never been big on emotions or full of words, but she speaks through her eyes and it's easy to see when she is struggling to string her thoughts together. "Mila, we have plenty of whatever you need for him in the guest closet upstairs," she says.

"Don't worry," Mila says. "I'll take care of him."

She's patient and understanding as it takes much longer for me to climb up the stairwell as it does for her. Her grip around my hand is tight, worried she might have to stop me from tripping or falling.

"You've been here all along?" I ask again.

"In the alcove in the loft, hiding mostly. The Nazis were big on house raids. They only came by a few times and the visits were brief, thankfully. They didn't know I was upstairs. Elias and Julia have taken wonderful care of me. They said it was the very least they could do after what happened to all of you. I tried to earn my keep here but they wouldn't allow me to do so. Neither of them hesitated for even a moment when I arrived at their door. I was afraid they would turn me away, but whatever your mother said to them last, it was enough to change their outlook on what we were going through."

I owe Elias my life in exchange for the gratitude I feel.

We make it to the top of the steps, and she leads me into the alcove. "I've been staying up here," she says.

The room is small with an old window. There's a mattress covered with a pile of blankets and a writing desk with a matching chair. In the middle of the desk, I spot a familiar belonging. I lift it up, recalling the sensation of holding it in my hands.

"Your notebook of poems gave me hope that you would come back. I went so long believing if I didn't open the book, it would mean you hadn't gone away forever. But when the village was tormented with tremors from nearby air raids, I didn't know what was going to happen and I needed your words more than I needed air. With the words from just one of your poems, I knew our fate was something I could rely on. Your beautiful prose offered me bravery at a time when I wanted to cower and hide."

I recall filling up many of the pages just after I met Mila.

I lift the notebook into my hand, noticing the distinct difference between the worn leather and my torn-up hands. The pages flip like a fan until I reach the end, finding the words I poured into this book when I knew I had felt true love for the first time in my life. Next to the last page are folded papers. I unfold them, finding the title to the estate.

"I kept it safe. I didn't want your family to lose your history too."

I sniffle, trying to wane away another wave of tears. My focus drifts to the words in the poem and with just the reminder of the first line, I recall each word I wrote.

I close the notebook and place it back down, turning for the hands I need to hold in mine.

"Mila," I whisper:

A million years ago is when I found you
Minutes became hours, days, months, and years
Nothing measured by the logic of time
For souls join long before we knew

The meaning of reason is wondrous and
    nonsensical
Because love is not a feeling
It's another sense of being
Imprinting a heart against another is imper-
    ceptible

Once together, never apart
Infinite existence never to be undone
Since one stark, brittle lifetime
Could never be enough from even the start

I pull Mila to me and cup my hands around her rosy cheeks.
I lean down and kiss her soft lips, long for my life to reignite like
a motor powered by the force of everlasting electrical currents.

EPILOGUE

MILA, APRIL 1947

.

There were once thirteen people, each with a different purpose, plan, and timeline. We're born blind, unknowing, but instilled with the belief that we shall carry on until we're unaware we've reached a second past the end.

Of our two families, only four of us survived. We knew the chances of finding even one living family member wasn't likely, especially since the rest of Ben's family was on the initial list at the Red Cross station. I didn't have much hope of finding my family, following that news.

It took nearly a full year to reach the bottom of our small list before we found out Lela was the sole survivor of my family, who were taken against their will while living in the settlement here, then moved through two countries and into a ghetto, then re-established in the same camp where Ben and his family were sent. Papa was executed for being the head of our "Gypsy" family and Mama starved to death, giving all her food rations to my four siblings. Lela was the only one who found herself in a position to maintain a job that kept her alive. The other three weren't as fortunate and were listed as being sent to Auschwitz, where they perished. Reason, still unknown. It seems anyone who was deported to Auschwitz was sent for one reason. I'm not sure if the wait to find out about my family was more painful than learning the truth right away, but the more days that passed without an update, the less chance there was of good news at the end. By the time their names appeared on a list, my burdening pain lessened into a form of relief, knowing I had an answer, learning they didn't have to suffer for as long as some did. Romani may have been chased into the lifestyle of a nomad, but the days we spend on earth are the ones leading up to our next life. There is no end, just new beginnings. I know I will someday be surrounded by their souls again.

Even two years after the war came to an end and the prison camps were liberated across Europe, families are still torn apart, children are orphans, and those like me who managed to escape all brutalities live to give back to those who suffered.

Ben wanted to leave the estate behind, to never set foot inside, and let the beautiful structure filled with generations of memories crumble to the earth as time naturally took its course. I wasn't sure how to argue when I myself couldn't fathom walking into a home that was once filled with an abundance of life, but now represents something different.

Sleeping beneath the stars was no longer a dream for Ben. Neither was cooking over an open fire outdoors. Everything he thought he once wanted was no longer something he could imagine enjoying.

We considered searching for a sponsor in the United States so we could emigrate, but the longer we sat on the idea, the more I realized I couldn't leave the Beckers behind. They had become family to me, and we had no others left.

With all the space we were fortunate to have on the estate, Ben settled on the idea of helping displaced people with no means of anywhere to go. We took in several orphaned children and made space for those who needed a temporary place to stay while they found what they were looking for next.

We redecorated every room, bringing in a modern feel filled with warmth and casual comfort—a place where we could form new memories without losing the old. We filled the gallery hall with portraits of everyone we lost, and it has become a place we can walk through with a sense of knowing they are watching over us.

The exterior façade has remained the same with its rich stoic baroque architecture surrounded by freshly painted pillars and stacked framed dormers. We restored the former gardens and even blocked off more space for Nova, Twister, and Krása to roam freely within a gated area.

Ben recovered the assets buried deep underground by Mister Bohdan, which were carefully hidden in a safe below a set of pipes, within the area behind the false wall. The wealth is more than anyone could need in a lifetime. To take care of others gives us both meaning and a way to repent for our lucky fate.

Pavel is attending university and going for a degree in law, a place where he can ensure justice is served correctly.

Lela has come to live with us and is best with the children under our care. I enjoy cooking and putting food on the table for every eager mouth that fills up the dining room table. She would like to become a teacher but has turned the library into a classroom of her own. Each of the children here ranging from the ages of six to twelve is fluent in three languages and has surpassed their expected grade level of education by over a year.

Our life isn't perfect. There is pain to be felt in every direction we look, but to help is to heal, and for that, we will be okay together.

"Mila," Ben calls into the kitchen, "I need to run down to the village to pick up a few groceries. Do you have the key to the motorbike?"

My cheeks burn upon being caught holding on to the key. "No, I don't believe I do."

"I heard the engine running this morning when I was feeding the horses," he says, raising a brow.

I look around the kitchen, trying to find a way to distract Ben so I can remove the key from my dress pocket, but before I'm able to twist away, his arms gather around me, his lips are on my neck, and his hand is in my pocket. "Got it," he mutters against my hot skin.

"I don't know how it got in there," I say, pursing my lips.

"You can't fool me, Misses Bohdan. You are a sweet, innocent woman who has not only stolen my heart, and my last name, but also my beloved bike."

"I warned you about us Romani girls," I tease.

"No, no. Lela is not as feisty or as daring as you."

"That's only what you assume," I argue.

"I'm not sure I know what you mean, nor do I want to know."

I take Ben's hand and lead him to the far end of the kitchen to look out the window toward the stables. I lift the curtain so he can see what I'm witnessing. A blossoming tree next to the stables offers the perfect amount of privacy for anyone who wants to enjoy a few minutes of quiet.

Wildflowers decorate the grass beneath a wooden swing hanging from two ropes secured to a sturdy branch. Ben hung a swing from the tree for the kids to enjoy during their playtime, but they aren't the only ones who seem to enjoy it.

Lela's hair billows in the wind as she soars back and forth between the trees and garden. Pavel waits for the swing to slow and wraps his arms around my sister to place a sweet kiss on her cheek, one he thinks no one can see.

"What am I looking at right now?" he asks, exasperated.

I chuckle because it's been going on for months right under his nose. "Lela and Pavel are enjoying each other's company in the very same spot we once did. Of course, we didn't have a swing then, but they seem to be enjoying it," I reply.

"Is this a secret?" Ben isn't angry, just flustered and oddly taken aback when Lela and Pavel have been obvious with their flirtatious behavior.

"Once a maid, always a maid—I'm entitled to my secrets." Ben doesn't appreciate the ear-to-ear grin on my face. He takes the curtain from my hand, letting it fall in front of his face.

"Who is with all the kids? Lela should be with them. Pavel should be in class!"

"The kids are reading in the library in the next room over. It's eleven in the morning. They read for an hour at the same time every morning, darling. And Pavel is home for lunch and will go back to class at one."

"Are you sure? I can go sit with the kids at least," he says.

I pull him away from the window and loop my arms around his neck. "You no longer need to oversee everything. Our family can do this together if you let us. We both know your father spent every minute of his life trying to take care of all of you at the same time. It's more than one man should ever have to handle, Ben. You said the last thing he did was give you the food off his plate so you would be less hungry that day. You have followed in his footsteps in every God-given way. Take pride in who you have become and relax knowing everything is as it must be in this lifetime."

Ben sweeps a long, loose curl from in front of my eye and loops it behind my ear as a coy smile tugs at his lips. "You have saved me in this life, my love, and I hope to repay you in the next."

A LETTER FROM SHARI

Dear reader,

I'm thrilled you chose to read *The Maid's Secret*. If you enjoyed it and want to keep up to date with all my latest releases, just sign up at the following link. Your email address will never be shared, and you can unsubscribe at any time.

www.bookouture.com/shari-j-ryan

To live during the World War II era is hard for me to imagine, which is why I spend a great deal of time collecting research and sometimes old newspapers and antiques to assist me in standing behind the words I write. Those who suffered during this time deserve stories that represent their hardship to be shared with detail, truth, and realism. These stories are a challenge I take on with passion and devotion. My yearning to concentrate on the Holocaust has developed from my upbringing and heritage. As the granddaughter of two Holocaust survivors, I feel a sense of determination when it comes to keeping the truth of their past experiences alive. While the subject matter is heavy, I feel stronger at the end of each book I write.

I truly hope you enjoyed the book, and if so, I would be very appreciative if you could write a review. Since the feedback from readers helps me grow as a writer, I would love to hear what you think, and it makes such a difference helping new readers to discover one of my books for the first time.

There's no greater pleasure than hearing from my readers – you can get in touch on my Facebook page, through Twitter, Goodreads, or my website.

Thank you for reading!

xoxo

Shari

www.sharijryan.com

 facebook.com/authorsharijryan
twitter.com/sharijryan

ACKNOWLEDGMENTS

The Maid's Secret was an incredible learning experience in my writing career. Nothing makes me happier than to pour my heart and soul into each story I write.

I'd like to thank Bookouture for being an outstanding publishing house—the compassion, kindness, and care is something I appreciate with every interaction of the time. I'm grateful to be a part of such a wonderful team. Thank you!

Christina, working with you brings a smile to my face every day. You've helped me grow with each book we've worked on together, and I'm beyond grateful for your diligence and extraordinary effort to bring these stories to another level. I feel very fortunate for the opportunity to work with you.

Linda, thank you for always cheering me on and supporting my endeavors. Our friendship means everything to me, and I don't know what I'd do without having you as a constant in my life.

Tracey, Gabby, and Elaine—thank you for sticking by my side and being my sounding board. I'm forever grateful for the time and support you offer me, but most of all, your friendship. I don't know what I'd do without you ladies!

To the wonderful ARC readers, bloggers, influencers, and readers: Being in this community has given me a different outlook on life, and I can't think of a better industry to be a part of than this one with all of you. Thank you for your support and encouragement to continue living out my dream.

Lori, the greatest little sister in the universe. Thank you for always being my #1 reader and my very best friend in the whole universe. Love you!

My family—Mom, Dad, Mark, Ev, and Papa—thank you for always keeping track of my every deadline, asking me the ridiculous questions most wouldn't think to ask—like *how many words I've written today*, and telling me I can achieve anything I put my mind to—because sometimes my dreams are bigger than life. To know how greatly you love and support me gives me the constant motivation to go higher. I love you all.

Grandma, I feel you over my shoulder, keeping me upright when I'm tired, and whispering the next best idea into my ear. I miss you more than anything in the world.

Bryce and Brayden—my wonderful boys—thank you for always showing your pride for me and the books I write. As children, I never expect you to admire something I do, for me, but you do and scream it out to anyone who will listen, and it means more than I could ever explain to you.

Josh, thank you for always being the person who will talk scenes out with me, offer advice when I feel stuck, or just hand me a cookie when it's time to close the laptop for the day. To have your support is all I ever need in life. Ten years ago, you told me I should try and write a book. So, this is all because of you, and I love you for pushing me to a place I may never have found on my own.

Made in United States
North Haven, CT
06 July 2023

38634662R00233